LAW AND
DISORDER

BY
HEATHER GRAHAM

MILLS & BOON

First Published in Great Britain 2017
By Mills & Boon, an imprint of HarperCollins*Publishers*
1 London Bridge Street, London, SE1 9GF

ISBN: 978-0-263-92858-7

46-0217

Printed and bound in Spain
by CPI, Barcelona

New York Times and *USA TODAY* bestselling author **Heather Graham** has written more than a hundred novels. She's a winner of the RWA's Lifetime Achievement Award and the International Thriller Writers' Silver Bullet. She is an active member of International Thriller Writers and Mystery Writers of America. For more information, check out her website: www.theoriginalheathergraham.com. You can also find Heather on Facebook.

For Kathy Pickering, Traci Hall and Karen Kendall
Great and crazy road trips
Florida's MWA and FRA...
And my magnificent state, Florida

Chapter One

Dakota Cameron was stunned to turn and find a gun in her face. It was held by a tall, broad-shouldered man in a hoodie and a mask. The full-face rubber mask—like the Halloween "Tricky Dickie" masks of Richard Nixon—was familiar. It was a mask to denote a historic criminal, she thought, but which one?

The most ridiculous thing was that she almost giggled. She couldn't help but think back to when they were kids; all of them here, playing, imagining themselves notorious criminals. It had been the coolest thing in the world when her dad had inherited the old Crystal Manor on Crystal Island, off the Rickenbacker Causeway, between Miami and South Beach—despite the violence that was part of the estate's history, or maybe because of it.

She and her friends had been young, in grammar school at the time, and they'd loved the estate and all the rumors that had gone with it. They hadn't played cops and robbers—they had played cops and *gangsters*, calling each other G-Man or Leftie, or some other such silly name. Because her father was strict and there was no way crime would ever be glorified here—even if the place had once belonged to Anthony Green, one of the biggest mobsters to hit the causeway islands in the late

1940s and early 1950s—crime of any kind was seen as very, very bad. When the kids played games here, the coppers and the G-men always won.

Because of those old games, when Kody turned to find the gun in her face, she felt a smile twitching at her lips. But then the large man holding the gun fired over her head and the sign that bore the name Crystal Manor exploded into a million bits.

The gun-wielder was serious. It was not, as she had thought possible, a joke—not an old friend, someone who had heard she was back in Miami for the week, someone playing a prank.

No. No one she knew would play such a sick joke.

"Move!" a husky voice commanded her.

She was so stunned at the truth of the situation, the masked man staring at her, the bits of wood exploding around her, that she didn't give way to the weakness in her knees or the growing fear shooting through her. She simply responded.

"Move? To where? What do you want?"

"Out of the booth, up to the house, now. And fast!"

The "booth" was the old guardhouse that sat just inside the great wrought-iron gates on the road. It dated back to the early years of the 1900s when pioneer Jimmy Crystal had first decided upon the spit of high ground— a good three feet above the water level—to found his fishing camp. Coral rock had been dug out of nearby quarries for the foundations of what had then been the caretaker's cottage. Over the next decade, Jimmy Crystal's "fishing camp" had become a playground for the rich and famous. The grand house on the water had been built—pieces of it coming from decaying castles and palaces in Europe—the gardens had been planted and the dock had slowly extended out into Biscayne Bay.

In the 1930s, Jimmy Crystal had mysteriously disappeared at sea. The house and grounds had been swept up by the gangster Anthony Green. He had ruled there for years—until being brought down by a hail of bullets at his club on Miami Beach by "assailants unknown."

The Crystal family had come back in then. The last of them had died when Kody had been just six; that's when her father had discovered that Amelia Crystal— the last assumed member of the old family—had actually been his great-great-great-aunt.

Daniel Cameron had inherited the grandeur—and the ton of bills—that went with the estate.

"Now!" the gun wielder said.

Kody was amazed that her trembling legs could actually move.

"All right," she said, surprised by the even tone of her voice. "I'll have to open the door to get out. And, of course, you're aware that there are cameras all over this estate?"

"Don't worry about the cameras," he said.

She shrugged and moved from the open ticket window to the door. In the few feet between her and the heavy wooden door she tried to think of something she could do.

How in the hell could she sound the alarm?

Maybe it had already been sounded. Crystal Manor was far from the biggest tourist attraction in the area, but still, it *was* an attraction. The cops were aware of it. And Celestial Island—the bigger island that led to Crystal Island—was small, easily accessible by boat but, from the mainland, only accessible via the causeway and then the bridge. To reach Crystal Island, you needed to take the smaller bridge from Celestial

Island—or, as with all the islands, arrive by boat. If help had been alerted, it might take time for it to get here.

Jose Marquez, their security man, often walked the walled area down to the water, around the back of the house and the lawn and the gardens and the maze, to the front. He was on his radio at all times. But, of course, with the gun in her face, she had no chance to call him.

Was Jose all right? she wondered. Had the gunman already gotten to him?

"What! Are you eighty? Move!"

The voice was oddly familiar. Was this an old friend? Had someone in her family even set this up, taunting her with a little bit of reproach for the decision she'd made to move up to New York City? She did love her home; leaving hadn't been easy. But she'd been offered a role in a "living theater" piece in an old hotel in the city, a part-time job at an old Irish pub through the acting friend who was part owner—and a rent-controlled apartment for the duration. She was home for a week— just a week—to set some affairs straight before final rehearsals and preview performances.

"Now! Get moving—now!" The man fired again and a large section of coral rock exploded.

Her mind began to race. She hadn't heard many good things about women who'd given in to knife- or gun-wielding strangers. They usually wound up dead anyway.

She ducked low, hurrying to the push button that would lower the aluminum shutter over the open window above the counter at the booth. Diving for her purse, she rolled away with it toward the stairway to the storage area above, dumping her purse as she did so. Her cell phone fell out and she grabbed for it.

But before she could reach it, there was another explosion. The gunman had shot through the lock on the heavy wooden door; it pushed inward.

He seemed to move with the speed of light. Her fingers had just closed around the phone when he straddled over her, wrenching the phone from her hand and throwing it across the small room. He hunkered down on his knees, looming large over her.

There wasn't a way that she was going to survive this! She thought, too, of the people up at the house, imagining distant days of grandeur, the staff, every one of which adored the house and the history. Thought of them all…with bullets in their heads.

With all she had she fought him, trying to buck him off her.

"For the love of God, stop," he whispered harshly, holding her down. "Do as I tell you. Now!"

"So you can kill me later?" she demanded, and stared up at him, trying not to shake. She was basically a coward and couldn't begin to imagine where any of her courage was coming from.

Instinctual desperation? The primal urge to survive?

Before he could answer there was a shout from behind him.

"Barrow! What the hell is going on in there?"

"We're good, Capone!" the man over her shouted back.

Capone?

"Cameras are all sizzled," the man called Capone called out. She couldn't see him. "Closed for Renovation signs up on the gates."

"Great. I've got this. You can get back to the house. We're good here. On the way now!"

"You're slower than molasses!" Capone barked.

"Hurry the hell up! Dillinger and Floyd are securing the house."

Capone? As in "Al" Capone, who had made Miami his playground, along with Anthony Green? Dillinger—as in John Dillinger? Floyd—as in Pretty Boy Floyd?

Barrow—or the muscle-bound twit on top of her now—stared at her hard through the eye holes in his mask.

Barrow—as in Clyde Barrow. Yes, he was wearing a Clyde Barrow mask!

She couldn't help but grasp at hope. If they had all given themselves ridiculous 1930's gangster names and were wearing hoodies and masks, maybe cold-blooded murder might be avoided. These men may think their identities were well hidden and they wouldn't need to kill to avoid having any eye witnesses.

"Come with me!" Barrow said. She noted his eyes then. They were blue; an intense blue, almost navy.

Again something of recognition flickered within her. They were such unusual eyes...

"Come with me!"

She couldn't begin to imagine why she laughed, but she did.

"Wow, isn't that a movie line?" she asked. "*Terminator*! Good old Arnie Schwarzenegger. But aren't you supposed to say, 'Come with me—if you want to live'?"

He wasn't amused.

"Come with me—if you want to live," he said, emphasis on the last.

What was she supposed to do? He was a wall of a man, six-feet plus, shoulders like a linebacker.

"Then get off me," she snapped.

He moved, standing with easy agility, reaching a hand down to her.

She ignored the hand and rose on her own accord, heading for the shattered doorway. He quickly came to her side, still holding the gun but slipping an arm around her shoulders.

She started to shake him off.

"Dammit, do you want them to shoot you the second you step out?" He swore.

She gritted her teeth and allowed the touch until they were outside the guardhouse. Once they were in the clear, she shook him off.

"Now, I think you just have to point that gun at my back," she said, her voice hard and cold.

"Head to the main house," he told her.

The old tile path, cutting handsomely through the manicured front lawn of the estate, lay before her. It was nearing twilight and she couldn't help but notice that the air was perfect—neither too cold nor too hot—and that the setting sun was painting a palette of colors in the sky. She could smell the salt in the air and hear the waves as they splashed against the concrete breakers at the rear of the house.

All that made the area so beautiful—and, in particular, the house out on the island—had never seemed to be quite so evident and potent as when she walked toward the house. Jimmy Crystal had not actually named the place for himself; he'd written in his old journal that the island had seemed to sit in a sea of crystals, shimmering beneath the sun. And so it was. And now, through the years, the estate had become something glimmering and dazzling, as well. It sat in homage to days gone by, to memories of a time when the international city of Miami had been little more than a mosquito-ridden swamp and only those with vision had seen what might come in the future.

She and her parents had never lived in the house; they'd stayed in their home in the Roads section of the city, just north of Coconut Grove, where they'd always lived. They managed the estate, but even in that, a board had been brought in and a trust set up. The expenses to keep such an estate going were staggering.

While it had begun as a simple fishing shack, time and the additions of several generations had made Crystal Manor into something much more. It resembled both an Italianate palace and a medieval castle with tile and marble everywhere, grand columns, turrets and more. The manor was literally a square built around a center courtyard, with turrets at each corner that afforded four tower rooms above the regular two stories of the structure.

As she walked toward the sweeping, grand steps that led to the entry, she looked around. She had heard one of the other thugs, but, at that moment, she didn't see anyone.

Glancing back, she saw that a chain had been looped around the main gate. The gate arched to fifteen feet; the coral rock wall that surrounded the house to the water was a good twelve feet. Certainly not insurmountable by the right law-enforcement troops, but, still, a barrier against those who might come in to save the day.

She looked back at her masked abductor. She could see nothing of his face—except for those eyes.

Why were they so…eerily familiar? If she really knew him, if she had known him growing up, she'd have remembered who went with those eyes! They were striking, intense. The darkest, deepest blue she had ever seen.

What was she thinking? He was a crook! She didn't make friends with crooks!

The double entryway doors suddenly opened and she saw another man in its maw.

Kody stopped. She stared at the doors. They were really beautiful, hardwood enhanced with stained-glass images of pineapples—symbols of welcome. Quite ironic at the moment.

"Get her in here!" the second masked man told the one called Barrow.

"Go," Barrow said softly from behind her.

She walked up the steps and into the entry.

It was grand now, though the entry itself had once been the whole house built by Jimmy Crystal when he had first fallen in love with the little island that, back then, had been untouched, isolated—a haven only for mangroves and mosquitos. Since then, of course, the island—along with Star and Hibiscus islands—had become prime property.

But the foyer still contained vestiges of the original. The floor was coral rock. The columns were the original columns that Jimmy Crystal had poured. Dade country pine still graced the side walls.

The rear wall had been taken down to allow for glass barriers to the courtyard; more columns had been added. The foyer contained only an 1890's rocking horse to the right side of the double doors and an elegant, old fortune-telling machine to the left. And, of course, the masked man who stood between the majestic staircases that led to the second floor at each side of the space.

She cast her eyes around but saw no one else.

There had still been four or five guests on the property when Kody had started to close down for the day. And five staff members: Stacey Carlson, the estate manager, Nan Masters, his assistant, and Vince Jenkins, Brandi Johnson and Betsy Rodriguez, guides. Manny

Diaz, the caretaker, had been off the property all day.
And, of course, Jose Marquez was there somewhere.

"So, this is Miss Cameron?" the masked man in the
house asked.

"Yes, Dillinger. This is Miss Cameron," Barrow said.

Dillinger. She was right—this guy's mask was that
of the long-ago killer John Dillinger.

"Well, well, well. I can't tell you, Miss Cameron,
what a delight it is to meet you!" the man said. "Imagine! When I heard that you were here—cuddle time with
the family before the final big move to the Big Apple—
I knew it was time we had to step in."

The man seemed to know about her—and her family.

"If you think I'm worth some kind of ransom," she
said, truly puzzled—and hoping she wasn't sealing her
own doom, "I'm not. We may own this estate, but it's
in some kind of agreement and trust with the state of
Florida. It survives off of grants and tourist dollars."
She hesitated. "My family isn't rich. They just love this
old place."

"Yeah, yeah, yeah, Daddy is an archeologist and
Mom travels with him. Right now they're on their way
back from South America so they can head up north
with their baby girl to get her all settled into New York
City. Yes! I have the prize right here, don't I?"

"I have no idea what you're talking about," Kody told
him. "I wish I could say that someone would give you
trillions of dollars for me, but I'm not anyone's prize.
I'm a bartender-waitress at an Irish pub who's struggling to make ends meet as an actress."

"Oh, honey," Dillinger said, "I don't give a damn if
you're a bad actress."

"Hey! I never said I was a *bad* actress!" she protested. And then, of course, she thought that he was making her crazy—heck, the whole situation was making her crazy—because who the hell cared if she was a bad actress or a good actress if she wasn't even alive?

Dillinger waved a hand in the air. "That's neither here nor there. You're going to lead us to the Anthony Green stash."

Startled, Kody went silent.

Everyone, of course, had heard about the Anthony Green *stash*.

Green was known to have knocked over the long-defunct Miami Bank of the Pioneers, making off with the bank's safe-deposit boxes that had supposedly contained millions in diamonds, jewels, gold and more. It was worth millions. But Anthony Green had died in a hail of bullets—with his mouth shut. The stash was never found. It had always been suspected that Anthony Green—before his demise—had seen to it that the haul had been hidden somewhere in one of his shacks deep in the Everglades, miles from his Biscayne Bay home.

Rumor followed rumor. It was said that Guillermo Salazar—a South American drug lord—had actually found the stash about a decade ago and added a small fortune in ill-gotten heroin-sales gains to it—before he, in turn, had been shot down by a rival drug cartel.

Who the hell knew? One way or the other, it was supposedly a very large fortune.

She didn't doubt that Salazar had sold drugs; the Coast Guard in South Florida was always busy stopping the drug trade. But she sure as hell didn't believe that Salazar had found the Green stash at the house, because she really didn't believe the stash was here.

Chills suddenly rose up her spine.

If she was supposed to find a stash that didn't exist here…

They were all dead.

"Where is everyone?" she asked.

"Safe," Dillinger said.

"Safe where?"

No one answered Kody. "Where?" she repeated.

"They're all fine, Miss Cameron."

It was the man behind her—Barrow—who finally spoke up. "Dillinger, she needs to know that they're all fine," he added.

"I assure you," Dillinger continued. "They're all fine. They're in the music room."

The music room took up most of the left side of the downstairs. It would be the right place to hold a group of people.

Except...

Someone, somewhere, had to know that something was going on here. Surely one of the employees or guests had had a chance to get out a cell phone warning.

"I want to see them," she said. "I want to see that everyone is all right."

"Listen, missy, what you do and don't want doesn't matter here. What you're going to do for us matters," Dillinger told her.

"I don't know where the stash is. If I did, the world would have known about it long ago," she said. "And, if you know everything, you surely know that history says Anthony Green hid his bank treasure in some hut somewhere out in the Everglades."

"She sure as hell isn't rich, Dillinger," Barrow said. "Everything is true—she's taken a part-time job because what she's working is off-off Broadway. If she knew about the stash, I don't think she'd be slow-pouring Guinness at an old pub in the city."

Dillinger seemed annoyed. Kody was, in fact, surprised by what she could read in his eyes—and in his movements.

"No one asked your opinion, Barrow," Dillinger said. "She's the only one who can find it. I went through every newspaper clipping—she's loved the place since she was a kid. She's read everything on Jimmy Crystal and Anthony Green and the mob days on Miami Beach. She knows what rooms in this place were built what years, when any restoration was done. She knows it all. She knows how to find the stash. And she's going to help us find it."

"Don't be foolish," Kody said. "You can get out now. No one knows who you guys are—the masks, I'll grant you, are good. Well, they're not good. They're cheap and lousy masks, but they create the effect you want and no one here knows what your real faces look like. Pretty soon, though, walls or not, cops will swarm the place. Someone will come snooping around. Someone probably got something out on a cell phone."

She couldn't see his face but she knew that Dillinger smiled. "Cell phones? No, we secured those pretty quickly," he said. "And your security guard? He's resting—he's got a bit of a headache." He shook his head. "Face it, young lady. You have me and Barrow here. Floyd is with your friends, Capone is on his way to help, and the overall estate is being guarded by Baby Face Nelson and Machine Gun Kelly and our concept of modern security and communication and, you know, we've got good old Dutch—as in Schultz—working it all, too. I think we're good for a while. Long enough for you to figure out where the stash is. And, let's see, you are going to help us."

"I won't do anything," she told him. "Nothing. Nothing at all—not until I know that my friends and our

guests are safe and that Jose isn't suffering from anything more than a headache."

Not that she'd help them even then—if she even
could. The stash had been missing since the 1930s. In
fact, Anthony Green had used a similar ruse when he
had committed the bank robbery. He'd come in fast with
six men—all wearing masks. He'd gotten out just as
fast. The cops had never gotten him. They'd suspected
him, but they'd never had proof. They'd still been trying to find witnesses and build a case against him when
he'd been gunned down on Miami Beach.

But her demands must have hit home because Dillinger turned to Barrow. "Fine. Bring her through."

He turned to head down the hallway that led into
the music room—the first large room on the left side
of the house.

It was a gorgeous room, graced with exquisite crown
molding, rich burgundy carpets and old seascapes of
famous ports, all painted by various masters in colors
that complemented the carpet. There was a wooden
dais at one end of the room that accommodated a grand
piano, a harp, music stands and room for another three
or four musicians.

There were sofas, chairs and love seats backed to all
the walls, and a massive marble fireplace for those times
when it did actually get cold on the water.

Kody knew about every piece in the room, but at
that moment all she saw was the group huddled together on the floor.

Quickly searching the crowd, she found Stacey Carlson, the estate manager. He was sixty or so with salt-
and-pepper hair, old-fashioned sideburns and a small
mustache and goatee. A dignified older man, he was
quick to smile, slow to follow a joke—but brilliant.

Nan Masters was huddled to his side. If it was possible to have platonic affairs, the two of them were hot and heavy. Nothing ever went on beyond their love of Miami, the beaches and all that made up their home. Nan was red-haired, but not in the least fiery. Slim and tiny, she looked like a cornered mouse huddled next to Stacey.

Vince Jenkins sat cross-legged on a Persian rug that lay over the carpet, straight and angry. There was a bruise forming on the side of his face. He'd apparently started out by fighting back.

Beside him, Betsy Rodriguez and Brandi Johnson were close to one another. Betsy, the tinier of the two, but by far the most out-there and sarcastic, had her arm around Brandi, who was nearly six feet, blond, blue-eyed, beautiful and shy.

Jose Marquez had been laid on the largest love seat. His forehead was bleeding, but, Kody quickly saw, he was breathing.

The staff had been somewhat separated from the few guests who had remained on the property, finishing up in the gardens after closing. She couldn't remember all their names but she recalled the couple, Victor and Melissa Arden. They were on their honeymoon, yet they'd just been in Texas, visiting the graves of Bonnie Parker and Clyde Barrow in their separate cemeteries. They loved studying old gangsters, which was beyond ironic, Kody thought now. Another young woman from Indiana, an older man and a fellow of about forty rounded out the group.

They were all huddled low, apparently respecting the twin guns carried by another man in an identity-concealing mask.

"Kody!" Stacey said, breathing out a sigh of relief.

She realized that her friends might have been worrying for her life.

She turned to Dillinger. "You'd better not hurt them!"

"Hurt them?" Dillinger said. "I don't want to hurt any of you, really. Okay, okay, so, quite frankly, I don't give a rat's ass. But Barrow there, he's kind of squeamish when it comes to blood and guts. Capone—my friend with the guns—is kind of rabid. Like he really had syphilis or rabies or something. He'd just as soon shoot you as look at you. So, here's my suggestion." He paused, staring Cody up and down. "You find out what I need to know. You come up to that library—and you start using everything you know and going through everything in the books, every news brief, every everything. You find that stash for me. Their lives depend on it."

"What if I can't find it?" she asked. "No one has found this stash in eighty-plus years!"

"You'd better find it," Dillinger said.

"Help will come!" Betsy said defiantly. "This is crazy—you're crazy! SWAT teams aren't but a few miles away. Someone—"

"You'd better hope no one comes," Dillinger said. He walked over to hunker down in front of her. "Because that's the whole point of hostages. They want you to live. They probably don't give a rat's ass one way or the other, either, but that's what they're paid to do. Get the hostages out alive. But, to prove we mean business, we'll have to start by killing someone and tossing out the body. And guess what? We like to start with the big-mouths, the wise-asses!"

He reached out to Betsy and that was all the impetus Kody needed. She sure as hell wasn't particularly courageous but she didn't waste a second to think. She just bolted toward Dillinger, smashing into him with such force that he went flying down.

With her.

He was strong, really strong.

He was up in two seconds, dragging her up with him.

"Why you little bitch!" he exclaimed as he hauled his arm back, ready to slam a jaw-breaking fist into her face.

His hand never reached her.

Barrow—with swift speed and agility—was on the two of them. She felt a moment of pain as he wrenched her out of Dillinger's grasp, thrusting himself between them.

"No, Dillinger, no. Keep the hostages in good shape. This one especially! We need her, Dillinger. We need her!"

"Bitch! You saw her—she tackled me."

"We need her!"

The hostages had started to move, scrambling back, restless, frightened, and Capone shoved someone with the butt of his gun.

Barrow lifted his gun and shot the ceiling.

Plaster fell around them all like rain.

And the room went silent.

"Let's get her out of here and up to the library, Dillinger. Dammit, now. Come on—let's do what we came here to do!" he insisted. "I'm into money—not a body count."

Kody felt his hand as he gripped her arm, ready to drag her along.

Dillinger stared at him a long moment.

Was there a struggle going on? she wondered. A power play? Dillinger seemed to be the boss, but then Barrow had stepped in. He'd saved her from a good beating, at the least. She couldn't help but feel that there was something better about him.

She was even drawn to him.

Oh, that was sick, she told herself. He was a crook, maybe even a killer.

Still, he didn't seem to be as bloodthirsty as Dillinger.

Dillinger stepped around her and Barrow, heading for the stairs to the library. Barrow followed with her.

"Hey!"

They heard the call when they had nearly cleared the room.

She turned to see Capone standing next to Betsy Rodriguez. He wasn't touching her; he was just close to her.

He moved his gun, running the muzzle through her hair.

"Dakota Cameron!" he said. "The world—well, your world—is dependent on your every thought and word!"

She started to move toward him but Barrow stopped her, whispering in her ear, "Don't get them going!"

She couldn't help herself. She called out to Capone. "You're here because you want something? Well, if you want it from me, step the hell away from my friend!"

To her surprise, Dillinger started to laugh.

"We've got a wild card on our hands, for sure. Come on, Capone. Let's accommodate the lady. Step away from her friend."

From behind her, Barrow added, "Come on, Capone. I'm in this for the money and a quick trip out of the country. Let's get her started working and get this the hell done, huh? Beat her to pieces or put a bullet in her, and she's worthless."

"Miss Cameron?" Dillinger said, sweeping an elegant bow to her. "My men will behave like gentlemen—as long as your friends let them. You hear that, right?"

"I can be a perfect gentleman!" Capone called back to him.

"Tell them all to sit tight and not make trouble—that you will manage to get what we want," Barrow said to her.

She looked at him again.

Those eyes of his! So deep, dark, blue and intense!

Surely, if she really knew him, she'd recognize him now.

She didn't. Still, she couldn't help but feel that she did, and that the man she knew wasn't a criminal, and that she had been drawn to those eyes before.

She shivered suddenly, looking at him.

He didn't like blood and guts—that's what Dillinger had said.

Maybe he was a thief, a hood—but hated the idea of being a murderer. Maybe, just maybe, he did want to keep them all alive.

"Hey!" she called back to the huddled group of captives. "I know everything about the house and all about Anthony Green and the gangster days. Just hold tight and be cool, please. I can do this. I know I can do this!"

They all looked at her with hope in their faces.

She gazed at Barrow and said, "They need water. We keep cases of water bottles in the lower cabinet of the kitchen. Go through the music room and the dining room and you'll reach the kitchen. I would truly appreciate if you would give them all water. It will help me think."

But it was Dillinger who replied.

"Sure," he said. "You think—and we'll just be the nicest group of guys you've ever met!"

Chapter Two

Nick Connolly—known as Barrow to the Coconut Grove crew of murderers, thieves and drug runners who were careful not to share their real names, even with one another—was doing his best. His damned best.

Which wasn't easy.

Nick didn't mind undercover work. He could even look away from the drugs and the prostitution, knowing that what he was doing would stop the flow of some really bad stuff onto the city streets—and put away some really bad men.

From the moment he'd infiltrated this gang three weeks ago, the situation had been crazy, but he'd also thought it would work. This would be the time when he could either get them all together in an escape boat that the Coast Guard would be ready to swoop up, or, if that kind of maneuver failed, pick them off one by one. Each of these guys—Dillinger, Capone, Floyd, Nelson, Kelly and Schultz—had killed or committed some kind of an armed robbery. They were all ex-cons. Capone had been the one to believe in Nick's off-color stories in an old dive bar in Coconut Grove, and as far as Capone knew, Nick had been locked up in Leavenworth, convicted of a number of crimes. Of course, Capone had met Nick as Ted—Ted Johnson had been the pseudonym Nick had been using in South Florida. There really had been a Ted Johnson; he'd died in the prison hospital ward of a knife wound. But no one knew that. No one except certain members of the FBI and the hospital staff and warden and other higher ups at the prison.

None of these men—especially "Dillinger"—had any idea that Nick had full dossiers on them. As far as they all knew, they were anonymous, even with each other.

Undercover was always tricky.

It should have been over today; he should have been able to give up the undercover work and head back to New York City. Not that he minded winter in Miami.

He just hated the men with whom he had now aligned himself—even if it was to bring them down, and even if it was important work.

Today should have been it.

But all the plans he'd discussed with his local liaisons and with Craig Frasier—part of the task force from New York that had been chasing the drug-and-murder-trail of the man called Dillinger from New York City down through the South—had gone to hell.

And the stakes had risen like a rocket—because of a situation he'd just found out about that morning.

Without the aid, knowledge or consent of the others, for added protection, Dillinger had kidnapped a boy right before they had all met to begin their takeover of the Crystal Estate.

It wouldn't have mattered who the kid was to Nick—he'd have done everything humanly possible to save him—but the kidnapped boy was the child of Holden Burke, mayor of South Beach. Dillinger had assured them all that he had the kid safely hidden somewhere—where, exactly, he wasn't telling any of them. They all knew that people could talk, so it was safer that only he knew the whereabouts of little Adrian Burke. And not to worry—the kid was alive. He was their pass-go ace in the hole.

That was one thing.

Then, there was Dakota Cameron.

To be fair, Nick didn't exactly know Kody Cameron but he had seen her—and she had seen him—in New York City.

And the one time that he'd seen her, he'd known immediately that he'd wanted to see her again.

And now, here they were. In a thousand years he'd never imagined their second meeting would be like this.

No one had known that Dillinger's game plan ended with speculation—the vague concept that he could kidnap Dakota, take her prisoner—and *hope* she could find the stash!

Dillinger planned the heists and the drug runs; he worked with a field of prostitution that included the pimps and the girls. He had South American contacts. No one had figured he'd plan on taking over the old Crystal Estate, certain that he could find a Cameron family member who knew where to find the old mob treasure.

So, now, here he was—surprised and somewhat anxious to realize that the lovely young brunette with the fascinating eyes he'd brushed by at Finnegan's on Broadway in New York City would show up at the ticket booth at a Florida estate and tourist attraction.

Craig Frasier, one of the main men on the task force Director Egan had formed to trace and track "Dillinger," aka Nathan Appleby, along the Eastern seaboard, spent a lot of time at Finnegan's. The new love of his life was co-owner, along with her brothers, of the hundred-and-fifty-year-old pub in downtown Manhattan.

Nick and Kody Cameron had passed briefly, like

proverbial ships in the night, but he hadn't had the least problem recognizing her today. He knew her, because they had both paused to stare at one another at the pub.

Instant attraction? Definitely on his part and he could have sworn on hers, too.

Then she'd muttered some kind of swift apology and Craig's new girlfriend, who'd come over to greet them, explained, "That's Kody Cameron. She's working a living theater piece with my brother. Sounds kind of cool, right? And she's working here part-time now, making the transition to New York."

"What's living theater?" Nick had asked Kieran Finnegan.

"Kevin could tell you better than me," she had explained, "but it's taking a show more as a concept than as a structured piece and working with the lines loosely while interacting with the audience as your character."

Whatever she did, he'd hoped that he'd see her again; he'd even figured that he could. While Kieran Finnegan actually worked as a psychologist and therapist for a pair of psychiatrists who often came in as consultants for the New York office of the Bureau, she was also often at Finnegan's. And since he was working tightly with Craig and his partner, Mike, and a cyber-force on this case, he'd figured he'd be back in Finnegan's, too. But then, of course, Dillinger had come south, met up with old prison mates Capone, Nelson, Kelly, Floyd and Schultz, and Nick—who had gone through high school in South Florida and still had family in the area—had been sent down to infiltrate the gang.

The rest, as the saying went, was history.

Now, if Dakota Cameron saw his face, if she gave any indication that she knew him, and knew that he was an FBI man...

They'd both be dead.

And it didn't help the situation that she was battle ready—ready to lay down her life for her friends.

Then again, there should have been a way for him to stop this. If it hadn't been for the little boy who had been taken…

He had to find out where the kid was. Had Dillinger stashed him with friends or associates? Had he hidden him somewhere? It wasn't as hard to hide somewhere here as one would think, with the land being just about at sea level and flat as a pancake. There were enough crack houses and abandoned tenements. Of course, Nick was pretty sure Dillinger couldn't have snatched the kid at a bus station, hidden him wherever, and made it to the estate at their appointed time, if he had gone far.

But that knowledge didn't help much.

Nick's first case when he'd started with the Bureau in the Miami offices had been finding the truth behind the bodies stuffed in barrels, covered with acid and tossed in the Everglades.

He refused to think of that image along with his fear for the child; the boy was alive. Adrian Burke wouldn't be worth anything in an escape situation if he was dead.

Nick wiped away that thought and leaned against the door frame as he stood guard over Kody. Capone was now just on the other side of the door.

Like the entire estate, the library was kept in pristine shape, but it also held an air of fading and decaying elegance, making one feel a sense of nostalgia. The floors were marble, covered here and there by Persian throw rugs, and built-in bookshelves were filled with volumes that appeared older than the estate itself, along with sea charts and more.

Kody Cameron had a ledger opened before her, but she was looking at him. Quizzically.

It seemed as if she suspected she knew him but couldn't figure out from where.

"You're not as crazy as the others," she said softly. "I can sense that about you. But you need to do something to stop this. That treasure he's talking about has been missing for years and years. God knows, maybe it's in the Everglades, swallowed up in a sinkhole. You don't want to be a part of this—I know you don't. And those guys are lethal. They'll hurt someone…kill someone. This is still a death penalty state, you know. Please, if you would just—"

He found himself walking over to her at the desk and replying in a heated whisper, "Just do what he says and find the damned treasure. Lie if you have to! Find something that will make Dillinger believe that you know where the treasure is. Give him a damned map to find it. He won't think twice about killing people, but he won't kill just for the hell of it. Don't give him a reason."

"You're not one of them. You have to stop this. Get away from them," she said.

She was beautiful, earnest, passionate. He wanted to reassure her. To rip off his mask and tell her that law enforcement was on it all.

But that was impossible, lest they all die quickly.

He had to keep his distance and keep her, the kidnapped child and the others in the house alive.

Capone was growing curious. He left his post at the archway and walked in. "Hey. What's going on here? Don't interrupt the woman, Barrow. I want to get the hell out of here! I've done some wild things with Dillinger, but this is taking the cake. Makes me more nervous than twenty cartel members in a gunboat. Leave her be."

"Yeah. I'm going to leave her be. And she's going to come up with something," Barrow said.

He'd barely spoken when Schultz came rushing in. While Capone knew how to rig a central box and stop cameras and security systems, Schultz was an expert sharpshooter. He was tall and thin, not much in the muscles department, but Nick had seen him take long shots that were just about impossible.

"News is out that we're here," he said. "Cops are surrounding the gates. I fired a few warning shots and Dillinger answered the phone—told them we have a pack of hostages. You should see them all out there at the gates," he added, his grin evident in his voice. "They look like a pack of chickens. Guess they're calling for a hostage negotiator. Dillinger is deciding whether to give them a live one or a body."

Kody Cameron stood. "They give him a body and I'm done. If he gives them one body, it won't make any difference to him if he kills the rest of us."

"And just how far are you getting, sweet thing?" Schultz asked, coming close to her. He reached out to lift the young woman's chin.

Nick struggled to control himself. Hell, she wasn't just a captive. Not just someone he had to keep alive.

She worked for Finnegan's. She was connected to Kevin Finnegan and Kieran Finnegan—and therefore, to Craig Frasier.

And he noticed her the first time he'd ever seen her. Known that he'd wanted to see her again.

He'd never imagined it could be in this way.

For a moment he managed to keep his peace. But, damn her, she just had to react. Schultz cradled her face and she stepped back and pushed his hand away.

"Hey, hey, hey, little girl. You don't want to get hurt, do you? Be nice."

Nick stepped up, swinging Schultz around.

"Leave her alone, dammit. We're here for a reason."

"What? Are you sweet on her yourself?" Schultz asked him, his tone edgy. "You think this is merchandise you keep all for yourself?"

"I'm not merchandise!" Kody snapped.

"I want her to find what Dillinger wants, and I want to get the hell out of here!" Nick said. He was as tall as Schultz; he had a lot more muscle and he was well trained. In a fair fight, Schultz wouldn't stand a chance against him.

There were no fair fights here, he reminded himself. He had to keep an even keel.

"Leave her alone and let her get back to work," he said. "Get your mind on the job to be done here."

"Shouldn't you be up in one of the front towers?" Capone asked Schultz. "Isn't that your job in all this?"

Schultz gave them all a sweeping and withering glare. Then he turned and left.

Capone was staring at Nick. "Maybe you should get your mind on the job, too, Barrow," he suggested.

"And you," Nick added softly.

Capone continued to stare at him.

It went no further as Dillinger came striding into the room. He ignored Capone and Nick and walked straight to the desk and Kody.

"How long?" he asked her.

"How long? You're asking me to do something no one has managed in decades," Kody said.

"You're got two hours," Dillinger said. "Two hours. They're bringing in a hostage negotiator. Don't make me prove that I will kill."

"I'm doing my best," Kody said.

"Where's the phone in this room?" Dillinger asked.

"On the table by the door, next to the Tiffany lamp," Kody said.

"What the hell is a Tiffany lamp?" Dillinger demanded, leaning in on Kody.

"There. Right there, boss," Nick said, pointing out the elegant little side table with the lamp and the white trim-line phone. He walked over to it and saw that the volume was off.

"Ready for calls," he told Dillinger.

"Good. We'll manage it from here. Capone, get on down and help Nelson with the hostages. Schultz is in the eagle's seat in the right tower. Floyd's in the left. And we've got our good old boy, our very own private Machine Gun Kelly, in the back. Don't trust those hostages, though. I'm thinking if we have to get rid of a few, we'll be in better shape."

"No, we won't be," Nick said flatly. "You hurt a hostage, it tells the cops that they're not doing any good with negotiation. We have to keep them believing they're getting everyone back okay. That's the reason they'll hold off. If they think we're just going to kill people, they'll storm us, figuring to kill us before we kill the hostages. That's the logic they teach, trust me," Nick told Dillinger.

Dillinger shrugged, looking at the phone. "Well, we'll give them a little time, if nothing else. So, Miss Cameron, just how are you doing?"

Dakota Cameron looked up and stared at Dillinger, then cocked her head at an angle. "Looking for a needle in a haystack?" she asked. "I'm moving some hay out of the way, but there's still a great deal to go. You do realize—"

"Yes, yes," Dillinger said impatiently. "Yes, everyone has looked for years. But not because their lives were at stake. You're holding so many precious souls in your hands, Miss Cameron. I'm just so sure that will help you follow every tiny lead to just where the treasure can be found."

"Well, I'll try to keep a clear head here," she said. "At the moment, my mind is not hampered with grief over losing anyone, and you really should keep it that way. I mean, if you want me to find out anything for you."

Nick wished he could have shut her up somehow; he couldn't believe she was taunting a man who was half-crazy and holding the lives of so many people in his hands.

He had to admire her bravado—even as he wished she didn't have it.

But Dillinger laughed softly beneath his mask.

"My dear Miss Cameron, you do have more balls than half the men I find myself working with!" Dillinger told her. "Excellent—if you have results. If you don't, well, it will just make it all the easier to shut you up!"

She wasn't even looking at Dillinger anymore. She'd turned her attention back to the journal spread open before her.

"Let me work," she said softly.

Dillinger grunted. He took a seat in one of the chairs by the wall of the library, near the phone.

Nick walked to the windows, looking out at the gardens in the front of the house, the driveway and—at a distance—the wall and the great iron gates that led up to the house.

More and more cars were beginning to arrive—marked police cars, unmarked cars belonging to the FBI and other law-enforcement agencies.

He wondered how Dillinger could believe he might get out of this alive.

And then he wondered just how the hell any of them were going to get out alive.

The phone began to ring. Dakota Cameron jumped in her chair, nearly leaping from it.

Nick nearly jumped himself.

Dillinger rose and picked up the phone. "Hello? Dillinger here. How can I help you? Other than keeping the hostages alive… Let's see, how can you help me? Well, I'll begin to explain. Right now, everyone in the house is breathing. We have some employees, we have some guests… What we want is more time, really good speed boats—cigarettes or Donzis will do. Now, of course, we need a couple because a few of these good people will be going with us for just a bit when we leave. We'll see to it that you get them all back alive and well as long as we get what we want."

Nick wished he was on an extension. He wanted to hear what was being said.

He saw Dillinger nod. "How bright of you to ask so quickly! Yes, there is a missing child, too, isn't there? An important little boy—son of a mayor! Ah, well, all children are important, aren't they…? Mr. Frasier? Ah! Sorry, Special Agent Frasier. FBI. They've brought in the big guns. Let's go with this—right now, I want time. You give me some time and you arrange for those boats. To be honest, I'm working on a way to give you back that kid I scooped up. Not a bad kid, in the least. I liked him. I'd hate for him to die of neglect, caged and chained and forgotten. So, you work on those boats."

Nick saw Dakota Cameron frown as she'd heard the name Frasier. Not that Frasier was a rare name, but Kody was good friends with Kevin Finnegan and therefore friends with his sister Kieran—and so she knew Craig. She had to be puzzled, wondering first if he was indeed the same man a friend was dating and, if so, what he was doing in South Florida.

She looked up from her ledger. She was staring at Dillinger hard, brows knit in a frown.

A moment later Dillinger set the receiver back in the cradle. He seemed to be pleased with himself.

"You kidnapped a child?" she asked.

"I like to have a backup plan," Dillinger said.

"You have all of us."

"Yes. But, hey, maybe nobody cares about any of you. They will care about a kid."

"Yep, they will," Nick interrupted. "But I think they need to believe in us, too. Hey, man, you want time for Miss Cameron to find the treasure, the stash, or whatever might be hidden? If we're going to buy that time, we need to play to them. I say we give them the security guard. He needs medical attention. Best we get him out of here. An injured hostage is just a liability. Let's give him up as a measure of good faith."

"Maybe," Dillinger said. He looked at Kody. "How are you doing?"

"I'd do a lot better if you didn't ask me every other minute," she said. "And," she added softly, "if I wasn't so worried about Jose."

"Who the hell is Jose?" Dillinger asked.

"Our security guard. The injured man," Kody said.

Dillinger glanced restlessly at his watch and then at the phone. "Give them a few minutes to get back to me."

He walked out of the room, leaving Nick alone with Kody.

"How *are* you doing?" he asked her.

She shrugged and then looked up at him. "So far, I have all the same information everyone has had for years. Anthony Green robbed the bank, but the police couldn't pin it on him, couldn't make an arrest. He wrote in his own journal that it was great watching them all run around like chickens with no heads. Of course, it wouldn't be easy for anyone to find the stash. What it seems to me—from what I've read—is that he did plan on disappearing. Leaving the country. And he was talking about boats, as well—"

She broke off, staring at the old journal she was reading and then flipping pages over.

"What is it?" Nick asked.

She looked up at him, her expression suddenly guarded. He realized that—to her—he was a death-dealing criminal.

"I'm not sure," she said. "I need time."

"You've got time right now. Use it," he said.

"We need to see some of the hostages out of here—returned to safety," she said firmly. "In good faith!"

They were both startled by the sound of a gunshot. Then a barrage of bullets seemed to come hailing down on the house.

A priceless vase on a table exploded.

Nick practically flew across the room, leaping over the desk to land on top of Kody—and bring her down to the floor.

The barrage of bullets continued for a moment—and then went silent.

He felt her move beneath him.

He looked down at her. Her eyes were wide on his as she studied him gravely. He hadn't just been intrigued, he realized. He hadn't just wanted to see her again.

He'd been attracted to her. Really attracted.

And now...

She was trembling slightly.

He leaped to his feet, drawing her up, pulling her

along with him as he raced down the hall to the stairs that led to the right tower where Schultz had been keeping guard.

Nick was pretty damned certain Schultz—a man who was crazy and more than a little trigger happy—had fired the first shots.

"What the hell are you doing?" he shouted.

As he did so, Dillinger came rushing along, as well. "What the hell?" he demanded furiously.

"I saw 'em moving, boss. I saw 'em moving!" Schultz shouted down.

The phone started ringing. Nick looked at Dillinger. "Let me take it. Let me see what I can do," he said.

Dillinger was already moving back toward the library. Nick followed, still clasping Kody's hand.

When they reached the library, Dillinger stepped back and let Nick answer the phone.

"Hello?" Nick said. "This is Barrow speaking now. We don't know what happened. We do know that you responded with the kind of violence that's going to get someone killed. Seriously, do you want everyone in here dead? What the hell was that?"

"Shots were fired at us," a voice said. "Who is this?"

"I told you. Barrow."

"Are you the head man?"

Nick glanced over at Dillinger.

"No. I'm spokesman for the head man. He's all into negotiation. What we want doesn't have anything to do with a bunch of dead men and women, but that's what we could wind up with if we don't get this going right," Nick said.

"We don't want dead people," the voice on the other end assured him.

"We don't, either," Nick said.

"Barrow. All right, let's talk. I think everyone got a little panicky. No one wants anyone to die here today. We're all working in the same direction, that being to see that everyone gets out alive. Okay?"

Nick knew who was doing the negotiating for the array of cops and FBI and law enforcement just on the other side of the gates.

He was speaking with Craig Frasier. Nick was glad the FBI and the local authorities had gotten it together to make the situation go smoothly. He knew Craig; Craig knew him. There was so much more he was going to be able to do with Craig at the other end.

"How are they doing on my boats?" Dillinger asked, staring at Nick.

"We're going to need those boats," Nick said. He needed to give Craig all the information he could about the situation, without making Dillinger suspicious, and he wanted, also, to maintain his position as spokesman for Dillinger.

"Yes, two boats, right?" Craig asked.

"Good ones. The best speedboats you can get your hands on. Now, we're not fools. You won't get all the information you need to save everyone until we're long gone and safe. But, right now, we're going to give you a man. Security guard. He's got a bit of a gash on his head. We're going to bring him out to the front and we'll see that the gate is opened long enough for one of you to get him out. Do you understand? The fate of everyone here may depend on this nice gesture on our part going well."

He knew that Craig understood; Nick had really just told him the guard had been the only one injured and that he did need help.

"No one else is hurt? Everyone is fine?"

Craig had to ask to keep their cover. But Nick knew

the agent was also concerned for Dakota Cameron. That the Cameron family owned this place—and that Kody was down here—was something Craig must have realized from the moment Dillinger made his move.

"No one is hurt. I'm trying to keep it that way," Nick assured him, glancing over at Dillinger.

Dillinger nodded. He seemed to approve of how Nick handled the negotiations. There was enough of a low-lying threat in Nick's tone to make it all sound very menacing, no matter what the words.

"That's good. Open the gate and we'll get the man. There will be no attempts to break in on you, no more bullets fired," Craig said.

Nick looked at Dillinger. *Yes?* he mouthed.

Dillinger nodded. "Keep an eye on her!"

As he hurried out, Kody stood and started after him, then paused herself, as if certain Nick would have stopped her if she hadn't. He held the phone and stared at her, wishing he dared tell her who he was and what his part was in all this.

But he couldn't.

He couldn't risk her betraying him.

He covered the mouthpiece on the house phone. "Don't leave the room."

"Jose Marquez…" she murmured.

"He's really letting him go," Nick said.

She walked over to him suddenly. He was afraid she was going to reach for the mask that covered his face.

She didn't touch him. Instead she spoke quickly. "You're not like that. You could stop this. You have a gun. You could—"

"Shoot them all down?" he asked her.

"Wound them, stop this—stop them from killing innocent people. I'd speak for you. I'd see that everyone in court knew that people survived because of you."

She was moving closer as she spoke—not to touch him, he realized, but to take his gun.

He set the phone down and grabbed her roughly by the wrists.

"Don't pull this on anyone else. Haven't you really grasped this yet? They're trigger happy and crazy. Just do as they say. Just find that damned stash!"

Something in her jaw seemed to be working. She looked away from him.

"You found it already?" he said incredulously. "You have, haven't you? But that's impossible so fast!"

She didn't confirm or deny; she gave no answer. He heard a crackle on the phone line and put it back to his ear. As he did so, he looked out the windows.

Dillinger, wielding a semiautomatic, was leading out two hostages carrying Jose Marquez. They brought him close to the gate, Dillinger keeping his weapon trained on them the entire time.

They left Jose and walked back into the house.

Dillinger followed them.

A second later the gate opened. Police rushed in and scooped up the security guard. They hurried out with him.

The gates closed and locked.

"Barrow! Barrow? Hey, you there?"

"Yes," Nick replied into the phone.

"We have the security guard. We'll get him to the hospital. What about the others? Do they need food, water?"

Kody was staring at him. He heard footsteps pounding up the stairs, as well.

Dillinger was back.

"Sit!" he told Kody. "Figure out what we need to do in order to get our hands on that stash."

To his surprise, she sat. She sat—and had the journal up in her hands before Dillinger returned to the room.

"Well?" Dillinger said to Nick.

Nick spoke into the phone. "We've given you the hostage in good faith. We really would like to see that all these good folks live, but, hey, they call bad guys bad guys because…they're bad. So back away from the gates and start making things happen. What about our boats?"

"I swear, we're getting you the best boats," Craig said.

"I want them now," Dillinger said.

"We need you to supply those boats now," Nick said, nodding to Dillinger and repeating his demand over the phone. "We need them out back, by the docks, and then we need you and your people to be far, far away."

"The boats will be there soon," Craig told Nick.

"Soon? Make that six or *seven* minutes at most!" he said.

He hoped Craig picked up on the clue. Stressing the word told him there were seven in this merry band of thieves.

"Don't push it too far!" Nick added. "Maybe we'll give you to ten or *eleven* minutes to get it together, but… well, you don't want hostages to start dying, do you?"

Easy enough. That told him there were eleven hostages, including Dakota Cameron, being held.

Dillinger looked at Nick and nodded, satisfied.

"We've got one of the boats," Craig said. "How do I get my man to bring it around and not get killed or become a hostage himself?" he asked.

"One boat?"

"So far. Getting our hands on what you want isn't easy," Craig said. "If we give you that one boat, what do we get?"

"You just got a man."

"We could find a second boat more quickly if we had a second man—or woman," Craig said.

They had to be careful; the negotiator's voice carried on the land line.

Of course, Craig Frasier knew that. He would be careful, but Nick knew that he had to be more so. Dakota could hear Craig, as well.

"Please," she said softly, "give them Stacey Carlson and Nan Masters. They're older. They'll just be like bricks around your neck when you need hostages for cover. Please, let them leave."

"Please," Dillinger said, mimicking her plea, "find what I want to know!"

"I might have," Kody said very softly.

"You might have?"

"Give the cops two more hostages. Give them Stacey and Nan," she said. "I'll show you what I think I've figured out once you've done that. Please."

Dillinger looked at Nick. "Hey, the lady said please. Let's accommodate her. Get on the phone and tell them to get the hell away from the gate. We'll give them two more solid, stand-up citizens." His eyes narrowed. "But I want my boats. Two boats. And I want them now. No ten minutes. No eleven minutes. I want them now!"

He looked at Kody. She was staring gravely at him.

"We have a present for you," he told Craig over the phone. "Two more hostages. Only we want two boats. Now. We want them right now."

"And if we don't get those boats soon…" Dillinger murmured.

He looked over at Kody.

And his eyes seemed to smile.

Chapter Three

"It's done. He's let them go. Three of the hostages. Your security man, Marquez, and the manager and his assistant."

Kody looked up from the journal she'd been reading.

Concentration had not been an easy feat; men were walking around with guns threatening to kill people. That made her task all the more impossible.

But it was Barrow who had walked in to speak with her. And the news was good. Three of her coworkers were safe.

And she was sure it was Craig Frasier out there doing the negotiating with them on the phone. Craig Frasier. From New York. In Miami.

But then, at Finnegan's, Kieran had been saying that Craig was going on the road; they'd been tracking a career criminal who'd recently gotten out of prison and was already starting up in NYC, and undercover agents in the city had warned that he was moving south.

Dillinger?

Was Craig Frasier here in Miami after Dillinger?

The masked man with the intense blue eyes was staring at her. She schooled her expression, not wanting to give away any of her thoughts or let on that she knew the negotiator and might know about their leader.

"So what happens now?" she asked. Capone was once again standing just outside the library, near the arched doorway to the room. He was, however, out of earshot, she thought, as long as they spoke softly.

"We need getaway boats. And, of course, Anthony Green's bank haul stash. How are you doing?" Barrow asked her.

How the hell was she doing?

Maybe—*maybe*—with days or weeks to work and every bit of reference from every conceivable source, she might have an answer. So far she had found some interesting information about the old gangster, Miami in the mob heyday, and even geography. She'd gone through specs and architectural plans on the house. But she was pretty sure she'd been right from the beginning—the stash was not at the house on Crystal Island. It was in the Everglades—somewhere.

To say that to find something in the Everglades was worse than finding a needle in a haystack was just about the understatement of the year. The Everglades was actually a river—"a river of grass," as one called it. On its own, it was ever-changing. Man, dams, the surge of sugar and beef plantations from the middle of the state on down, kept the rise and flow eternally moving, right along with nature. There were hammocks or islands of high land here and there. The Everglades also offered quicksand, dangerous native snakes and now, sixty-thousand-plus pythons and boas that had been let loose in the marsh and swamps, not to mention both alligators and, down in the brackish water, crocodiles, as well.

Great place to hide something!

"Well?" Barrow asked quietly.

"I don't think the stash is here," she said honestly. "Anthony Green talks about having a shack out in the

Everglades. My dad and his University of Miami buddies used to have one. They went hunting—they had their licenses and their permits to take two alligators each. But usually they just went to their shack, talked about school and sports and women—and then shot up beer cans. The shacks were outlawed twenty or thirty years ago. But that didn't mean the shacks all went down, or that some of the old-timers who run airboat rides or tours off of the Tamiami Trail don't remember where a lot of them are."

"So, the stash is in one of the old cabins," Barrow murmured. "But you don't know which—or where." He hesitated. "A place like Lost City?"

Kody stared at the man, surprised. Most of the people she knew who had grown up in the area hadn't even heard about Lost City.

Lost City was an area of about three acres, perhaps eight miles or so south of Alligator Alley, now part of I-75, a stretch of highway that crossed the state from northwestern Broward County over to the Naples/Ft. Myers area on the west coast of the state. It was suspected that Confederate soldiers had hidden out there after the Civil War, and many historians speculated that either Miccosukee or Seminole Indians had come upon them and massacred them all. Scholars believed it had been a major Seminole village at some point—and that it had been in use for hundreds of years.

But, most important, perhaps, was the fact that Al Capone—the real prohibition era gangster—had used the area to create his bootleg liquor.

She hesitated, not sure how much information to share—and how much to hold close.

Then again, she didn't have a single thing that was solid.

But…

It was evident he knew the area. Possibly, he'd grown up in South Florida, too. With the millions of people living in Miami-Dade and Broward counties alone, it was easy to believe they'd never met.

And yet, they had.

She knew his eyes.

And she had to believe that, slimy thief that he was, he was not a killer.

Yes, she had to believe it. Because she was depending on him, leaning on him, believing that he was the one who might save them—at the least, save their lives! She had to believe it because…

It wasn't right.

But, when she looked at him. When he spoke, when he made a move to protect one of them…

There was just something about him. And it made her burn inside and wish that…

Wish that he was the good guy.

"Something like that," she said, "except there's another version of the Al Capone distillery farther south. Supposedly, Anthony Green had a spot in the Everglades where he, too, distilled liquor. Near it, he had one of the old shacks. The place is up on an old hammock and, like the Capone site, it was once a Native American village, in this case, Miccosukee."

"You know where this place is?" Barrow asked her.

"Well, theoretically," she said with a shrug. "Almost all the Everglades is part of the national parks system, or belonging to either the Miccosukee or the Seminole tribes. But from what I understand, Anthony Green had his personal distillery on a hammock in the Shark Valley Slough—which empties out when you get to the Ten Thousand Islands, which are actually in Monroe

County. But I don't think that it's far from the observation tower at Shark Valley. There's a hammock—"

Kody stopped speaking when she noticed him staring down at one of the glass-framed historic notes she had set next to the Anthony Green journal she'd been cross-referencing.

"Chakaika," he said quietly.

She started, staring at him when he looked up and seemed to be smiling at her.

"A very different leader," he said. "Known as the 'Biggest Indian.' He was most likely of Spanish heritage, with mixed blood from the Creek perhaps, or another tribe that had members flee down to South Florida. Anyway, he was active from the center of the state on down—had his own mix of Spanish and Native American tongues and traded with other Native Americans, but seemed to have a hatred for the whites who wanted to ship the Indians to the west. He attacked the fort and he headed down to Pigeon Key, where he murdered Dr. Henry Perrine—who really was, by all historic record, a cool guy who just wanted to use his plants to find cures for diseases.

"Anyway, in revenge, Colonel Harney disguised himself and his men as Native Americans and brought canoes down after Chakaika, who thought they could not find him in the swamp. But they found a runaway slave of the leader's who led them right to the hammock where the man lived. They didn't let him surrender— they shot him and his braves, and then they hanged him. And the hammock became known as Hanging People Kay. I know certain park rangers believe they know exactly where it is."

Kody lowered her head, keeping silent for a minute. Her parents had been slightly crazy environmentalists. She knew all kinds of trivia about the state and its history. But while most people who had grown up down here might know the capital and the year the territory had become a state or the state bird or motto, few of them knew about Chakaika. Tourists sometimes stopped at the museum heading south on Pidgeon Key where Dr. Henry Perrine had once lived and worked, but nothing beyond that.

"Chakaika," he said again. "It's written clearly on the corner of that letter."

"Yes, well…they found oil barrels sunk in the area once," she murmured. "They were filled with two of Anthony Green's henchmen who apparently fell into ill favor with their boss. I know that the rangers out there are pretty certain they know the old Green stomping grounds—just like they know all about Chakaika. The thing is, of course, it's a river of grass. An entire ecosystem starting up at Lake Kissimmee and heading around Lake Okeechobee and down. Storms have come and gone, new drainage systems have gone in… I just don't know."

"It's enough to give him," Barrow said. "Enough to make him move."

Kody leaned forward suddenly. "You don't want to kill people. You hate the man. So why don't you shoot him in the kneecap or something?"

"And then Capone would shoot us all," Barrow said. "Do you really think that I could just gun them all down?"

"No, but you could—"

"Injure a man like that, and you might as well shoot yourself," he told her. "And, never mind. I have my reasons for doing what I'm doing. There's no other choice."

"There's always a choice," Kody said.

"No," he told her flatly, "there's not. So, if you want to keep breathing and keep all your friends alive, as well—"

Dillinger came striding in. "So, Miss Cameron. Where is my treasure?"

"Dammit! Listen to me and believe me! It's not here, not in the house, not on the island," she told him. She realized that while she was speaking fairly calmly, she was shivering, shaking from head to toe.

It was Dillinger and Barrow in the room then.

If Dillinger attacked her, what would Barrow do? Risk himself to defend her?

There certainly was no treasure at the house—other than the house itself—to give Dillinger. She'd told him the truth.

"So, where is it?" he demanded.

Thankfully he didn't seem to be surprised that it wasn't in the Crystal Manor.

"I have no guarantees for you," she said. "But I do have a working theory. This letter," she said, pausing to tap the historic, framed note that had been hand-penned by Anthony Green, "refers to the 'lovely hammock beneath the sun.' It was written to Lila Bay, Green's favorite mistress. In summary, Green tells her that when he's about on business and she's missing him, she should rest awhile in the hammock, and find there the diamond-like luster of the sun and the emerald green of the landscape."

"What's that on the corner?" Dillinger demanded suspiciously.

"It's the name of a long-ago chief or leader who was killed there. I think it was a further reference for Green when he was trying to see to it that Lila found the stash from the bank," Kody said.

Dillinger stood back, balancing the rifle he carried as he crossed his arms over his chest and stared at her.

"So, my treasure is in an alligator-laden swamp—along with rattlers, coral snakes, cottonmouths and whatever else! And we're just supposed to go out to the swamp and start digging in the saw grass and the muck?" Dillinger said.

"I'm still reading his personal references," Kody said. "But, yes. I can't put this treasure where it isn't. I'm afraid I'd falter and you'd know me for a liar in an instant."

"And you think you can find this treasure in acres of swamp land?" he asked.

Everything in Kody seemed to recoil. She shook her head. "I'm not going into the swamp. I don't care about the treasure or the stash. You do. I mean, I can keep reading and give you directions, all kinds of suggestions, but I—"

"Come on, Dillinger," Barrow said. "She'd be a pain in the ass out in the swamp!"

Dillinger turned to stare at Barrow. "She's going with us, one way or the other."

"What?" Barrow asked.

"Did you think I'm crazy? No way in hell we're leaving here without a hostage. We'll take Miss Cameron here for sure. I can't wait to see her dig in the muck and the old gator holes until she finds the diamonds and the emeralds! Come on, Barrow, you can't be that naive. They're not going to just give us speedboats. They're going to have the Coast Guard out. They're going to be following us. Now, I'm not without friends, and I'm pretty damned good at losing people who are chasing me, but…hey, you need to have a living hostage." He turned to Kody. "And, of course, Miss Cameron, if you're going to send us on a wild-goose chase, you have to understand just how it will end for you."

The house line began to ring again.

Dillinger looked at Barrow. "Get it! See if they have my boats for me now. You!" He pointed a finger at Kody. "You figure it out—or you will be the one in the snake and gator waters!"

Kody looked down quickly at the journal she was reading. She prayed he couldn't see just how badly she was shaking.

She knew local lore. She'd walked the trails at Shark Valley. She'd driven out from the city a few times just to buy pumpkin bread at the restaurant across from the park.

But she'd never camped in the Everglades. She'd never even gotten out of her car on the trail once it had grown dark.

Tramping out in alligator- and snake-infested swamps? No way.

"Get the line," Dillinger told Barrow again when the phone continued to ring.

Barrow answered.

"Where are the boats? We're doing our best to make sure that this works but you need to start moving on your end. And, be warned—no cops, no Coast Guard, no nothing coming after us!" he said.

He looked over at Dillinger. "He's getting us a pair of Donzi racers."

"That will do," Dillinger said. "As long as he starts getting it done. As long as he backs off some."

"You keep your men in check—I mean stay back," Barrow said to the person on the other end of the line.

Barrow covered the phone with his hand. "He swears they won't fire unless they're fired on. You've made that clear to the others, Dillinger, right? I don't want one of those trigger-happy psychos getting me killed."

"Hey, we fire on them, they fire back," Dillinger said with a shrug. "Like the saying goes, no one lives forever. If they shoot, they take a chance on killing a hostage!"

Barrow politely relayed Dillinger's threat. Then he walked out of the room, leaving Kody alone with Dillinger.

She kept telling herself that Craig was out there. He was playing a careful game, all that any man could do when hostages were involved.

Did Craig know she was in there? Of course, she knew him, she'd had meals with him and Kieran and the Finnegan family, and they'd talked about her home in Miami and the estate on Crystal Island with all its mob ties...

She blinked, determined that she not give anything away.

Dillinger just looked at her and tapped his fingers on the desk. "We need you, Miss Cameron. Isn't that nice? As long as you're needed, you know that you'll live. Remember that."

Then Dillinger, too, walked out of the room.

Kody looked around, wondering what was near her that might possibly be used as a weapon.

Nothing.

Nothing in the room stood up to a gun.

NICK STOOD WITH Dillinger in the ballroom—the large stretch on the left side of the house that connected two of the towers. Crown moldings and silk wallpaper made the room a work of real, old-artisan beauty, but, at the moment, it felt empty and their soft-spoken conversation seemed to echo loudly with the acoustics of the room.

"You played us all," he told Dillinger. "You made us all think that coming here was the job—that there was something here we'd be taking. In and out. Quick and easy. Round up people as a safety net and then get the hell out."

"I said the house was the key to great riches!" Dillinger said. "And this is an easy gig. We have some scared people. We have the cops keeping their distance at the gate. The guard is going to be okay. At worst, he'll have some stitches and a concussion. So, Barrow, don't be a pansy. You know what? I'm not so fond of the killing part myself. But, hell, when a job needs to be done…" He let Nick complete the thought himself.

Instead, Nick went on the offensive. "If Miss Cameron is right, we've got to go south from here and then west into the Everglades. Donzi speedboats aren't going to take us in to where we need to be. I don't think you planned this out."

"You don't think?" Dillinger said, tapping Nick on the forehead. "You don't think? Well, my friend, you're wrong. I know where Donzis won't take us— and I know where airboats will take us! I've done lots of thinking."

"This isn't an in and out!" Nick snapped.

"No. But the reward will be worth the effort."

So, Dillinger had known all along that what he'd wanted wouldn't be found on the property. And he had other plans in the works already. Who else was in on it? Any of the men? None of them? Was Dillinger so uptight and paranoid that he hadn't trusted a single person in their group?

Nick was pretty sure he was doing a decent job of

maintaining his cover while giving his real coworkers as much information as possible. Craig and their local FBI counterparts and law enforcement knew how many men were in the house—and how many hostages remained. He hadn't been able to risk a call to Craig—other than those he made as Barrow. While the agent didn't know the who, how or where, he now knew Dillinger had expected he'd have to leave the house to find his treasure. Would he assume that he'd be heading out to the Everglades, given the legends?

Dillinger had to have people lined up and waiting to help him. As he'd said, to get where they wanted to go, a Donzi would be just about worthless. They'd need an airboat.

Dillinger had no doubt been playing this game for the long run from the get-go.

It was still crazy. There was no real treasure they were taking from the house. There was just information—a major league *maybe* on where treasure might be found.

Dillinger was, in Nick's mind, extremely dangerous. He was crazy enough to have taken a house—a historic property—for what might possibly have been found in it.

And while none of them had even so much as suspected Dillinger would go off and do something like kidnap a child, he had done so—and been smug when he'd let them all know that he had the child for extra leverage.

The kid changed everything. Everything.

Nick couldn't wait for that moment when Dillinger was off guard and the others were in different places and he could take him down and then wait for the others. He couldn't risk losing Dillinger—not until he knew where the man was holding the little boy.

First thing now, though, Nick knew, was to get them all out of the house—alive.

Then he'd just have to keep Dakota Cameron—and himself—alive until Dillinger somehow slipped and told them where to find little Adrian Burke. Then he'd have to get himself and Kody away from Dillinger and whoever the hell else he had in on it and—

Baby steps, he warned himself.

"Here's the thing—we haven't done anything yet, not really," he told Dillinger. "Okay, assault—that's what they can get us on. They don't understand what we're doing, why in God's name we've taken this place, why we've taken hostages…and they really don't have anything. What you really want—what we all want—is the Anthony Green bank-job treasure. They just promised that they're getting the boats—that they'll be here right away. The young woman whose family owns this place is still reading records and I do think she's gotten something in two hours that no one else thought of in decades. Not that it doesn't mean we'll be digging in the muck forever but…I really suggest that you let more hostages go," Nick said.

"I don't know," Dillinger said. "Yeah, maybe… maybe we should get rid of that one woman—the one with the mouth on her. She might be stupid enough to attempt something."

"Good idea. Here's the thing—the hostages are weakening us. We have the hostages in the front and the front towers covered, and you've proven you have sharpshooters up there who will pick off men and happily join in a gunfight. But, with everyone moving around and everything going on, we are missing a man for sound protection in back. I'm afraid they'll eventually figure that out. Let go a few more hostages, and we'll be in a better position to control the ones we do keep."

Dillinger seemed to weigh his words.

Then they heard shots—individual rat-a-tats and then a spray of gunfire.

Dillinger swore, staring at Nick. "What the hell? What the bloody hell?"

"I guarantee you, the cops and the Feds were clean on that," Nick snapped. "One of your boys just went crazy with a pistol and an automatic."

He raced down the length of the room to the stairs to the tower. He was certain the first shots had come from that direction.

Another round of gunfire sounded. Nick ran on up the stairs.

Schultz was there, spraying rounds everywhere.

"What the hell is the matter with you?" Nick shouted.

The man was wielding a semiautomatic. He had to take great care.

Schultz gave him a wild-eyed look before he turned back to the window. Nick made a flying leap at him, hitting him in his midsection, bringing him down.

The semiautomatic went flying across the floor.

Nick rose, ready to yell at Schultz. But the man was staring up at him with swiftly glazing eyes. He was dead. A crack police marksman had evidently returned the spray of bullets with true accuracy.

"Hey, Barrow! Schultz!" Dillinger shouted from below.

Nick inhaled. He stood and went to the stairs.

"You brought in an idiot on this, Dillinger!" he called down. "They've taken down Schultz. The idiot just went crazy and the police returned his fire. A sharpshooter got him. We need to play for a little time while those boats get here. We need to let more of the hostages go—now. If they figure out just how weak we are in numbers, they might storm the house."

"They do, and everybody dies!" Dillinger swore.

"Don't think with your ass, Dillinger. We can pull this off if no one else acts like we're in the wild, wild, West! I want to live. I didn't come in on a frigging suicide mission! We came here for something. We need to keep calm and figure out the best way to get it. Let me offer up more hostages."

"The girl almost has it. We can grab up whatever journals and all she's using and take the boats. I want them now!"

"The boats are coming. Let me free a hostage!" Nick pleaded.

Dillinger was quiet for a minute. "Yeah, fine. Just one."

"Two would be better. There's a young couple down there—"

"No, only one of them. And tell the cops if another one of our number dies, they'll have all dead hostages. One way or the other!" Dillinger snapped. "Schultz is dead," he reminded Nick. "We should retaliate. Kill someone—not let them go."

Nick hurried along the hall back to the library, Dillinger close at his heels.

The phone was already ringing when they reached the room.

Dakota Cameron remained behind the library desk.

Her face was white, but rather than afraid she looked uneasy. Guilty of something.

For the moment Nick ignored her. He picked up the

phone. Once again Craig was on the other end and they were going to play their parts.

"What happened?" Craig asked.

"Your people got a little carried away with fire," Nick said. "We now have a dead man. We should kill a hostage."

"No. The boats are coming. And your man started the firing. He was trying to kill people out here. Our people had to fire back."

"Do it again, the hostages die."

"We don't want to fire."

"Yeah, well, we have anxious people up here carrying semiautomatic weapons. But just to prove that we can keep our side of a bargain, we're going to give you another hostage. Then we want the boats."

"Yes, all right. That can be done."

"We'll have someone for you, so watch the gate. No tricks or someone will die."

"No tricks," Craig said.

Nick hung up. Dillinger was looking at him.

"Okay, we give them a hostage," Nick said. "Or two."

"Two? I said—"

"Two. We'll give them the sassy girl—Betsy, I think her name is—and then a guest. All right?"

"Fine. Do it," Dillinger said.

"You want me out there?" Nick asked.

"Yes, you, Mr. Diplomacy. Get out there."

Nick was surprised. "You're leaving her alone upstairs?" he asked.

"No." Dillinger looked over at Kody, smiled and headed over to her. "I'll be close. But just to be careful..." He reached into his pocket and pulled out police-issue plastic cuffs.

"Miss Cameron, one wrist will do. We just need to

see that you don't leave the desk. I can attach you right here, to the very pretty little whirligig in the wood," Dillinger said.

Nick was relieved to see that Kody offered him her left wrist and just watched and waited in silence as he secured it to the desk. She didn't protest; she didn't cause trouble. She was probably just glad they were letting another hostage free.

But Nick didn't trust her. She was a fighter.

"Miss Cameron, you have all the clues, clues that are like a road map, right? You know what we need to do?" Dillinger asked her.

"I have an area. I have an idea," Kody said.

"Don't lie to me," Dillinger said.

She shook her head. "I told you—no guarantees. This treasure has been missing for decades. I believe I know where you can dig, but whether it's still there or not, I don't know. Even the earth shifts with time."

"I knew you could find it, my dear Miss Cameron!"

"Me? How did you even know I'd be here? I don't even live here anymore. I live in New York," Kody said.

"Oh, Miss Cameron. Of course, I checked out my information about the stash, the house—and you. It was possible but I doubted that the treasure would be in the house. I knew that you were here. I knew how much you loved this old house…and, yeah, I knew you'd be leaving soon. So it was time to act." He shrugged, as if he was done explaining. "Now let me get rid of your big-mouthed friend. You help me, I help you. That's the way it works."

Dillinger turned and looked at Nick.

Nick gritted down hard on his teeth.

Yeah, they'd all been taken on this one. Dillinger

had known damned well that he hadn't gotten them all to take the house for the treasure.

They'd taken the house for Dakota Cameron.

Because Dillinger believed that she was the map to the treasure.

"Get going, Barrow. Do it. I'll be watching from the top of the stairs. I mean, I really wouldn't want to leave Miss Cameron completely alone," Dillinger said.

Nick headed on out and down the sweeping marble stairs to the first floor.

He was loath to leave the upstairs, especially now that Schultz had been killed. He was afraid Dillinger would lose all logic in a frenzied moment of anger and start shooting.

But he had no choice. And Dillinger needed Kody Cameron. He wouldn't hurt her.

Dillinger was at the top of the stairs.

Watching Kody.

Watching Nick.

And there was nothing to do but play out the man's game…

And make it to the finish line.

Chapter Four

Capone and Nelson were with the hostages when Nick arrived in the living room. The group of them was still huddled together.

The group, at least, was a little smaller now.

"You," he said quietly, pointing at the tiny woman who had given them the hardest time. "What's your name?"

"What's it to you?" she demanded.

He fired his gun—aiming at a mirror on the wall. It exploded. He waited in silence.

"Betsy Rodriguez!" the young woman answered him.

"Thank you," he told her. "Come on."

"What?" she asked.

"Come on. You're going out."

"Me. Just me?"

"No," he said and pointed to another young woman. She appeared to be in her mid- to late-twenties; she was clinging to the arm of the man beside her. They were a couple. It was going to be hard to split them up.

But it was what Dillinger wanted.

"You," he said to the young woman.

"Us?" she asked. As he'd expected, she didn't want to be separated from the man she was with.

"No. Just you," he said softly.

The young woman began to sob. "No," she said stubbornly. "No, no, no!"

"Please, miss," Nick said. "Honestly, none of us wants any of you dead. Help me try to see that no one does wind up dead."

"Go, Melissa, please go," the dark-haired man who was with her said. "Go!" he told her. "Please. I need to know that you're all right."

"Victor, I can't leave you," the woman—whom he now knew to be named Melissa—said.

Melissa hugged the man she had called Victor. He pulled away from her, saying, "You can and you must."

"How touching! How sweet!" Capone said.

"Nauseating!" Nelson agreed. He walked over as if about to strike one of them with the butt of his gun.

Nick moved more quickly, walking through the huddled crowd to reach Melissa and pull her to her feet. He looked down at Victor as he did so. There was something cold and hateful in the man's eyes. Cold, hateful—and oddly calm.

The guy was a cop! Nick thought. Some kind of a cop or law enforcement. He just knew it. He also knew the man wasn't going to cause trouble when he couldn't win.

Nick thought about the situation quickly. It would be good to have another cop around—except this guy didn't know that he was FBI and he could easily kill Nick thinking he was with the bad guys—which he was, by all appearances.

He reached down and grasped the man's arm.

"Victor, you're coming, too."

The man stood and looked at him. "No, don't take me. Take the young woman who is one of the guides here. She's very scared. I'm scared—just not as scared," Victor said.

Nick liked him.

He wished he could keep him around, that they were in a situation where they could trust one another.

They weren't.

"No, I think we're going to let you lovebirds go together. I don't want my friends here becoming nauseated."

"Hey!" Nelson said. "He told you to go. You don't want us shooting up your lovey-dovey young wife, do you?"

Staring at Nick with a gaze that could cut steel, Victor took his wife's arm and started out of the room, followed by Betsy Rodriguez and then Nick.

He had to be careful now. Dillinger was watching from upstairs and Nelson was following him out to the porch.

Nick walked out toward the gate, making his way slightly past Betsy Rodriguez. He came as close to Victor as he dared and spoke swiftly.

"Cop? Please, for the love of God, tell me the truth," Nick said urgently.

Victor stared at him and then nodded.

"Tell Agent Frasier that the main man plans to get out to the Everglades, down south of the Trail, near Shark Valley. Keep his distance. Watch for men abetting along the way."

It was all he dared say. He shoved the man forward, shouting to the assembled police, agents and whoever else at the gate, "Get the hell back! Take these three— and remember, sharpshooters have a bead on you and inside there are a few guns aimed at the skulls of a few hostages."

Craig Frasier stepped forward, his hands raised, showing that he was unarmed.

"No trouble! And boats will show up at the docks

almost as we speak. But what's the guarantee for the rest of the hostages?"

"You'll find them once we're gone. Most of them," he added quietly. "But we need assurances that we won't be followed. Get too close and— Well, just keep your distance."

He stepped back behind the gate and locked it again.

Betsy Rodriguez and Melissa went running toward officers who were waiting to greet them with blankets.

Only Victor held back a moment, nodding imperceptibly to Nick.

"Wait!" Craig called. "I need more...more on the hostages to give you the two boats."

"As soon as I can see them from the back, I'll bring out a few more," he promised.

"I'll be here. Waiting."

Nick nodded gravely. He turned and headed back toward the house.

As he'd suspected, Capone had waited and watched from the porch.

Nelson was with the rest of the hostages. Dillinger was still upstairs and Floyd and Kelly would be manning the towers.

He doubted that anyone other than himself and Dillinger knew Schultz was dead. Dillinger wouldn't have shared that news, fearing the others might have wanted revenge.

Dillinger only wanted one thing: the treasure.

Capone walked with him through the grand foyer and into the music room. "Good call, by the way, on getting rid of that cop," Capone said.

Nick looked at him; Capone was no idiot. "You saw that, too?"

"Yep. That kind of guy is dangerous. We don't want any heroes around here, you know."

"No heroes," Nick agreed. He shook his head. "I've got to admit—it's got me a little worried. Getting out of here, I mean." He hesitated. A man really wouldn't want to be bad-talking an accomplice in an evil deed. "I kind of thought that Dillinger was sure what he wanted was here. I guess he had the idea we might be heading someplace else to find it all along—and that's why he took the kid. More leverage."

"Yeah, I'm figuring that's the leverage he's using to get us all out of here. Do the cops even know he's the one who took the boy?" Capone asked. "You know, I've done some bad things, but I've never hurt a kid. That's why he didn't tell us. Hell, even in prison, the men who hurt, kill or molest kids are the ones in trouble. I'd never hurt a kid!"

"Nor would I—and probably not our other guys, either, but who knows. And I don't know if the cops know that Dillinger took the boy yet, but I'm figuring they do. And if they find the kid…"

"If they find the kid, we may all be screwed," Capone said.

"Do you know where he stashed him?"

Capone shrugged. "He didn't tell me. Dillinger isn't the trusting kind. Let's just hope he knows what the hell he's doing."

Nick nodded.

He really hoped to hell he knew what he was doing himself.

KODY HAD A letter opener.

Not just any letter opener, she told herself. This was a

letter opener that was now considered a historic or collectible piece. It was fashioned to look like a shiv—the same kind of weapon often carried by Anthony Green and his thugs. They'd been sold at almost every tourist shop in Miami right after Green had been gunned down on the beach.

Now, they were rare. And collectible.

And she had slid the one the property had proudly displayed on the library desk into the pocket of her jeans.

Yep, she thought, a letter opener. Against automatic weapons. Still, it was something.

Maybe it would help once they got to the Everglades. She didn't imagine it would do much against a full-size alligator if one came upon her while she was trying to find the place in the glades where Anthony Green might have hidden his stash—or even one of the thousands of pythons. But at least it was something.

She looked up as Dillinger came striding back into the room.

"How are you doing?" he asked her.

She stared back at him. "Um, just great?" she suggested.

He laughed softly. "You are something, Miss Cameron. You see, I do know what I'm doing. I know that you know what you're doing. See, if you were to go online and Google yourself, you'd find some of your acting pages or your SAG page or whatever it is, and you'd find some promo pictures and play reviews and things like that. But when you keep going, you find out that you were quite the little writer when you were in college and that you did a feature for the school paper on the mob in Miami. You'd already done a lot of studying up on Anthony Green—and why not? Your dad inherited this place! Now, of course, I know you're not rich, that he runs it all in a trust. But I knew that if anyone knew how to get rich, it would be you. As in—if anyone could find the stash, it would be you."

Kody tried not to blink too much as she looked back at him. The man wasn't just scary. He was creepy. He was some kind of an intellectual stalker—and knew things about her that she'd half forgotten herself. It was terrifying to realize he'd really gone on a cyber-hunt for her—and that he'd found far more than most people would ever want to find.

Her skin seemed to crawl.

"I keep telling you this—there's no guarantee. Most people who have studied Anthony Green and Crystal Island and even the mob in general have believed that Green stashed his treasure out in the Everglades. I think I've found verification of that—and that's all," she said.

"But you know just about where. Everyone has looked around Shark Valley—but you know more precisely where. Because you also studied the Seminole Wars, and you loved the Tamiami Trail growing up—and made your parents drive you back and forth from the east to the west of the Florida peninsula all the time."

"I didn't make them," Kody protested, noting how ridiculous her words were under the circumstances. "And you really are counting on what may not exist at all."

"The stash exists!"

"Unless it was found years ago. Unless it's sunk so deep no one will ever find it. Oh, my God, come on! Criminals have written volumes on people killed and tossed into the Everglades, criminals through time who never did a day of time because the Everglades can hide just about anything—and anyone! I can try. I can try with everything I've learned now that I've been put to the fire, and everything that I know from what I've heard and what I've read through the years. But—"

She broke off. He was, she was certain, smiling—even if she couldn't exactly see his face.

"That's right," he said softly. "Bodies have disappeared out there. You might want to remember that."

"Maybe you should remember not to threaten people and scare them and make them totally unnerved when you want them to do calculated thinking!" she countered quickly.

He held still, quiet for a minute. "It will be fun when we reach the peak, Miss Cameron. It will be fun," he promised.

Ice seemed to stir and settle in her veins.

It would be fun...

He meant to kill her.

And still, she'd play it out. Right now, of course, because many lives were resting on her managing to keep this man believing...

And then, of course, because her life depended on it.

Barrow came striding into the room, his blue eyes blazing from his mask. As they lit on her, she felt the intensity of their stare and once again she had a strange feeling that she'd been touched by those eyes before.

"We're closing in on time to go. What are you going to need here, Miss Cameron?" he asked. Then he turned to Dillinger. "I'd wrap up whatever books and journals she wants to take. We'll be getting wet, getting out of here in speedboats."

"Well, what do you need, Miss Cameron?" Dillinger asked.

Barrow had walked over to the windows that looked out over the water.

"They're coming now," he said.

Dillinger walked over to join him. "They've stopped about a mile out."

"I'll give them a few more people and they'll bring the boats in to the docks. Their people will clear the area and we'll leave the last of the hostages on the dock for them," Barrow said.

"Not good enough," Dillinger said. "We need at least a couple of them with us."

"All right, how's this? We let three go. We take two with us—and leave them off once we're a safe distance away."

"I say when it's a safe distance. And if they follow us, the hostages are dead," Dillinger said flatly.

"I'm telling you, hostages will be like bricks around our necks once we start moving," Barrow said.

"Let the guests go. There are a couple of people who work here left—keep them," Dillinger said.

Kody jumped up. "If you're taking them, let me talk to my friends. The guides who work here. Let me talk to them. It will make it easier for you."

Dillinger pulled out a knife. For a moment she thought that Barrow was going to fly across the room and stop him from stabbing her.

But he didn't intend to stab her.

He cut through the plastic cuffs that held her to the desk.

"Go down. I'll warn our guys in the turrets about what's going on," he said.

Barrow caught Kody by the arm. She wanted to wrench free but she didn't. She felt the strength of his hold—and the pressure of her shiv letter opener in her pocket.

She glanced at him as they headed down the stairs.

"This isn't the time," he said.

"The time for what?"

"Any kind of trick."

"I wasn't planning one, but if I had, wouldn't this be the right time—I mean, before we're in a bog or marsh and saw grass and Dillinger shoots me down?"

Those blue eyes of his lit on her with the strangest assessment.

"Now is not the time," he repeated.

She looked away quickly. The man put out such mixed signals. He didn't like blood and guts, yet he didn't want any escape attempts.

He headed with her into the music room where they joined Capone and Nelson.

"You, you, and you!" he said, pointing out the two male and the one female guests.

They stood, looking at one another anxiously. Kody was amazed at how clearly she remembered their names now. The men were Gary Goodwin and Kevin Dean. The woman was Carey Herring.

"No, no, no! They're getting out—and we're not!"

Kody turned quickly to see that Brandi Johnson, her face damp with tears, was looking at the trio who was then standing.

She left Barrow's side, hurrying over to the young woman. "It's okay. It's okay, Brandi," she said. She squeezed the girl's hand and then pulled her close, talking to her and to the young man with the thick glasses at her side. "Brandi, Vince, we're all going to be together. We're going to be fine. Don't you worry. They need us."

"I'm good, Kody. I'm good," Vince told her. She smiled at him grimly. She really loved Vince; he was as smart as a whip and loved everything about his job at the estate. He had contacts that he seldom wore and he was a runner—a marathon runner. He'd told her once that he liked to look like a nerd—which, of course, he was, in a way—because nerds were in.

He would be good to have at her side. Except…

She was very afraid that Brandi was right; they were the ones who would end up dead.

But not now. Right now, she was still needed. All she had to do was to make sure that Dillinger believed they could all be important in finding his precious Anthony Green treasure.

"Come on, you three, it's your lucky day," Barrow said quietly to the guests. "Let's go."

Kody stayed behind with the two guides, taking their arms in hers. "Just hang tight with me," she whispered to a trembling Brandi.

"Stop it. Move away from each other," Nelson told them.

"She's scared!" Kody informed him. "We're not doing anything. She's just scared."

Barrow—who almost had the three being released out the door—paused and looked back. "They're okay, Nelson. Trust me." He turned to Kody. "No tricks at this moment in time, right?"

She met those eyes and, for whatever reason, she had a feeling he was giving her advice she needed to heed. "No tricks."

ALL THE WAY to the gate, the young woman who was being set free looked back at Nick, tripped and had to grasp someone to keep standing.

"We're almost at the gate," Nick told her. "Look, it's all right. You're going!"

"Someone is going to shoot me in the back!" she whispered tearfully.

"No, you're safe. You're out of here."

When he got the gate open, Craig Frasier raised his arms to show that he was unarmed then stepped forward to accept the hostages.

As he did so, they heard a short blast of gunfire.

"What the hell!" Nick muttered, spinning around furiously. The angle meant the shot had come from one of the towers—and it hadn't been aimed at one of the hostages, him or Craig.

The shot had been aimed at the sky.

Dillinger. He'd headed up to one of the towers himself.

He leaned out over the coral rock balustrade to shout out to the FBI.

"We've got three young people left. They will die if you don't back off completely. You follow us, they die. It's that simple. Do you understand?"

Craig pushed the three hostages through the gate, then stepped back from the fence, lifting his hands. "We aren't following. How do we get the last three?" he shouted.

"We'll call you. Give Barrow there a number. If we get out safe and sound, they'll be safe. Even deal. Got it?"

Craig reached into his pocket and handed Nick his card. Nick shoved the card into the pocket of his shirt. Barely perceptible, Craig nodded. Then he shouted again, calling out to Dillinger, "You have someone else. The boy that was kidnapped this morning. When are you going to give us the boy?"

For a moment Dillinger was silent. Then he spoke.

"When I'm ready. When you keep your word. When

you get these hostages back, you'll know how to find the boy."

"Give us the boy now—in good faith. He's just a kid," Craig said, looking at Nick for some sign. But Nick shook his head. So far, he hadn't gotten Dillinger to say anything.

"Kids are resilient!" Dillinger called. "You keep your word, you get the kid."

Craig looked at Nick again. Nick did his best to silently convey the fact that he knew it was imperative they keep everyone alive—and that he figured out where Dillinger had stashed Adrian Burke before it was too late.

The cop—Victor Arden—had apparently repeated word for word what Nick had said earlier. Craig knew what Nick knew so far; they wouldn't have to follow the Donzis at a discreet distance. Dillinger would take his band the sixty-plus miles from their location there on the island down and around the peninsula, curving around Homestead and Florida City, to Everglades National Park.

Every available law-enforcement officer from every agency—Coast Guard, U.S. Marshals, State Police, Rangers, FBI, Miccosukee Police and so forth—would be on the lookout. At a distance.

While that was promising, the sheer size of the Everglades kept Nick from having a good feeling. Too many people got lost in the great "river of grass" and were never seen again.

He needed to actually speak with Craig—without being watched or heard.

"The boats are docking now in back," Craig told him. "How will my men get back?" He looked up at the tower and raised his voice. "If they're assaulted in any way—"

A shot was fired—into the sky once again.

And Dillinger spoke, shouting out his words. "They just walk off onto the dock. You stay where you are. My friend, Mr. Barrow there, is going to walk around and bring them to you. You know that I have sharpshooters up here in the towers. No tricks. Hey, if I'm going to die here today, everybody can die here today!"

"We don't want anyone to die," Craig said.

"So, my boats best not run out of gas," Dillinger said. "Fix it now…or a hostage dies, I guarantee you."

"You're not going to run out of gas. You have good boats, in sound working order," Craig promised him. "My men will leave the boats' keys in the ignitions, and give Barrow here backups. As soon as my men are safely off the property, we'll all back away."

"Go get 'em, Barrow!" Dillinger shouted.

Nick backed away from the fence and then turned to follow the tile path around the house and out to the back. He traversed the gardens to the docks.

There were two Donzis there, both a good size, both compact and tight. They were exactly what Dillinger had wanted.

Two men, Metro-Dade police, Nick thought, leaped up onto the dock as they saw Nick. They eyed him carefully as he came to meet them. He figured they knew his undercover part in this, but they would still carry out the charade for his safety.

He reached for the keys then he pretended to jerk the two men around and push them forward. He lowered his head and spoke softly. "Tell Frasier and the powers that be to concentrate south of Shark Valley. Around Anthony Green's old distillery grounds."

"Gotcha," one of the men murmured, turning back

to look at Nick and raise his hands higher, as if trying to make sure Nick wouldn't shoot him.

"They're after Green's treasure?" the second man asked, incredulous. "Asses!" he murmured. "Everyone is still…okay?"

"Yeah. I'm trying to keep it that way," Nick said. He fell silent. They had come closer to the house on the path. In a few steps they'd be turning the corner to the front. He couldn't risk Dillinger so much as looking at his lip movement suspiciously.

He got the two men to the gate, opened it and shoved them out.

He carefully locked the gate again, looking at Craig.

There was no shout and there were no instructions from the tower. Dillinger, he knew, had already moved on. He'd have gotten what books and materials Dakota Cameron was using and he'd have headed on down and out.

Nick walked backward for a few minutes and then headed back into the house.

As he'd expected, it was empty.

He went through the music room, checked the courtyard and made his way through the vast back porch to look out to the docks.

The cons were already on their way to the boats with the hostages. Dillinger himself was escorting Kody Cameron.

Nick reached the docks just as Dillinger was handing out boat assignments.

Nelson, Capone, Kelly and the young woman, Brandi Johnson, were to take one boat.

Dillinger would take the second with Floyd, Vince and Kody Cameron.

And Barrow, of course.

"Barrow, move it!"

"No!" Brandi cried, trying to break free from Capone to reach Kody and Vince. "No, please, no. Please don't make me be alone, please…"

"You don't need to be alone. I can shoot you right here," Dillinger said.

"Then you can shoot me, too!" Kody snapped. "You let her come with us or you let me go with her, one or the other!"

"I should shoot you!" Dillinger flared, gripping Kody by the front of her tailored shirt.

"Hey!" Barrow stepped in, extracting Kody from Dillinger's grip—a little less than gently—and staring down Dillinger. "Eyes on the prize, remember? Can we get out of here, dammit! Let's go while the going is good. Vince, just go with the nice Mr. Nelson, nice Mr. Capone, and nice Mr. Kelly, please. Brandi—Miss Johnson, step aboard that boat, please!"

Everyone seemed to freeze in response to his words to Dillinger for a minute.

Then Dillinger ripped off his cheap costume shop mask and glared around at everyone.

Nick had his hand on Kody's arm. He could feel the trembling that began.

Now they all knew what Dillinger looked like. They could identify him. Until now, the hostages weren't at much of a risk.

Now they were.

"What are you doing?" Capone began.

"What's the difference?" Dillinger spat. "Who cares? We'll be long gone, and we'll leave these guys in the Everglades. By the time they're found—if they're found—we'll be gone."

The others hesitated and then took off their masks.

And Barrow had no choice. He took off his mask and stared at Kody—praying.

The instant he pulled it off, he detected the flare in her eyes.

She recognized him, of course. Knew that she knew him…immediately. He'd always had the feeling she'd suspected he was familiar, but now that she could see his face, she was certain.

But from the look of confusion that overtook her face, he knew she couldn't place him exactly. And if she did figure it out, he'd have to pray she was bright enough to not say anything. She had to be. Both their lives depended on it.

"Let's get going!"

Nick moved them along, hopping into the front Donzi himself without giving Dillinger a chance to protest.

Dillinger followed, allowing his changes.

Nick turned the key in the ignition, shouting back to Capone after his boat roared to life, "You good back there?"

"She's purring like a kitten!" Capone called to him.

Nick led the way. He looked anxiously to the horizon and the shoreline. He skirted the other islands, shot under the causeway, joining the numerous other boats.

There was no way to tell which might be pleasure boats and which might be police. He had to trust in Craig to see that law enforcement got in front of them, that officers would be in the Everglades to greet them.

He drove hard for forty-five minutes. The day was cool and clear; under different circumstances, it would have been a beautiful day for boating.

Dillinger suddenly stood by him at the helm. "Cut the motor!" he commanded.

"I thought you wanted—"

"Cut the motor!"

Nick did so. "What are you doing?"

"See that fine-looking vessel up there? Not quite a yacht, but I'd say she's a good thirty feet of sleek speed."

"Yeah, so?"

"We're taking her."

"Ah, come on, Dillinger! She's not the prize," Nick protested.

The second Donzi came up next to them. "That one?" Kelly shouted to Dillinger.

"Looks good to me," Dillinger shouted back.

Nick realized they'd come up with this game plan while he'd been working with the hostages.

"No," Nick said. "No, no, this isn't good."

"What are you, an ass?" Dillinger asked him. "You don't think the cops won't be looking for these Donzis soon enough? Even if they know we have hostages— even they know I took the kid. We're taking that boat!"

Kelly was already moving his boat around the larger vessel. He started shouting. A grizzly-looking fellow with bright red skin and a captain's hat appeared at the rail. "What the hell are you carrying on about, boy?" he demanded.

Kelly lifted his semiautomatic and pointed it at the old man. "Move over, sir! We're coming aboard!"

"Son of a bitch!" Nick roared. He kicked his vessel back into gear, flooring it on a course toward the second Donzi.

Kelly turned to him, gun in hand.

"What the hell is the matter with you?" Nick demanded of Kelly.

"What the hell is the matter with *you*?" Dillinger asked him.

"We're not killing the old bastard," Nick said, snapping his head around to stare at Dillinger. "We're not doing it. I am not risking a death penalty for you stupid asses!"

Huddled together in the seat that skirted the wheel, Kody and Brandi Johnson were staring at him.

For the moment, he ignored them.

They were safe for now.

The old man wasn't.

Not giving a damn about damage or bumpers, Nick shoved the Donzi close to the larger vessel; she was called *Lady Tranquility*.

Nick found a hold on the hull and lifted himself up and over onto the deck. The old man just stared at him, shaking his head. "You think I'm grateful? You think I'm grateful you didn't kill me? You're still a thug. And you should still be strung up by the heels."

"You got a dinghy of any kind?" Nick asked, ignoring him.

"Yeah, I got a blow-up emergency boat."

"This is an emergency. Blow it up and get the hell out of here!" Nick said.

By then, he heard Dillinger yelling at him again. Floyd was coming up on board, using a cleat the same way Nick had, and Dillinger was pushing Kody upward.

He helped Floyd on, and Kody, and then Brandi.

"Get him in his inflatable dinghy and get him out of here!" Nick urged Floyd.

Floyd stared at him. Then he shrugged and grabbed the old man. "Let's do it, you old salt. Let's do it."

"Make sure he stays the hell away from the radio!" Dillinger ordered, crawling up onto the deck at last. "Come on, get on up here!" Dillinger called to the men in the second Donzi.

Nick left them at the bow, heading toward the aft.

He got a quick look down the few stairs that led to the cabin. Seemed there was a galley, dining area, couches—and a sleeping cabin beyond.

The storage was aft; the old man had gotten his inflatable out.

Floyd was keeping an eye on him. "Hurry it up, geezer!" Floyd commanded.

Nick took a quick look down into the cabin and toyed with the idea of using the radio quickly. He made it down the steps, but heard movement above.

"Who the hell does he think he is?" Nick heard. It was Kelly—and he was furious that Nick had stopped him. "Like he thinks he's the boss? Well, the pansy sure as hell isn't my boss!"

Nick looked up the stairs and saw Kelly's gun aimed at the old man again.

Nick couldn't shoot but he couldn't let the man die. His hand reached out for the nearest weapon—a frying pan that hung on a hook above the galley sink. He grabbed it in an instant and aimed it at Kelly's head.

His aim was good—and the old frying pan was solid. Kelly stumbled right to the portside and over the deck and into the water.

Floyd stared at him.

"We're not killing anyone!" Nick snapped.

Floyd shrugged and turned to the old man. "Better get in that boat, then, mister. If he's alive, Kelly will be coming back meaner than hell."

Nick looked at Floyd.

Floyd wasn't a killer, he realized.

Good to know.

Of course, Floyd wasn't a model of citizenry, either. It was still good to know that in this number, there was at least one more man who didn't want the bay to run red with blood.

"Hey, Barrow!"

It was Dillinger shouting for him. He hurried around to the front.

"Get her moving!" Dillinger said.

"Aye, aye, sir," Nick said. He hurried back to the helm, set the motor and turned the great wheel.

A minute later Dillinger came and stood by him. "Hey, where the hell is Kelly?"

Nick tensed. "I think he went for a swim." Dillinger was silent.

"Hmm. At this point, good riddance." Dillinger shrugged and then turned toward the cabin. "Well, I'll bet the old guy didn't know much about fine wine, but there's bound to be some beer aboard. You know the course, right? Hold to it. We'll be around the bend to some mangrove swamps I know and love soon enough."

Dillinger left him, heading down to the cabin.

Nick spared a moment to take stock. This mission was definitely not going the way they'd planned when he'd signed on to go undercover. But he was playing the hand he'd been dealt. He had no other choice.

At least they were down to three hostages. Dakota Cameron, Brandi Johnson and Vince Jenkins.

And down to four cons. Nelson, Capone, Floyd and Dillinger.

And, of course, there was still a kidnapped boy out there...

And they were heading for the Everglades. Where, soon enough, the winter sun would set.

Chapter Five

"God, it's dark!" Brandi whispered to Kody.

"Yes, it's dark," Kody whispered back. She wasn't sure why they were whispering. She, Vince and Brandi were the only ones down in the cabin. They were hardly sharing any type of useful secrets.

Above them, on deck, were their captors. Men she could see clearly now.

Dillinger, the oldest and the craziest in the group, had a lean face with hollow cheeks, and eyes that darted in a way that made her think of a gecko. Floyd was almost as much of a "pretty boy" as his borrowed gangster name implied. Nelson, also whipcord-lean, tense, reminded her of a very nervous poodle. Capone was muscular and somewhat stout, with brown eyes and chubby cheeks.

And Barrow.

Yes, she knew him. She knew his face. She recognized him.

From where? She still couldn't pinpoint just when she'd seen him before. So how could she possibly be so certain they had met? But she was.

Why did she feel a strange sense of attraction to him, as if he were some kind of an old friend, or an acquaintance, or even someone she had seen and thought...

I need to know him.

"Where are we? Do you think we're still in Florida?" Brandi asked. "I mean…we're on the water, I know that, but we're not really moving anymore. I don't think. Or we're going really slow."

"We're right off the tip of the peninsula," Vince said. "Kind of out in the swamps that would make us really hard to find. But, in truth, a pretty cool place, really. You know crocodiles usually hang out in salt water, and alligators like fresh water, but here, we have both— yeah, both. Alligators and crocodiles. 'Cause of the way the Everglades is like a river of grass, you got the brackish thing going…"

Brandi was staring at him in horror.

Kody set a hand on his arm. "Come on, all three of us grew up here. I know I've been to Shark Valley a couple of dozen times. The wildlife is just there—snakes and alligators in the canals and on the trails—and people don't bother them and they don't bother people. We're going to be fine," she told Brandi.

"They're going to leave us out here, aren't they?" she asked, tilting her head to indicate the men on the deck.

"Don't be silly," Kody said.

"Yeah, don't be silly," Vince said. "They're not going to leave us—not alive anyway."

Brandi let out a whimper; Kody pulled her in close and glared at Vince.

"Sorry!" he whispered. "But, really, what do you think is going on?"

"I don't know," Kody admitted.

Vince looked over at her, obviously sorry he'd been so pessimistic when Brandi was barely hanging in.

"I've come down this way a lot," he said. "Hop on the turnpike and take it all the way down to Florida City, hop off, take a right and you get to the Ernest F.

Coe Visitor Center, or head a little farther west and go to the Royal Palm Visitor Center and you can take the Anhinga Trail walk and see some of the most amazing and spectacular birds ever!"

Brandi turned and looked at him sourly. "Birds. Yep, great. Birds."

Vince looked at Kody a little desperately.

"Let me see what's going on," she whispered.

She left her position at the main cabin's table and inched her way to the stairs.

As she did so, she heard a long, terrified scream. She ran up the few stairs to reach the deck and paused right when she could see the men. Vince and Brandi came up behind her, shoving her forward so that she nearly lost her balance as the three of them landed on the highest step.

"What the hell?" Dillinger demanded angrily.

Yeah, what the hell? Kody wondered.

The boat's lights cast off a little glow but beyond that the world seemed ridiculously dark out on the water. Except, of course, Kody realized, the moon was out—and it was high up in the sky, bathing in soft light the growth of mangroves, lilies, pines and whatever else had taken root around them.

Kody wasn't a boater, or a nature freak. But she did know enough to be pretty sure they were hugging a mangrove shoreline and that the boat they were on had basically run aground—if that was what you called it when you tangled up in the mangrove roots.

And now it appeared that Nelson was heading back to the boat across the water, walking—or rather running—on water. He wasn't, of course. He was moving across submerged roots and branches and the build-up of sediment that occurred when the trees, sometimes in conjunction with oyster beds, formed coastlines and islands.

"What the hell are you doing, running like a slimy coward?" Dillinger thundered. "Where the hell is Capone?"

"Back there… We were shining the lights and trying to see around us but it's pitch-dark out here. We were a few feet apart. We kept flashing the lights, trying to attract your friend who is supposed to come help us, just like you told us… There was a huge splash, a huge splash, can't tell you how it sounded," Nelson said. He held a gun. He was shaking so badly, Kody was afraid he'd shoot somebody by accident. He worked his jaw and kept speaking. "I saw…I saw eyes. Like the devil's eyes. I heard Capone scream…it was…it was…not much of a scream…a choking scream… It's out there. A monster. And it got him. It got Capone."

"You mean you two were attacked by the wildlife and you just left Capone out there to fight it alone? You have a gun! No, wait! You don't just have a gun—you have an automatic!"

"I couldn't see a damned thing. I couldn't shoot—I couldn't shoot. I could have hit Capone."

"You left Capone!" Dillinger said.

Nelson stared back at him. "Yeah, I left Capone. He was—he was being eaten. He was dead. Dead already. There wasn't anything I could have done."

Kody heard a shot ring out. She saw Nelson continue to stare at Dillinger as if he was in shock. Then, he keeled over backward, right over the hull of the boat, gripping his chest as blood spewed from it.

He crashed into the water.

And Brandi began to scream.

Dillinger spun around. "Shut her up!" he ordered. He was still holding his smoking gun.

Kody was ice cold herself, shaking and terrified. She turned to Brandi and pulled her against her, begging, "Stop, Brandi. Stop, please!"

Vince caught hold of Brandi, pulling her back down the stairs to the cabin, out of harm's way.

There was silence on deck then.

Barrow, Floyd and Dillinger—and Kody—stood there in silence, staring at one another.

"He was one of us!" Floyd said.

"He wasn't one of us!" Dillinger argued. "He let a prehistoric monster eat Capone, eat my friend." He swore savagely and then continued. "Capone was my friend. My real friend. And that idiot led him right into the jaws of a croc or gator or whatever the hell it was!"

"I don't think it was his fault," Floyd said. "I mean—"

Dillinger raised his gun again. Barrow stepped between the two men, reaching out to set his hand on the barrel of Dillinger's gun and press it downward.

"Stop," Barrow said. "Stop this here and now. What's happened has happened. No more killing!"

Dillinger stared at Barrow. Maybe even he saw Barrow as the one voice of sanity in the chaos of their situation.

But, Kody realized, she was still shaking herself. Cold—and shaking so badly she could hardly remain on her feet.

She shouldn't be so horrified; the two dead men were criminals. Criminals who had been threatening her life.

But it was still horrible. Horrible to think that a man had been eaten alive. Horrible to have watched a man's face as a bullet hit his chest, as he splashed over into the water...

"I never heard such a thing," Floyd murmured as if speaking to himself. "An alligator taking a full-grown man like that."

"Maybe that idiot Nelson panicked too soon and Capone is still out there?" Dillinger asked.

Kody jerked around, startled when she heard Vince speaking from behind her.

"In the Everglades, alligator attacks on humans are very rare. I think the worst year was supposed to be back in 2001. Sixteen attacks, three fatal. You know all those things you see on TV about killer crocodilians are usually filmed in Africa along the Nile somewhere. Crocs are known to be more aggressive, and of course, we do have them here, but… Capone is a big man… not at all usual." He spoke in a monotone; probably as stunned as she was by the events in the last few minutes.

"Someone has to look," Dillinger said. "The airboat is still due. Someone has to look, has to find Capone. Has to make sure…"

No one volunteered.

"Go," Dillinger told Barrow.

"What about the hostages? Three of them and three of us," Barrow noted.

Kody had to wonder if he was worried about Dillinger managing the hostages—or if he was afraid for the hostages.

"I've got the hostages," Dillinger said. "Floyd is here with me. We're good. Go on, Barrow. You're the one with the steel balls—get out there. Find Capone. See if—"

"Alligators drown their victims. They twist them around and around until they drown them," Vince offered.

Kody gave him a good shove in the ribs with her elbow.

He fell silent.

Luckily, Dillinger hadn't seemed to have heard him. Barrow had.

He suddenly turned and pointed at Vince. "Right, you know a fair amount, so it seems. You come with me."

Kody could feel Vince's tension. Huddled behind him, Brandi whimpered.

Kody had to wonder if Barrow hadn't told Vince to come with him because he was afraid for Vince—afraid that Vince would say something that would send Dillinger into a fit of rage again.

"Um...all right," Vince said.

He looked at Kody, his eyes wide with fear. But then, as he stared at her, something in him seemed to change. As if, maybe, he'd realized himself that Barrow was actually trying to keep them all alive. He smiled. He crawled on past her up the rest of the cabin steps and out onto the deck.

Barrow was already crawling over the hull.

"There's a good tangle of roots right here," Barrow said. "Watch your step, and cling to the trees this way. Dillinger!"

"Yeah?" Dillinger asked.

"The boat's spotlight—throw it in that direction," Barrow said.

"Yeah, yeah, should have done that before."

Kody heard some splashes. For a few minutes she could see Barrow leading, Vince following, and the two men walking off into the mangrove swamp. Then they disappeared into the darkness of the night.

Everything seemed still, except for the constant low hum of insects…

And the occasional sound of something, somewhere, splashing the water.

Victim or prey.

"THEY REALLY DON'T," Vince said, his voice still a monotone as he followed Nick across the mangroves, slipping and sliding into several feet of water here and there. "Alligators, I mean. They don't usually attack people. We're not a good food supply. And since the python invasion down here, gators don't get big enough anymore."

"Tell that to the alligators," Nick murmured. He didn't know what the hell had happened himself. It was unlikely that a man Capone's size had been taken down by an alligator, but it wasn't impossible.

And he didn't know who the hell Dillinger was supposed to be meeting, but it was someone coming with an airboat.

Dillinger had taken over at the helm once they'd headed around the tip of the peninsula; Nick had known that he'd force them to come aground. But Dillinger had a one-track thing going with his mind. There'd been no stopping him.

Now, of course, he'd taken Vince with him to keep him alive. Dillinger was trigger happy at the moment.

Nick had been stunned himself when Dillinger had gunned down Nelson without blinking. They were all at risk. What he really needed to do was to take Dillinger down. Take him out of the equation altogether— no matter what it took.

But what about the boy? Adrian Burke. Where was the child? Only Dillinger knew.

Then again, what about the hostages?

Dillinger seemed to get even crazier the deeper they got into the Glades. Did Nick risk Vince, Brandi and Kody in the hope of saving a child who might be dead already by now?

"Help!"

He was startled to hear someone calling out weakly.

"Hey…for the love of God, help me. Please…"

The voice was barely a whisper. It was, however, Capone's voice.

"I hear him!" Vince said.

"Yeah, this way," Nick murmured.

He was startled when Vince suddenly grabbed him by the arm, so startled, he swung around with the Smith & Wesson he was carrying trained on the man.

"Whoa!" Vince said. "I guess you are one of them!"

"What?"

"You, uh, you've kept us alive a few times. I thought that maybe you were a good guy, but, hey…never mind."

Nick said nothing in response. He couldn't risk letting Vince in on the truth. The man talked too much. Instead, he turned, heading for the sound of Capone's weak voice.

Nick came upon him in a tangle of mangrove roots. Capone seemed to be caught beneath branches and roots that had actually tangled together.

"We thought a gator got you," Vince said.

"Gator? That Nelson is an idiot!" Capone said. "The branch broke, splashed down and pinned me here like a sitting duck. If there is some kind of major predator around… " He paused, looking up at Nick. "My leg is broken. I won't be able to make it to…wherever it is exactly that Dillinger wants to go. You gotta help me somehow, Barrow. You gotta help me. He'll kill me if I'm useless. Dillinger will kill me!"

Nick hesitated but Vince didn't.

"No, no, he likes you!" Vince said. "He just shot that other guy—Nelson—for leaving you!"

"He shot Nelson?" Capone demanded, staring at Nick.

"Yeah," Nick said quietly.

He reached down. First things first. He had to get Capone out of the mire he was tangled in.

There was a sudden fluttering sound as Nick lifted a heavy branch off the man. He had disturbed a flock of egrets, he saw. A loud buzzing sounded; he'd also attracted a nice swarm of mosquitos.

Vince swore, slapping at himself.

"Help me!" Nick snapped.

Vince went to work, slapping at his neck as he did so. "Amazing. Amazing that people actually came and stayed to live in these swamps."

He rambled on but Nick tuned him out. He was too busy detangling Capone.

When they lifted off the last branch and pile of brush, Capone let out a pained cry.

"My leg," he wailed. He looked at Nick desperately. "What the hell do I do? He'll kill me. No, no, we have to kill him, Nick. We have to kill him before he kills all of us."

"We can't just kill him, Capone," Nick said.

"Why the hell not? The hostages are free or with us. Once we kill him—"

"We don't know who he has coming. He made plans for this. Someone is bringing an airboat here. We're stuck, if you haven't noticed. And this may be a national park, but if you've ever spent any time in the Everglades, you know that we could be somewhere where no one will ever find us."

"We have guns."

"And he's got a kid stashed somewhere, too, Capone. A little kid."

"I know. He made sure we all knew. I'm sorry about the kid but—"

"I won't tell him that you wanted to kill him," Nick said firmly.

Capone stared at him and nodded.

"Yeah. Okay. But you watch. He's going to want to kill me."

"I can see that you're left behind. On the boat. The one we stole from that poor old man. Someone will come upon it eventually," Nick said.

"You can make that happen?"

Nick shrugged. "I can try. If you stay behind, it'll probably be the cops who find you. But, hey, these guys might speak nicely for you when it comes to sentencing."

Capone suddenly pulled back and shot him a look. "You're a cop!"

Nick didn't miss a beat. "I swear I am not a cop." Without a moment's hesitation he called to Vince for help lifting Capone.

With Capone shrieking in pain, they got the man up on his one good leg.

Just as they did, they heard the whirr of an airboat and saw a blinding light flood the area.

Sleeping birds shrieked and fluttered and rose high in flight.

Nick noticed the glassy eyes of a number of nearby gators; they'd been hidden in the darkness.

The sound of one engine sputtered and stopped; a second did so just a moment after.

Two airboats had arrived.

"Hey, are you having trouble?" someone shouted.

Nick couldn't see a thing; he was blinded.

But he didn't have to. He knew this had to be Dillinger's associate, whoever he had been waiting for to bring him the airboat.

"Broken leg!" Nick shouted.

The light seemed to lower. He saw the first airboat and a second airboat in back.

A man jumped off the first one and came sloshing through the water. He was quickly followed by another. Both men were tall and muscular and quick to help support Capone.

"Where's Dillinger?" the older of the two, a man with dark graying hair and a mustache and beard to match, asked Nick.

"Back at the boat we took this afternoon," Nick said.

"Cops have been looking for that ever since the old man who owned her got picked up by a Coast Guard vessel about an hour ago."

"You gotta ditch it," the younger man said. He looked just like the older man.

Father and son, Nick figured.

"Everyone is all right?" the older one asked, sounding nervous.

"Do I look all right?" Capone moaned.

"I meant…"

"The hostages are all alive. We've had a few difficulties," Nick said. "There—ahead, there's the boat!"

"Dillinger!"

Dillinger looked over the bow as Nick, Vince, Capone and the two unnamed newcomers came along, nearing the boat.

"Capone!" Dillinger cried. "I knew it. I just knew you weren't dead. You're too damned mean for any alligator to eat!" He frowned then, realizing how heavily Capone leaned upon the men at his sides. "What happened?" he asked darkly.

"We've brought you an airboat—just as you asked," the older of the men shouted.

"Good. How will you get back?" Dillinger asked.

"We've got a second boat. We'll get out of here and back to our business," the older man said.

"All right, go."

"We're even then, right?" the older man demanded. "We did what you wanted."

"Yep. You did what I wanted. Head to the old cemetery in the Grove. Find the grave of Daniel Paul Allegro. Dig at the foot. You'll find what you want. You've evened the score enough, so go," Dillinger said.

"How do I know that the papers are there?" the older man asked.

"You're going to have to trust me. But I've always been good to my word," Dillinger said.

The man with the graying dark hair and beard looked at Nick. "If you would help us…?"

"Yes, of course," Nick said. He took Capone's arm and wrapped it around his shoulder. The night was cool but Capone was still sweating profusely.

The men who had brought the airboat nodded and walked away.

Nick watched as they left, water splashing around them as they returned to the second airboat.

They'd owed Dillinger; he'd been holding something over them. Now all they wanted was to get away as quickly as possible, get to a graveyard and dig something up.

What hold could Dillinger have had on the men?

It didn't matter at the moment. What mattered was

the fact that one man was dead and Capone couldn't move an inch on his own.

"My leg is broken!" Capone shouted up to Dillinger. "I'm in bad shape. I tripped, fell, Nelson went running off…"

Dillinger started swearing. "We've got to get you up here." He paced the deck, grabbing his head, swearing. "Floyd! Floyd, get up here, help!"

Floyd appeared on deck, looking around anxiously. He saw Capone. "Hey, you're alive!"

"Well, somewhat," Capone said.

It wasn't easy, but with help from Floyd and Vince, they got Capone onto the boat.

Nick crawled over the hull.

By then, Kody and Brandi had pillows and sheets taken from the boat's cabin stretched out and ready on the deck. In a few minutes, they had Capone comfortably situated. Vince had noted a broken plank caught up in a nearby mangrove. He hurried to get it and, between them all, they splinted Capone's leg.

"He needs medical care," Kody said.

"He can't go slogging through the Everglades, up on the hammocks, through the saw grass and the wetlands," Nick agreed quietly.

"I'll make it! I'll make whatever!" Capone said. "Don't…don't…"

"He thinks you're going to kill him," Vince told Dillinger.

"What?" Dillinger asked. He truly looked surprised.

"I'm like a lame horse," Capone said quietly.

Kody had been kneeling on the deck by him. She stood, retreated down the steps for a minute, and came back with a bottle of vodka.

"This will help," she said.

"I killed Nelson for leaving you, because we don't turn on each other," Dillinger said. He looked at his friend and reassured him.

"Then you have to leave me," Capone said, looking at Dillinger and taking a long swig of the vodka. He sighed softly, easing back as the alcohol eased some of his pain. "I swear there's nothing I will tell them. There's nothing I can tell them. I don't even know where you're going. Just leave me."

"You'll do time. You know you'll do time," Dillinger told him.

"Yes, yes, I will. But I may live long enough to get out," he said. "If I try to go with you..."

Dillinger thought about his words. He lowered his head. After a long moment he nodded.

He walked over to the big man on the ground, leaned down and embraced him.

Then he jerked up, his gun trained on the others.

"He stays. We go," he said.

Nick was startled when Kody spoke up. "You can't leave him, not like this."

"Miss Cameron," Nick said, trying to step in, trying to stop whatever bad things her words might do to Dillinger's mind.

"He needs help. Look," Kody said, determined. "Brandi is screaming and scared and freaking us all out. She needs to be picked up as soon as possible. And Capone here needs help. Leave the two of them. Capone still has his gun, and Brandi isn't a cruel person. They have enough supplies on the boat to get them through the night okay. I say we leave them both." She turned to Dillinger. "That leaves five of us. Five of us in good health and good shape and not prone to hysterics in any way. We can make it."

Dillinger stared back at her. Nick barely dared to breathe.

Dillinger smiled. "You are quite something, Miss Cameron. I think you might have something. All right! Get supplies together. We leave Capone and little Miss Cry Baby here. Actually, Blondie, you really were starting to get on my nerves. Let's do it."

"You want to move deep into the Everglades by night?" Vince asked Dillinger.

"Well, hell, yes, of course!" Dillinger said. "The cops or someone will be around here very soon. We've got to get deep into the swamp and the muck and the hell of it all before the law comes around. Darkness, my boy! Yes, great. Into the abyss! Indeed, into the abyss!"

Chapter Six

The airboat was a flat-bottomed, aluminum-and-fiberglass craft with the engine and propeller held in a giant metal cage at the rear. Dillinger prodded everyone in.

Kody recalled the two men who had come to deliver the boat. They hadn't looked like bad men.

Once again she asked herself, *So what did bad men look like?*

Why didn't Barrow look like a bad man? Was he a good man—somehow under the influence of real criminals because he was between a rock and a hard place? He had a child somewhere being held, perhaps. Somehow, he was being coerced…either that, or she was simply being really drawn to someone really, really bad—and she couldn't accept that!

She had a hard time understanding what was going on with any of the men. She wished she could close her eyes and open them to find out that everything that had happened had occurred in her imagination.

But it was real. Too real.

At least she was grateful that Dillinger had listened to her and left both Capone and Brandi behind.

Alive.

As she was. For now…

Amid the deafening sounds of the motors she looked out into the night.

It was dark. Darker than any darkness Kody had ever known before. There was a haze before her to the north, and she knew the haze she saw was the light that illuminated the city of Miami and beyond up the coast.

But it was far away.

Out here Kody had no concept of time. She realized suddenly that she was tired, exhausted. It had to be getting close to the middle of the night. It seemed they'd been moving forever, but, of course, out here, that didn't mean much. Unless you were a ranger or a native of the area, each canal, new hammock and twist and zig or zag of the waterways seemed the same. The glow of gator eyes—caught by the headlights of the airboat—was truly chilling.

And despite it all, she'd nearly drifted to sleep twice. Vince had caught her both times.

Suddenly the whirr of the airboat stopped. She jerked awake—as did Vince at her side.

"Where are we?" Vince murmured.

Kody didn't know. But as she blinked in the darkness, Barrow and Floyd jumped out of the airboat and caught hold of the hull, pulling it—with the others still aboard—up on a hammock of higher, dry land. The lights still shone for a moment, long enough for Kody to see there was a chickee hut before them. It was the kind of abode the Seminole and Miccosukee tribes of Florida had learned to use years before—built up off the ground, open to allow for any breeze, and covered with the palms and fronds that were so abundant.

She was still staring blankly at the chickee hut when she realized Barrow had come back to the airboat— and that he had a hand out to assist her from her chair.

She was so tired that she didn't think; she accepted his hand. And she was so tired that she slipped coming off the airboat.

He swept her up quickly. Instinctively she wound her arms around his neck.

It felt right; it felt good to hold on to him...

She wanted to cry out and pull away. And she didn't know why she felt with such certainty that he would protect her and that he'd keep her from harm.

He set her down on dry ground. "Hop on up. I'm going to light a fire," he said, indicating the chickee hut.

It was just a few feet off the ground. Vince was already there. He offered her an assist up and she took it.

There was nothing in the little hut—nothing at all. But it was dry and safe, Kody thought. Floyd was up on the platform with them and he indicated that the two of them should sit. "Make yourselves as comfortable as you can. Grab what sleep you can. This isn't exactly the Waldorf but..."

Kody took a seat in the rear of the chickee hut and Vince followed her. She could hear Dillinger and Barrow talking, but they kept their argument low and nothing of it could be heard.

Vince shook his head. "What the hell?" he murmured.

Kody reached for his hand and squeezed it. "Hey. We're going to be okay."

"Yeah."

"Just follow directions and you'll be okay," Floyd said.

They were both silent. Then Vince spoke, as if he just had to have something to fill the silence of the night.

"Did you know that Alexander Graham Bell led the team that created the first airboat?" Vince asked idly as they sat there. "And it was up in Nova Scotia? The thing was called the *Ugly Duckling*. Cool, huh? The things are useful down here—and on ice for rescues. Go figure."

"Sure, cool," Kody agreed. "I had not known that," she said lightly.

"Alexander Graham Bell, huh, go figure!" Floyd said.

Kody thought Floyd was just as interested in what the others were saying as she and Vince were. He kept trying to listen. He had his gun on his lap—ready to grab up—but Kody was getting a different feeling from the man than she had earlier. Somehow, right now, he didn't seem as dangerous.

Floyd inched closer. "Do you really think you can find this treasure stash Dillinger thinks you can find?" he asked, looking first at Kody and then on to Vince. "I guess I never knew the guy. I mean, I hope you can find that treasure. Seems like the only one who can kind of keep Dillinger in check right now is Barrow, but even then…" His voice trailed. He squinted—as if squinting might make him hear more clearly.

Kody glanced at Vince and then at Floyd. "I don't know. I mean…we're following a written trail. Things change. The land out here changes, too." She hesitated and then asked, "Do you think he's going to kill us all?"

Floyd shrugged. "Hell, I don't know. I actually wish I was Capone! Yeah, they'll get him. Yeah, he'll go to jail. But he won't die out here in this godforsaken swamp!"

"Why don't you just shoot him?" Vince asked. "You just shoot Dillinger dead when he least expects it. Kody and I disappear until we can get help. You disappear into the world somewhere, too. You don't want to hurt us, and we won't turn you in. The three of us—we live."

Floyd hesitated, looking away. "Dillinger won't do it—he, um, he won't kill us."

"He might! Why take a chance?" Vince said.

Floyd smiled. "Don't kid yourself. I could never out-draw Barrow. I could never even take him by surprise." He lifted his shoulders in a hunch and then let them fall. "If I could...no. You've got to be careful, toe the line! Barrow is freaked out that Dillinger kidnapped that kid. Barrow can't take the kid thing and I think he's pretty sure the boy is stashed somewhere and he'll wind up dying if we don't get the truth from Dillinger. He won't do anything until Dillinger gives up the kid, and now that we're out here...I don't know how in hell that's going to happen."

Kody swatted hard at an insect, her mind racing. "If the police just got their hands on Dillinger, they could make him talk."

Floyd shook his head. "Dillinger's real name is Nathan Appleby. I'm not supposed to know any of this. None of us is supposed to know about the others. But I was at this place Dillinger was staying at in the Grove one day and I found some of his papers and then I looked up anything I could about him. He served fifteen years of a life sentence up north. He and some other guys had kidnapped a white-collar executive. He wouldn't give up the guys he was working with to the cops—or the old crack house where they were holding their hostage. The hostage wound up dying of an overdose shot up into his veins by the people holding him. Nathan's gang on that one did get away with the money. But one of them betrayed Nathan. That guy wound up in the Hudson River.

"See, that's just it—he holds things over on people. Like the guys who brought the airboat. He had papers on them, I'm willing to bet, which would have proven the older man's—the dad's, I'm pretty sure—illegal status here in the USA. And, I'm willing to bet, when Nathan gets what he wants here, he's got some other poor idiot he's blackmailing somehow to have a mode of transportation available for him that will get him out of the country. Not so hard from here, you know. He can get to the Bahamas or Cuba damned easily, and move on from there."

Kody had been so intent on Floyd's words that she didn't hear or see Dillinger approaching until Vince nudged her. She turned to see that Dillinger and Barrow had come up on the platform. She wasn't sure if Dillinger had heard what Floyd had been saying.

"What's going on here?" Dillinger asked.

"I'm telling them that they'd be crazy to try to escape," Floyd said. "Nowhere to go."

"I don't believe you," Dillinger said. There was ice in his voice. He raised his gun.

Kody wasn't sure what might have happened if she hadn't moved, and she wasn't the least sure of what she was doing.

She was just very afraid that Dillinger was about to shoot Floyd.

She rolled off the ledge of the chickee hut and landed down on the ground of the little hardwood hammock they had come upon.

And she began to run.

He wouldn't fire at her, would he? Dillinger wouldn't fire at her!

She heard a shot. It was a warning shot, she knew. It went far over her head.

And she stopped running. She couldn't see anything at all, except for large shadowlike things in the night, created by the weak moonlight that filtered through here and there. She tried to turn and her foot went into some kind of a mud hole. She stood for a moment, breathing deeply, wondering what the hell she had done—and what the hell she could do now.

She could hide and maybe they wouldn't find her.

"Kody."

She heard her name spoken softly. It was Barrow. She turned but she couldn't see him.

"Stay where you are," he whispered. "Don't move."

She stood still, puzzled, afraid—and lost.

And then she understood. At first it sounded as if she was hearing pigs rooting around in a sty. Then she realized the sound was a little different.

She felt Barrow's hand on her upper arm, at the same time gentle and firm. He jerked her back, playing a light over the muck she'd just stepped into.

And right there in the mud hole she saw a good-size group of alligators. They weren't particularly big, but there were plenty of them gathered together on the surface of the mud.

She froze and her breath stalled in her throat.

"Come on!" he said, pulling her away.

With his urging, she managed to move back. She realized she had come fairly far—the chickee hut and the fire Barrow had built were a distance ahead through a maze of brush and trees. She knew then that this was the opportunity she'd been waiting for. She turned to Barrow.

"He's going to kill everyone and you know it," Kody said.

"I don't intend to let him kill everyone," he said. "You have to believe me."

He looked directly into her eyes then and, in the light

of the flashlight, she saw his face clearly. She wasn't sure why, but at that moment she remembered where and when she had seen Barrow before.

In New York City. She and Kevin had been walking out of Finnegan's. He'd been telling her that he had a secret new love in his life, and he was very excited. And she had been laughing and telling him she was glad she was all into her career and the move to New York, because she didn't have anyone who resembled a love—new or old—in her life at all.

And that's when she'd plowed into him. Run right into him. He'd been there with another man—Craig Frasier. Of course, she knew Craig Frasier because she knew his girlfriend Kieran Finnegan.

They paused to look at one another, both apologizing and then...

She'd thought instantly that he felt great, smelled great, had a wonderful smile, and that she wanted to find out more about him. She'd hoped he wasn't married, engaged or dating, that she'd be able to see him and...

Then Kevin had grasped her arm and they'd hurried on out and...

Her mind whirled as the memories assailed her.

"You're FBI!" she said.

His hand on her arm tensed and he pulled her closer. "Shh!"

"All along, you're FBI. You could have shot him dead several times now. We're here, out in the true wilds, the Everglades where even the naturalists and the Native Americans and park rangers don't come! You could have shot him, you—"

"Shh! Please!"

"You didn't say anything to me! Not a word," Kody

told him. She was shaking, furiously—and still scared as could be.

"I couldn't risk it," he said.

"But I recognize you—"

"It took you a while," he said. "Look, if you'd recognized me and it had shown, and Dillinger had known, or Schultz, or even one of the others, we could all be dead now. I just infiltrated this gang not long ago. It should have been easy enough. We should have gotten into the house. I should have been able to design a way in for the cops and the FBI, but…there's a little boy out there. Dillinger kidnapped a kid. I have to get him to tell me where he's holding that boy."

She stared at him, sensing his dilemma, because she herself felt torn.

On the one hand, her desire to survive was strong.

And on the other hand, she couldn't let an innocent child die.

"You've had opportunities to tell me," she said. "I could maybe help."

"How?"

"You're forgetting—he believes he needs me. He thinks I know all about Anthony Green and the stash of riches from the bank heist Green pulled off years and years ago. Maybe he'll talk to me. Maybe he will—you don't know!"

"And maybe he won't. And maybe he'll figure out that Vince is really more up on history than you are and that he needs him—and doesn't need you. Dammit, I'm trying to keep everyone alive," Barrow said to her.

Barrow. His real name was Nick. Nicholas Connolly. Now she remembered clear as day.

She remembered everything. She'd asked Kieran and

Craig about him later, and they'd told her his name—
and what he did!

"You're on some kind of a team with Craig Frasier.
He's the one you've been talking to all along on the negotiations," Kody said.

"A task force. And, yes. Our task force has followed
Dillinger—actually, Nathan Appleby—from New York
on down. And now…we've got to stop him here. But
we've seen what he's capable of. We have to find that
boy before Nathan knows that he's trapped." He was
staring at her and he let out a long breath.

"What do we do?" she whispered. "He's—he's crazy.
Even Floyd thinks he's crazy. He shot and killed one
of his own men!"

"We go back. We make it through the night," he told
her. "There's nowhere to go out here. We're north of the
tip of the peninsula and south of Tamiami Trail and the
Shark Valley entrance up that way. A mile here is like a
hundred miles somewhere else. The chickee is the safest
place to be for the night." When she shivered, he added,
"One of us will be on guard through the darkness."

She looked at him.

He was right about one thing.

She didn't want to just walk into the darkness of the
Everglades.

Vipers, constrictors and crocodilians, oh, my.

"Okay," Kody said quietly. "Okay. So we go back.
Morning comes. We head to what I believe to be the
area where Anthony Green had his distillery, his Everglades hideout. And what happens if I can't find the
treasure he wants? What happens if you can't find the
boy?"

"I have to believe that we'll get what we need—that
somewhere in all this, Dillinger will trust me and that

I can get him talking. And if not, I pray that the cops and the FBI and everyone else working the kid's disappearance will find a clue. One way or the other, I will see to it that you and your friend, Vince, are safe by tomorrow morning. I got information to Craig. They know where to go. They'll have a very carefully laid ambush for tomorrow. We just have to get to that time."

Kody nodded dully. Okay. She'd go back.

He suddenly pulled her into his arms; she swallowed hard, looking up at him, seeing the emotion conflicting in his eyes.

"I'll keep you safe!" he vowed. "I'll keep you safe!"

"I know!" she whispered, hoping there was more courage in her voice than she felt.

"I have to make this look real," he told her.

She felt the muzzle of his gun against her back. "Of course."

Dillinger was standing by the edge of the chickee hut ledge when they returned—watching for them.

"My dear Miss Cameron! Foolish girl. Where were you going to go?" he asked.

"She's not going anywhere. She's going to be by my side from here on out," Barrow—or, rather, Nick Connolly—told him.

"Let's hope not. It's getting late. We could all use a little sleep. Oh, but, please, don't go thinking that my fellows are sweet on you, Miss Cameron, or that if I sleep, you can run again," Dillinger said. "I wake at a whisper in the wind. You will not pull things over on me.

"Not to mention…the coral snake doesn't have much of a mouth span, but the bite can be lethal. There are pygmy rattlers out there and Eastern diamondbacks. And the cottonmouth. Nasty, all of them. Not to mention the pythons and boas. But, since I'm being honest here, I haven't heard of anyone being snuffed out by one of them yet. There are the alligators and the crocs—mostly alligators where we are right now, but, hey, if you're going to get mauled or eaten by an alligator or a croc, do you really care which one?"

"I'm not going anywhere," Kody said. "You scared me. You scared me worse than the thought of a snake or an alligator or whatever else might be out here." She inhaled air as if she could breathe in courage. So far, it seemed to work with him. "You have to stop. You got mad at your own man for nothing. You—you shot one of your own men."

"He betrayed the brotherhood," Dillinger said.

"I want us all to live. You want Vince and me to find your treasure. So quit scaring everyone so much and we'll find your treasure."

Dillinger smiled and glanced at Barrow where he stood right behind her.

"This one is a little firecracker, isn't she?" Dillinger asked.

"And you need her," Barrow said softly. "And you do have your code of honor, Dillinger. None of these people has betrayed anyone, so let's just let them be. Meanwhile it's you, me and Floyd taking turns on guard. We'll get some sleep."

"Sure," he said. "Floyd, there's some water and some kind of food bars on the airboat. Go get 'em."

"On it, boss," Floyd said.

Kody realized that she was desperately parched for water—and that she was starving, too.

Barrow—Nick—walked around her, leaped up onto the platform and then reached a hand down to help her up.

She accepted it.

And when Floyd came with the water and power bars, she gratefully accepted those, as well.

After she ate, she found herself curling into a little ball on the wooden platform. Vince was to her one side. Nick was to her other side, leaning against one of the support poles.

"I'll take the first hours," Dillinger said. "Floyd, you're up next."

Hours later, Kody realized she had fallen asleep. She opened her eyes and Nick was still by her side, sitting close beside her, awake, keeping guard. She could feel his warmth, he was so close, and it was good.

The night had been cold, and she was scared, but she'd slept, knowing Nick Connolly remained at her side.

She looked up at him. His eyes were open and he was watching her. She was startled to feel a flood of warmth streak through her.

Of course, she remembered now when she had initially met him. Her reaction had been quite a normal one for a woman meeting such a striking man. He was really attractive with his fit build and dark blue, intense eyes. She'd had to hurry out that night at Finnegan's, but she'd thought that maybe she'd see him again.

Then life, work and other things had intervened.

And now…

He was good, she thought. Good at what he did. He had kept all the hostages alive so far. He had gotten many of them to safety.

He was still a very attractive man. Even covered in Everglades' mud and muck. With his broad shoulders and muscled arms he looked like security. Strength. And she was so tempted to draw closer to him, to step into the safe haven of those arms…

What was she thinking? This had to be some kind of syndrome, she told herself. Kieran Finnegan would be able to explain it to her. It was a syndrome wherein women fell in love with their captors.

No, she wasn't in love. And he wasn't really a captor. He was as G-man and he worked with Craig Frasier!

"You okay?" he whispered.

She nodded.

"I will get you out of this."

"Yes…I believe you."

He nodded grimly.

"Vince? Is Vince all right."

"Right now? He's quite all right. Take a look."

Kody rolled carefully to take a look at Vince. He was actually snoring softly.

She turned back to Nick. She nodded and offered him a small, grim smile.

"Hey! You're up, Barrow!" Dillinger suddenly called out.

"Yep, I'm on it," Nick called back to him.

He stood. Kody saw that he'd never let go of his gun, that it was held tightly in his hands.

It would be so easy! So easy for Nick just to walk over and shoot the man who was holding them all hostage, threatening their lives.

But she saw the way that Dillinger was sleeping. His gun in his lap.

The man even slept with his damned eyes open!

Kody didn't sleep again. She watched as the sun came up. It was oddly beautiful. The colors that streaked the sky were magnificent. Herons and cranes, white and colorful, flew to the water's edge. Then nature called.

She stood and saw that Floyd and Dillinger and Nick were all up. Nick had gone over to kick the fire out.

There was little preparation to be made for them to move on, but they were obviously ready to go.

She cleared her throat.

"I…I need a few moments alone," Kody said. "I need privacy."

"Don't we all," Dillinger said.

"I'm serious. I need to take a little walk. As you've pointed out, there's really nowhere for me to go. I insist. I mean it, or you can shoot me now!"

Dillinger started to laugh. "Okay, Barrow, take Miss Cameron down a path. Give her some space—but not too much. You seem to be good at hunting her down, but we're ready to move on and I don't want to waste any time."

"Yeah, fine," Nick said.

"Don't worry. Hey, I'm fine right here!" Vince said. "It's a guy thing, right? No one cares about my privacy, huh?"

They all ignored Vince.

"Go. Move! There's a trail there," Nick told her.

She walked ahead of him, aware that Dillinger was watching. Nick kept his gun trained on her.

A great blue heron stood in her way. The bird looked at her a moment and then lifted into flight. It was beautiful…and it was all so wrong.

Fifty feet out and into the trees, she turned and told Nick, "I really need privacy. I won't go anywhere, I swear."

"Scream bloody murder if you need me," he said and stopped.

She'd really only need a few seconds—what they used to call *necessary* seconds for the nonexistent facilities out here—but she was one of those people who absolutely needed to be alone.

The hammock was riddled with what they called gator holes—little areas of mud and muck dug out by gators when they tried to cool themselves off in summer. It was winter now, but the holes remained. One was full of water and she dared dip her hands in, anxious to pretend she was dealing with something that resembled normalcy and hygiene.

She looked up, ready to rise—and a scream caught in her throat.

She was staring at a man. He had coal-dark eyes and long dark braids, and he was dressed in greenish-brown khaki jeans and a cotton shirt. He was, she knew, either Miccosukee or Seminole, and he was capable of being as silent as a whisper in the air.

He quickly showed her a badge and brought his finger to his lips. "Tell Nick that Jason Tiger is here," he said softly. Then he disappeared back into the brush by the gator hole.

He might never have been there.

Chapter Seven

"Jason Tiger," Kody said, whispering as she returned to Nick. "He showed me his badge!"

Instead of taking her by the arm to lead her back, Nick reached down and pretended to tie his shoes. "Tiger?" he said. He didn't know why he needed the affirmation. If Kody had said the name, she had certainly seen the man.

His heart skipped a beat.

He silently sent up a little prayer of thanks.

He'd known Jason Tiger from years before, when they'd both attended the same Florida state university. Neither of them had been FBI then. Since then he'd seen Jason only once, just briefly, right before he'd gone undercover.

The name Tiger signified one of the dominant clans of the Miccosukee. Jason had been proud to tell him that his family clan was that of William Buffalo Tiger, who was just recently deceased, and had been the first elected tribal chairman when the Miccosukee had been recognized as a tribe in the 1960s. Jason knew the Everglades as few others. He'd been recognized by the FBI for the contributions he'd made in bringing down murderers and drug lords—those who had used what Jason considered to be the precious beauty and diversity of the Everglades to promote their criminal activities.

If Kody had seen Jason Tiger, they were going to be all right.

Jason would be reporting to Craig and the county police and the tribal police and every other law enforcement officer out there.

It was good.

It was more than good; it was a tremendous relief. Jason was out there and Nick wasn't working this alone anymore.

He stood and grabbed her arm. "All right." He nodded, knowing that was all the reassurance he could give her right now. Just fifty feet away, he felt Dillinger looking their way.

He held her arm tighter as they returned to the chickee. He couldn't show the relief he was feeling. He didn't dare defy Dillinger as yet—not until they knew the whereabouts of the boy. And still, the lives of Kody and Vince were at stake.

Kody wrenched free from his hold as they neared the airboat. He wasn't prepared. She managed the feat easily.

She walked over to Dillinger. He followed closely, ready to intervene.

"I don't care about the money or your treasure or whatever," she told him. "I'm more than willing to help you find it and you are just welcome to it. But if you want my help—or Vince's help—you better tell us where that little boy is. You kidnapped a kid. We've been out overnight now. That little boy is somewhere terrified, I imagine. Let him go, and I will dig from here until eternity to find the treasure for you."

Nick realized he was holding his breath, standing as tense as steel—and ready to draw on Dillinger or throw himself in front of Kody Cameron.

But Dillinger laughed softly.

He stared at Kody, obviously amused. "Wow. Hey, Vince, is that true? You don't care about yourself, right? You'll work yourself to the bone for me—if I tell you where the kid is, right? Yeah, Vince, you ready to throw your own life away for a kid you've never seen?"

Vince didn't answer. He pushed his glasses up the bridge of his nose, looking nervous.

"Okay, Miss Cameron, you want to know where the kid is? He's up in the northwest area, an abandoned crack house that's ridiculously close to the fancy new theater they've got up there north of the stadium. So, there's your kid. Yeah, it's probably getting bad for him. He was a pain in the ass, you know. I had to tie him up and stuff a gag in his mouth. So, I'm going to suggest you find this treasure for me as quickly as possible. Then I'll leave you where—if you're lucky—some kind of cop will find you before the wildlife does. And you can tell the cops where to look. You happy now?"

For a moment the air seemed to ring with his words. And then everyone and everything was silent, down to the insects.

"Yes, thank you!" Kody snapped at last, and she hurried past Dillinger, ready to hop aboard the airboat.

Dillinger studied Nick for a long moment. Nick was afraid he was on to something.

Then Dillinger smiled. "I will get what I want!" he said softly.

"I'm sure you will. I have to tell you, I'm confused. What the hell is the idea with the boy? I mean, we're in the Everglades. The boy is in an abandoned crack house."

"If they find us—not an impossible feat, even out here—I may need to use that boy to get free," Dillinger said.

"You have hostages."

"And by the time we find the treasure, we may not," Dillinger said. He shook his head, swearing. "Here we are, end of the road, the prize in sight. And I'm down at the finish line with you and Floyd, the two most squeamish crooks I've come across in a long career."

"I told you, I'm not in this to kill people. I never was. I like the finer things in life. I've been around, too. You can survive without killing people," Nick said. "I'm also against the jail terms or the needle that can come with killing people."

"Ah, well, they can only stick a needle in once," Dillinger said. "And we've already killed people, haven't we?"

"You killed Nelson. I sure as hell had no part in that. The hostages... Thanks to me, we're not going to die because of them."

"Ah, but you did kill Schultz, didn't you?" Dillinger accused him. "It's so obvious, my friend. You've got a thing for the woman. Schultz was getting too close. You took care of him, huh?" Barrow asked, his grin broad—eerie and frightening—as he stared at Nick.

And Nick was good at this, the mind game—delving into the psyche of criminals, following the trails of sick minds.

But he wasn't sure about Dillinger. Nick had studied this man. But, right now, he wasn't sure.

"You'll never really know, will you?" he asked Dillinger quietly, and he was pleased to see a worried frown crease the man's brow. Dillinger didn't know; the man really didn't know if Barrow would go ballistic on him or not.

Pull a trigger—or not.

It was good. It was very good to keep Dillinger off guard.

"Thing is, no one has any idea who killed old Schultz. You shot Nelson in front of the hostages. Oh, yeah, so you don't intend that Dakota and the young man should live, right? Well, start thinking anew. I'll help make sure you get the hell out of here. But you aren't killing that girl. You've got it right. I've got a thing for her. And she's coming with me."

"And then what, you idiot?" Dillinger demanded angrily. "You're going to just keep her? Keep her alive? You will rot in jail, you idiot."

"You'll be long gone—what will you care?"

"She'd better find what I want, that's all I've got to say. You want her alive? She'd better find it."

Nick looked at the ground and then shook his head as he looked back up at Dillinger. "You want to know if I can be a killer? Touch a hair on her head. You'll find out."

"Really?" Dillinger said, intrigued.

"Yeah. Really."

With that he shoved his way past Dillinger and headed toward the airboat.

In minutes, it seemed that they indeed flew, the craft moving swiftly across the shallow water and marshes of the Everglades.

"Such an interesting place," Dillinger said, "this 'River of Grass!' If one wants to be poetic, I mean. Imagine Anthony Green. Out here, in pretty good shape. But he's out of ammunition and there are a dozen deadly creatures you can encounter in every direction—with no real defense. Imagine being here. Deserted. Alone. With nothing."

Kody didn't answer him or even respond, even

though Vince looked at her nervously, apparently praying she had some clue as to what they were doing.

They'd traveled for hours until she'd told them to stop. Now she held a map unfolded from the back page of one of the journals. She pointed in what she truly hoped was the right direction. "Anthony Green's illegal liquor operation was out here, right on this hammock. When he had the place, he had workstations set up—chickees. But there was a main chickee where he set up a desk and papers and did his bookkeeping."

"Obviously, not here anymore, right?" Dillinger asked, eyes narrowed as he stared at her.

"You're sure this is the right place?" Floyd asked her.

"I'm not *sure* of anything," Kody said. "I know that there were four chickees and all the parts for having a distillery. I'm thinking that they were set about the hammock in a square formation, with the 'cooking' going on right in the middle by the water. Remember, land floods and land washes away. But I do think that we have the right hammock area..." She paused and looked over at Vince. "Right?"

"The Everglades is full of hammocks," Vince murmured. "Hardwood hammocks, with gumbo limbo trees, mahogany and more, and there are pine islands. Unless you really know the Everglades, it can all be the same."

"My sense of direction isn't great," Kody said. "But I believe that we did follow the known byways from the southern entrance to the park and that, if we were to continue to the north, we would come upon Shark Valley and Tamiami Trail. Naturally, we've really got to hope that this was the hammock. But—"

"Great," Floyd murmured. "We have to hope!"

Kody ignored him. "Okay, so, the heating source they used was fire, but anything they might have used to create fire would have been swallowed up long ago into nature. But Green had a massive stainless-steel still and a smaller copper still—a present to Green from the real Al Capone—and other tools that were made of copper or stainless steel. If we can find even the remnants of any of the containers, we'll know we're in the right place."

"This is ridiculous," Floyd told Dillinger. "Even if we find a piece of stainless steel, how are we going to find out where the chickees were? This has been an idiot's quest from the get-go, Dillinger!"

The way Dillinger looked at Floyd was frightening.

Floyd quickly realized his mistake and lifted a hand. "Sorry, man. I just don't see how we're going to find this."

"There is hope," Kody said quickly. "There are notes in Anthony Green's journal about his chickees. He didn't intend that his operations be washed away in a storm. Each one of the chickees was built with pilings that went deep into the earth. If we see any sign of pilings or of the remnants of a still, we'll know we're in the right place."

"Well, we know what we need to do." Nick stepped forward, defusing the tension and getting the group to focus on the task at hand. "We need to all start looking. Span out over the hammock, but be careful. There are snakes that like to hide in the tall grasses. Vince and Kody, you stay to the center and see if you can find remnants of a still. Floyd, you and Dillinger, try the upper left quadrant over there. I'll head to the right. We're looking for any one of the sections where the workmen's chickees might have stood."

It was like looking for a needle in a haystack. Time passed. Decades. There were so few of them; there was so much ground to cover.

"Let's cover each other, crossing positions around here," Vince suggested to Kody.

She looked at him, smiled and nodded. He was a good guy, she thought. Afraid, certainly, but doing his best to be courageous when it didn't look good at all for them.

Vince didn't know that "Barrow" was FBI. She longed to tell him but she wasn't sure if that would be wise. Vince could still panic, say something.

"We're going to be okay," she told him.

"Yeah. We're going to have to make a break for it somehow," he told her. "Do you realize that if we really find this stash—oh, so impossible!—Dillinger will kill us?"

"Maybe he'll let us go," Kody said.

"He killed one of his own men!"

"Yes, but that man deserted one of his friends. Maybe he does have some kind of criminal code of honor," Kody said.

Vince shook his head. "We have to get out of here," he said.

"But what is your suggestion on how?" Kody asked. "We're in the center. The three guys with guns can focus on us in a matter of seconds."

"Two of them won't kill us—neither Floyd nor Barrow," Vince said, his voice filled with certainty. "We just have to watch out for Dillinger."

"Who has an automatic weapon," Kody murmured. "We might be all right, Vince. Help will be on the way."

Vince let out a snort. "Yeah. Help. In the middle of the Everglades."

"Okay, so, to us it's a big swamp. But there are people who know it well, down to each mangrove tree, just about. It's going to be okay."

"Hey!" Dillinger suddenly called. "Are you two working out there?"

"Yes!" Kody shouted.

"Anything?" Nick asked.

Kody turned, hearing Nick's voice behind her. He was walking in quickly toward where they stood.

But before he could speak, Vince stood and stared at her, shaking his head, a look of desperation in his eyes. "We're going to die. If we just stay here, we're going to die. I'd rather feed a gator than take one of that asshole's bullets. I'm sorry, Kody."

He turned, ducking low into the high grasses, and began to run.

"What the hell?" Dillinger shouted.

He began to fire.

Nick threw himself on top of Kody, bringing her down to the damp, marshy earth. The gunfire continued and then stopped.

"Now, take my hand. Run!" Nick told her. He had her hand; he was pulling her. He came halfway to his feet and let go with a spray of bullets.

Then, hunched low, and all but dragging her behind him, he started to run.

Kody was stunned; she had no idea where they were going or why they had chosen that moment to leave. Vince had wanted to run...

Where was he?

Had he been shot?

What about Floyd? Was he shooting at them along with Dillinger?

Kody just knew that, for the moment, they were racing through a sea of grass and marsh. Her feet sank into mush with their every movement. Grass rose high around her, the saw grass tearing into her flesh here and there.

"Low! Keep low!" Nick told her.

Keep low and run? So difficult!

She could still hear Dillinger firing, but the sound was nowhere near as loud as it had been.

While Kody had no idea where they were running to, apparently Nick did. She felt the ground beneath her feet harden. They had come to a definite rise of high hammock ground, possibly a limestone shelf. She was gasping for breath and tugged back hard on Nick's hand.

"Breathe. Just breathe!" she gasped out.

And he stood still, pulling her against him as she dragged in breath after breath.

Suddenly the sound of gunfire stopped.

Now they could hear Dillinger shouting. "You're a dead man, Barrow! You're dead. I'll find you. And I'll let you watch me rip your pretty little pet to shreds before I kill you both. You're an ass. If the cops get you, you'll face a needle just like me!"

Nick remained still, just holding Kody.

"You can come back! You, too, Floyd! You can come back and we'll find the treasure, and we'll go on, free as the birds. I know where to go from here. I've got friends, you know that! They'll see that we get out of here safely. We can be sipping on silly drinks with umbrellas in them. Hey, come on now. Barrow, just bring her on back. I won't kill her, I promise. I just want that damned treasure!"

Nick held still and then brought his finger to his lips. He started to walk again—away from the sound of Dillinger ranting.

As they moved, though, they could still hear the man. "Vince! You idiot. Why did you run? I wouldn't have killed you. I just need the knowledge that you have. You're going to die out here. You have no way back in. I'm your way back in. Floyd! Oh, Floyd. You'd better be running. You are such a dead man. Such a namby-pamby dead man. I will find you. I will see that you die in agony, do you hear me? You are dead! You're all dead! I will find you!"

Only when Dillinger's voice had grown fainter did Kody dare to speak. "What the hell was that? What just happened? You said that a child would die. That—"

"Jason Tiger is out here," Nick said. "I'm going to get you to him as quickly as possible, and then I'll try to find your friend Vince."

"But the child. The little boy…"

"Adrian Burke," Nick said, smiling at her. He was studying her with a strange mixture of awe and disbelief. "Jason was still out there when we took off this morning. I met up with him earlier, looking for the pilings. Jason overheard Dillinger give up the boy's location. He got a message through to Craig Frasier and the local cops. They searched all the buildings in the area that Dillinger mentioned and they found the little boy. He's safe."

"Oh, my God! Really?" Kody asked. She wasn't sure if she believed it herself. She was so relieved that she felt ridiculously weak—almost as if she would fall.

"They found him—because of me confronting Dillinger?" she asked incredulously.

"Yep." He looked uncomfortable for a minute. "I should have trusted you," he said softly. "I should have trusted in you earlier."

"I'm just—I'm just so grateful!"

"Me, too. The kids…finding kids. It's always the hardest!"

She was still standing God-alone-knew-where in the middle of deadly wilderness, and it would be wise not to fall. She blindly reached out. Nick caught her hands, steadying her.

"I have to get back around to where I can leave you with Jason Tiger," he told her. "Then I can look for your friend."

"There was so much gunfire," Kody said. "But Vince… Vince is smart. There's a chance he made it." She paused, as if to reassure herself, then said, "He was determined to escape. He was certain that Dillinger would have killed us."

Nick was quiet.

"He would have killed us," Kody said.

"Most likely. Come on. We're on solid ground here, and I think I know where I'm going, but I haven't worked down here in Florida for years."

"You worked here—in Florida?"

"I did. I'm from Florida."

"Ah. But…you know Craig?"

"I work in New York City now," he told her. "I often work with him there. I've been on a task force with Craig and his partner. We've been following Dillinger—Nathan Appleby—all the way down the coast. I was the one who had never been seen, and I know the area, so I fit the bill to infiltrate. Especially once we knew that Dillinger was down here. That he was forming a gang and pulling off narcotic sales, prostitution, kidnapping…murder."

She was really shivering, she realized.

But it wasn't just fear. The sun was going down.

A South Florida winter was nothing like a northeastern winter, but here, on the water, with the sun going down, it was suddenly chilly. She was cold, teeth chattering, limbs quaking. And he was watching her with those eyes of his, holding her, and he seemed to be a bastion of heat and strength. She didn't want to lean on him so heavily. They were still in danger—very real, serious danger. And yet she felt ridiculously attracted to him. They'd both been hot, covered in swamp water, tinged with long grasses…

She was certain that, at the moment, her hair could best be described as stringy.

Her flesh was burned and scratched and raw…

And she was still breathing!

Was that it? She had survived. Nick had been a captor at first, and now he was a savior. Did all of that mess with the mind? Was she desperate to lean on the man because there was really something chemical and physical and real between them, or was she suffering some kind of mental break brought on by all that had happened?

She never got the chance to figure out which.

"Come on," he urged her.

And they began to move again, deep into the swamp. She felt his hand on hers. She felt a strange warmth sweeping through her.

Even as she shivered.

THEY WEREN'T IN a good position, but once Vince had suddenly decided to run, there had been no help for it.

Nick couldn't have gone after Vince and brought him down and go on pretending he was still part of Dillinger's plan. If he'd brought Vince back to Dillinger, the man would have killed Vince.

There had been nothing else to do but run then. Now all he could do was hope that Vince was smart enough to stay far, far away from Dillinger. And while Nick hadn't seen Floyd disappear, it was pretty clear from

Dillinger's shouting that he'd used the opportunity to get away, as well.

It was one thing to be a criminal. It was another to be a crazed murderer.

Hurrying along at his side, Kody tugged at his hand, gasping.

"Wait, just one minute. I just have to breathe!" she said.

And Kody breathed, bending over, bracing her hands on her knees, sweeping in great gulps of air.

Nick looked around anxiously as she did so. Naturally, Dillinger had seen the direction in which they had run.

Nick believed he knew the Everglades better than Dillinger, at any rate. But, even then, he was praying that Jason Tiger had been watching them, that Tiger had followed him after they had spoken.

"You…you think that Vince will be okay?" Kody asked him.

"He's smart. He needs a good hiding place and he needs to hole up. Dillinger has studied the Everglades on paper, I'm sure. Though he was hoping that the treasure might have been at the mansion, he thought that it might be out here. He had communication going with men who owed him or needed him. I'm sure he has someone coming out here for him soon. But he's not a native. Vince is, right? He seems knowledgeable."

Kody stared at him. "He's knowledgeable. I'm knowledgeable. But this? We're on foot in the swamps! Oh, please! Who is at home out here and knows what they're doing—except for the park rangers and maybe some members of the local tribes and maybe a few members of the Audubon Society. Dillinger was right—we don't know what we're doing out here."

"But Jason Tiger does," Nick reminded her gently.

"Oh! But where is he?"

"He's been watching, I'm sure. He'll find us. Don't worry. Ready?"

She nodded. He grabbed her hand again and hurried in a northwesterly direction, hoping he had followed the directions he'd received from Jason Tiger.

He'd been out in the Everglades often enough. His dad had brought him out here to learn to shoot, and his grandfather had kept a little cabin not far from where they were now. But most of what he knew about the Everglades he'd learned from a friend, Jimmy Eagle. Jimmy's dad had been a pilot from Virginia but his mom had been Miccosukee.

One of the most important things he'd ever learned from Jimmy was that it was easy to lose track of where you were, easy to think one hammock was another. Waterways changed, and there could be danger in every step for the unsuspecting.

He heard a bird call and stopped walking, returning the call.

A moment later Jason Tiger stepped out onto the path, almost as if he had materialized from the shrubs and trees.

"Right on the mark," he told Nick. "Miss Cameron, excellent."

Kody flushed at the compliment.

"I was excellent at running," she murmured. "But…" She paused, looking at Nick and telling him, "Your expression when you came toward me…it was so…determined."

"I was trying to let you know that we'd be able to do something," Nick told her. "I was going to let you know that Jason had found me while I was looking for the pilings of Anthony Green's distillery operations."

"And Vince chose that moment to run," Kody murmured.

"You think he's alive?" Jason Tiger asked Nick.

"I think it's possible."

"I'll get you to the cabin, then I'll look," Jason said.

"I wanted Kody safe with you," Nick said. "As long as Kody is safe, I can go back out and search until I find Vince—and Floyd. Floyd deserves jail time, but he doesn't deserve a bullet in the back from Dillinger."

"This way," Jason Tiger said.

He led them through a barely discernible trail until they came to the water.

He had a canoe there.

"Hop in," he told them.

Nick steadied the craft and gave Kody a hand. He stepped in carefully himself. Jason hopped in after, shoving his oar into the earth to send them out into the water.

They were in an area of cypress swamps; the trees grew here and there in the water. Egrets, cranes and herons seemed to abound and fish jumped all around them. Nick saw a number of small gators, lazy and seeking the heat of the waning sun.

The sun was going down, he realized. Night was coming again.

Jason drew the canoe toward the shore and then leaped out. Nick did the same, helping to drag the canoe up on the shore.

He wasn't sure what he was expecting, but not the pleasant cabin in the woods he and Kody saw as they burst through the last thick foliage on the trail.

It wasn't any kind of chickee. It was a log cabin, on high ground.

Nick looked at Jason Tiger, who seemed amused.

"There are a lot of houses out here. A lot on tribal lands. We're not completely living in the past, you know. Hey, guys, if it were summer, there's even an air conditioner. Everything here is run on a generator," Jason told them.

"Wow, so, there are a lot of these out here? For the Miccosukee and Seminole?" Kody asked.

Jason laughed. "No. Actually, this one belongs to the United States government. A lot of drug traffic goes through here."

Jason had a key; he used it, letting them into the cabin. It was rustic, offering a sofa in worn leather, a group of chairs, a center stove and a few throw rugs.

"There are bedrooms to the right and left. Hot showers are available—naturally, we ask you to conserve water. I have lots of coffee and power bars and other food."

"You live out here?" Kody asked him.

"When I need to. When we're watching the flow of illegal drugs through the area. I work with a newbie, Sophia Gray, and when she's in residence, she uses the second bedroom. You'll find clean clothing there, Miss Cameron. Anyway, I've been in touch with Special Agent Frasier and the police. We are actually on the edge of National Park land. You're at a safe house. You'll be fine, and we'll have you out of here by morning," Jason told Kody. "And now..."

"I need to get back out there," Nick said. "Find Vince first...and hope that I can find Floyd, as well."

"And Dillinger," Kody said. "He's still out there. He has to be stopped. I think that he really is crazy—dangerously crazy."

"Yes, and Dillinger," Nick said. "And, yes, he is crazy. Functionally crazy, if you will, and that makes him very dangerous." His tone softened as he added directions. "You stay here and obey anything Jason says, and stay safe."

"Of course," Kody said.

"Wait, this is backward. You need to watch over Miss Cameron," Jason said. "I'll see if I can find your friend, Vince, and the others."

"I can't ask you to take on my case," Nick said.

"You have to ask me. I know these hammocks and waterways like the back of my hand. You don't. I'll find them." When Nick was about to protest, he added, "I'm right, and you know that I'm right. I'm better out here than you are, no disrespect intended."

Nick was quiet for a moment and then lowered his head. "All right," he said.

"You're still armed?" Jason asked Nick.

Nick reached for the little holster at his back and the Glock there. "I am armed."

"All right, then. I'm going to head right back out. My superiors at the FBI know this place. We're remote, but they'll get here."

"I should go out with you—"

"But you won't," Jason told him.

Nick nodded. "You're right. You're far better for this job than me."

He felt Kody's fingers slip around his arm. "I'm sorry. You could both go if it weren't for me. Honestly, I know how to lock a door. I can watch out for myself here."

"No way. You're a witness who can put Dillinger away forever," Jason said.

"He's right. We can't risk you."

"Great. Because I'm a witness," Kody murmured.

Jason smiled at them both. "You're okay here for the moment. Take showers, relax. You were both amazing. Miss Cameron, you behaved selflessly, with great courage, and Special Agent Connolly, you're the stuff that makes the Bureau the place to belong. So, take this time. Sit, breathe... Hey, there's real coffee here."

"Thanks, Jason," Nick murmured.

Kody stepped over to Jason and took his hand, shaking it. "Thank you! And the child...the child is really all right?"

"Yes. Thanks to you, they knew where to search. He's safe and sound."

"I'm so glad," Kody murmured.

Jason nodded then and headed to the door. "Lock up," he told Nick. "Not that I'm expecting you'll have any company, but—"

"You just never know," Nick finished for Jason. He offered him a hand, as well. "Thank you, my friend."

"We're all in this together," Jason assured him.

When he left, Nick locked the door.

Kody was heading toward the kitchen. "Coffee!" she said. "Food."

"Yes."

"He's an agent. You're an agent." She spoke while searching the cabinets.

"Yes."

"But you didn't know him before?"

"Yes."

"He's from here and you're from here."

Nick laughed softly. "A lot of people are from here. But, yes—Jason and I went to college together," he said.

"It's ironic, isn't it, that I saw you in New York City? Never here," she said.

He grinned at that. "Millions of people live in this

area. I don't suppose it's odd in any way that people from South Florida never met. It's just odd that we wound up here together in this way after we did see each other in New York. I was probably a few years ahead of you in school. I went to Killian—and then on to the University of Florida. I was in Miami-Dade Homicide…and then the FBI," Nick told her. "And, for the last ten months or so, I've been on the task force with Craig. For the last few weeks, I've been undercover as Barrow."

"Incredible," she murmured.

"Not really."

She stared at him a moment longer and then smiled. And he thought that she really was beautiful—a perfect ingénue for whatever play it was she was doing.

She walked over to him.

"Well, I'm alive, thanks to you," she murmured.

"It's my job," he said. "It never should have gone this far. I should have been able to stop Dillinger at the mansion. I should have—"

He suddenly remembered the day she'd brushed by him at Finnegan's. He knew then he would have liked to have met her. Now…

They were safe—relatively safe, at any rate. They'd come far from Dillinger and his insanity. Jason Tiger was a great agent who knew this area and loved it, knew the good, the bad and the ugly of it, and would find and save Vince and Flynn if anyone could.

He would have given so much to smile, think they were back, way back before any of this, imagine that they'd really met, gone out…that he could pull her into his arms, hold her, feel her, kiss her lips…

But Nick was still an agent.

He was still on duty.

"Should have what?" she asked softly.

"Should have been able to finish it all earlier," he said softly.

She still held the bag of coffee. He took it gently from her fingers and headed into the kitchen to measure it out. In no time, he heard the sound as it began to perc.

She still stood in the living room of the cabin, looking out. He saw that she walked to the door to assure herself it was locked. She turned, probably aware that he was studying her.

"Windows?" she asked with a grimace. "I'm usually not the paranoid type."

"They've got locks, I'm sure," Nick said. He crossed the room to join her at the left window to check.

It was impossible.

They'd been crawling around in fetid swamp water, muck and more. Yet there was still something sweet and alluring in her scent.

She looked at him. Her face was close, so close. Her lips…so tempting.

Get a grip! he told himself.

"We should check them all," she said.

"That's a plan. Then all we need fear is a raccoon coming down the chimney," he said, grinning at her.

They checked and double-checked one another, close and closer. He headed to each of the two bedrooms. Simple, rustic, charming, clean…

Equipped with beds.

"This is good, right?" Kody asked him, tugging at the left bedroom window. It was evidently Jason Tiger's room. It was neat as a pin, but there were toiletries on the dresser and some folded clothes on the footrest.

"Yeah." Nick double-checked the window. "One more room," he said.

In the second room, the guest room, he could almost smell the scent of crisp, cool, cotton sheets.

Kody checked a window; he walked over to her.

How the hell could her hair still smell like some kind of subtle, sweet shampoo?

"Good, right?" she asked.

He inhaled the scent. "Yep, excellent."

"And you're still armed?" she asked.

"I am. Glock in the holster at the back of my belt."

"Then it's good. It's really all good. We aren't in any danger."

Nick arched a brow.

They weren't in any danger?

He was pretty sure he was in the worst danger he'd been in since he'd started on his undercover odyssey.

Because she was danger.

Because he was falling into love/lust/respect/admiration...

And he was an agent.

And she was the bartending actress he was duty-bound to protect.

And yet the mind could be a cruel beast at times. No matter what the circumstances, no matter what their danger, his position, her position, he couldn't help but believe there was a future. And in that future they were together.

Or was that just his mind teasing him?

For the moment he needed to shape up and damn the taunting beast of a voice within him that made him picture her as she headed for the shower.

Chapter Eight

Clean!

There was nothing like the feeling of being clean.

Kody could have stayed in the shower forever, except, of course, she knew the water was being heated by a generator. Special Agent Nick Connolly certainly deserved his share of the water.

And Vince was still out there, somewhere. Was he safe? He surely knew more about the Everglades than Dillinger, but just living in the area and knowing history and geography did not ensure survival. There were just too many pitfalls. Crocodilians, snakes, insects—and, of course, a madman running around with a gun.

And what about Floyd?

Floyd was a criminal but not a killer; he had never wanted to hurt them.

She couldn't help but be worried about them both.

She had to believe that Jason Tiger would find Vince. Meanwhile, Vince was smart enough to watch out for sinkholes, gator holes and quicksand. He knew which snakes were harmful and which were not. He probably even had a sense of direction. He would head straight for the observation tower at Shark Valley—and the Tamiami Trail. He was going to be okay.

Hair washed, flesh scrubbed, Kody emerged from

the shower. A towel had been easy to find in the bathroom. She hesitated when she was dry, feeling as if she was somewhat of an invader as she headed to the dresser and found clothing that belonged to Jason Tiger's "newbie" associate. "Forgive me," she murmured aloud, finding panties and a bra and then a pair of jeans and a tailored cotton shirt.

When she returned to the living room, Nick was sipping coffee at the little dining table that sat between the kitchen and the living room. He'd obviously showered; his hair was wet and slicked back. She couldn't help but notice the definition of his muscles in a borrowed polo shirt and jeans. She met his eyes, so beyond blue, and she felt such a tug of attraction that she needed to remind herself they were still in a perilous position.

And that Nick had been her captor—who had turned into her savior.

There was surely a name for the confusion plaguing her!

"Hey," he said softly.

"Hey."

"Feel better?"

"I feel terrific," she told him. "Clean. Strong. Okay—still worried."

"Jason will find Vince," he assured her.

She nodded and pulled out a chair to join him at the table. "What are you doing?" she asked him.

He swept an arm out, indicating the maps on the table. "I'm following your lead. This map was created by a park ranger about ten years ago. Now, of course, mangrove islands pop up here and there, water washes away what was almost solid. You have your hardwood hammocks and you have areas where the hardwood hammocks almost collide with the limestone shelves.

From what I'm seeing here and where we've been, I'm convinced that we were in the right place. Anthony Green's still sat on a limestone shelf."

"Where we were today, I'm pretty sure," Kody agreed.

"Exactly. Well, on this map, the ranger—Howard Reece—also made note of the manmade structures he found, or the remnants thereof. Kody, you were right, I believe." He paused and pointed out notations on the map. "There are the pilings for different chickee huts he had going there. Back quarter—that's the one where Anthony Green did his bookkeeping. So, if you're right, that's where we'll find the buried treasure."

"If it does exist," she said.

"I believe that it does."

"And you want to go find it—now?"

He laughed softly. "Nope. I want to stay right here now. Stay right here until you're picked up by my people and taken to safety. Then I want to help Jason Tiger and the forces we'll get out here to find Vince and Floyd. And then, at some point, get the right people with the right equipment out here to see if we're right or wrong."

She nodded and bit into her lower lip.

He reached out, laying his hand over hers where it rested on the table. "I know that you're worried. It will be okay. Jason will find Vince, and, I hope, Floyd."

"What if he can't find them? What if he can't find either of them?" Kody asked.

"He will." The conviction with which he spoke the words sank into her, giving her hope. "For now," he said, "let's find something to eat. There's not a lot of food here, nothing fresh, but there are a lot of cans and, as Jason said, power bars."

"There's soup," Kody said, pointing to a shelf in the kitchen area.

"Anything sounds good. Want me to cook for you?"

"You mean open a can?"

"Exactly."

Kody laughed. "Yes, I'd love you to open a can for me."

The both rose. Nick dug around for a can-opener. Kody found bowls, spoons and even napkins. She set the table.

"Nice," Nick told her.

"Well, we want to be civilized, right?"

"I don't know. I could suck the stone-cold food out of a can right now, but, hey, you're right. Heated is going to be better."

She smiled. It was an oddly domestic scene as they put their meal of soup and crackers together. Jason kept a hefty supply of bottled water at the cabin, and the water tasted delicious.

"So, when you're not playing the part of a thug and holding up historic properties, what are you doing?" Kody asked as she ate.

"I'm with the same unit as Craig Frasier—criminal investigation," Nick told her. "New York City is my home office. The man you know as Dillinger was carrying out a number of criminal activities in New York that included extortion and murder. He served time. He should have served more time, after. The cops had arrested him again a few years ago on an armed robbery, but the one witness was found floating in the East River. Then he started to move south, so we followed his activities. And as I said, I was a natural to slide into the gang he was forming down here."

"And you like your work?" Kody asked. "I know that Craig likes his work and his office."

"I love what I do. It feels right," he said. "What about you—what do you do when you're not guarding the booth? Ah, yes! Acting. And you're friends with Kevin Finnegan." He was quiet for a minute. "Well, this is just rude, but what kind of friends?"

She laughed. "Real friends. We've struggled together on a number of occasions. We met on the set of a long-running cop show that we both had a few short roles on." She grinned. "He was the victim and I was the killer once in the same episode. And we've gone to some of the same workshops together. But, trust me, we were never anything but friends."

"Kevin is a good-looking, great guy," Nick said.

"That he is," she agreed. "And it's cool to have a friend like him for auditioning and heading out and trying to see what's going on. We were both accepted to a really prestigious class once because we could call on one another right away and work together. We decided long ago that we'd never ruin what we had by dating or becoming friends with benefits, or anything like that." She hesitated, flushing. That was way too much information, she told herself. "And, by the way, Kevin is in love. It's even a secret from me, it's such a hush-hush thing. I hope it works out for him. I do love him—as a friend."

"Nice," he murmured.

He was watching her, his eyes so intense she looked away uncomfortably.

She rose uneasily, afraid it sounded as if she was determined he know she wasn't involved with Kevin. She wandered closer to the stove and nervously poured more coffee into her cup. "So. What happens now? I mean,

Jason Tiger has been in contact with Craig and the FBI and the local police, right? They'll be out soon, right?"

"They'll be out soon," he agreed. "We're just in an area where there is no easy access. But they'll get here. Why don't you try to get some sleep? You have to be exhausted."

"I'm fine, really. Well, I'm not fine. I'm worried about Vince. I just wish—"

"Jason Tiger is good. For all we know, he might have found Vince by now."

"Right," she murmured. She smiled at him. "I can't believe that I didn't know you right away. I mean, it's not as if we got to know one another that night at Finnegan's. But you do have a really unusual eye color and…"

"I was afraid that you'd recognize me," he said quietly. "That, naturally, you would call me out, and we would all be dead."

"Yes, well…"

"I just wasn't that memorable," he said, a slight smile teasing his lips.

"Oh, no! I had been thinking…"

"Yes?"

Kody flushed, shaking her head.

"You know what I was thinking?" he asked.

"What's that?"

"I was thinking that it was a damned shame that I was on this assignment, that I never had asked you out, that I was meeting you as an armed and masked criminal."

"Oh," she said softly.

He stood and joined her by the stove. Stopping close to her, he touched her chin, lifting it slightly.

"What if it had been different? What if we'd met again in New York and I'd asked you to a show...to dinner? Would you have said yes?"

Kody was afraid her knees would give way. She was usually so confident. Okay, so maybe being under siege, kidnapped at gunpoint and still trapped in a swamp was making her a little too emotional. She was still shaky. Still caught by those eyes. And she was attracted to him as she couldn't remember being attracted to anyone before.

"Yes," she said softly.

He smiled, his fingers still gentle on her chin. He moved toward her and she could almost taste his kiss, imagine the hunger, the sweetness.

Then there was a pounding on the door.

Dropping his hands from her chin, he moved quickly away from her, heading to the door.

"It's Tiger!" came a call.

Nick opened the bolt on the door. Jason Tiger was there with Vince. Vince was shaking.

And bleeding.

"Oh, get in, get in! Sit him down. I'll boil water. Is an ambulance coming? Can an ambulance come?" Kody demanded.

Nick took Vince's weight, leading him to a chair. Apparently both men were adept at dealing with wounds. Nick had Vince's shirt ripped, while Jason went for his first-aid box.

Kody did set water to boil.

"It's just a flesh wound," Nick said.

"We'll get it cleaned, get some antiseptic on it," Jason murmured.

Nick took the clean, hot towel Kody provided and

in moments they discovered he had been right; it was just a flesh wound.

"Dillinger didn't shoot you?" Kody asked.

Vince looked up at her with a shrug. "I tripped on a root. Scratched myself on a branch."

"Oh," she said, relieved, sliding down to sit in one of the chairs.

"Floyd?" Nick asked Jason Tiger.

"No sign of him—nor have I been able to find Dillinger. The airboat is where it was. He hasn't taken off from where you were, by the old distillery."

Vince suddenly turned and grabbed Nick's arm. "You weren't one of them. You're not a crook."

"No," Nick said, hunkering down and easing himself from Vince's hold. There wasn't time to give him the background of his undercover investigation right now. They had to find Dillinger. "You were smart—and lucky. When Dillinger started shooting, you went down low. But he is still out there. As long as he's out there, other people are in danger. Did you see him again? Did you hear him stalking you?"

Vince looked from Nick to Jason and then at Nick again. "I think he chased me through half of the hammock. Then he was gone."

"I didn't see him," Jason said.

Nick stood. "All right." He looked over at Jason Tiger. "This time, I think it's me. I think that I need to go," he said.

Tiger nodded.

"You're going out there again?" Kody asked him.

"Yes, we need to stop Dillinger and, hopefully, find Floyd alive."

He turned, heading out of the little cabin in the

swamp. Even as he did so, they heard shouts. Kody hurried to the door behind Jason.

An airboat had arrived; it bore a number of men in khaki uniforms.

Men with guns.

They were going after the killer in the swamps.

"Kody!"

One of the men, she saw, was hurrying toward her. It was Craig Frasier. He caught her up in a hug.

"Thank God. Kieran and Kevin have been going insane, they've been so worried about you. Not to mention your family. We'll get you home. We'll get you back to safety."

She gave him a hug back. Craig was truly an amazing man. Kody was happy that he and Kieran Finnegan were together—and happy that he was a good friend to Kevin and all of the Finnegan family.

She was grateful to know him, and everyone involved with Finnegan's on Broadway.

He was there for her.

She and Vince were safe.

And yet, at that moment—right when she was surrounded by law enforcement—she felt bereft.

Nick was gone. He was off with the teams of officers that had come out to find Dillinger and Floyd.

EMTs had arrived with the officers; they were looking at Vince's wounds. They were asking her if she was all right.

Soon, she was escorted onto an airboat. And before she knew it, she was back on the Tamiami Trail, headed toward downtown Miami and to the home in the Roads section of the city, just north of Coconut Grove, where she had grown up. A policewoman came with her, took her statement and promised to watch her house through the night—just in case Dillinger found his way to her before they were able to find Dillinger.

And there was nothing left to do except watch the television to see how the rest of it all began to unfold.

DILLINGER WAS OUT THERE. He was determined to get the treasure, and so, Nick was certain, he had to have stayed in the general area where they had been.

Law enforcement had fanned out, but by the time they reached the hammock again, the airboat that Dillinger had extorted from the men he had been blackmailing was gone. He was off, somewhere.

The forces that had come out for the search were from Miami-Dade and Monroe counties, Florida Highway Patrol, the U.S. Marshal's Office and the FBI.

But, as the hours went by, they found nothing.

Nick was about to give it up himself when he determined one more time to search the original hammock. The grasses grew high there, and a twisted pattern of pines might hide just about anything along the northern edge of the hammock.

He came out alone and stood in the center, as still as he could manage. And that was when he was certain he heard movement. He cautiously took a step, and then another, and drew his weapon and gave out a warning. "FBI. Show yourself, hands above your head."

Floyd emerged out of the grass. He was shaking visibly.

"I don't want to die. I don't want to die. They can lock me up, but I don't want to die."

"You're not going to die. But you are under arrest."

"Barrow. You," Floyd said. "I should have known you were a cop. I mean, I don't like blood and guts. But you…? Wow. I should have guessed it. It's cool. It doesn't matter. Get me in. Protect me. He was running around here crazy. Dillinger, I mean. He wants me dead. He wants you dead more but…" He shook his head as he stepped forward. "Get me out of here. Quickly. He'll shoot me dead right here in front of all of you, he just wants me dead so badly."

"All right, all right," Nick said, and cuffed the man. He caught him by the elbow and hurried back toward the airboat where other officers were waiting. "Come on, we'll get you in. You'll be safe."

"Did you get him? Did you get Dillinger?" Floyd asked.

"Not yet."

"You have to get him."

"Yes, we know."

But while Floyd was brought in, and they worked through the night, there was no sign of Dillinger to be found.

When morning dawned, he was still on the loose.

KODY SIPPED COFFEE and watched the news.

She should have slept, but she hadn't.

Her parents had arrived as soon as humanly possible, of course. They'd been worried sick about her, and she understood.

They'd nearly crushed her. Her mother had cried. Her father had cursed the day he'd discovered he'd been related to the Crystal family. Emotions had soared and then, thankfully, fallen back to earth and she had finally managed to make her parents behave normally once again.

She'd gotten a call from Mayor Holden Burke. He'd nearly been in tears as they had spoken. He'd been told by the police that it had been her courage against the kidnappers that had led to his son being found. She'd told him how grateful she was that the boy, Adrian, was alive, and she'd begged him not to do anything publicly for her—she wanted it all to remain low key.

"Yes, but I hear you're an actress—don't you want the publicity?" he'd asked.

She'd laughed. "No, I want to create characters and read well for auditions and, of course, get great reviews," she told him. "The only publicity I want is for great performances. As far as my home goes…I just worry."

"Oh, trust me," he assured her, "more people than ever will want to tour the house now. And I will thank you with my whole heart and remain low key."

When she hung up, she'd smiled, glad of a new friend.

She needed to sleep.

But hours later she was back up, staring at the television. She wanted to hear about Nick.

Every local channel and even the national channels had covered the news.

Nathan Appleby, aka Dillinger, was still on the loose. The FBI had been on his trail for nearly a year, from the northeast down to the far south. Thanks, however, to the combined efforts of various law-enforcement groups, the hostages taken at the Crystal Manor were safe, as were those who had been forced to accompany the criminals. Three of the gang had been killed; their bodies had been recovered by the Coast Guard and the Miccosukee police.

Dillinger, however, was still at large. The local populace was advised that he was armed and extremely dangerous.

There was nothing said about Nick Connolly.

"Hey!"

She had been sitting in the living room, quietly

watching the television. She turned to see that her father was already up, as well.

She smiled and patted the sofa next to her. He came and sat with her.

"The manhunt continues?" he asked.

"Here's the thing. Dillinger manipulates people. The men who brought him the airboat—they weren't bad. I mean, I don't think they would ever want to hurt anyone. Dillinger put them into a desperate situation, like he does with everyone."

With an arm around her shoulders, her father said, "I didn't want you moving to New York. And I didn't want to stop you. You have to follow your dreams, and you're responsible and…well, now I'm glad you're going to be in New York—far, far away from wherever the Anthony Green stash might be. I thank God that you were rescued. I can't imagine what your mom and I would have gone through if we had made it home and…and you hadn't been found."

"I'm very thankful."

"You don't ever have to work at that awful mansion again—under any circumstances!"

"Dad, the house wasn't at fault. I love the old house and the history—and we don't throw it all away because of a very bad man. They will find him."

He nodded. "I know. For your mom and me, you're everything, though. We thought it was tough when you decided to move to New York, when you landed the role and you got the part-time gig at Finnegan's. But…you were safer there."

"None of us can ever expect something like what happened, Dad. Anywhere. Bad people exist everywhere."

"I know," he told her quietly. "Because of New York,

though, you already knew that FBI man who brought you home."

"Craig Frasier. Yes, I know him through Kieran Finnegan, who is Kevin's sister. You met Kevin—I introduced you to him when we were in an infomercial together."

"Right."

"His family owns the pub where I'll be working part-time. And you will love it when you come up," Kody assured her father.

"And he's the one who saved you?"

Kody shook her head. "No. That was Nick."

"They haven't even mentioned a Nick on the news, you know."

"I know. He was working undercover. But… " Her voice trailed.

"Well, if he weren't all right and still working this thing, you'd be hearing about a dead agent," her father said.

"Dad!"

"Am I right?"

"Yes, you're right."

She leaned against his shoulder. "Don't blame the house on Crystal Island, Dad. Don't stop loving it. Don't stop caring about it. If we do that, we let the bad guys win, you know."

"Very nobly said," her father told her, a slight smile twisting his lips. "But…I say screw all noble thoughts when it comes to your safety!"

"Dad!"

"Not really. I just want them to catch that guy!"

Kody agreed.

And she longed to hear that Nick Connolly was fine, as well.

TWO DAYS LATER there were still a number of officers searching through the miles and miles that encompassed the enormous geographical body known as the Everglades.

Nick was no longer among them.

The chase now would fall to the men who knew the area.

He spent a day being debriefed and a day on paperwork. That was part of it, too.

He was going to be given a commendation. Thanks to his work, according to Director Egan via a video conference, a kidnapped child had been found and not a hostage had been harmed.

In his debriefing, Nick was determined that the agency understand it had been Dakota Cameron who had gotten the information out of Nathan Appleby and that Jason Tiger had been the one to convey it to the police and the FBI back in Miami. He was told that Kody had completely downplayed her role in the entire event, hoping that life could get back to normal.

He, too, would stay out of the public eye. It didn't pay, in his position, to have his face plastered on newspapers across the country.

Floyd—aka Gary Forman—had told the police everything he knew about Dillinger, the gang and the various enterprises that Dillinger had been into. What seemed surprising to Nick at the end of it all was that Dillinger was an amazing crook. The man had worked with a scope that Nick, even as part of the gang, had merely been able to guess about.

Sitting with Craig Frasier in the Miami Bureau offices, he shook his head and said, "Why did the man become so obsessed with a treasure that may not exist?

If he stayed away from Crystal Island, he could still be fronting all his illicit operations."

"Who says he isn't? The man is still out there," Craig reminded him.

"So he is. But he's known. His face is known. The thing is, of course, that he does use people."

"Exactly. He may well be deep in Mexico now, on an island somewhere—or headed for the Rockies. No one knows with a man like that."

"True," Nick said. "There was just something about him and that treasure. He was obsessed, like an addict. He still means to get that treasure somehow."

"Well, Jason Tiger and the local Miccosukee police as well as the FBI and city and county police are still on it."

"Yes," Nick murmured. "Good people. And still…I don't feel right. I don't feel that we should be turning it over now. You and me—we followed Nathan Appleby all the way down the east coast. I was the one chosen to go undercover."

"Something that is completely blown now, of course—albeit in the best way."

"Yes. It doesn't feel right, though."

"And we're due on a plane back to New York tomorrow. It's over for us. I thought you'd be glad. I know that you didn't mind and accepted the undercover—but, it's also damned good to get out of it."

"I am ready, I don't mind doing what's needed, but you're right—there's a time you're ready for out. There's always the point where you may have to give yourself away or commit a criminal act. And then you have guys like Nathan Appleby—guys who kidnap kids and don't give a damn if they live or die, as long as the act gives them their leverage. I am glad it's over. I just wanted it to be over with Nathan Appleby behind bars."

"We don't win every time. We try our best. That's what we do."

Nick stood and grinned at Craig. "Tomorrow, hmm. What time?"

"Plane leaves at 11:00 a.m."

"I'll be there."

"And tonight?"

"Tonight...I want to stop by and see a girl. I want to pretend that months and months haven't gone by and that I just saw her say hi to you and smile at me as she left a restaurant."

"And?"

Nick laughed softly. "And, hopefully, I'm going on a date."

Chapter Nine

An iconic pop singer died. An earthquake rattled Central America. A boatload of refugees made landfall just south of Homestead, and a rising politician threw his hat into the ring for a vacated senate seat.

Given all that, the news about the assault on the historic mansion on Crystal Island at last died down.

Kody had spent hours with her folks, assuring them she was fine. She had made arrangements for them to fly to New York when the show opened, and she'd told them about her apartment, her part-time job and her friends, especially the Finnegans. She told them about the four siblings who owned the pub. How Declan was the boss and Kieran was a clinical psychologist and therapist who often worked with the police and the FBI. How Danny was a super tour guide and would take them around and, as they knew, Kevin was an actor.

It was all good.

She went back out to the mansion. She and her co-workers and friends who had been taken hostage hugged and cried and did all the things that survivors did. She was somewhat surprised to discover that none of them was leaving.

"I just don't see it happening again," Vince said.

"You don't give in to violence," Stacey Carlson told her.

Nan Masters, his supportive assistant, as always, smiled. "Stacey does not give in. He hires more security. That's the way we roll."

Jose was still in the hospital, but doing well.

Brandi was fine, as well—traumatized, but fine.

Kody felt relieved and almost happy when she left them. Everything was perfect.

She'd called Craig; he'd assured her that Nick Connolly was fine. They were all disappointed, of course, that they hadn't been able to find Nathan Appleby.

Her parents were still at a board meeting, seeing to the trust, when Kody came back from the mansion and turned on the news.

Yes. The story had already fallen to the back burner.

The doorbell rang as she was staring at the television.

When she looked through the peephole, her heart skipped a beat. It was Nick.

She instantly thrust the door open.

"Hey! You're supposed to be cautious!" he began.

He was barely able to speak. She threw her arms around him, holding him fiercely.

"Um, cautious…or not!" he said, looking down into her eyes, half detangling himself and half sweeping her closer. And he just looked at her and then his mouth touched down on hers and he kissed her.

Her mouth parted and she tasted the sweet heat of his lips and tongue. The warmth swept into her limbs, magical and wonderful, and causing her to tremble. He lifted his mouth from hers, searching out her eyes.

"You're okay," she said as if she needed him to confirm it.

"Yes. And you?"

"Absolutely fine, thank you. I… You're here. Thank you. I mean, thank you for knowing that I would be worried about you. And thank you for letting me know that you're okay."

"That's not why I'm here," he said. "Although I'm grateful to know that you were worried."

"Of course," she murmured. "So, why are you here?"

"Ah, yes. Well, you're not being held by a demonic kidnapper anymore. I'm not working undercover. In fact, I'm free until tomorrow, when I fly back to New York. I'm here to ask you to dinner. This is your family home, though, I understand. Should I ask your folks, too?"

"No! Oh, don't get me wrong. I love them dearly. But I don't need their approval to tell you this. I would love to go to dinner with you. That would be great. Where should we go?"

"I'm staying at the Legend, the new place on the bay. They have a chef who just won the grand prize on a reality show," he said with a rueful smile. "Want to try it?"

"Yes. Give me one minute." She started into the house, leaving him on the steps, then went back to invite him in. Gathering her wits, she ran to the kitchen counter to leave a note for her parents so they wouldn't worry, grabbed her purse and headed back. He smiled, watching her.

"What?" she asked.

"I was nervous coming here to ask you out, and I can see you're nervous, too. But we shouldn't be so nervous. We know each other, right? We slept together—kind of—in a hut."

"Yes…but it's different now, huh?"

He offered her his arm. She took it and then headed down the walk to his rental car, a black Subaru. He opened the door for her; she slid in.

"They still haven't found Dillinger—Nathan Appleby?" she asked.

"No. It's amazing that he's managed to disappear the way he has—and yet, not. He has such a network going. He had a way to reach someone who got him out—or got him into hiding in the Everglades, one or the other."

"But you're going home, right?"

"Yes. I wouldn't be useful anymore undercover. He knows me. Craig Frasier is heading back, too. The operation will be handled from here now. Every agency down here is on the lookout."

"You don't sound happy about it," Kody said.

"I'm not. I hate it when we haven't finished what we started out to do. Dillinger has been a step ahead of us down the eastern seaboard. I'm not happy, but…" He shrugged, glancing over at her. "But you're heading to New York City, too, right?"

"The play opens in a few weeks."

"Living theater?" he asked. "I mean, isn't most theater living? Not to sound too ignorant or anything, but…"

Kody laughed. "Interactive would be a better description. It's been done before in a similar manner. We're doing a Shakespeare play, except that it all takes place on different floors within an old hotel. I love what we're doing. It's never the same thing, different every night. Basically, we are the characters. We work with the script and draw people in from the audience. And the audience moves from place to place while we have our scenes in which we work."

"I can't wait to see it."

"You'd really come?"

"Sure. We can have FBI night at the theater."

"Very amusing."

"I'm serious. I'm sure that Craig and Kieran will come, and Craig's partner. And once I'm home, I'm hoping to be paired again with my old partner, Sherri Haskell."

"Ah, Sherri."

"Married to Mo."

"I didn't ask."

"Yes, you did."

Nick drew up to valet parking and they left the car behind.

He caught Kody's hand, hurrying up the planked ramp that led out to the bay and along the water. The moon was a crescent, dozens of stars were shining and the glow of lights from the hotel and restaurant on the water was magical.

"Florida will always be home," Nick said.

"Always," Kody agreed. He pulled her into his arms and he kissed her again, and she thought that, indeed, it was all magic. She couldn't remember when she had met someone who made her feel this way, when she had longed for just such a touch and just such a kiss.

He drew away from her and leaned against the rail, just holding her, smoothing her hair, looking out on the water.

"You have a room?" she asked softly.

"That's a leading question, you know."

"Yes, I know."

He studied her eyes. "Room service?"

"That would be lovely."

He caught her hand again and led her to the elevator. When he opened the door to his room, she went straight to the large window that looked out on the night.

"Sorry, there's no balcony. Not on taxpayers' money," he said. "However, it is much better than the place I had before, when I was hanging with Dillinger's gang."

She turned to look at him.

"It wouldn't matter to me where you stayed," she said.

He strode to her, taking her into his arms. She drew the backs of her fingers down his face. He kissed her again, his fingers sliding to the zipper at the back of her dress. She allowed it to slip from her body.

"I wasn't…I'm not really prepared," he told her. Then he laughed. "I'm sure I can be—there're a dozen stores nearby."

"I'm on the pill," she told him.

"I'm not— There's no one else at the moment?" he asked.

She shook her head. "I've been working on the play, on the move…on life. But I've always been an optimist."

He laughed at that, pulled her closer. And he slid from his jacket, doffed his holster and gun, and kissed her neck and throat while she struggled with the buttons on his shirt. Still half dressed, they fell back on the bed. He kissed her again and then again, and stared down at her, and she reached up to him, drawing him back and tugging at his belt and his waistband.

Rolling, mingling passionate kisses with laughter, they finally stripped one another completely and lay breathlessly naked together, frozen for a moment of sweet anticipation and wonder. Then they tangled together again, seeking to press their lips upon one another's flesh here and there. He rose above her, staring down at her, straddled over her, and she reached for him, amazed that however it had come about, they were here together, and she was simply grateful.

He kissed her lips, her throat, and his mouth moved along her body, teasing her flesh. She lay still for a moment, not even breathing, swept up by the sensation. He caressed and teased, lower and lower, until she could stay still no longer, and she arched and writhed and rolled with him, and allowed her lips and tongue to tease in turn, bathing the length of him in kisses until breathless, they came together at last. He moved within her slowly at first. Their eyes were locked as the pace of their lovemaking began to increase, bit by bit, to a fever pitch.

Outside, the stars shone on the water. A breeze drifted by. The night was beautiful and, for Kody, these were intricate and unbelievable moments in which the world was nothing but stars, the scent of shimmering seawater and the man who held her.

Their climax was volatile and incredible, and holding one another in sweet aftershocks seemed just as wonderful. And then whispering and laughing and talking—and wondering if they should indeed order room service or just let the concept of dinner go—seemed as natural as if they had known one another forever.

"So there's been no one in your life for a long time?" he asked her.

"Not in a long time. I do love what I do. Rehearsals are long and hard—then there is the part-time work, as you know. And you?"

"Long hours, too. But I was engaged. To a designer."

"A designer?"

"Marissa works for a major clothing line. She wants her own one day."

"What happened?"

"Off hours, not enough time…we drifted apart. I have nothing bad to say about her. We just—we just weren't meant to be. Being with an agent isn't easy. Takes someone who understands that time is precious and elusive."

"It's a give and take," Kody said softly. She hoisted

up on an elbow and smiled down at him. "I had a similar problem with my last ex. Gerard."

"Ah. And what happened to him?"

Kody hesitated. "He met a teacher. She didn't work a second job to pay for the privilege of doing her main job. She just had much better hours."

"I'm sorry."

"I introduced him to the teacher," Kody said. "He was a good guy. I wasn't right for him."

"You think we might be right for each other?" Nick asked softly.

"I just...I hope," Kody said.

"Hmm. What made you...care about me?"

"Your ethics."

"As a crook?"

She laughed. "You wouldn't hurt people. That mattered. And you?"

"Well, there's nothing wrong with the way you look, you know," he teased.

"Ah. So it's all physical attraction, then?"

"And your courage, determination and attitude," he said.

She laughed softly. "For me it was your eyes. I knew your eyes. And I knew you, because of your eyes."

He smiled and pulled her down to him again. And what started as a kiss developed into another session of lovemaking.

By the time they finished, Kody jumped up after looking at her watch. "Oh! I have to go back. My parents...I mean, I was just home here to tie up loose ends. My mother and father are already a bit crazy."

"Say no more. I'll get you home right away," Nick promised.

They dressed quickly. "I really did intend to wine and dine you with a sumptuous meal," Nick said, his hand at the small of her back as they left the room and headed down.

"We'll both be in New York. There are tons of fabulous restaurants there, too, you know. I mean, I am assuming that we'll see one another in New York? Or is that maybe too much of an assumption? I was really worried about myself, you know. I was attracted to you—when you were with Dillinger. You weren't a killer—I knew that much…well, my feelings did make me question myself."

He smiled, holding her hand tight.

"Time is precious and elusive," he said. "I will gratefully accept any you can give me in the city—especially with your show starting."

"I'll find time," she promised. "I'm partial to old, historic restaurants."

"I know a great pub. I think we both get a discount there, too," Nick teased.

"A great pub!" she agreed.

The valet brought Nick's car. Kody glanced at her watch again. It was nearly 1:00 a.m. She was surprised that her mother or her father hadn't called her yet. Maybe they were happy she was out with an FBI agent.

The distance between the hotel and her parents' home wasn't great; she was there within minutes.

Nick walked her to the door.

"I'll really see you in New York?" she murmured.

He pulled her into his arms. "You will see me. You'll see so much of me…"

She moved into his kiss. The wonder of the night seemed to settle over her like a cloak. She was tempted to walk into her house and check on her family—and then just tell them she was off to sleep with her FBI agent before he had to get on his plane.

Kody managed to gather a sense of decorum.

"I should meet your parents," Nick said. "But I guess you shouldn't wake them up."

"Probably not the best idea," she agreed. "You'll meet them. They're coming up for opening night."

They kissed again. It seemed all but impossible to stop—to let him drive away.

But, finally, he broke away. "Kody, I…"

"Me, too," she said softly.

Then she slipped into the house, closed the door behind her and leaned against it. A sense of euphoria seemed to have settled over her.

She was walking on air.

But as she moved away from the front door, the lamp above her father's living room chair went on.

"Dad," she murmured.

Then she fell silent.

And she dead-stopped.

It wasn't her father, sitting in his chair.

It was Nathan Appleby—aka Dillinger.

NICK HEADED DOWN to the rental Subaru but paused as he reached the car. He looked up at the sky. It really was one of the most fantastic winter nights in Miami. Stars brilliant against the black velvet of the sky, a moon that seemed almost to smile in a half curve and a balmy temperature of maybe seventy degrees.

He would always love South Florida as home. There was nothing like it—even when it came to the Everglades with all its glory, from birds of uncanny beauty, endangered panthers—and deadly reptiles.

It would always be home to both of them, even as it seemed they both loved New York City and embraced all that could be found there. Actually, Nick had never cared much which office he was assigned to; he was just glad to be with the Bureau. Even if they didn't win every time.

Nathan Appleby was still out there.

But the hostages were safe. The hostages were alive. It was out of his hands and, after tonight, he could say that it had ended exceptionally well. The future loomed before them.

He turned the key in the ignition and drove out onto the street. His phone rang and he glanced at the Caller ID. It was Kody. He answered it quickly. "Hello?"

At first there was nothing. He almost hung up, thinking maybe she had pocket dialed him.

Then he heard Kody's voice. "You know me, Mr. Appleby. You know that I won't help you unless I'm sure others are safe. And this time, you have my parents. Do you really think that I'll do anything for you, anything at all, when I'm worried about their safety?"

"Right now, Miss Cameron, they are alive. You know me. I don't care a lot whether people live or die. You get that treasure for me and your parents live. It's that simple."

Nick quickly pulled the car to the side. He hadn't gone more than a block from the Cameron house. He cursed himself a thousand times over.

They had underestimated Nathan Appleby. They hadn't comprehended the depth of his obsession, realized that he would risk everything to find the Anthony Green treasure.

Appleby had known everything about the Crystal Island mansion, about Anthony Green. It was only natural that he should have known where the Cameron family lived, only natural that he had made his way out of the Everglades and into the city of Miami—and on to the Cameron house.

"You left Adrian Burke bound and gagged in an

abandoned crack house," Nick heard Kody say. "I need to know where my parents are—that they will be safe. That's the only way I help you."

"Okay, here it is. They are not in a crack house. They're out on a boat belonging to some very good friends of mine. Now, you help me and I get the treasure, I make a call and they go free. If you don't come with me—nicely!—I call and they take an eternal swim in Biscayne Bay. Oh, and added insurance—if they don't hear from me every hour, your parents take a dive."

"I'll go with you. But what guarantee do I have?"

"You don't have any guarantees. No guarantees at all. But…I can dial right now. Mommy and Daddy do love the water, right?"

"Do you mind if I put sneakers on?" Kody asked. "They beat the hell out of sandals for scrounging around in the Everglades!"

TORTURE WAS ILLEGAL.

But Nick still considered slipping into the Cameron house and slicing Nathan Appleby to ribbons in order to force him to tell the truth about Kody's parents.

But there were inherent dangers—such as Appleby getting a message through to the people holding Kody's parents, Kody herself protesting, and a million other things that could go wrong—along with torture being illegal. Appleby had said he had to make a call once an hour. The man was mean enough, manic enough, to die before making a call.

Nick didn't want to give up the phone; he couldn't reach Craig or anyone else unless he did hang up the phone.

He knew where Appleby would take Kody.

"Let's go!" he heard Appleby snap. "Ditch the

purse—you have a phone in there, right? Ditch the purse now!"

The line was still open but nothing else was coming from it. Nick hung up quickly and called Craig.

"We'll get the Coast Guard out in the bay along with local police," Craig said as soon as Nick apprised him of the situation. "We'll find them. Swing by for me at the hotel. We'll head out together. They'll alert Jason Tiger and he'll see that everyone out there is watching and ready."

"We know where they're going," Nick said.

"How damned crazy can that man be? He intends to dig in the swamp all night by himself?"

"He's not alone. He has Kody."

NATHAN APPLEBY MADE Kody drive.

Her own car.

She wasn't sure why that seemed to add insult to injury.

She didn't know how he'd gotten to her house; she hadn't seen a car, but then, he might have parked any-where on the street.

Wherever he had come from, he had come to her house and kidnapped her parents. They were out some-where in the bay. He'd come prepared; he had two back-packs—one she was certain she was supposed to be carrying through the Everglades. He'd managed all this with the news displaying his picture constantly and every law-enforcement agent in the city on the look-out for him.

He kept his gun trained on her as they drove, held low in the seat lest someone note that she was driving under stress.

Not that there were that many people out. Miami was truly a city that never slept, but here, in the residential areas that led from her home close to downtown and west toward the Everglades, there were few cars on the road.

"I'm not sure how you think I'm doing this. I mean, honestly? I don't know how I'm doing this. I've only ever dropped by the Everglades by daylight. I'm pretty sure there are gates or fences or something when you get to the park entrances," Kody said.

"We won't be taking a park entrance," he told her.

"What? You just happen to have friends with access driveways?" she asked, unable to avoid the sarcasm.

"I happen to know where to go," he said.

Kody checked the rearview mirror now and then, but she couldn't tell if any of the cars she saw behind them were following her or not.

She was fairly certain she had gotten a call out—that she'd managed to dial Nick's number without Appleby noting what she was doing as they'd spoken. Then, of course, he'd made her leave her purse.

But he'd never looked at the phone. He didn't know what she had done...

If, of course, she had actually done it.

She had, she assured herself.

They passed the Miccosukee casino where lights were still bright and the parking lot abounded with cars.

Then, as they continued west, there were almost no cars.

Businesses advertising airboat rides seemed to creep up on them. The lights were low and the darkness out there at night seemed almost surreal.

Kody had been driving nearly an hour when Appleby picked up his phone.

"My parents?" she asked.

"Yes, Miss Cameron. I'm making sure they'll be just fine."

Someone answered on the other end.

"Everything is good," he said. And he smiled at Kody and hung up. "Just keep on helping me and we'll be fine."

"You need more than just me," she said. "This is the kind of project you need a host of workers to accomplish. We have to find the pilings. We think we know that he buried the stash at the corner of the main chickee, but we're not sure. And how deep? Exactly where? We need more people to look."

"Maybe," he told her.

"Just how many friends do you have? And do you really trust these people? Okay, so I've seen you in action. You extorted an airboat from people who were forced to help you. But remember, people you bribe and threaten just might want to bite back, you know," Kody told him.

"Would you bite back?" he asked her.

"If you keep threatening my parents, I promise you, I'll bite back!"

"Not if you want them alive. And slow down!"

Kody slowed down. She had no idea what he was looking for. If she were to turn to the right at the moment, she'd wind up in a canal. Not a pleasant thought. If she turned to the left, as far as she could see, there was nothing but soupy marsh. They were, she knew, near Shark Valley, but it was still ahead of them on the trail by a mile or two.

"Here," he said.

"Where's 'here'?" Kody demanded.

"Slow down!"

She slowed even more and glanced in the rearview mirror.

There were no lights behind them.

She wasn't being followed. Her heart seemed to sink.

"Right there!" Appleby told her. "See there? See the

road? And don't get any ideas. You sink us in a canal or a bog out here, your parents die. Oh, and you die, too. So, drive, and drive carefully."

"Do you know how pitch-dark it is out here?" Kody demanded.

"Do you know that's why they give cars bright lights?" Appleby retorted.

Kody grated her teeth. She turned to the left and slowly, carefully, followed the dirt road Appleby had indicated. It seemed to head into nothing but dense green grass and it slowly disappeared.

"That's good," Appleby said. "Here. This is fine. It's as far as we go by car, my dear."

She's already been dragged through the swamp. She'd spent a night in a chickee. She'd walked, not knowing if she'd disturb a rattler or a coral snake, or if she'd step on a log that turned out to be an alligator. She shouldn't have been so terrified.

And yet she was.

Appleby shoved his gun into his waistband and tossed her a backpack. "Get your flashlight," he commanded her.

She found a large flashlight in the pack along with water, a folded shovel, a pick and a power bar.

They might have been on a planned hike or tour into the wilderness!

"Turn your light on," he said.

She did so, as did he. The flashlights illuminated great circles of brush and grass and trees. "There," he said.

Where?

And then she saw an airboat before them.

"Let's go!" he said.

She took a step; the ground was no longer solid.

She stepped into swamp and prayed she wasn't disturbing a cottonmouth.

It was only a few steps to the airboat. She was grateful to climb aboard it.

And then Appleby was with her, the motor was revving and they were moving deeper into the abyss of the night.

"I WILL BE there when they arrive," Jason Tiger assured Nick. "I'll have Miccosukee police with me. They know how to hide in the night. We'll be on it, I promise."

"But don't approach until we're out there," Nick said. "We're trying to find her parents. We'll be behind them. We have a ranger meeting us to take us out to the hammock. We'll take the first miles by airboat and then switch to canoes so that we're not heard."

"We won't approach. Unless, of course, we see that Miss Cameron is in imminent danger."

"Of course," Nick agreed.

Nick spoke with Tiger as he waited for Craig to join him. He hung up just as his teammate joined him in the car.

"You know, I keep thinking about this," Nick said.

"We haven't thought of anything but for days now," Craig said grimly.

"No. I mean the timing. I went to Kody's house at 8:00 p.m. Her mom and dad were still out—at a board meeting. We came to the hotel. We were at the hotel about three hours or so. That would mean that Appleby got to her house, either charmed or laid a trap for her parents when they returned, and then found someone to threaten who had a boat, and got Kody's mom and dad out on the boat. At least, that's what he told Kody."

"And?" Craig asked him. "Ah. Yeah, timing. You don't think that he really got them out on a boat. We have the Coast Guard out, but, of course, there are so many boats out there. And they can search for the Cameron couple. Thing is…"

"There are hundreds of boats out on the water. It's dark, and the bay stretches forever, and boats move," Nick said. He shook his head. "But I don't think they're on a boat."

"Where do you think they are?"

"Somewhere near the house," Nick said. "I can't look, though. I have to get out there. I have to get out there as quickly as possible. I know what Kody was doing, where she was looking, what she believed. I need—"

"To be there. I get it. Drop me at the Cameron house. I'll find her parents, if they are anywhere near the house," Craig said firmly.

Nick nodded. "Thank you."

"It's a plan, my friend. It's a good plan. I'll get some help out to the house with me. If Mr. and Mrs. Cameron are anywhere near, we'll find them. And, if they're on the water, the Coast Guard will find them. Appleby knows Kody. He knows that she'll do anything he says as long as she's worried about her parents."

"We're ahead of him by one step this time," Nick said. "He didn't know that she got a call through on her phone, that I heard what went on between them. As far as he knows, we don't have a clue that Kody has been taken, that he has her out in the Everglades."

"She's really the right stuff," Craig said lightly.

She's perfect! Nick thought, and it felt as if the blood burned in his veins.

He knew he probably shouldn't be on the case now. Because he would kill, he would die, to see that she was safe. And that was just the way it was.

Chapter Ten

The airboat drifted onto the marshy land just before the rise of the hammock.

Kody's heart sank when she thought about the impossibility of the task before them. People had known about the Anthony Green stash forever. Scholars had mused and pondered on it.

They'd agreed that the treasure was in the Everglades.

Where bodies and more had disappeared since the coming of man.

"Get your pack. We'll head straight back," Appleby told her. "That bastard G-man had it down right, just before everything went to hell, before your silly friend freaked out and ran. You know, this could have all been over. We could have found the treasure. I'd have left you out here, where one of those rangers or Miccosukee police would have found you.

"Yep. It could have all been over. You know, letting that man in was the only mistake I made," Appleby said, and shrugged. "He talked a good story—he pulled it off. He acted as if he could be tough when needed." He grinned at Kody. "Maybe that's why you two hit it off so well. Two actors, cast in different roles in life."

Appleby laughed, amused by his observation. "Okay,

let's go. Get back there. We're going to find the site of the pilings, and we're going to start digging."

"Don't you think that this is a little crazy?" Kody asked him. "The local police know that you were here, the FBI know that you were here…they'll have someone out here."

"Why would they have someone out here?"

"It was a crime scene!"

Appleby laughed. "They looked for me here. They didn't find me here. They've moved on. They're checking the airlines and private planes. They're going to be certain that I've fled the area. They won't be looking for me here. So let's get started."

"This is ridiculous. It's dark. I can step on a snake. You can step on a snake. I saw gator holes back there. You could piss off a gator—"

"Yep. So let's hurry. Over here. That's where your lover boy seemed to be when all hell broke loose. And he was going by your determination."

It was insane. Maybe by daylight. Maybe with a dozen people digging and working…

"It could be worse," Appleby said.

"Really?"

"It could be summer." Appleby laughed and swatted his neck. "If it was summer, the mosquitos would be unbearable."

Every step in the night was torture. At least, once they had moved in from the edges of the hammock, the ground was sturdy, a true limestone shelf.

It was difficult to get a bearing in the darkness. While the stars remained in the sky, the glow of the flashlights only illuminated circles of light; large, yes, but not large enough. She heard the chirping of crickets and, now and then, something else. Something that slunk into the water from the land. Something that moved through the trees. There were wild boars out here, she knew. Dangerous creatures if threatened. There were Florida panthers, too. Horribly endangered, and yet, if one was there, and threatened…

She kept walking, searching the ground, a sense of panic beginning to rise within her as she thought about the hopelessness of what she was doing. And then she came upon an indentation in the earth. She paused and shone her light down.

The dry area of the heavy pine piling would have eroded with time. But beneath the limestone and far into the water, the wood had been preserved.

She'd found it.

A piling that indicated the corner of the main chickee where, decades ago, Anthony Green had maintained the Everglades "office" for his illicit distillery.

She looked up; Appleby was staring at her.

"Time to dig!"

"WE'VE BEEN WATCHING HER. She has been safe," Jason Tiger told Nick. "You don't see them, but there are three men with me, watching from different angles. Oliver Osceola is in a tree over there—he's closest. Appleby has kept his gun out, so we've been exceptionally careful not to be seen or to startle him in any way." He was quiet for a minute. "We have a sniper. A good one. David Cypress served three tours of duty in the Middle East. If we need—"

"We need to keep watching now. My partner is searching for Kody Cameron's parents. She'll throw herself in front of him, if she's worried about what will happen to her folks." The burning sensation remained with Nick, something that he fought—reminding himself over and over again that he was a federal agent, responsible to his calling. He would make every move the way a federal agent would—and that included killing Appleby point-blank if necessary to save a civilian.

The time taken to reach the hammock deep in the Everglades behind Shark Valley had seemed to be a lifetime.

He was here now.

He could see Appleby and Kody.

"All right, we're ready," Jason Tiger said. "You call the shots."

Nick nodded and ducked low into the grass. He kept as close to the ground as he could, making his way around to the area where Kody and Appleby were standing. He came close enough to hear them speaking.

"That's it! Now dig. It's there somewhere! You see! Ah, you were such a doubter, Miss Cameron! Dig! We have found it."

Kody was trying to assemble a foldable spade.

"You need to make a phone call," she said.

"I need you to dig."

"Make the call. It's been an hour again. I mean it— make the call."

"What if I just cut you up a little bit, Miss Cameron?"

"Then you'd have to dig yourself," Kody told him. "Make the call."

"You want me to make a call? Fine, I'll make a call."

Appleby pulled out his phone. He placed a call. He appeared to be speaking to someone.

But Nick wondered if there was actually anyone on the other end.

Had the man really taken Kody's parents out on a boat somewhere? Did he have new accomplices watching over them, actually ready to kill?

Or had Nick been right? Were they somewhere near their own home?

Still a safe distance, hunkered low in the rich grasses, Nick put a call through to Craig. "Anything yet?"

"No. But we have search-and-rescue dogs on the way. We're going to find them. What's going on at your end? Have you found Kody and Appleby?"

"We have them. Jason Tiger has had them in sight. We're good here. Just…just find Kody's parents."

As he spoke he heard the dogs start to bay. They were on to something. He suddenly found himself praying that Craig and the men and the dogs weren't going to find corpses. The corpses of two people he had never met.

"Bones," Craig said over the phone.

"Bones?"

"And a little gravestone. For JoJo, a little dog who died about a decade ago."

"Oh, lord. Craig—"

"Hold up. We've got something. The dogs are heading across the street. There's a park over there. I think he has them in the park, Nick. Right back with you!"

KODY DIDN'T TRUST APPLEBY. She knew the man really didn't care if people lived or died.

She wondered with a terrible, sinking feeling if her parents weren't already dead. If Appleby hadn't come into the house, waited for them and shot them down in cold blood…

"I want to talk to my mother," she said.

"What?"

"I want to talk to my mother. I want to know that she's alive. I don't believe you and I don't trust you. And this is sick and ridiculous, and if I'm going to continue to search and help you, I want to know that my mother is alive!" Kody said determinedly.

"Do you know what I could do, little girl?" Appleby asked her. "Do you have any idea of what I could do to you? Let me describe a few possibilities. Your knee-caps. You can't imagine the pain of having your knee-cap shot out. I could shoot them both—and then leave you here. Eventually birds of prey and other creatures would come along and then the fun would really start. They would eat you alive. Slowly. They're very fond of soft tissue, especially birds of prey. They love to pluck out eyes…you can't begin to imagine. With any luck, you'd be dead by then."

Kody wasn't about to be swayed. "I want to talk to my mother."

"You can't talk to your mother."

"Why not? Is she dead? If she's dead, I don't give a damn what you do to me."

"She can't talk because there isn't anyone with her to hand her a phone!"

"I thought she was being held on a boat by people who would kill her."

"She's alive and well, Kody. Okay, maybe not so *well*, but she is alive. She's just tied up at the moment."

"Tied up where?"

"Does it matter? She can't talk right now." Appleby let out a growl of aggravation. "She can't talk. I knocked them out, left them tied up. They're alive, Kody."

"How do I trust you?"

"How do you not? You don't have a choice. Start moving. The longer you take, the more danger there is for your mom and dad."

"Maybe you've never even had them!" Kody said.

Appleby grinned. "Mom. Her name is Elizabeth,

nickname Beth. She's about five feet, six inches. A pretty brunette with short, bobbed hair. Dad—Daniel. Six-two, blue eyes, graying dark hair. Yep, not to worry, Kody, dear, I do know the folks."

Kody managed to snap her shovel into working condition. For a moment she stared at Appleby, then she studied the ground and jumped back.

"What?" Appleby demanded.

"Snake."

"It will move."

"Yes, I'm trying to let it. It's a very big snake."

"It's just a ball python," Appleby said. "Someone's pet they let loose out here. Damn, but I hate that! People being so irresponsible. They've ruined the ecosystem."

Kody stared at him. He hadn't minded shooting an accomplice at close range. But he was worried about the ecosystem.

Thankfully, the snake at her feet was a non-native constrictor instead of a viper.

She swallowed hard.

The snake was gone.

She started to dig.

"TELL ME YOU'VE got something!" Nick whispered to Craig.

"Yes! We've got them. They were left under the bridge at the edge of the park. They couldn't twist or turn a lot or they'd have been in a canal. But we have them. We have them both. Elizabeth and Daniel Cameron are safe."

"Roger that. Thank you," Nick said. He clicked the phone closed, then inched through the grass and rose slightly, giving a signal to Jason Tiger to hold for his cue.

Kody suddenly let out a little cry, stepping backward.

"What?" Appleby demanded.

"Another snake…it's a coral snake. A little coral snake, but they can be really dangerous."

"No, that's not a coral snake. It's just a rat snake. Rat snakes are not poisonous."

"'Red touch yellow, kill a fellow. Black touch yellow, friend of Jack,'" Kody said, quoting the age-old way children were taught to recognize coral snakes from their non-venomous cousins.

"Yeah! Look, black on yellow!" Appleby said.

"No, red is touching yellow!"

"You want to get your nose down there and check?" he demanded.

"I am not touching that snake!" Kody said.

Appleby made a move. Nick could judge the man's body motion, the way that he crouched. He was getting ready to strike out.

And that was it.

Nick went flying across the remaining distance between them.

Appleby spun around, but he never knew Nick was coming, never saw what hit him. Nick head-butted the man, bringing him down to the ground.

The man's gun went flying.

They could all hear the popping sound as it was sucked into the swamp.

Appleby made no effort to struggle. Nick had raised a fist; Appleby just stared at him. He started to laugh. "You won't do it, will you? Pansy lawman. You won't do it. In fact…"

Nick didn't listen to the rest; he was already rising. Jason Tiger and his men were coming in to take the prisoner.

He looked over at Kody, who was standing there,

shaking. She hadn't moved from her position; she was just staring at him.

Then she flew at him, her fists banging against his chest. "Nick! You idiot, he has my mom and dad. He's going to kill my mom and dad. He'll never tell us—"

"That's right! They'll die!" Appleby chortled.

Nick caught Kody's hands. He turned and glanced at Appleby. "No, actually, Dan and Beth are just fine. They're being checked out at Mercy Hospital as we speak, but I imagine they'll be home by the time Kody and I manage to get back in."

Kody went limp, falling against him. "Really?"

"Really," he said.

He started to lead her back toward the police boat that had brought him to the hammock.

"Thank you!" she whispered.

"You did it, you know. Getting the call through. If you hadn't managed that, no one would have known. You did it, Kody."

She looked up at him. "I called the right guy, huh?" she said softly.

He kissed her lightly, holding her close, and heedless of who might see.

Appleby let out a horrendous scream. "It got me! It got me! Son of a bitch, it got me! Help, you've got to get me help, fast. You have to slice it, suck the poison out... It got me. You bastards, do something!"

"Oh, I don't know," Jason Tiger said. "David, did you see the snake?"

"Had to be a rat snake."

With Appleby supported between them, Jason Tiger and David Cypress walked by them. Jason Tiger winked. *Rat snake*, he mouthed to Nick.

And Nick grinned.

Yep…

Let Appleby do a little wondering, after what he had done to others.

The winter's night was nearly over. Morning's light was on the way. And with it, Nick felt, all good things.

It was done. Case over, the way he liked it.

Appleby would rot beyond bars.

And Kody was safe, in his arms.

"'HE HATH, MY LORD, of late made many tenders of his affection to me!'"

Beyond a doubt, Dakota Cameron made the most stunning Ophelia that Nick had ever seen.

The play was definitely different; not that, until now, he'd really been an expert on plays.

He was learning.

But even with what he knew, *Hamlet Thus They Say* was a different kind of show. Of course, Kody was beyond stupendous and Nick could hear the buzz among the people around him.

It was going to be a hit.

There was no real curtain call; the play just continued for four hours each night. There was no intermission. It was "living theater."

And it was FBI night.

Craig was there with Kieran. Mike, Craig's partner, was there. Nick had been glad to learn that he would be repartnered with Sherri Haskell, and she was there with her New York City cop husband, Mo.

Director Egan had even come out for the night.

They waited in front of the theater for the last of the attendees to leave.

"I can't believe that they didn't break character—not once!" Kieran said, smiling at Nick. "Okay, so, actually,

I can't believe you disappear, Kody goes home to settle some things, and you come back a duo, having caught a man who held a spot on the Ten Most Wanted list—and found a treasure that's been missing for decades."

"Ah, but we didn't find the treasure!" Nick told her.

"I think you did."

Nick laughed softly, looking at Craig. "Poor Ophelia, going mad for love! I think Craig and I did a bit of the same. The county, the federal government and the Miccosukee Tribe all got together—and that's when they found the treasure. None of us stayed because, as we know, the FBI is a commitment—and because the show must go on. That's a commitment for Kody.

"We stayed in Miami just long enough for her to spend a day with her parents. Then we all had to be back up here. But, yes, Kody's research and logic led those forces to the stash. They had to dig pretty deep. I don't think that Nathan Appleby would have managed to get it all out. He might have found some pieces, though. It had been buried in leather cases, and they were coming apart. But, yes, the stash was filled with gold pieces—South African—and emeralds, diamonds, you name it."

"What will happen with it all?" Kieran asked.

"I understand some of the pieces will wind up in a museum. Some will go to the state and some will wind up helping to keep the Crystal Manor going. It will be part of the trust that runs the place—along with Kody's family. And speaking of Kody's family…" He paused, waving as Daniel and Beth Cameron exited the theater. Nick drew them over and introduced them to those in their group they hadn't met already.

Of course, on arrival in the city, they'd been brought to Finnegan's and feted with stout from excellent taps and the world's best shepherd's pie.

"Wow. And you're FBI, too?" Daniel asked Sherri.

"Yes, sir. I am."

"Well, our girl will be hanging around with a good crowd," Daniel told his wife.

"Yes, certainly," Beth Cameron said, but she looked a little puzzled.

"Is anything wrong?" Nick asked her.

"No, no, of course not. I'm not so sure that I get it. I mean, living theater, or whatever it is. I'm used to the actors just…acting on stage. I've never talked with the actors before during a performance," she said. "But, of course, Kody and Kevin were wonderful!"

Kieran laughed. "Yes, they were. They were both wonderful."

"She talked to me—but as if she didn't know me!" Daniel said.

"Well, she doesn't know you. Not as Ophelia," Nick explained.

"Yes, yes, of course. She's playing a role. I guess. I mean, of course. It's just strange," Beth said. She sighed. "She has a beautiful voice. Maybe it will be a musical next. Oh, look!" she murmured, catching Nick by the hand. "There—do you know who that is?"

Nick looked. No, he didn't.

"That's Mayor Holden Burke. With his little boy, Adrian. And his wife, Monica."

The man, next to the boy who appeared to be about nine, noted Beth just as she was whispering about him.

He waved and came over, catching the hands of his wife and son so they would join him. Adrian Burke was carrying a large bouquet of flowers.

Beth introduced people all around.

"We're so grateful," he said, and his wife nodded, looking around. "You're the agents who were involved?"

"Craig and I were down there," Nick said. "But, like I said in my debriefing, in all honesty, Kody was the one who got Nathan Appleby to say where Adrian was being held. And an agent down in South Florida, Jason Tiger, got the information back to the city."

The cast door opened and the actors were all coming out. There was a round of applause that sounded up and down the street.

Nick saw Kody, and saw that she was searching through the crowd.

Looking for him, he thought. He waved and then watched her chat and smile with grace and courtesy as she spoke to fans and signed programs.

"Excuse us," Mayor Burke said.

Nick realized, as the mayor and his family approached Kody, that she'd never actually met them.

She took the flowers from Adrian, hugged him and planted a kiss on his cheek. She was hugged by the mayor and his wife.

The three left then, waving to the others.

And, finally, the crowd around the performers had just about thinned out.

He, Kody's parents, the Finnegans and the extended FBI family made their way over to the group, congratulating the actors. Nick bypassed everyone, going directly to Kody and taking her in his arms.

Her kiss was magnificent. Her eyes touched his with promise. She was filled with the excitement and adrenaline of opening night; she was also anxious, he knew, for their time together.

But first, of course, they all made their way to Finnegan's for a late-night supper and a phenomenal Irish band.

And, at last, it was time for him and Kody to leave.

In his company car they saw her parents to their hotel in midtown. Then they headed for his apartment.

When they'd first returned to the city a few weeks ago, they'd kept both apartments. That had proved to be a total waste. They both worked, and worked hard, but their free time was spent together.

When a night bartender at Finnegan's was about to lose his lease—his apartments were being turned into condos—Kody offered her apartment to him, and so, just last week, she had made the official move into Nick's place.

It was simply the best accommodation: a full bedroom, an office, a parlor, two baths. Plus it was situated right on the subway line that connected Finnegan's and the FBI offices and midtown.

Kody, of course, had already made some changes, and Nick loved them.

There were posters on the wall—show posters and band posters—and there was artwork, as well. Seascapes, mostly, from Florida, and paintings from New York City, too.

One of his favorite pieces they had bought together down in the Village. It was a signed painting of the Brooklyn Bridge.

"A new artist—who will be a famous artist one day," Kody had said. "And if not, it's still a brilliant painting and I love it."

She was, he thought, everything he needed.

Life, as he saw it, was too often grim. But Kody looked for the best, always. And she saw the best that way. She showed it to him, as well.

"So, what did you think of the play? What did you really think?" she asked when they stepped into the apartment, alone at last.

"I loved it," he said.

"Really?"

"I really did. But I do believe you have to have the right cast for that kind of theater. Your cast is truly amazing. Powerful performers—they all engaged the audience."

"I don't think my mom saw it that way."

Nick laughed. "She admitted to a bit of confusion."

"But you really thought that it was good?" she asked.

"I, like the critics, raved!"

She flew into his arms, kissing him. "Are you a liar?" she asked.

"No!"

She laughed. "Doesn't matter," she said. "You were there for me, on FBI night."

"I'll come to the show whenever I can."

"You don't have to. It's okay. We'll settle in and we'll figure it all out—the time, the FBI, the theater…"

"I know we will," he told her. And he kissed her again, shrugging out of his jacket as he did so. It had been a chilly night. Kody was in a heavy wool coat and it, too, hit the floor.

She kicked off her shoes, their lips never parting.

Nick suddenly dipped low and swept her off her feet. She laughed as she looked up at him.

"It's been a dramatic night. Thought I should be dramatic, too."

"You really are quite the actor. You know, down in Florida when I first saw you, I really thought you were a bad guy."

"But not really. You said you knew I wasn't a killer."

"You played the part very well."

"Thank you. If the law-enforcement thing fails…"

She touched his face gently, studying his eyes. "It

won't. You love what you do, and you're very good, and I would never want anything different for you."

"Nor would I change a thing about you," he told her huskily.

She smiled.

They headed into the bedroom and Nick laid Kody carefully upon the sheets, kneeling beside her. He kissed her lips again, but she was impatient and rose against him, crawling over him, straddling him, while she tore away her clothes.

"Ah, my lady! Wait, I have a surprise for you," he said.

She laughed softly. "And I have a surprise for you! I can wait for nothing." And she shoved him down. She lay against him, teased his shoulders, chest and abdomen with her kisses as she tugged at his clothing, entangled them both in it, and laughed as they finally managed to strip down completely. She whispered to him, touching him, making love to him with a combination of tenderness and fierceness that drove him wild.

It was later, much later, when he lay sated and incredulous, cradling her to him, his chin atop her head, that she said, "You told me you had a surprise for me."

"Ah, yes!"

He got out of bed and Kody sat up to watch him, curious as he left the room.

He'd never been with an actress before.

This one, he knew he would love all his life. Therefore, he had figured, he would get it right.

He plucked the champagne from the refrigerator and prepared the ice bucket.

The plate of chocolate-covered strawberries was ready, as well.

Along with the long-stemmed roses. And a tiny box.

He swept up the bucket, the plate balanced atop it, the roses in his mouth. And he walked back into the bedroom.

Kody cried out with delight, clapping her hands.

"Oh, but you are perfect! Perfect! Roses, chocolate-covered strawberries, champagne—and a naked FBI guy! What more could one want?"

They both burst into laughter.

And he joined her in the bed.

They popped the cork on the champagne, laughed as it spilled over. They shared the strawberries and Kody smelled the roses and looked at him seriously.

"I love you so much," she whispered. "Is it…is it all right to say that? I tend to speak quickly, rashly, sometimes. I mean…well, you know. I probably could have gotten myself or someone else killed back in Florida if you weren't you. If you hadn't been undercover. If—"

He pulled her into his arms. "I wouldn't have you any other way at all. I love that you said what you did. I love you. And…"

He realized he was terribly nervous. He might be a well-trained agent, but his fingers were trembling as he reached for the little box.

Kody took the box, her eyes on his. She opened it and stared in silence.

His heart sank. "It's too soon, too much," he murmured. "I—"

She threw her arms around him, and kissed him, and kissed him, and kissed him.

"Is that a yes?"

"Yes!" She laughed. "Not even I am that good an actress!"

He took the ring and slipped it on her finger. "Since we're living in sin…?"

"This kind of love could never be a sin," she assured him.

"You're really so beautiful...in every way," he told her.

She smiled—a mischievous smile. "With the pick-up line you gave me in Florida, who would have thought that we would wind up here!"

"Go figure," he agreed.

He kissed her and lay her back on the bed.

"Go figure," he repeated.

And he started kissing her again and again...

It was, after all, opening night. For the show.

And for the rest of their lives.

* * * * *

*Keep reading for a special preview of
the next novel from*
New York Times *bestselling author
Heather Graham*
A PERFECT OBSESSION
The second thrilling story in the
NEW YORK CONFIDENTIAL *series.*
Coming soon from MIRA Books.

Chapter One

"Horrible! Oh, God, horrible—tragic!" John Shaw said, shaking his head with a dazed look as he sat on his bar stool at Finnegan's Pub.

Kieran nodded sympathetically. Construction crews had found old graves when they were working on the foundations at the hot new downtown venue Le Club Vampyre.

Anthropologists had found the new body among the old graves the next day.

It wasn't just *any* body.

It was the body of supermodel Jeannette Gilbert.

Finding the old graves wasn't much of a shock—not in New York City, and not in a building that was close to two centuries old. The structure that housed Le Club Vampyre was a deconsecrated Episcopal church. The church's congregation had moved to a facility it had purchased from the Catholic church—whose congregation was now in a sparkling new basilica over on Park Avenue. While many had bemoaned the fact that such a venerable old institution had been turned into an establishment for those into sex, drugs, and rock and roll, life—and business—went on.

And with life going on…

Well, work on the building's foundations went on, too.

It was while investigators were still being called in following the discovery of the newly deceased body—moments before it hit the news—that Kieran Finnegan learned about it, and that was because she was helping out at her family's establishment, Finnegan's on Broadway. Like the old church/nightclub behind it, Finnegan's dated back to just before the Civil War, and had been a pub for most of those years. Since it was geographically the closest place to the church with liquor, it had apparently seemed the right spot at that moment for Professor John Shaw. They'd barely opened; it was still morning, and it was a Friday, and Kieran was only there at that time because her bosses had decided on a day off following their participation in a lengthy trial. She'd just come up from the cellar, fetching a few bottles of a vintage chardonnay for her brother that had been ordered specifically for a lunch that day, when John Shaw had caught her attention, desperate to talk.

"I can't tell you how excited I was, being called in as an expert on a find like that," the professor told Kieran. "They both wanted me! By they, I mean Henry Willoughby, president of Preserve our Past, and Roger Gleason, owner and manager of the club. I was so honored. It was exciting to think of finding the *old* bodies—not the new body. But then...opening a decaying coffin and finding Jeannette Gilbert! And the university was entirely behind me, allowing me the time to be at my site, giving me a chance to bring my grad students here. Oh, my God! I found her! Oh, it was..."

John Shaw was shaking as he spoke. He was a man who'd seen all kinds of antiquated horrors, an expert in the past. He fit the stereotype of an academic with his lean physique, his thatch of wild white hair and his little gold-framed glasses. He held doctorate degrees in archaeology and anthropology, and science and history meant everything to him.

Kieran realized that he'd been about to say once again that it was horrible, like nothing he'd ever experienced. He clearly realized that he was speaking about a recently living woman, adored by adolescent boys and heterosexual males of all ages—a woman who was going to be deeply mourned.

Jeannette Gilbert. Media princess. The model and actress had disappeared two weeks ago after the launch party for a new cosmetics line. Her agent and manager, Oswald Martin, had gone on the news, begging kidnappers for her safe return.

At that time, no one knew if she actually *had* been kidnapped. One reporter speculated that she'd disappeared on purpose, determined to get away from the very man begging kidnappers for her release: her agent and manager.

Kieran hadn't really paid much attention; she'd assumed that the young woman—who'd been made famous by the same Oswald Martin—had just had enough of being adored and fawned over and told what to do at every move, and she'd decided to take a hiatus. Or it might have been some kind of publicity gig; her disappearance had certainly ruled the headlines. There were always tabloid pictures of Jeannette with this or that man, and then speculation in the same tabloids that her manager had furiously burst into a hotel room, sending Jeannette Gilbert's latest lover—gold digger, as Martin referred to any young man she dated—flying out the door.

In the past few weeks the "celebrity" magazines had run rampant with rumors of a mystery man in her life.

A secret love. Kieran knew that only because her twin brother, Kevin, was an actor—struggling his way into TV, movies and theater. He read the tabloids avidly, telling Kieran that he was "reading between the lines," and being up on what was going on was critical to his career. There were too many actors—even good ones!—out there and too few roles. Any edge was a good edge.

While all the speculation had been going on, Kieran couldn't help wondering if Jeannette's secret lover had killed her—or if, maybe, her steel-handed manager had done so.

Or, since this was New York City with a population in the millions, it was possible that some deranged person had murdered her. Perhaps this person felt that if she was relieved of her life, she'd be out of the misery caused by being such a beautiful, glittering star, always the focus of attention.

It was fine to speculate when you believed that someone was just pulling a major publicity stunt.

Now Kieran felt bad, of course. From what she *knew* now, it seemed evident that the woman had indeed been murdered.

Not that she had any of the facts other than that Jeannette had been found in the bowels of the earth in a nineteenth-century tomb, but it was unlikely that Jeannette Gilbert had crawled into a historic coffin in a lost catacomb to die of natural causes.

"It was so horrible!" John Shaw repeated woefully. "When we found her, we just stared. One of my silly young grad students screamed, and she wasn't the only one. We called the police immediately. The club wasn't open then, of course—except to us, those of us who were working. I was there for hours while they grilled me. And now...now, I need this!" His hand shook as he picked up his double shot of single-malt scotch to swallow in a gulp.

He was usually a beer man. Ultra light.

It was horrible, yes, as Shaw kept saying. But, of course, he realized he'd be in the news, interviewed for dozens of papers and magazines and television, as well.

After all…

He'd been the one to find Jeannette Gilbert dead. In a coffin, in a deconsecrated church now turned into the Le Club Vampyre. Well, that was news.

The pub would soon be buzzing, especially since it was on the other side of the block from Le Club Vampyre.

The whole situation, aside from the grief of a young woman's untimely death, was interesting to Kieran. In her "real" job during the week she worked as a psychologist and therapist for psychiatrists Bentley Fuller and Allison Miro. But, like her brothers, she often filled in at the pub; it was kind of a home away from home for them all. The pub had been in the family—belonging to a distant great-great uncle—from the mid–nineteenth century. Her own parents were gone now, and that made the pub even more precious to her and her older brother, Declan, her twin, Kevin, and her "baby" brother, Daniel.

So, while Declan actually managed the pub and made it his life's work, Kieran was employed by doctors Fuller and Miro, Kevin pursued his acting career and Danny strove to become the city's best tour guide. And they all spent a great deal of time at Finnegan's.

The tragic death of Jeannette Gilbert would soon have all their patrons gossiping about this latest outrage regarding Le Club Vampyre. They'd been talking about it now and then for six months, ever since the sale of the old church to Dark Doors Incorporated. Patrons had become extremely glum when the club had opened a month ago. A club! Like that! In an old church!

The club had also, of course, been the main topic of conversation yesterday, when the news had come out that unknown gravesites had been found—and Professor John Shaw had been called in.

Of course, people were still talking about the old catacombs today. Not that finding graves while digging in foundations was unusual in New York. It was just creepy-cool enough.

Creepy-cool was fine when you were talking about very old gravesites.

Because they were old—they were the site of the earthly remains of people who'd lived and died long ago.

Not the newly deceased.

At the moment, though, Kieran was one of the few people who knew that the body of Jeannette Gilbert had been discovered. Kieran had been among the first to find out; that was because she knew Dr. John Shaw—professor of archaeology and anthropology at NYU, famed in academic circles for his work on sites from Jamestown, Virginia, to Beijing, China—very well. He and a group of his colleagues had met at Finnegan's Pub one night a month as long as she could remember.

When she'd see him looking so distressed, she'd ushered him into one of the small booths against the wall that divided the pub's general area from the offices. She'd gotten him his scotch—and she'd sat down with him so she could try to calm him down.

"Oh, my God! I can just imagine when it hits the news!" he said, looking at her with stricken eyes. And yet, she recognized a bit of awe in them...

Of course, he hadn't known Jeannette Gilbert. Kieran hadn't, either. She'd seen her once, on a red carpet, heading to the premiere of a new movie in a theater near Times Square.

Sadly, Jeannette hadn't been an especially talented actress. But she'd been too beautiful for most people to care.

"I'm so sorry you're the one who found her," Kieran said. That should've been the right thing to say; usually, people didn't want to find others dead. Though John Shaw was going to be famous in the pop-culture world now, as well as the academic world.

But it was obvious that he was badly shaken.

He was accustomed to studying bones and mummies—not a woman who'd been recently murdered.

"I was—I am!—very excited about the project. I don't understand how the church could have lost all those graves. Can you imagine? Okay, so, you know how they built St. Paul's to accommodate folks farther north of Trinity back in the day? Well, they built St. Augustine's for those a little north of St. Paul's. And, according to my research so far, the church was fine until about 1860, when way too many people went off to fight in the Civil War. It wasn't deconsecrated—just more or less abandoned because the congregations were so much smaller. Then, according to records, Father O'Hara passed away, and it took the church forever to send out a new priest. Apparently, there was structural damage by then, which closed off that section of the catacombs. You see, there was, until about seventy-five years ago, an entrance to the catacombs from the street, and I suppose everyone—church officials, city organizers, engineers, what have you—believed all the graves had been removed. Of course, most of the dead were buried then in wooden coffins, and in the ground area outside, most of those became dirt and bone. But there were underground catacombs, too. Coffins set upon shelves... Some of the dead were just shrouded, but some were in old wooden coffins, and they were decaying and falling apart and I had workers taking them down so carefully—and then there she was!"

He sipped his scotch again and looked at her intently. "Kieran, you're not to say a word, not yet. The police... they asked me not to speak about this until...until someone was notified. I don't think either of her parents are living, but she must have family..." His voice trailed off. "My God. It was ghastly!" he said a moment later. "Gruesome—ghastly!"

This time, he didn't sip his scotch. He swallowed it down in a gulp.

Kieran wasn't sure why she turned to look at the front door when she did; it was always opening and closing. Maybe she wanted to look anywhere except at John Shaw. She was a working psychologist, and yet she wasn't sure what to say to the man.

She glanced up just in time to see Craig Frasier come in and blink to adjust to the light.

She wasn't surprised Craig was there; they were seeing each other and had been since the affair over the "flawless" Capeletti diamond. They were talking about giving up their current situation, in which they each had dresser drawers at the other's apartment, and moving in together.

But while she had truly fallen in love with Craig, she was a little hesitant—and a little worried about the fact that the man she believed to be her soul mate also happened to be a special agent with the FBI. Her family was striving to be legitimate now, which hadn't always been the case. Growing up, her brothers had had a few brushes with the law.

And trusting her beloved brothers to behave wasn't

easy. They were never malicious; however, their ways of helping friends out of bad situations weren't always the best.

Then again, she'd met Craig because of the Capeletti diamond and Danny's determination to do the right thing...

And because of some criminal clientele.

"Excuse me," she murmured to John, assuming that Craig had come to see her.

The door was still open; he stood in a pool of light and her heart leaped as she saw him. Craig was, in her mind, entirely impressive, tall and broad shouldered, with extraordinary eyes that seemed to take everything in.

But he had not, apparently, come to see her.

He greeted Kieran with a nod, held her shoulders for a minute—and then offered her a grim smile as he gently set her aside so he could move past her.

Something was up. Craig spent his free time here with her and her family. Her friends, coworkers and the usual clientele all knew that Craig and Kieran were a couple.

Today, however, there wasn't even a quick kiss. Craig was being very official.

He was heading straight to the booth where John Shaw was seated.

Kieran stood there for a minute, perplexed.

Of course, Craig was FBI. But a local woman had been killed, and no matter how famous she'd been, it should've remained a matter for the NYPD. And John Shaw had left the old church/screaming-hot nightclub less than an hour ago.

Why would Craig be here so quickly? And more to the point, why was the FBI involved?

She didn't get a chance to slide back into the booth

and find out what was going on; she felt a tap on her shoulder and turned around.

Her brother Kevin was next to her. Kevin was a striking man—in *anyone's* opinion, she thought. He was tall and fit with fine features, dark red hair and deep blue eyes; their coloring was the same. They were twins, and it showed. She loved her brother and she felt that acting was the perfect career for him. Like all of them, however, he worked at the pub when he could.

"I have to talk to you!" he said urgently.

"Sure," she said.

"Not here. In the office," he told her. To her surprise, he glanced uneasily at Craig—whom he liked and with whom he was pretty good friends.

Her brother whirled her around and headed her down the entry aisle toward the bar and then to the left and down the hallway to the business office. He peered in, as if afraid their older brother might be there, since it was, basically, Declan's office.

He closed the door behind them.

"She's dead, Kieran! She's dead!" Kevin said, looking at her and shaking his head with dismay and anxiety.

She stared at him for a moment. He couldn't be talking about Jeannette Gilbert—no one knew she'd been found at the church yet, not according to John Shaw.

Her heart quaked with fear. She was afraid he was talking about an old friend, or a longtime customer of the pub.

Someone he cared about deeply.

"Kevin, *who*?" she asked.

"Jeannette."

She frowned. "Jeannette Gilbert?"

He nodded.

"Okay," she said slowly. "*I* know that, because John

Shaw just told me. But he only found her a few hours ago. The police asked him not to say anything."

Kevin took a deep breath. "Well, John Shaw might not have said anything, but one of the workers down there—a grunt? A student? I don't know—came out and told people on the street, and the story was picked up, and there are already media crews there."

She studied her brother. "Kevin, it's terrible. A young and beautiful young woman who was very popular has—I'm assuming—been murdered. But, Kevin, I'm afraid that terrible things do happen. But…we didn't know Jeannette Gilbert. Not personally."

"Yes," he said. "We did."

"We did?"

"*I* did," he corrected. "Kieran, I was the so-called 'mystery man' she was dating! I might have been the last one to see her alive."

The NYPD had been called in first; that was proper protocol, since New York City was where the body had been found.

Jeannette Gilbert hadn't been kidnapped in another state and subsequently killed in New York. She'd last been seen by her doorman entering her apartment; she was a longtime Manhattan resident. She had, in fact, grown up in Harlem, a little girl who'd lost both parents and gone on to live in a household filled with children and an aunt who hadn't wanted another mouth to feed.

At the age of seventeen, however, she had an affair with a rock star.

While the rock star denied any kind of intimate relationship with her at the time, he'd gone on to put her in one of his music videos soon after.

An agent had picked her up and it had been a classic tale—little girl lost had become a megastar. By twenty-five, she was gracing runways and doing cameo spots on television shows and even appearing in small roles in several movies. She was considered a true supernova.

Because Jeannette's physical appearance had been called *perfect* by every critic out there.

She could walk a runway.

She had beautiful skin, luscious hair, long legs and a body that didn't quit.

Craig Frasier had learned all this about Jeannette in the past few hours. Before that, she'd been a face he might have recognized on a magazine cover.

But he'd made it his business to read up on her quickly.

Because her death had suddenly become the focus of his life.

He'd been in his office, reading paperwork from witnesses about the murder of a known pimp, when he'd been summoned, along with his partner, Mike Dalton, to Assistant Director Richard Egan's office.

Craig and Mike had been partners for years. Craig had been assigned a young, new agent when Mike was laid up on medical—a shot to the buttocks—about a year ago. He'd learned then how much he appreciated his partner; they knew each other's minds. They naturally fell into a division of labor when it came to pounding the pavement and getting the inevitable paperwork done.

And there was no one Craig trusted more to have his back, especially in a shoot-out.

Egan, a good man himself, was hardcore Bureau. His personal life had suffered for it, but he never brought that into the office. He was the best kind of authority figure, as well—dignified, fair, compassionate. And efficient. He never wasted time. There were two chairs in front of his desk, but he hadn't waited for Craig and Mike to sit down. He'd started talking right away.

"I had a back-burner situation going on here," he'd told them. "We'd been given information, but the local police down in Fredericksburg, Virginia, were handling the case. A girl—a perfect-looking girl, an artist's model—disappeared about six months ago. A few weeks later, her body was found in a historic cemetery outside Fredericksburg. She'd been stabbed in the heart, then cleaned up, dressed up and laid out in a family mausoleum. She was discovered when the family's matriarch died, since she'd been put in the matriarch's space. As I said, it seemed to be a local matter, and the Fredericksburg police and Virginia state police had the murder. We were informed because of the unusual aspects."

Egan had paused, running his hands through his hair. Then he'd resumed speaking. "We're all aware of the high-profile disappearance of Jeannette Gilbert."

Mike had nodded. "Yeah, we were briefed with the cops about her disappearance when she went missing. We weren't really in on it, as you know. But we were on the lookout."

"Ms. Gilbert's been found. An archaeological dig at old St. Augustine's."

"You mean—" Mike began.

But Egan had cut him off. Yeah, he meant the new nightclub. Egan wasn't a fan. He'd gone on and ranted for a full minute about old historic places becoming nightclubs. In his opinion, that suggested New York City had no real respect for the past.

Craig knew Mike hadn't been asking his question because of the club; he'd been trying to ascertain if she'd been found dead.

Mike had glanced over at Craig; Craig shrugged.

They'd both just let Egan rant, figuring it was obvious. The poor girl was dead.

It had ended with Egan saying, "Yes, she's dead. And it is bizarre—as bizarre as that earlier case, maybe even more so. Because in this case, the perp had to know she'd be found quickly. He'd placed her in a historical site where anthropologists and archaeologists were expected to arrive imminently. Later, you can go over the info on the Virginia case, do some comparisons. We're part of the task force on this, but we're taking the lead, and you two are up for our division. Because, gentlemen, I believe we have a serial killer on our hands."

They'd asked about the security tapes.

Techs were going over those now.

"That's a bitch!" Egan had exclaimed. "Try looking for something out of the ordinary when every damned customer in the place is like an escapee from a Goth B flick or worse! Not to mention that the club closed down when the body was discovered. There's no club security at night other than the cameras, but cops have been patrolling the place since the historic folks stepped in."

From the office, he and Mike had gone straight to the church. The ME on duty was Anthony Andrews, a fine, detail-oriented doctor, but he hadn't really started yet.

Photographers were still taking pictures, trying to maintain the scene just as it had been after Professor Shaw had opened the first coffin—and had seen Jeannette Gilbert.

A half-dozen members of a forensic team had been moving around, but Dr. Andrews had delicately stopped the photo session to show Craig and Mike what he'd discovered. Gilbert had been killed in another location, stabbed through the heart, and then bathed and dressed and prepared before being placed in the old coffin.

Seeing her had been heartbreaking. He hadn't known the young woman or really anything about her until today, but she'd been young and beautiful and her life had been brutally taken. She lay in the old coffin, dressed in shimmering white, a wilted rose in her hands. With her eyes closed, it looked as if she slept.

Except, of course, she'd never wake again.

"Defensive wounds?" he'd asked Andrews.

"Not a one. She was taken by surprise. Whoever killed her stood close by—had to be someone who seemed trustworthy. Maybe someone she knew," the ME had speculated. "Or she could've had some kind of opiate in her system. Anyway, she didn't expect what was coming."

"Time of death?" Mike had asked. "She's been missing about two weeks."

"I'm thinking one to two weeks," Andrews had replied. "If she was abducted, perhaps soon after. And I don't believe she's been embalmed—but she was somehow preserved. Maybe in a freezer while he worked on her or made arrangements or…" He'd sighed. "I need to get her on the table."

Two patrol officers, the first on the scene, had closed off the area. Luckily, the club was closed, pending the investigation of the newly discovered crypt. Detective Larry McBride with the major crimes division had been the first to arrive. Craig and Mike had worked with him before. He was particularly mild mannered but he had a brilliant mind and nothing deterred his focus.

"Glad you guys are lead on this," McBride had told them. "This is… Well, I believe we definitely have a real psychopath on our hands. Bizarre! Wherever he killed her, he washed away the blood. I've got officers who'll be doing rounds with pictures of the dress. Pending notification of the so-called aunt who raised the girl, they'll be asking all her friends if she owned the dress, or if the killer obtained it."

"Checked the label," Andrews had said. "It's from Saks."

McBride had nodded. "Nice dress. She looks like a princess." He paused. "I have a daughter her age… So, anyway, no inside security by night—but cops watching on the street. The men on duty swore no one went in until Roger Gleason opened it up to wait for the archaeologists. Gleason says he comes in every day, even though the club's closed for a few days. I interviewed him and he seems to be on the up and up. Says he's personally not that interested in the historical stuff but seeing that the work goes well will actually make his club more famous. He's not one of those guys who lets his own property go unattended. He was working up here and heard Shaw's screams. Shaw swears there was no one down there at the time but him and a few of his grad students. I have names, et cetera, which I've emailed to you already. They were all questioned. I don't think they had anything to do with Ms. Gilbert's death. The mystery here is, *how the hell did the bastard get in with the body*? Anyway, the security footage is down at your office now. And, of course, we're hoping Forensics can come up with something. This killer…well, they're calling in shrinks. You know, profilers. The murder was cold, swift and brutal. But then he takes all this time with her. He comes in like a shadow—and then leaves her on display, waiting to be found. I talked with Egan, and I've been hanging around for you guys. Actually, I'm almost afraid to leave. It's a media frenzy out there."

By then the frenzy on the streets had involved more than just media. Word had spread; dozens of celebrity stalkers and those inclined to the macabre had congregated outside the club.

Craig had questioned Gleason himself before leaving. He seemed like a Wall Street type—and although his club might be Goth, he was far more prone to the elegant in his manner and dress.

New York City's finest were dealing with the facility and crowd control.

"I need to talk to Shaw," Craig had decided.

But Shaw wasn't there. They'd heard that when he'd first gotten up close and personal with the body, he'd screamed like a banshee.

And Allie Benoit, John Shaw's grad student and assistant, had told him that Shaw had spoken with the police, and then freaked out and fled. Allie was pretty sure he'd gone to the pub—the pub whose back wall abutted that of the old church-turned-nightclub.

And that *was* exactly what John Shaw had done.

Finnegan's!

Craig had sworn, walked around the corner and reached the pub.

The damned man just had to go to Finnegan's!

The pub had stood there almost as long as the church. It had seen the New York draft riots during the Civil War, and the violence of the Irish gangs that had once held huge sway in a city where immigrants poured in daily from around the world.

The pub had witnessed so much history.

Including the recent history of the diamond heist that had nearly cost Kieran Finnegan her life.

"She won't be involved!" he'd said firmly, speaking aloud.

But before he'd entered, he'd known, somewhere in his gut, that the die had already been cast.

Of all the pubs in all the world.

Finnegan's.

Chapter Two

As he'd entered the pub, Craig's attention was all for his search. With luck, Kieran would be at the office today or—

Naturally, she'd walked directly over to him.

And he hadn't been able to do what he wanted to do—tell her that she wasn't to have the least interaction with *anyone* connected to the murder.

He didn't have the right to make that kind of demand.

And since she was here, she might have already served John Shaw, and John Shaw would've talked to her…

At the moment, though, he needed Shaw. She'd understand that; he never had to explain himself or his intentions to Kieran.

She knew what he did for a living; he knew about her professional work for doctors Fuller and Miro. They respected each other's professions and discussed things when they could—or when the other might have a useful insight. Or when, as occasionally happened, they became involved in the same case.

Fuller and Miro worked with the police and the FBI. They often gave their opinion of a suspected criminal's state of mind or behavior.

They'd been involved, all four of them together, in a situation before—the so-called Diamond Affair.

But now...

He wanted to hold her and yet he couldn't; he was here professionally.

Even as he approached the booth where John Shaw was seated, he was still hating the fact that the church where Jeannette had been found was directly behind Finnegan's. He'd come to terms with being in love with Kieran—and the fact that she, too, dealt with criminals.

However, it was still difficult for him to accept that she was sometimes too quick to put herself in danger in defense of others.

Yes, it seemed to be a Casablanca *moment.*

Of all the old abandoned dug-out holes in Manhattan....

The damned catacombs just had to be close to Finnegan's!

Too close... This place was too close to where a young woman lay dead, where her body had been stashed with the bones of those long forgotten.

Craig knew John Shaw, and Shaw knew him; they'd met at the pub several times when Shaw had come for his professional meetings or get-togethers—or when he just wanted to sip one of his ultralight beers and chill.

"Craig!" John said, looking up at him with surprise. "I—oh, my. You're coming to see me. So I guess it should be Special Agent Frasier. Not Craig. Look, I'm not sure what else I can say to anyone. All I know is that we opened that coffin and...and there she was."

Craig slid into the booth and smiled at him. "You must be pretty rattled."

"Yes. You're here officially? The police told me not to say anything yet. They need to contact the poor girl's family. I mean, that's why you're here—coming to me and not Kieran, right?"

"Yes, John, this is official. The NYPD detectives are on the case, of course, but we're taking part, as well. We've put together a task force. This is a very high-profile murder."

John nodded, his white hair—something of a strange mullet cut—flapping beside his ears. His glasses slid down his nose with his effort and he pushed them back with his forefinger.

"Of course. This needs to be solved fast," John said. "But…" His expression grew even more perplexed. "I don't know how I can help anymore. I don't know how I can help, period. Professor Digby—Aldous Digby, one of my associates—and I were there, and three grad students. Oh, and two of the construction guys. The guys were watching—waiting to get back to work. I didn't let them touch the coffin. Nice guys, but, you know, that coffin might be two hundred years old—well, you need to have a delicate touch. And Ms. Gilbert. The second I saw her…I have to admit I screamed. I was rattled, as you said. But I made sure everyone got out. We did and then went up to the church, the—the club area, to wait for the police."

"Right. So there were seven of you. I have the names," Craig said. He was certain that the meticulous Detective McBride had sent his email.

He'd also seen Jeannette Gilbert's body at the site.

He winced, the picture of her still so clear in his mind. Her lovely, pale, perfect face. The white dress. The red rose.

John nodded. "Seven of us were in there—and seven of us got out quicker than a flash. And we were all interviewed." He sighed loudly. "Hell of a thing for the owner of that place. They've barely been open, what, a month or two? Then they have to stop work and close up because an engineer finds the coffins in the dirt and then the catacombs. They bring us in, and… Sad. So sad. By God, she was beautiful! Poor thing."

"Just to confirm, you were there yesterday?" Craig asked him.

"Of course. I was there as soon as the situation was reported." He paused. "Did you know that the land where the Waldorf Astoria sits was once a potter's field? Think of how old this city is. A number of the parks we enjoy today were originally cemeteries. I worked the old slave cemetery they discovered a few years back, so it was natural that I'd work on this one, too."

"You started on the church yesterday?"

"Yes, I did. I was called yesterday morning and I made arrangements to get there as fast as possible."

"And then?"

"I assessed the location. I called in Digby and my assistant, Allie Benoit. You don't pry apart ancient caskets willy-nilly. We researched church plans, but the original architect's plan is long gone." He shook his head. "You must be familiar with what happened. The church sold the property to the club people. There was an outcry, not that it made any difference. But the building is so historic. Everyone wants to shop Fifth Avenue, see a show, bank on Wall Street. They forget that Wall Street *was* a wall. Canal Street was a canal—or a cesspool, really. Those are all part of our city's origins and we need to preserve history!"

Craig nodded, although he wasn't convinced they'd needed to preserve the cesspool that had been Canal Street. He spoke quickly, not wanting the academic to bluster endlessly. "What time did you get in there?"

"Let's see… They called us right around ten in the morning. I was there within the hour."

"So, who was there then?" Craig asked. "Besides you and the colleagues and workers you've mentioned."

"Oh, lots of people. The manager—owner, too, I think—Roger Gleason. He'd been working down by the construction area. They stored their booze down there—in the old crypt they knew about, I mean, with the coffins and bodies all gone now. It's a foundation, a basement. The basement—the *crypts*—were far more extensive than people realized. The wall had hidden some of the old coffins and shrouded corpses, so when some of the corpses were moved, the 'second' crypt was missed."

"Okay. Anyone else know what was going on?"

"At least two construction workers and one of the barmaid-slash-dancers. Have you seen what they do in there? She was dressed up in a little black bra and skirt and wearing some wicked makeup. The girls dance on tables when they're not handing out booze."

"So, employees, construction workers—anyone else?"

"Oh, yeah, the rep from the historic preservation group. Henry Willoughby. Loves history. He's not a scientist, but he's a great hands-on guy, ready to protect the past and help out if he can. The man loves New York and studied history and architecture. His wife passed away a while back, and now he gives all his love to the city. He stayed long enough last night to check in with us, make sure we were ready to catalogue the bodies and the artifacts we found. I would've brought in more crew, but—"

"Who stayed, then? Who was actually there when you kept working?"

"The seven people you know about—me, Digby showed up, my grad students—plus a structural engineer and a construction worker, all to see that we didn't bring down a wall, I assume." He cleared his throat. "Of course, after I initially went in yesterday, the construction guys created a kind of door for us."

"How long were you there yesterday?"

"Oh, it was almost midnight before I left! I didn't touch or open anything. I stepped over the hole—where the wall broke when they were working on the foundations—into the crypt beyond. We make drawings and assessments and plan before we start the actual work, so, yes, I'd say it was midnight. By then, of course, the vampire dancers were gone and all the club people had been told to go home. Once they'd made the find—the second crypt—they closed down, of course, but people were hanging around. It's…it's history being reclaimed! Roger Gleason, the owner, seems like a nice guy. He has a conscience and some perspective on what's important. We didn't have to get court orders or anything. He simply agreed to close for a few days. They had patrol officers covering the place, making sure that once the news about the crypt got out, some Goth or necrophilia-pursuing freak didn't try to break in."

Craig nodded. He knew the answers to most of what he was asking; he just wanted it from Shaw and he wanted to ensure that their facts were straight.

"Yesterday," Shaw said, "you understand, it was *discovery* day. I planned where to put some lights. I judged the space for people and decided on equipment. I did all the assessments, got my ducks in a row, you know what I mean?"

Craig nodded again. "This morning when you arrived—were things exactly as you'd left them?" he asked.

"What?"

"Had anything you'd done been changed? Were tools missing, anything like that?"

Shaw frowned. "I...I don't think so. I don't get it. I'd roped off different areas in the basement for my people. We had our little brushes and chisels and...no, I'm positive that our work tables were the way we'd left them," he said. He leaned forward. "Didn't Ms. Gilbert disappear about two weeks ago? She didn't look as if she'd just been killed. She...she was beautiful as she lay there, but some decay had set in. I guess down there, with the cool temperature, natural decay wouldn't be what it would up here." He briefly closed his eyes. "If she was embalmed, she wasn't embalmed really well, but she was...dressed up. As if she'd been prepared for a viewing. Seeing her... It gave me chills! Chills! And I work with the dead all the time. When...when did she die?"

"The medical examiner is estimating her death to have been between one and two weeks ago. He'll tell us more definitively when he's done the autopsy."

"So, you think that..."

"I don't think anything yet," Craig said. "We need more information from the experts before I can even speculate. Go on, please, tell me about this morning."

"Oh. Oh," John said. "This morning." He looked longingly at his whiskey glass.

It was empty.

"You want another?" Craig asked.

"Yeah," John said huskily. "Yeah. The long dead are one thing. Fresh corpses...or not so fresh corpses..."

Craig knew what he meant.

He scanned the bar area but didn't see Kieran.

Declan Finnegan, however—looking like an old-time
Irish bartender as he dried a glass, decked in a white
apron tied around his waist—was behind the bar.

Craig walked over to him. Declan, he knew, had been
fully aware that Craig was in the pub and that he was
talking to John Shaw.

"You want another whiskey for him?" Declan asked.

Declan was the eldest of the Finnegans; he wore
his sense of responsibility and dignity well. All the
Finnegan family were attractive and charming people
with different degrees of red in their hair, and they all
had eyes in varying shades of blue. Even a casual observer had to note that they were related.

Declan tended to be the most serious in demeanor.
He didn't ask questions, not of Craig; he knew he'd
learn what was going on if and when it was appropriate.

"Thanks," Craig said. "Any idea where Kieran is?"

"She and Kevin were helping out. I'm not sure where
they went. Sorry you had to come to the bar. Anything
for you?"

"Soda water?"

Declan quickly poured him a glass from the foun-
tain, and Craig returned to the table. Where the hell
had Kieran gone?

She was helping her brother out today, which meant
she was working here somewhere. If he was going to
start worrying every time she wasn't in sight, he'd have
to get a psych evaluation himself.

John Shaw took the whiskey from him; it looked as
if he was going to gulp it down. Craig set a hand on his.
"Hey, that's prime stuff, my friend. Sip it."

"Yeah, yeah, of course," Shaw murmured.

"Okay, so, you got in today—"

"Early. Just after seven. This is an important true find. The historical value is immense."

"Of course. I understand," Craig assured him. "So, today. You haven't opened any of the other coffins in the catacomb, have you?"

"No. Some of the coffins have disintegrated, and the remains are down to bones and dust and spider webs. Remnants of fabric... Belt buckles, shoe buckles..." John said, studying the amber liquid in his glass.

"But you found Ms. Gilbert in the first coffin?"

Shaw nodded glumly.

"What made you open that one first?" Craig asked.

The question seemed to confuse Shaw for a minute. "It seemed to be the best preserved..." He paused, staring up at Craig. "Actually, it was at an odd angle on the shelf. As if it had been moved. Oh...that was obviously because someone had been there! They'd put her body in it!"

"Do you remember it being that way the day before?"

"No! That must've been it. There was something different!" John Shaw said. "I didn't realize it immediately. It was such a...subtle difference. The thing is, I thought I'd start with the best- preserved, but so did..." He frowned at Craig. "It was definitely the best preserved. And someone else knew that, too. Her killer."

Jeannette had been dead at least a week, possibly two. But she'd been placed in that coffin in a forgotten crypt much more recently than that.

The killer had learned about the archaeological find—he'd made use of it for his own designs.

"Excuse me," Craig said abruptly. "I'll be right back."

He wanted to see where Kieran was; it suddenly seemed important.

She wasn't at the bar. She wasn't on the floor.

He hurried down the hallway to the office and pushed open the door, not bothering to knock.

Kieran was there, and Craig let out a sigh of relief.

But then he saw that she wasn't alone. She was sitting on the sofa in front of the desk, talking earnestly with her twin brother, Kevin.

They both looked up at him, startled—and their expressions could only be described as guilty.

His heart stood still and his breath lodged in his lungs. Everything around him seemed to freeze. *No. It couldn't be.* **"How old is Lolly?"**

"Does it matter?" Charlie spun and walked toward the door. "If you want to see the threats, follow me."

He caught her arm and pulled her around to face him, his fingers digging into her skin. "How old is she?" he demanded, his lips tight, a thousand thoughts spinning in his head, zeroing in on one.

For a long moment, she met his gaze, refusing to back down. Finally, she tilted her chin upward a fraction and answered, "Six."

"Just six?" His gut clenched.

"Six and a few months."

Her words hit him like a punch in the gut. Ghost fought to remain upright when he wanted to double over with the impact. Instead, he dropped his hands to his sides and balled his fists. "Is she—"

"Yours?" She shrugged. "Does it matter? Will it change anything?"

HOT COMBAT

BY
ELLE JAMES

First Published in Great Britain 2017
By Mills & Boon, an imprint of HarperCollins*Publishers*
1 London Bridge Street, London, SE1 9GF

© 2017 Mary Jernigan

ISBN: 978-0-263-92858-7

46-0217

Our policy is to use papers that are natural, renewable and recyclable products and made from wood grown in sustainable forests. The logging and manufacturing processes conform to the legal environmental regulations of the country of origin.

Printed and bound in Spain
by CPI, Barcelona

Elle James, a *New York Times* bestselling author, started writing when her sister challenged her to write a romance novel. She has managed a full-time job and raised three wonderful children, and she and her husband even tried ranching exotic birds (ostriches, emus and rheas). Ask her, and she'll tell you what it's like to go toe-to-toe with an angry three-hundred-and-fifty-pound bird! Elle loves to hear from fans at ellejames@earthlink.net or www.ellejames.com.

This book is dedicated to my three lovely writing friends who encouraged me to write like my fingers were on fire during our annual writing retreat. If not for them and the timing of the retreat, this book might not have been written! Thank you, Cynthia D'Alba, Parker Kincade and Mandy Harbin.

Chapter One

Charlie McClain pinched the bridge of her nose and rubbed her eyes. Fifteen more minutes, and she'd call it a night. The computer screen was the only light shining in her house at eleven o'clock. She'd kissed her six-year-old daughter good-night nearly three hours ago, and made it a rule not to work past midnight. She was closing in on breaking that rule and knew she would pay for it in the morning.

She looked forward to the day when her student loans were paid off and a little money was socked away in the bank. Until then, she telecommuted developing software during the day and at night she moonlighted, earning additional money surfing the internet for the Department of Homeland Security.

Fortunately, she didn't have to use her own internet provider to do the DHS surfing. She lived on the edge of town, beside Grizzly Pass's small library with free Wi-Fi service.

Since she lived so close, she was able to tap in without any great difficulty. It had been one of the reasons she'd agreed to take on the task. As long as a hacker couldn't trace her searches back to her home address, she could surf with relative anonymity. She didn't know how sophisticated her targets were, but she didn't want to take any more chances than she had to. She refused to put her daughter at risk, should some terrorist she might root out decide to come after her.

Charlie had just about reached her limit when her search sent her to a social media group with some disturbing messages. The particular site was one the DHS had her monitor on a regular basis. Comprised of antigovernment supporters with axes to grind about local and national policy, it was cluttered with chatter tonight. The group called themselves Free America.

Charlie skimmed through the messages sent back and forth between the members of the group, searching for anything the DHS would be concerned about.

She'd just about decided there wasn't anything of interest when she found a conversation thread that made her page back to read through the entire communication.

Preparations are underway for TO of gov fac.

Citizen soldiers of WY be ready. Our time draws near.

A cold chill slid down Charlie's spine. TO could mean anything, but her gut told her TO stood for *takeover*. As a citizen of the US and the great state of Wyoming, she didn't like the idea of an antigovernment revolt taking place anywhere in the United States, especially in her home state.

Granted, Wyoming stretched across hundreds of miles of prairie, rugged canyons and mountains. But there weren't that many large cities with government facilities providing prime targets. Cheyenne, the state capital, was on the other side of the state from where Charlie and her daughter lived.

Charlie backed up to earlier posts on the site. She needed to understand what their grievances were and maybe find a clue as to what government facility they were planning to take over. The more information she could provide, the more ammunition DHS would have to stop a full-scale attack. What government facility? What city? Who would be involved in the takeover? Hell, for that matter, what constituted a takeover?

Several of the members of the group complained about the government confiscating their cattle herds when they refused to pay the increase in fees for grazing rights on federal land. Others were angry that the oil pipeline work had been brought to a complete halt. They blamed the tree huggers and the politicians in Washington.

Still others posted links to gun dealer sites and local gun ranges providing training on tactical fire and maneuver techniques used by the military.

The more she dug, the less she liked what she was finding. So far, nothing indicated a specific date or location for the government facility takeover. Without hard facts, she wasn't sure she had anything to hand over to DHS. But her woman's intuition was telling her she had something here. She tried to follow the post back to its orgin, but didn't get very far.

A message popped up in Charlie's personal message box.

Who is this?

Shocked at being caught, Charlie lifted her hands off the computer keyboard.

I can see you. Come, pretty lady, tell me your name.

Charlie's breath lodged in her lungs. Could he see her? Her laptop had a built-in webcam. Had he hacked into it? She slammed the laptop shut and stared at the device as if it was a snake poised to bite. Her pulse raced and her hands shook.

Had he really seen her?

Pushing back her office chair, Charlie stood. If he had seen her, so what? She could be anyone who just stumbled onto the site. No harm, no foul. She shoved a hand through her thick hair and walked out of her office and down the hallway to the little bedroom where her six-year-old daughter lay peacefully sleeping.

The message had shaken her and left her rethinking her promise to help DHS monitor for terrorists.

Charlie tucked the blankets up around her daughter's chin and straightened. She shouldn't let the message bother her. It wasn't as if just anyone could trace her efforts at snooping back to her laptop. To track her down would require the skills of a master hacker. And they'd only get as far as the library's free Wi-Fi.

Too wound up to sleep, Charlie walked around her small cottage, checking the locks on the windows and doors, wishing she had a big bruiser of a dog to protect her if someone was to breach the locks.

Charlie grabbed a piece of masking tape, opened the laptop and covered the lens of the webcam. Feeling a little better, she took a seat at her desk and drafted an email to Kevin Garner, her handler at DHS. She'd typed This might not be anything, but check it out. Then she went back to the social media site and was in the middle of copying the site's location URL where she'd found the damning call to arms when another message popped up on her screen.

You're trespassing on a private group. Cease and desist.

Charlie closed the message and went back to pasting the URL into her email.

Another message popped up.

I know what you look like and it won't take long to trace your location. Pass on any information from this group and we'll find you.

The next thing to pop up was an image of herself, staring down at her laptop.

A horrible feeling pooled in the pit of Charlie's belly. Could he find her? Would he really come after her?

Suddenly the dead bolt locks didn't seem to be enough protection against whoever was at the other end of the computer messaging.

Charlie grabbed her phone and dialed Kevin's number. Yeah, it was after eleven o'clock, but she needed to hear the sound of someone's voice.

"I got it," Kevin's wife, Misty, answered with a groggy voice. "Hello."

"Misty, it's Charlie."

"Charlie. Good to hear from you. But what time is it? Oh, my, it's almost midnight. Is anything wrong?"

Charlie hesitated, feeling foolish, but unwilling to end the call now. She squared her shoulders. "I need to talk to Kevin."

A moment later, Kevin's voice sounded in her ear. "Charlie, what's up?"

She drew in a deep breath and let it out, willing her voice to quit shaking as she relayed the information. "I was surfing the Free America social media site and found something. I'm not sure it's anything, but it set off alarm bells in my head."

"Shoot."

She told him about the message and waited for his response.

"Doesn't sound good. Got anything else?"

"I looked, but couldn't find anything detailing a specific location or government facility."

"I don't like it, but I can't get a search warrant if I don't have a name or location."

"That's what I figured, but that isn't all."

"What else have you got for me?"

"While I was searching through the social media site, a message popped up."

"A message?" he asked.

Charlie read the messages verbatim from her laptop. "He has my picture."

"Hmm. That he was able to determine you were looking at the site and then able to take command of your laptop long enough to snap a picture has me concerned."

"You're not the only one." She scrubbed a hand down her face, tired, but too agitated to go to sleep. "I was using the library's Wi-Fi. He won't be able to trace back to my computer."

"That's good. More than likely he's near the state capital."

"Are you willing to bet your life on that?" she asked.

"My life, yes."

"What about the life of your son or daughter?" Charlie asked. She knew he had two kids, both under the age of four. "Would you be able to sleep knowing someone is threatening you? And by threatening you, they threaten your family."

"Look, can you make it through the night?" Kevin asked. "It'll be tomorrow before I can do anything."

"I'll manage."

"Do you want me to come over?"

She shook her head, then remembered she was on the phone. "No. I have a gun. I know how to use it.

And I really don't think he'll trace me to my home address so quickly. We don't even know if he has that ability."

"He snapped a picture of you," Kevin reminded her. "I'd say he's internet savvy and probably pretty good at hacking."

"Great." Charlie sighed. "I'll do okay tonight with my H&K .40 caliber pistol. But tomorrow, I might want some help protecting my daughter."

"On it. I'm expecting reinforcements this week. As soon as they arrive, I'll send someone over to assess the situation."

"Thanks." Charlie gripped the phone, not in a hurry to hang up. As if by so doing, she'd sever her contact permanently with the outside world and be exposed to the potential terrorist on the other end of the computer network.

"Look, Charlie, I can be there in fifteen minutes."

"No, really. I'll be fine." And she would be, as soon as she pulled herself together. "Sorry to bother you so late."

"Call me in the morning. Or call me anytime you need to," Kevin urged.

She ended the call and continued to hold the phone so tightly her fingers hurt.

What was supposed to have been an easy way to make a little extra cash had just become a problem. Or she was overreacting.

Just to be safe, she entered her bedroom and opened her nightstand where she kept the pistol her father had purchased for her when she'd graduated college. She could call her parents, but they were on a river cruise in Europe. Why bother them if this turned out to be nothing?

She found her pistol beneath a bottle of hand lotion and a romance novel. The safety lock was in place from the last time she'd taken it to Deputy Frazier's ranch for target practice six months ago. She removed the lock, dropped the magazine full of bullets and slid back the bolt. Everything appeared to be in working order. She released the bolt, slammed the magazine into the handle and left the lock on. She'd sleep in the lounge chair in the living room so that she would be ready for anything. She settled in the chair, her gun in her hand, hoping she didn't fall asleep, have a bad dream and shoot a hole in her leg.

She positioned herself in the chair, her gaze on the front door, her ears tuned in to the slightest sound. Not that she expected anyone to find her that night, but, if they did, she'd be ready.

Jon "Ghost" Caspar woke to the sun glaring through his windshield on its early morning rise from the horizon. He'd arrived in Grizzly Pass sometime around two o'clock. The town had so little to offer in the way of amenities, he didn't bother looking for a hotel, instead parking his truck in the empty parking lot of a small grocery store.

Not ten minutes after he'd reclined his seat and closed his eyes, a sheriff's deputy had rolled up beside him and shone a flashlight through his window.

Ghost had sat up, rolled down his window and

explained to the deputy he'd arrived later than he'd expected and would find a hotel the next day. He just needed a few hours of sleep.

The deputy had nodded, warned him not to do any monkey business and left him alone. To make certain Ghost didn't perform any unsavory acts, the deputy made it his sole mission to circle the parking lot every half hour like clockwork until shift change around six in the morning.

Ghost was too tired to care. He opened his eyes briefly for every pass, but dropped back into the troubled sleep of the recently reassigned.

He resented being shuffled off to Wyoming when he'd rather be back with his SEAL team. But if he had to spend his convalescence as a loaner to the Department of Homeland Security, it might as well be in his home state of Wyoming, and the hometown he hadn't visited in a long time.

Seven years had passed since the last time he'd come back. He didn't have much reason to return. His parents had moved to a Florida retirement community after his father had served as ranch foreman for a major cattle ranch for the better part of forty years. Ranching was a young man's work, hard on a body and unforgiving when it came to accidents. The man deserved the life of leisure, soaking up the warm winter sunrays and playing golf to his heart's content.

Ghost adjusted his seat to the upright position and ran a hand through his hair. He needed a shower and a toothbrush. But a cup of coffee would have to do. He was supposed to report in to his contact, Kevin Garner, that morning to receive instructions. He hoped like hell he'd clarify just what would be entailed in the Safe Haven Task Force. To Ghost, it sounded like a quick path to boredom.

Ghost didn't do boredom well. It nearly got him kicked out of the Navy while in rehab in Bethesda, Maryland, at the Walter Reed National Military Medical Center. He was a SEAL, damn it. They had their own set of rules.

Not according to Joe, his physical therapist. He'd nearly come to blows with the man several times. Now that Ghost was back on his own feet without need of crutches, he regretted the idiot he'd been and had gone back to the therapy center to apologize.

Joe had laughed it off, saying he'd been threatened with far worse.

A smile curled Ghost's lips at the memory. Then the smile faded. He could get around without crutches or a cane, but the Navy hadn't seen fit to assign him back to his team at the Naval Special Warfare Group, or DEVGRU, in Virginia. Instead he'd been given Temporary Duty assignment in Wyoming, having been personally requested by a DHS task force leader.

What could possibly be so hot that a DHS task force leader could pull enough strings to get a highly trained Navy SEAL to play in his homeland security game? All Ghost could think was that man had some major strings to pull in DC. As soon as he met with the DHS guy, he hoped to make it clear he wanted off the assignment and back to his unit.

The sooner the better.

He'd left Grizzly Pass as a teen, fresh out of high school. Though his father loved the life of a ranch foreman, Ghost had wanted to get out of Wyoming and see the world. He'd returned several times, the last to help his parents pack up their things to move to Florida. He'd taken a month of leave to guide his parents through the biggest change in their lives and to say goodbye to his childhood home one last time.

With his parents leaving Wyoming, he had no reason to return. Having recently graduated from the Basic Underwater Demolition/SEAL training and having just completed his first deployment in his new role, Ghost was on a path to being exactly what he wanted—the best Navy SEAL he could be. A month on leave in Grizzly Pass reminded him why he couldn't live there anymore. At the same time, it reminded him of why he'd loved it so much.

He'd been home for two weeks when he'd run into a girl he'd known since grade school, one who'd been his friend through high school, whom he'd lost touch with when he'd joined the Navy. She'd been the tagalong friend he couldn't quite get rid of, who'd listened to all of his dreams and jokes. She was as quirky and lovable as her name, never asking anything of him but a chance to hang around.

With no intention of starting a lasting relationship, he'd asked her out. He'd told her up front he wasn't there to stay and he wouldn't be calling her after he left. She'd been okay with that, stating she had no intention of leaving Wyoming and she wouldn't be happy with a man who would be gone for eleven months of the year. But she wouldn't mind having someone to go out with while he was there.

No strings attached. No hearts broken.

Her words.

Looking back, Ghost realized those two weeks had been the best of his life. He'd recaptured the beauty of his home and his love of the mountains and prairies.

Charlie had taken him back to his old haunts in her Jeep, on horseback and on foot. They'd hiked, camped and explored everywhere they'd been as kids, topping it off by skinny-dipping in Bear Paw Creek.

That was when the magic multiplied exponentially. Their fun-loving romp as friends changed in an instant. Gone was the gangly girl with the braid hanging down her back. Naked, with nothing but the sun touching her pale skin, she'd walked into the water and changed his life forever.

He wondered if she still lived in Grizzly Pass. Hell, for the past seven years, he'd wanted to call her and ask her how she was doing and if she still thought about that incredible summer.

He supposed in the past seven years, she'd gone on to marry a local rancher and had two or three kids by now.

Ghost sighed. Since they'd made love in the fresh mountain air, he'd thought of her often. He still car-

ried a picture of the two of them together. A shot
his father had taken of them riding double on horseback at the ranch. He remembered that day the most.
That was the day they'd gone to the creek. The day
they'd first made love. The first day of the last week
of his leave.

Having just graduated from college, she'd started
work with a small business in town. She worked half
days and spent every hour she wasn't working with
Ghost. When he worried about her lack of sleep,
she'd laughed and said she could sleep when he was
gone. She wanted to enjoy every minute she could
with him. Again, no strings attached. No hearts broken.

Now, back in the same town, Ghost glanced
around the early morning streets. A couple of trucks
rumbled past the grocery parking lot and stopped
at the local diner, pulling in between several other
weathered ranch trucks.

Apparently the food was still good there.

A Jeep zipped into the diner's parking lot and
parked between two of the trucks.

As his gaze fixed on the driver's door as it opened,
Ghost's heartbeat stuttered, stopped and raced on.

A man in dark jeans and a dark polo shirt climbed
out and entered the diner.

His pulse slowing, Ghost let out a sigh, squared
his shoulders and twisted the key in the ignition. He
was there to work, not rekindle an old flame, not
when he was going to meet a man about his new assignment and promptly ask to be released to go back

to his unit. The diner was the designated meeting place and it was nearing seven o'clock—the hour they'd agreed on.

Feeling grungy and road-weary, Ghost promised himself he'd find a hotel for a shower, catch some real sleep and then drive back to Virginia over the next couple of days.

He drove out of the parking lot and onto Main Street. He could have walked to the diner, but he wanted to leave straight from there to find that hotel and the shower he so desperately needed. Thirty minutes max before he could leave and get some rest.

Ghost parked in an empty space in the lot, cut the engine, climbed out of his truck and nearly crumpled to the ground before he got his leg straight. Pain shot through his thigh and kneecap. The therapist said that would happen if he didn't keep it moving. After his marathon drive from Virginia to Wyoming in under two days, what did he expect? He held on to the door until the pain subsided and his leg straightened to the point it could hold his weight.

Once he was confident he wouldn't fall flat on his face, he closed the truck door and walked slowly into the diner, trying hard not to limp. Even the DHS wouldn't want a man who couldn't go the distance because of an injury. Not that he wanted to keep the job with DHS. No. He wanted to be back with his unit. The sooner the better. They'd get him in shape better than any physical therapist. The competition and camaraderie kept them going and made them better, stronger men.

Once inside the diner, he glanced around at the men seated at the tables. Most wore jeans and cowboy boots. Their faces were deeply tanned and leathery from years of riding the range in all sorts of weather.

One man stood out among the others. He was tall and broad-shouldered, certainly capable of hard work, but his jeans and cowboy boots appeared new. His face, though tanned, wasn't rugged or hardened by the elements. He sat in a corner booth, his gaze narrowing on Ghost.

Figuring the guy was the one who didn't belong, Ghost ambled toward him. "DHS?" he asked, his tone low, barely carrying to the next booth.

The man stood and held out his hand. "Kevin Garner. You must be Jon Caspar."

Ghost shook the man's hand. "Most folks call me Ghost."

"Nice to meet you, Ghost." Garner had a firm grip, belying his fresh-from-the-Western-store look. "Have a seat."

Not really wanting to stay, Ghost took the chair indicated.

The DHS man remained standing long enough to wave to a waitress. Once he got her attention, he sat opposite Ghost.

On close inspection, his contact appeared to be in his early thirties, trim and fit. "I was expecting someone older," Ghost commented.

Garner snorted. "Trust me, I get a lot of push-back

for what I'm attempting. Most think I'm too young and inexperienced to lead this effort."

Ghost leaned back in his seat and crossed his arms over his chest. "And just what effort is that?"

Before the DHS representative could respond, the waitress arrived bearing a pot of coffee and an empty mug. She poured a cup and slapped a laminated menu on the table. "I'll be back."

As soon as she left, Garner leaned forward, resting his elbows on the table. "Safe Haven Task Force was my idea. If it works, great. If it fails, I'll be looking for another job. I'm just lucky they gave me a chance to experiment."

"Frankly, I'm not much on experiments, but I'll give you the benefit of a doubt. What's the experiment?"

"The team you will be part of will consist of some of the best of the best from whatever branch of service. They will be the best tacticians, the most skilled snipers and the smartest men our military has produced."

"Sorry." Ghost shook his head. "How do I fit into that team?"

Garner slid a file across the table and opened it to display a dossier on Ghost.

Ghost frowned. SEALs kept a low profile, their records available to only a very few. "How did you get that file?"

He sat back, his lips forming a hint of a smile. "I asked for it."

"Who the hell are you? Better still, what politician is in your pocket to pull me out of my unit for this boondoggle gig?" Ghost leaned toward Garner, anger simmering barely below the surface. "Look, I didn't ask for this assignment. I don't even want to be here. I have a job with the Navy. I don't need this."

Garner's eyes narrowed into slits. "Like it or not, you're on loan to me until I can prove out my theory. Call it a Temporary Duty assignment. I don't care what you call it. I just need you until I don't need you anymore."

"There are much bigger fish to fry in the world than in Grizzly Pass, Wyoming."

"Are you sure of that?" Garner's brow rose. "While you and your teammates are out fighting on foreign soil, we've had a few homegrown terrorists surface. Is fighting on foreign soil more important than defending your home turf?"

"I might fall for your line of reasoning if we were in New York, or DC." Ghost shook his head. "We're in Grizzly Pass. We're far away from politicians, presidents and wealthy billionaires. We're in the backside of the backwoods. What could possibly be of interest here?"

"You realize there's a significant amount of oil running through this state at any given time. Not to mention, it's also the state with the most active volcano."

"Not buying it." Ghost sat back again, unimpressed. "It would take a hell of an explosion to get things stirred up with the volcano at Yellowstone."

"Well, this area is a hotbed for antigovernment movements. There are enough weapons being stashed and men being trained to form a sizable army. And we're getting chatter on the social media sites indicating something's about to go down."

"Can you be more specific?"

Garner sighed. "Unfortunately, not yet."

"If you're done speculating, I have a two-day drive ahead of me to get back to my unit." Ghost started to rise, but the waitress arrived at that time, blocking his exit from the booth.

"Are you ready to order?"

"I'm not hungry."

Garner gave the waitress a tight smile. "I'd like the Cowboy Special, Marta."

Marta faced Ghost. "It's not too late to change your mind."

"The coffee will hold me." Until he could get to Cheyenne where he'd stop for food.

After Marta left, Garner leaned toward Ghost. "Give me a week. That's all I ask. One week. If you think we're still tilting at windmills, you can go back to your unit."

"How did I get the privilege of being your star guinea pig?"

Garner's face turned a ruddy shade of red and he pressed his lips together. "I got you because you weren't cleared for active duty." He raised his hand. "Don't get me wrong. You have a remarkable record and I would have chosen you anyway, once you'd fully recovered."

That hurt. The Navy had thrown the DHS a bone by sending a Navy SEAL with a bummed-up leg.

Great. So they didn't think he was ready to return to duty either. The anger surged inside him, making him mad enough to prove them wrong. "All right. I'll give you a week. If we can't prove your theory about something about to go down, I'm heading back to Virginia."

Garner let out a long breath. "That's all I can ask."

Ghost smacked his hand on the table. "So, what exactly am I supposed to do?"

"One of our operatives was threatened last night. I need you to work with her while she tries to figure out who exactly it is and why they would feel the need to harass her." He handed Ghost his business card, flipping it over to the backside where he'd written an address. "This is her home address here in Grizzly Pass."

"I know where that is." Orva Davis lived there back when he was a kid. She used to chase the kids out of her yard, waving a switch. She'd been ancient back then, she couldn't possibly be alive now. "She's expecting me this morning?"

"She'll be happy to see anyone this morning. The sooner the better."

"Who is she?"

At that exact moment Garner's cell phone buzzed. He glanced down at the caller ID, his brows pulling together. "Sorry, I have to take this. If you have any questions, you can call me at the number on the front of that card." He pushed to his feet and walked out of the building, pressing the phone to his ear.

After tossing back the last of his coffee, Ghost

pulled a couple of bills from his wallet and laid them on the table. He took the card and left, passing Garner on his way to his truck.

The DHS man was deep in conversation, turned completely away from Ghost.

Ghost shrugged. He'd had enough time off that he was feeling next to useless and antsy. But he could handle one more week. He might even get in some fly-fishing.

He slid behind the wheel of his pickup and glanced down at the address. Old Orva Davis couldn't possibly still be alive, could she? If not her, who was the woman who'd felt threatened in this backwater town? Probably some nervous Nellie.

He'd find out soon enough.

And then…one week.

Chapter Two

Charlie had nodded off once or twice during the night, waking with a jerk every time. Thankfully, she hadn't pulled the trigger and blown a hole in the door, her leg or her foot.

She was up and doing laundry when Lolly padded barefoot out of her bedroom, dragging her giant teddy bear. "I'm hungry."

"Waffles or cereal?" Charlie asked, forcing a cheerful smile to her tired face.

"Waffles," Lolly said. "With blueberry syrup."

"I'll start cooking, while you get dressed." Charlie plugged in her waffle iron, mixed the batter and had a waffle cooking in no time. She cleaned off the small dinette table that looked like a throwback to the fifties, with its speckled Formica top and chrome legs. In actuality, the table did date back to the fifties. It was one of the items of furniture that had come with the house when she'd bought it. She'd been fortunate enough to find the bright red vinyl fabric to recover the seats, making them look like new.

On a tight budget, with only one income-producing person in the family, a car payment and student loans to pay, she couldn't afford to be extravagant.

She was rinsing fresh blueberries in the sink when a dark figure suddenly appeared in the window in front of her. Charlie jumped, her heart knocking against her ribs. She laughed when she realized it was Shadow, the stray she and Lolly had fed through the winter. Charlie was far too jumpy that morning. The messages from the night before were probably all bluster, no substance, and she'd wasted a night she could have been sleeping, worrying about nothing.

The cat rubbed her fur against the window screen. When that didn't get enough attention, she stretched out her claws and sank them into the screen netting.

"Hey! Get down." Charlie tapped her knuckles against the glass and the cat jumped down from the ledge. "Lolly! Shadow's hungry and my hands are full."

Lolly entered the room dressed in jeans, a pink T-shirt and the pink cowboy boots she loved so much. The boots had been a great find on one of their rare trips to the thrift shop in Bozeman, Montana. "I'll get the bowl." She started for the back door.

I'll find you.

The message echoed in Charlie's head and she dropped the strainer of blueberries into the sink and hurried toward her daughter. "Wait, Lolly. I'll get the cat bowl. Tell you what, you grab a brush, and we'll braid your hair this morning."

Charlie waited until her daughter had left the kitchen, then she unlocked the dead bolt and glanced out at the fresh green landscape of early summer in the Rockies. The sun rose in the east and a few puffy clouds skittered across the sky. Snow still capped the higher peaks in stunning contrast to the lush greenery. How could anything be wrong on such a beautiful day?

A loud ringing made her jump and then grab for the telephone mounted on the wall beside her.

"Hello," she said, her voice cracking, her body trembling from being startled.

"Charlie, it's me, Kevin."

"Thank goodness." She laughed, the sound even shakier than her knees.

"Any more trouble last night?"

She shook her head and then remembered he couldn't see her. "No. I'm beginning to think I'm paranoid."

"Not at all. In fact, I'm sending someone over to check things out. He should be there in a few minutes."

"Oh. Okay. Thanks, Kevin."

"The guy I'm sending is one hundred percent trustworthy. I'd only send the best to you and Lolly." He broke off suddenly. "Sorry. I have an incoming call. We'll talk later."

"Thanks, Kevin." Feeling only slightly better, Charlie returned the phone to its charger and stepped out onto the porch.

Shadow rubbed against her legs and trotted to the empty bowl on the back porch steps.

"Impatient, are we?" Charlie walked out onto the

porch, shaking off the feeling of being watched, calling herself all kinds of a fool for being so paranoid. She dropped to her haunches to rub the cat behind the ears.

Shadow nipped at her fingers, preferring food to fondling. Charlie smiled. "Greedy thing." She bent to grab the dish. When she rose, she caught movement in the corner of her eyes and then there were jean-clad legs standing in front of her.

She gasped and backed up so fast, she forgot she was still squatting and fell on her bottom. A scream lodged in her throat and she couldn't get a sound to emerge.

The man looming over her was huge. He stood with his back to the sun, his face in the shadows, and he had hands big enough to snap her bones like twigs. He extended one of those hands.

Charlie slapped it away and crab-walked backward toward the door. "Wh-who are you? What do you want?" she whispered, her gaze darting to the left and the right, searching for anything she could use as a weapon.

"Geez, Charlie, you'd think you'd remember me." He climbed the steps and, for the second time, reached for her hand. Before she could jerk hers away, he yanked her to her feet. A little harder than either of them expected.

Charlie slammed against a wall of muscle, the air knocked from her chest. Or had her lungs seized at his words? She knew that voice. Her pulse pounded against her eardrums, making it difficult for her to hear. "Jon?"

He brushed a strand of her hair from her face. "Hey, Charlie, I didn't know you were my assignment." He chuckled, that low, sexy sound that made her knees melt like butter.

Her heart burst with joy. He'd come back. Then as quickly as her joy spread, anger and fear followed. She flattened her palms against his chest and pushed herself far enough way, Jon was forced to drop his hands from around her waist. "What are you doing here?" she demanded.

"I'm on assignment." He grinned. "And it appears you're it."

She shook her head. "I don't understand."

"Kevin Garner sent me. The Navy loaned me to the Department of Homeland Security for a special task force. I thought it was going to be a boondoggle, and actually asked to be released from the assignment. But it looks like it won't be nearly as bad as I'd anticipated."

Charlie straightened her shirt, her heartbeat hammering, her ears perked to the sound of little footsteps. "You were right. Get Kevin to release you. Go back to the Navy. They need you more there."

"Whoa. Wait a minute. I promised Kevin I'd give it a week." Jon gripped her arms. "Why the hurry to get rid of me? As I recall, we used to have chemistry."

She shrugged off his hand. "That was a long time

ago. A lot has changed since then. Please. Just go. I can handle the situation myself."

"If you're in trouble, let me help."

"No." God, why did he have to come back now? And why was it so hard to get rid of him? He'd certainly left without a care, never looking back or contacting her. Well, he could stay gone, for all she gave a damn. "I'm pretty sure I don't need you. Ask Kevin to assign you elsewhere."

"Mommy, I found the brush." Lolly pushed through the back door, waving a purple-handled hairbrush. "You can braid my hair now." Charlie's daughter, with her clear blue eyes and fiery auburn hair tumbling down her back, stepped through the door and stopped. Her mouth dropped open and her head tilted way back as she stared up at the big man standing on her porch. "Mommy?" she whispered. "Who is the big man?"

Charlie's heart tightened in her chest. If only her daughter knew. But she couldn't tell her and she couldn't tell Jon. Not after all these years. Not when he'd be gone again as soon as he could get Kevin to release him. "This is Mr. Caspar. He was just leaving." Thankfully, her daughter looked like a miniature replica of herself, but for the eyes. No one had guessed who the father was, except for her parents, and they'd been very discreet about the knowledge, never throwing it up in her face or giving her a hard time for sleeping with him without a wedding ring.

Jon dropped to his haunches and held out his

hand. "Would you like for me to brush your hair? I used to do it for your mother."

The memory of Jon brushing the hay and tangles out of her hair brought back a rush of memories Charlie would rather not have resurrected. Not now. Not when it had taken seven years to push those memories to the back of her mind. She had too much at stake.

Charlie laid a hand on her daughter's shoulder. "Mr. Caspar was leaving."

He shook his head and crossed his arms over his chest. "Sorry. I promised to stay for a week. I don't go back on my word."

No, he didn't. He'd told her he wasn't looking for a long-term relationship when he'd last been in town. He'd lived up to his word then, leaving without once looking back. "Well, you'll have to keep your promise somewhere else besides my back porch."

Her daughter tugged on the hem of her T-shirt. "Mommy, are you mad at the man?"

With a sigh, Charlie shook her head. "No, sweetie, I'm not mad at him." Well, maybe a little angry that he'd bothered to come back after seven years. Or more that he'd waited seven years to return. Hell, she didn't know what to feel. Her emotions seemed to be out of control at the moment, bouncing between happiness at seeing him again and terror that he would discover her secret.

Since Jon seemed in no hurry to leave, she'd have to get tougher. Charlie turned her little girl and gave her a nudge toward the door. "Go back inside, Lolly. We adults need to have a talk."

Lolly grabbed her hand and clung to it. "I don't want to go." She frowned at Jon. "What if the big man hurts you?"

Lord, he'd already done that by breaking her heart. How could he hurt her worse?

GHOST WATCHED AS the little girl, who looked so much like her mother that it made his chest hurt, turned and entered the house, the screen door closing behind her.

Charlie hadn't waited around for him to come back. She'd gone on with her life, had a kid and probably had a husband lurking around somewhere. "Are you married?" He glanced over her shoulder, trying to see through the screen of the back door.

"Since you're not staying, does it matter?" She walked past him and down the stairs, grabbed a bowl from the ground and nearly tripped over a dark gray cat twisting around her ankles.

When Charlie stepped over the animal and started up the steps, the feline ran ahead and stopped in front of Ghost. She touched her nose to his leg as if testing him.

Ghost grew up on a ranch with barn cats. His father made sure they had two or three at any given time, but had them spayed and neutered to keep from populating the countryside with too many feral animals with the potential for carrying disease or rabies around the family and livestock.

He bent to let the cat sniff his hand and then scratched the animal's neck. "You didn't answer my question," he said. Why would she avoid the simple yes or no question?

"I don't feel like I owe you an explanation for what I've been doing for the past seven years." Her tone was tight, her shoulders stiff.

When he'd first seen her on the deck, he hadn't immediately recognized her. Her hair was longer and loose around her shoulders. When they'd been together, all those years ago, she'd worn her hair in a perpetual braid to keep it out of her face.

Her hips and breasts were fuller, even more enticing than before. Motherhood suited her. If possible, she was more beautiful and sexier than ever.

His gut twisted. But who was the father? Lolly was small. Maybe five? Though he didn't have a claim on Charlie, he never could stomach the idea of another man touching her the way he'd touched her.

The fact was babies didn't come from storks. So Charlie wasn't the open, straightforward woman she'd been all those years ago. She probably had a reason for being more reserved. Having a child might have factored into her current stance.

He straightened. "So, tell me about the threats."

"You're not going away, are you?" Her brows drew together, the lines a little deeper than when she'd been twenty-two. She sighed. "I really wish you would just go. I have enough going on."

"Without me getting in the way?" He shook his head. "I'm only going to be here a week. Unless you have a husband who is willing to take care of you, let me help you and your family for the week." He smiled, hoping to ease the frown from her brow. "Show me a husband and I'll leave." He cocked his brows.

She stared at him for a long, and what appeared to be wary, moment before she shook her head. "There isn't a husband to take care of us."

"Is he out of town?" He wasn't going to let it go. The thought of Charlie and her little girl being threatened didn't sit well with him. Who would do that to a lone woman and child? "I could stay until he returns."

"I told you. There isn't a husband. Never has been."

He couldn't help a little thrill at the news. But if no husband, who was the jerk who'd gotten her pregnant and left her to raise the child alone?

His heart stood still and his breath lodged in his lungs. Everything around him seemed to freeze. *No. It couldn't be.* "How old is Lolly?"

"Does it matter?" Charlie spun and walked toward the door. "If you want to see the threats, follow me."

He caught her arm and pulled her around to face him, his fingers digging into her skin. "How old is she?" he demanded, his lips tight, a thousand thoughts spinning in his head, zeroing in on one.

For a long moment, she met his gaze, refusing to back down. Finally, she tilted her chin upward a fraction and answered, "Six."

"Just six?" His gut clenched.

"Six and a few months."

Her words hit him like a punch in the gut. Ghost fought to remain upright when he wanted to double over with the impact. Instead, he dropped his hands to his sides and balled his fists. "Is she—"

"Yours?" She shrugged. "Does it matter? Will it change anything?"

"My God, Charlie!" He grabbed her arms wanting to shake her like a rag doll. But he didn't. "I have a daughter, and you never told me?"

"You were going places. You had a plan, and a family wasn't part of it. What did you expect me to do? Get an abortion? Give her up for adoption?"

"Hell, no." He choked on the words and shoved a hand through his hair. "I can't believe it." His knees wobbled and his eyes stung.

He turned toward the back door. The little auburn-haired girl-child stood watching them, her features muted by the screen.

That little human with the beautiful red hair, curling around her face was his daughter.

Chapter Three

Charlie walked toward the house. As she reached for the doorknob, her hands shook. Now that Jon knew about his daughter, what would he do? Would he fight for custody? Would he take her away for long periods of time? Would he hate her forever for keeping Lolly from him?

Questions spiraled out of control in Charlie's mind.

Lolly stood in the doorway, watching the two adults. Had she heard what had passed between them? Did she now know the big man was her father?

Up until Lolly had started school, she hadn't asked why she didn't have a father. Her world had revolved around Charlie. She didn't know enough about having a father to miss it.

Charlie pulled open the screen door, gathered her daughter in her arms and lifted her. "Hey, sweetie. Do you still have that brush?"

Her daughter held up the brush. "Is the big man going to stay?" She shot a glare at Jon. "I don't like him."

"Oh, baby, he's a nice man. How can you say you don't like him when you don't know him yet?"

That stubborn frown that reminded Charlie so much of Jon grew deeper. "I don't want to know him."

Charlie cringed and shot a glance over her shoulder at the father of her child. Had she been wrong to keep news of his daughter from him? Would he have wanted to be a part of her life from birth?

Jon's expression was inscrutable. If he was angry, he wasn't showing it. If Lolly's words hurt...again, he wasn't letting on.

Then he smiled. Though the effort appeared forced to Charlie, it had no less of an impact on her. She remembered how he'd smiled and laughed and played with her when he'd been there seven years ago.

She still had a picture they'd taken together. He'd been laughing at something she said when she'd snapped the photo of them together.

Her heart pinched in her chest. No matter how much she might want it, they couldn't go back in time. What they had was gone. They had to move on with their lives. How Jon would fit into Lolly's world had yet to be determined, if he chose to see her again. Now that Jon knew about her, Charlie couldn't keep him from being with her. She just hoped he didn't break Lolly's heart like he'd broken Charlie's all those years ago.

"Lolly, Mr. Caspar is going to be visiting for the next week. I think you'll like him." She stared into her daughter's eyes. "Please, give him a chance."

Lolly stared over Charlie's shoulder at the man

standing behind her. She didn't say anything for a few seconds and then nodded. "Okay." Then she extended the hand with the brush toward Jon. "You can brush my hair."

A burst of laughter erupted from Charlie. She clapped her hand over her mouth, realizing it sounded more hysterical than filled with humor. Trust her daughter to put the man to the test first thing.

Charlie set her daughter on her feet.

Jon nodded, his face set, his gaze connecting with Lolly's. "I'd be honored." He took the brush from her and glanced around.

"You can have a seat in the kitchen," Charlie said. "I'll make some coffee. Have you had breakfast? I'm making blueberry waffles."

She went through the motions of being a good hostess when all she wanted to do was run out of the room screaming, lock herself in her room and cry until she had no more tears left. With a daughter watching her every move, Charlie couldn't give in to hysterics.

She'd cried more than enough tears over this man. No longer a young woman on the verge of life, she was a mother with responsibilities. Her number one priority was the well-being of her little girl.

Charlie rinsed the bowl in the sink, poured cat food into it and set it aside. Shadow jumped into the window again, startling her. "Cat, you're going to give me a heart attack," she muttered. "I'll be back."

As she left the kitchen with the cat food, she watched Jon and Lolly.

Jon had taken a seat at the kitchen table and stood Lolly with her back to him between his knees.

Charlie swallowed hard on the lump forming in her throat.

The Navy SEAL, with his broad shoulders and rugged good looks, eased the brush through Lolly's hair with a gentleness no one would expect from a man conditioned for combat.

Once outside, Charlie stood for a moment on the porch, reminding herself how to breathe. What was happening? She didn't know which was worse, being threatened by a potential domestic terrorist, or facing the man she'd fallen so deeply in love with all those years ago. Her life couldn't be more of a mess.

An insistent pressure on her ankles brought her out of her own overwhelming thoughts and back to a hungry cat, purring at her feet.

"Sorry, Shadow. I keep forgetting that I'm not the only one in this world." She set the bowl on the porch, straightened and was about to turn when she saw movement in the brush near the edge of the tree line behind her house.

Narrowing her eyes, she stared into the shadows. Sometimes deer and coyotes made their way into her backyard. An occasional black bear wandered into town, causing a little excitement among residents. Nothing emerged and nothing stirred. Yet awareness rippled across her skin, raising gooseflesh.

Charlie rubbed her hands over her arms, the chill she felt having nothing to do with the temperature of the mountain air. She retreated behind the screen door where she stood just out of view from an outside observer. A minute passed, then another.

A rabbit hopped out of the shadows and sniffed the air, then bent to nibble on the clover.

Releasing the breath she'd been holding, Charlie turned toward the kitchen. Out of the corner of her eye, she saw the rabbit dart across the yard, away from the underbrush of the tree line.

Charlie shook off that creepy feeling and told herself not to be paranoid. Just because someone threatened her on the internet didn't mean someone would follow through on his threat.

She closed the back door and twisted the dead bolt. It didn't hurt to be careful. Walking back into the kitchen, she couldn't help feeling safer with Jon there. He had Lolly's hair brushed and braided into two matching plaits.

Her daughter leaned against Jon's knee, showing him her favorite doll.

Jon glanced up, his eyes narrowing slightly.

Oh, yeah. He was angry.

Charlie didn't doubt in the least he'd have a few choice words for her when Lolly wasn't in the room. And he had every right to be mad. He'd missed the first six years of his daughter's life.

Glad she had a bit of respite from a much-deserved verbal flogging, Charlie rescued a waffle from burning, poured batter into the iron and mixed up more in order to make enough for a grown man. Flavorful scents filled the air as the waffles rose.

Milking the excuse of giving her full attention to

the production of the waffles, Charlie kept her back to Lolly and Jon. Yes, she was avoiding looking at Jon, afraid he'd see in her gaze that she wasn't totally over him. Afraid he'd aim that accusing glance at her and she'd feel even worse than she already did about not telling him.

"Here. Let me." A hand curled around hers and removed the fork from her fingers. "You're burning the waffles."

Charlie couldn't move—couldn't breathe. Jon stood so close he almost touched her. If she backed even a fraction of a step, her body would press against his.

God, she could smell that all too familiar scent that belonged to Jon, and only Jon—that outdoorsy, fresh mountain scent. She closed her eyes and swayed, bumping her back into his chest.

With his empty hand, he gripped her elbow, steadying her. Then he reached around her with the fork, opened the waffle iron and lifted out a perfect waffle. "Plates?" he said.

His mouth was so close to her ear, she could feel the warmth of his breath, causing uncontrollable shivers to skitter across her body.

Plates. Oh, yeah. She reached up to her right and started to pluck two plates from a cabinet. Then she remembered there were three of them now. After setting the plates on the counter, she turned away from the stove, desperate to put distance between her and Jon. Her body was on fire, her senses on alert for even the slightest of touches.

"Come on, Lolly, let's set the table while Mr. Caspar cooks." She grabbed the plates and started around Jon.

He shifted, blocking her path. "We *will* talk."

She stared at his chest, refusing to make eye contact. "Of course."

He stepped aside, allowing her to pass.

Charlie wanted to run from the room, but she knew she couldn't. Her daughter was a very observant child. She'd already figured out something wasn't right between her and Jon. Besides, running away would solve nothing.

Lolly gathered flatware from the drawer beside the sink.

Charlie set the plates on the table and went back to the cabinets for glasses. While she filled them with orange juice, she took the opportunity to study Jon while his back was to her.

The Navy SEALs had shaped him into even more of a man than he'd been before. His body was a finely honed weapon, his bulging muscles rippling with every movement. He'd been in great shape when he'd come home on leave seven years ago, but he was somehow more rugged, with a few new tattoos and scars on his exposed surfaces.

Charlie yearned to go to him, slip her arms around his waist and lean her cheek against his back like she had those weeks they'd been together. She longed to explore the new scars and tattoos, running her fingers across every inch of him.

He slipped waffles onto a platter and turned toward her, catching her gaze before she could look away.

Charlie froze, her eyes widening. Shoot, he'd caught her staring. Could he see the longing in her eyes?

She dragged her gaze away and darted for the stove and the pan of blueberry syrup simmering on the back burner. Her hand trembled as she poured the hot syrup into a small pitcher.

"Careful, you might get burned." Jon took the pan from her and set it on the stove.

You're telling me? She'd been burned by him before. She had no intention of falling for him again. Her life was hectic enough as a single parent trying to make a living in a small town.

She hurried away from Jon and set the syrup in front of her daughter.

Lolly pointed to the end of the table. "Mr. Caspar, you can sit there." She climbed into her chair and waited for the adults to take their seats.

Charlie felt like she and Jon were two predatory cats circling the kill. She eased into her chair, her knees bent, ready to launch if things got too intense.

Jon frowned. "Are you sure you don't want your mother to sit here?"

Lolly shook her head. "She always sits across from me so we can talk."

Jon glanced at Charlie.

Charlie gave half of a smile. "That's the way we roll."

"Before we got our house, we sat on the couch to eat," Lolly offered.

"How long have you been in your house?" Jon asked.

"We moved in on my birthday." Lolly grinned. "I had my first birthday party here."

"What a special way to celebrate." Jon reached for the syrup and poured it over his stack of waffles. "Where did you live before?"

Charlie tensed.

Lolly shrugged. "Somewhere else." Her face brightened. "Did you know mommies go to school, too?"

Jon smiled. "Is that so?"

Lolly nodded. "Mommy went to school."

His brows hiked as he glanced toward Charlie.

Heat rose up her cheeks. She didn't want to talk about herself. They didn't need to go into all the details of their lives for the past seven years.

Jon didn't need to know that the years before they'd moved into the little house in Grizzly Pass had been lean. Too many times, Charlie had skipped a meal to have enough money to feed Lolly and pay for the babysitter. Working as a waitress during the day kept a roof over their heads and school at night didn't leave much time for her to be with her daughter. But they'd made their time together special. Now that she worked from home, Charlie was making up for all the times she couldn't be home.

Her daughter shoved a bite of waffle into her mouth and sighed. "Mmm."

Charlie almost laughed at the pure satisfaction on Lolly's face. They hadn't always eaten this well, and it hadn't been that long since she'd landed a job paying enough money that she could afford to buy a small house in her hometown.

Jon took a bite of the waffle, closed his eyes and echoed Lolly's approval. "Mmm. Your mother makes good waffles."

"You helped," Lolly pointed out.

"So he did." Charlie pushed her food around on her plate, her stomach too knotted to handle anything. Not with Jon Caspar sitting at her table.

Hell, Jon Caspar, the man she'd dreamed about for years, was sitting at her table. She pushed her chair back. "If you'll excuse me, I just remembered something."

She took her plate to the sink and was about to scrape the waffles into the garbage disposal when Jon's voice spoke up. "If you aren't going to eat them, I will."

She stopped with her fork poised over the sink. Walking back to the table, she set her plate down beside Jon's and then ran from the room.

So, I'm a big fat chicken. Sue me.

In an attempt to take her mind off the man in the kitchen, Charlie entered the guest bedroom she'd converted into an office. A futon doubled as a couch and a guest bed. The small desk in the corner that she'd purchased from a resale shop was just the right size for her. She spent most of her day in her office, working for a software developer she'd interned with during the pursuit of her second degree in Information Systems.

The shiny new business degree she'd finished right before that summer with Jon had landed her nothing in the way of a decent job. She'd stayed in Grizzly Pass with her parents through Lolly's birth, making plans and taking online courses.

She'd moved to Bozeman to return to school for a degree in Information Systems, looking for skills that wouldn't require her to move to a big city to make a living. She'd chosen that degree because of the opportunities available to telecommute. It had been a terrific choice, giving her the flexibility she needed to raise Lolly where she wanted and provide the family support her daughter needed. She had no regrets over her decision and now had the time to dedicate to her work and her small family of two.

She booted up her laptop and waited for the screen to come to life. As she waited, she glanced around the small room, wondering if Jon could fit his six-foot-three-inch frame on the futon. Ha! Fat chance. But he wasn't going to sleep in her room. Seven years apart changed everything.

Everything but the way her body reacted to his nearness.

Hell, he'd probably had a dozen other women.

Her heart stopped for a moment as another thought occurred. An image of Jon standing beside a woman wearing a wedding dress popped into her head and a led weight settled in her belly. He might have a wife somewhere. He'd said he was there for only a week. He might have someone waiting for him back home.

And kids.

Charlie pressed her hand to her mouth, her heart aching for Lolly. How would she feel about sharing her father with other children? Would she get along with a stepmother?

Her eyes stung and her throat tightened. Lolly's life had just gotten a lot more complicated.

The screen on her laptop blinked to life. No sooner had she opened her browser than a message popped up on her screen.

You told.
Beware retribution.

"Damn." She shut the laptop and laid her head on top of it. If only wishing could fix everything, she'd wish her problems away.

"Are you okay?" A large hand descended on her shoulder.

For a moment Charlie let the warmth chase away the chill inside her. Jon had always had a knack for making everything all right. He would help her figure out this problem. In one week, they'd solve the mystery of who was threatening her and possibly a government facility in the state of Wyoming. Just one week. And then she could get back to life as usual.

Who was she kidding? Jon wouldn't leave for good. He'd be back. For Lolly.

Charlie shrugged Jon's hand off her shoulder and sat straight, opening her laptop again. "I've had another message." When the screen lit, she leaned back, allowing Jon to read the message.

"Do you think it's some kid yanking your chain?" Jon asked.

"I wish it was." Charlie pushed her hair back from her forehead. She clicked the keyboard until she found the URL she'd bookmarked and brought it up. Scrolling through the messages, she searched for the one that had started it all. She backed up through the messages from around the date and time the call to arms had been made. It was gone.

"What the hell?" Charlie scrolled farther back. "It was here last night."

"Whoever posted it could have come back in and erased the message."

Charlie snorted. "That's fine. I saved a screenshot, just in case." She pulled up the picture and sat back, giving Jon a moment to read and digest the words. "Do you think I was overreacting by reporting it to DHS?"

Jon shook his head. "With everything happening in the country and around the world, you can't be too cautious." He reached around her and brought up the social media site and scrolled through the messages again.

"Yesterday, there were a lot more messages expressing dissatisfaction with the way the government was handling the grazing rights and pipeline work."

"Apparently, someone scrubbed the messages. These all appear to be regular chatter."

Charlie sighed. "I'm beginning to think I imagined it."

"You did the right thing by alerting DHS." He straightened and crossed his arms over his chest. "Let them handle it. They have access to people who can trace sites like this back to the IP address."

The phone on her desk rang, making Charlie jump. She grabbed the receiver and hit the talk button. "Hello."

"Charlie, Kevin here. I take it you've met Ghost?"

"Ghost?" She glanced up at Jon.

He nodded and whispered, "My call sign."

Heat rose in her chest and up into her cheeks. "Yes, I've met him." She'd met him a long time ago, but she didn't want to go into the details with her DHS handler. Kevin wasn't from Grizzly Pass, and there were certain things he didn't need to know.

"Is he there now?" Kevin asked.

"Yes."

"Let me talk to him."

Charlie handed the phone to Jon. "It's Kevin."

Jon took the phone.

When their fingers touched, that same electric shock she'd experienced the first time he'd touched her shot up her arm and into her chest. She couldn't do this. Being close to him brought up all the same physical reactions she'd felt when she was a young and impressionable twenty-two-year-old.

She pushed back in her chair and rose, putting distance between them. It wasn't enough. Being in the same room as Jon, aka Ghost, made her ultra aware of him. She wasn't sure how long she could handle being this close and not touching him.

"GHOST HERE." HE HELD the receiver to his ear, unused to using landlines. But then cell phones were practically useless in the remote towns of Wyoming.

"The rest of the team has arrived. I'd like you to meet them and talk through a game plan for the security of the area."

"I thought you wanted me to stay with Ms. McClain."

"I wanted you to assess the situation and give me feedback. I think she'll be okay in broad daylight. For now, you need to come to my digs above the Blue Moose Tavern and meet the rest of the men."

Ghost glanced at Charlie.

She paced the length of the small office, chewing on her fingernail.

"I'll bring her and the child with me." His gaze locked on her.

Charlie's head shot up and she met his glance with a frown. "Wherever you're going, you'll have to go by yourself. I had plans to take Lolly with me to the grocery store and the library. You don't need to come with me. We can take care of ourselves."

"Is that Charlie talking?" Kevin asked.

Ghost nodded. "It is."

"Tell her I only need you for about an hour. Then she can have you back."

Ghost covered the mouthpiece with his hand.

"Garner said he only needs me for an hour. Are you sure you and Lolly will be okay for that time?"

She nodded. "Nobody will attack us in broad daylight."

Ghost snorted. Too many people assumed that same sentiment and were dead because of it. "Stay out of the open and report in every time you come and go from a location."

"I really think we might be paranoid, but okay." She raised her hands. "I'll stay out of the open, and I'll report my comings and goings." Charlie crossed her arms over her chest and tilted her head back. "Happy?"

"Not really," he said, his lips pressing together. "I'd rather drop you where you want to go and pick you up later."

Her lips pressed into a thin line.

Ghost decided it was better not to argue while Garner waited on the phone.

"Everything set?" Garner asked.

Ghost stared at Charlie, not sure he was happy with the arrangement, but Charlie wasn't budging. "Yes. I'll see you in twenty minutes. That will give me time to take a shower."

"Will do." Garner ended the call.

"I have to meet with DHS and the team Garner is assimilating. Are you sure you'll be okay?"

She gave a firm nod. "Positive."

How she could be so certain was unfathomable to Ghost. He wasn't sure *he* was okay. Being near Charlie brought back too many memories and a resurgence of the passion he'd felt for the woman seven years ago.

When he met with Garner, he'd have to tell him that he might not be the right man for the job. They had a huge conflict of interest. He and Charlie had slept together. Hell, they had a child together.

Tired and grungy, he couldn't think straight. "I need a shower."

"What do you want me to do about it?" She stood with her arms crossed, a semibelligerent frown on her face.

The corners of his lips twitched. Ghost stepped up to her and tipped her chin with his finger. "There was a time when you would have offered to shower with me."

"I was young and stupid."

He chuckled. "And you don't want to get stupid together? There's a lot to be said for being stupid. Especially when you do this—" Before he could talk sense into his own head, he bent and touched his lips to her forehead. "And this." He moved from her forehead to the tip of her nose.

She closed her eyes and her chest rose on a deep, indrawn breath. She unwound her arms and laid her hands on his chest.

At first he thought she would push away, but her fingers curled into his shirt, giving him just enough encouragement.

"And this." Ghost pressed his lips to hers, tasting what he'd missed for all those years, drinking in her sweetness. Sweet ecstasy, he couldn't get enough. He slid his hands to her lower back and pressed her closer. Why had he stayed away so long?

He skimmed the seam of her lips with his tongue. When she opened her mouth on a gasp, he dived in, caressing her tongue with his in a long, slick slide, reestablishing his claim on her mouth.

She felt different, her curves fuller, her arms stronger, her hair longer, but she was the same inside. This woman was the only one who'd stayed with him over the years, her image tucked in the recesses of his mind as he prepared for combat. She was the reason he'd dedicated his life to serving his country. To protect her and all the other people who depended on him to secure their freedom. He risked his life so that others could live free and safe.

For a long moment, he pushed every reason he'd had for leaving her out of his mind and reveled in the warm wetness of her kiss, the sweet taste of blueberry syrup on her lips and the heat of her body pressed to his. His groin tightened, the fly of his jeans pressing into her belly.

"Mommy?"

Ghost leaped back as if he'd been splashed with ice water.

"What do you need, Lolly?" Charlie pressed one hand to her swollen lips and the other smoothed her hair before she turned to face her daughter standing in the doorway.

"Why were you kissing Mr. Caspar?"

Ghost half turned away from the child, his lips twitching. He'd leave that answer for Charlie. Although, he'd like to know the answer to that question, too.

Chapter Four

"Sweetheart, let's get your shoes on. We're going to get groceries. After that, we're going to the library. So gather your books." Charlie didn't answer her daughter's question, choosing to hustle her daughter out of her office and away from the man who'd just kissed her socks off. She called over her shoulder, "Help yourself to the shower. There are towels in the linen closet and plenty of soap and shampoo."

Her lips tingled, and she could still taste the sweetness of his mouth. Dear, sweet heaven, how was she going to keep her hands off the man if he was around all the time?

She needed air. She needed space. What she wanted was another kiss just like that one. With her knees wobbling, Charlie left Lolly in her room and hurried into the master bedroom where the bed was still neatly made. She jammed her feet into her cowboy boots and yanked a brush through her hair, securing it at the nape of her neck in a ponytail. After checking that the safety switch was set on her handgun, she slid it into her purse, hooked the strap over her shoulder, braced herself and stepped into the hallway.

Thankfully, Jon wasn't anywhere in sight.

Charlie released the breath she'd held.

Lolly emerged from her room carrying a stack of children's books.

"Let's put those in a bag." She gathered the books and carried them back into Lolly's room where she found her book backpack and slid them inside.

Lolly slipped the backpack over her shoulders and led the way from the room.

She ran ahead to the living room.

Charlie shook her purse, listening for the jingle of keys. When she didn't hear it, she returned to her bedroom and grabbed them from the nightstand.

Hurrying into the hallway, with her head down, tucking the keys into her purse, she ran into a wall of muscles.

Big, coarse hands gripped her arms, steadying her.

"Are you all right?"

Hell no, she wasn't. Her pulse raced and she was out of breath before she'd even begun her day. "I'm fine," she said, studying her hands resting on his chest.

And boy, was he fine, too. Charlie couldn't help but stare at the expanse of skin peeking through his unbuttoned shirt. She remembered the smattering of hair on his chest and how she used to run her fingers through the curls. Her fingers curled into his skin, wanting to slide upward to test the springiness of those hairs.

"Are you ready?"

More than you'll ever know. Charlie shook herself and pushed way. "I'm taking my car since I have to stock up on groceries."

"I'll follow you there."

"No need. It's only a block from Kevin's office. If I run into any trouble, you won't be far away." She shook her head. "We'll be fine."

He stared at her for a long moment.

Charlie met his gaze and held it, refusing to back down. He'd been gone seven years. He couldn't just walk back into her life and take over.

"Okay." He started buttoning his shirt. "Let's go."

Charlie's glance dropped to where his fingers worked the buttons through the holes. Seven years ago, she would have helped him button up, and then undo them one at a time, kissing a path down his chest.

Ghost's fingers paused halfway up. "I remember, too," he said, his voice low and gravelly.

Shivers rippled through her body and Charlie swayed toward him. Then she stopped, mentally pulled herself together and said, "I don't know what you're talking about. And I don't care. Let's go."

She pushed past him, her arm bumping into his, the jolt of electricity generated in that slight touch turning her knees to jelly.

The sooner she got away from him, the sooner she'd get her mind back. What was it about the man that scrambled her brain and left her defenseless against his magnetism?

Lolly stood by the door, her thumbs hooked through the straps of her backpack.

Charlie grabbed her hand and stepped out. She waited for Ghost to exit as well before she turned to lock the door. Her hand shook as she tried to slide the key into the dead bolt lock. She fumbled and dropped them to the porch.

Ghost scooped them up, locked the door and dropped the keys into her open palm. "You sure you don't want me to come with you?"

Lolly looked up, a happy smile on her face. "Could he, Mommy?"

"Sweetheart, Mr. Caspar has to go to a meeting."

Ghost touched his daughter's chin and gave her a brief smile. "I'll see you in about an hour."

"Mommy, can we get ice cream at the Blue Moose?"

"Why don't we get ice cream at the grocery store and bring it home to eat?"

"Okay." Lolly skipped down the steps toward the Jeep.

Charlie followed, not wanting to prolong her time or conversation with Ghost. The more she was with him, the more she wanted to be with him, and the harder it would be when he left again.

The drive to the grocery store took less than three minutes. She could have walked the five blocks, but she didn't want Lolly to be exposed to the nutcase who was threatening her. And carrying enough groceries for them for the week would be difficult, especially since she planned to purchase enough for Ghost, if he stayed for the full week. A man that big had to have an appetite to match. If it was anything like it had been when he'd gotten back from BUD/S training, he could put away some groceries.

He'd looked thin and a little gaunt after his SEAL training. She'd read about BUD/S to understand a little more of what he'd gone through. They'd put him through hell. And those who stuck it out came out tougher and ready to take on anything.

He'd been tired but exhilarated at making it through.

Now, he appeared more battle weary than anything. And he limped. Had he been injured? Charlie pressed a hand to her belly. The thought of Ghost going into battle, being shot at and explosions going off around him, made her stomach twist. When he'd left her, she'd done her best to push him as far to the back of her mind as she could. But she couldn't turn off the television when she'd seen reports of Navy SEALs dying in a helicopter crash or risking their lives to save hostages in Africa or some other place halfway around the world.

Now that he was back and larger than life, all those fears would be even harder to suppress.

DESPITE HER ASSURANCE they'd be all right, Ghost followed Charlie all the way to the grocery store in his truck. He waited in the parking lot until they were safely inside the store. Then he drove the additional block to the Blue Moose Tavern. As he pulled into a parking space on Main Street, a disturbance in front of the feed store two blocks down caught his attention.

He climbed out of his truck and studied the gathering crowd.

"Ghost, glad you could make it." Kevin Garner stepped out of the tavern, followed by three other men. He stuck out his hand.

Ghost shook it. "Charlie and Lolly are getting groceries. What's going on at the feed store?"

"Some of the local ranchers are gathering to protest the Bureau of Land Management's increase in fees for grazing livestock on government land."

He'd read about the issues the ranchers were having and how BLM had confiscated entire herds of cattle from ranchers who refused to pay the fees in protest.

As the crowd got louder, a van rolled into town with antennas attached to the top. A cameraman and reporter leaped out and positioned themselves with a view of the angry ranchers behind them.

"Is this part of the problem we're here to help with?" one of the men standing near Kevin asked. He stuck out his hand to Ghost. "Name's Max Decker. My Delta team calls me Caveman."

Ghost gripped the man's hand. "Jon Caspar. Navy SEAL. Call me Ghost."

The next man stepped up and gripped Ghost's hand. "Trace Walsh. Marine. Expert marksman, earned the nickname Hawkeye."

A tall man with a crooked nose stepped up. "Rex Trainor. Army Airborne Ranger. They call me T-Rex."

Kevin turned back to the group. "Now that you've

all met, let's take it to the loft." He led the way up the stairs on the side of the tavern and entered a combination office-apartment.

Ghost followed and entered a large room with a fold-up table stretched across the center. A bank of computers stretched across one wall, the screens lit. A wiry young man sat in front of a keyboard, his gaze shifting between three monitors.

"That's Clive Jameson. We call him Hack. He's the brains behind the computer we're using to track movement and data."

"Movement of what?" Caveman asked.

"What data?" T-Rex stepped up behind Hack.

"Grab a seat, I'll explain." Garner waved his hand at the metal folding chairs leaning against the wall. "It's not the ideal location and can get pretty noisy on Friday and Saturday nights, but it gives me the space I need to run the operation."

"What operation?" Hawkeye asked.

Kevin pointed to a large monitor hung on the wall. "Hack, could you bring up the map?"

The computer guy behind them clicked several keys and a digital map came up on the monitor.

"This is the tristate area of Wyoming, Montana and Idaho. There's been a lot of rumbling going on for various reasons in the area. Between the pipeline layoffs and the cattle-grazing rights, things are getting pretty hot. We're afraid sleeper cells of terrorists are embedding in the groups and stirring them up even more and providing them with the funding and weaponry to create havoc."

"This is a hot area, anyway. Haven't there been rumblings from the Yellowstone Caldera?" T-Rex asked.

Garner nodded. "That's another reason why you four were brought into this effort. The scientists at the Yellowstone Volcano Observatory have been tracking specific trembles. They think there might be an eruption in the near future. They don't think it will be a catastrophic event, but it has generated a lot of interest and tourists are pouring into Yellowstone National Park."

"So, what specifically makes you think something big is about to happen?" Ghost asked.

"Last week, we had two men go missing from the BLM. They had been out riding four-wheelers in grizzly country near some of the park's active hot springs." Garner stared at each of the men, one at a time, then said, "They didn't come back.

"Because they were armed with GPS capability we were able to find their ATVs hidden in the brush near a particularly deadly spring. There was no sign of a bear attack, which was the rescue team's first inclination. But they did find a shoe near the spring and skid marks as if someone was either dragging or pushing a body toward the toxic water. If the BLM men found their way into that pool, either on their own, or by other more forceful means, there would be absolutely nothing left for a family member to claim. Their tissue and bones would have dissolved."

"The perfect place to hide the bodies," T-Rex said, his tone low, his eyes narrowed.

"Why bring in the military?" Ghost asked.

"DHS is spread thin, monitoring our boarders and the entrance and exit points of airports and ports. We don't have the manpower to provide assistance to a potentially volatile situation here. And frankly, I don't think we have sufficient combat training as afforded to active duty military." Kevin lifted his chin, his chest swelling. "I do know what our country is capable of, and what the best of the best could do to help the situation. You see, I'm prior military. Eight years as a Black Hawk helicopter pilot. I ferried troops in and out of combat as a member of the 160th Night Stalkers."

Ghost sat back in his chair. "So you've seen as much battle as any one of us."

"Not as intensely as you four have. But I've seen what you can do when the time comes. You're smart and you act instinctively when you need to."

Hawkeye tapped his fingers on the table. "We've been fighting in a war environment. That's not what this is."

"No? You saw that mob out there. It could escalate into a shooting match in seconds."

"Still, it's not up to us to police civilians," Caveman said. "That's why we have law enforcement."

"The law enforcement is either tapped out or worse." Garner shook his head. "We think some might be working with the people stirring things up."

Ghost leaned forward. "What exactly are you asking us to do here?"

"I need you to do several things. We have hot

spots in the tristate area." Garner pointed to the map. "One is a survivalist group on the edge of Yellowstone National Park. With all the tourists flooding the park, I'm afraid they'll use it as an excuse to stage something big. I need someone to get inside the group, spy and report back."

"I'll take that one." T-Rex raised his hand. "I can infiltrate the survivalists' group."

"All I'm looking for now is information. If they do anything, you are not to engage." One by one, Garner looked each man in the eye. "Repeat, you are not to engage."

Caveman scratched the back of his head, his brows twisting. "We're combat veterans. Why involve us if we're not to engage?"

"We want to reserve engagement until it's the last resort." The DHS task force leader placed both hands on the table and leaned toward the men. "Think of it as a reconnaissance mission. You infiltrate wherever I need you to go, assess the situation and report back."

Ghost studied Kevin, his gut telling him the man wasn't giving it to them straight. "What else are you not telling us?"

Kevin straightened, his eyes narrowing, his lips thinning into a thin line. "One of the folks we employ who monitors the internet for anything that could be construed as a potential attack, ran across a message last night. More or less, it was a call to arms to take over a government facility."

The Marine, Army Ranger and Delta Force man leaned forward.

Because he'd already heard this story, Ghost sat back in his chair and waited for the rest of whatever Kevin had to say.

"Where?" T-Rex asked.

"When?" Hawkeye wanted to know.

"We don't have that information. I need you all to keep an ear to the ground. If you hear anything, no matter how inconsequential it might sound, relay it to me."

Ghost shook his head. "The disappearing BLM men and a poorly worded message can't be all that has you calling in the cavalry. What else?"

Kevin met Ghost's gaze. "We've also been concerned about message traffic from some of the people we've been monitoring for the past six months. Men who are connected with ISIS. We intercepted a message we decoded indicating a weapons movement to this area. Enough guns and ammunition to stage a significant takeover of a state capital. Enough ammunition for a standoff. Or the murder of a great number of people."

Ghost's gut clenched. His daughter was in the area in question. If something went down, she could be caught in the cross fire. He'd just found his daughter. He'd be damned if he lost her so soon.

He couldn't wait to get out of the meeting and back to his family.

His family. Ha! If Charlie had her way, he wouldn't be anywhere near them. He'd just have to convince her she'd be better off with him sticking around.

Chapter Five

Once inside the grocery store, Charlie whirled the cart around the narrow aisles, hurrying through the tiny store, gathering only what she needed for the week. The shelves appeared barer than usual. When she got to the counter, Mrs. Penders, one of the owners of the mom-and-pop store checked her items.

"Why are the shelves so empty, Mrs. P?" Charlie asked, setting her items on the counter, one at a time. "Are you expecting a delivery today?"

She snorted and rang up a loaf of bread, the last one on the shelf. "I got a shipment this morning. We had a run on the store earlier. Did you see the crowd gathering in front of the feed store?"

She hadn't. Charlie had been more concerned about Ghost following her that she hadn't glanced farther down the street. "I'm sorry. I didn't see the crowd. What's going on?"

"A group of ranchers are taking a stand against the Bureau of Land Management over what they did."

"What did they do?"

"They confiscated half of LeRoy Vanders's herd.

He refused to pay his fees for grazing rights on federal land in protest of the increase."

"Confiscated a herd of cattle?" Charlie set the jug of milk on the counter. "Can they do that?"

Mrs. Penders nodded. "Can and did. Got all the local ranchers up in arms. Sheriff's talking to them now out front of the feed store.

"I hear Jon Caspar is back in town." Mrs. Penders rang up the milk and slid it into a bag, before she raised her gaze to capture Charlie's. "You two were a thing way back in the day, weren't you?"

Charlie shrugged. "We dated."

"If he needs a place to stay, I have a room over my garage," the store owner offered.

"Mr. Caspar is staying with us." Lolly tugged on her mother's shirt. "Isn't he, Mommy?"

Heat filled Charlie's cheeks. "Just for the week while he's in town. Then he'll have to go back to his job with the Navy."

"Can't he stay forever?" Lolly asked. "I like the way he brushes my hair."

"We'll discuss this later," Charlie said, hurriedly placing the last items on the counter.

Mrs. Penders was one of the worst gossips in town. By the time Charlie reached home, the older woman would have word spread across the county that Charlie and Ghost were shacking up. She wouldn't be surprised if she got a call from her parents all the way in Europe asking about the man sleeping in her little house.

Mrs. Penders gave her a total, Charlie paid and

pushed the cart out into the parking lot. Lolly helped her load the items into the back of her Jeep.

As she pulled out of the parking lot of the store, she glanced down the street toward the feed store. Just as Mrs. Penders had said, a crowd gathered, some of the men raised their hands, shaking fists in the air.

"This can't be good," Charlie muttered, turning the opposite direction, heading for her little house on the edge of town. She passed the library.

"Aren't we going to the library?" Lolly asked.

"After we unload and put the groceries away. It won't take long, and we can walk next door."

"Okay." Lolly helped her unload the groceries, carrying in the lighter bags.

Charlie put away the items, grabbed her own bag of books and Lolly's backpack. "Let's go see Ms. Florence. She might have some new books for you today."

Grizzly Pass was a very small town, but the residents were proud of the little library they'd helped to fund. Rebecca Florence was the preacher's daughter, with a fresh degree in library science. A quiet soul, she'd returned to her hometown, glad to escape the hustle and bustle of Denver, where she'd attended her father's alma mater.

Happy to take over duties of town librarian from her aging mother, she slipped into the role with ease. Though shy and quiet, she managed to bring the library up to twenty-first century standards, writing for grant money to have computers installed and providing Wi-Fi internet for those who couldn't afford their own satellite internet.

Charlie enjoyed talking with Rebecca about the latest books. The woman was a wealth of knowledge and read extensively in fiction and nonfiction.

Before Charlie left the house, she placed a call to Kevin. His computer guy, Hack, answered the call. "He stepped out front. Is this an emergency? Do you want me to run out and catch him?"

"No. Just have him relay to Mr. Caspar that Charlie made it home and is now taking Lolly to the library. Thank you." She ended the call, grabbed Lolly's hand and left the house.

Less than twenty steps brought them to the front of the old colonial house that had been converted into the library. The wide front porch had several rocking chairs for patrons to use when they just wanted to sit outside and read a book.

Charlie and Lolly had spent a few beautiful summer days reading on that front porch. Now, they pushed through the front door with the open sign hanging in the window.

"Ms. Florence?" Charlie called out.

When she got no answer, she didn't worry. Rebecca sometimes was in the back kitchen making tea.

Charlie and Lolly laid their books on the return counter and went in search of some they hadn't read.

After a few minutes, Charlie went in search of Rebecca. She hoped the librarian could help her find more information on grazing rights and what it meant to the ranchers in the area.

She understood many of the ranchers had grazed their cattle on government land for years. Some families had been grazing cattle on government land for several generations. Paying a grazing fee wasn't the only expense they incurred. They were responsible for maintaining the fences on the land where they grazed their cattle and providing for the water, if it wasn't readily available.

"Rebecca?" Charlie pushed through a swinging door leading into the back of the house where the kitchen was. As soon as she passed through the door, she heard a soft moan, coming from the other side of an island.

Her heart slammed hard against her ribs and she ran forward.

Rebecca lay on the floor, her strawberry blond hair tangled and matted with blood. A gash on her forehead dripped blood into her eyes and onto the floor.

"Rebecca?" Charlie leaned down and grabbed the woman's hand. "What happened to you?"

"Charlie?" she said, though her voice sounded muffled. She tried to open her eyes, but couldn't seem to. Instead she gripped Charlie's hand. "Get out."

"What?" Charlie shook her head. "I'm not leaving until I get you some help."

"Go," she said. "Not safe." She coughed and spit up blood.

"Is the man who attacked you still here?"

She lay still for a moment before answering. "I don't think so." Her words ended on a moan.

Anger burned in Charlie's gut. How could anyone do this to as gentle a soul as Rebecca?

Charlie smoothed a lock of her reddish-blond hair

from her face. "I'm calling the sheriff and an ambulance." She started to rise, but Rebecca tightened her hold on her hand.

"Angry. Said I told."

"Who was it?"

"Don't know." She coughed, her body tensing. "Wore a mask. Said I…was ruining…everything…" Her grip loosened and her hand dropped to the floor.

Her throat constricting, Charlie pressed her fingers to the base of Rebecca's throat, hoping to find a pulse and nearly crying when she felt the reassuring thump against her fingertips. She stood and feverishly searched the kitchen for a telephone. Thankfully, there was one on the wall near the back door.

Charlie grabbed the phone and dialed 911. After passing the information to the dispatcher, she hung up and dialed Kevin's number.

Kevin answered the phone on the first ring. "Garner speaking."

"Kevin. Thank God. It's Charlie."

"What's wrong?"

"Rebecca Florence was attacked here in the library. I've notified 911. But she was more worried about me than herself. She said the guy who attacked her was angry. She said he was mad because she told. Is Ghost with you?"

"He just left to go to your house. He should be there about now."

Charlie dropped the phone as the sound of a siren wailed toward the little house. She pushed through the swinging door, suddenly afraid for her daughter she'd left in the children's section of the library.

"Lolly!" she shouted.

Lolly emerged from the front room, carrying a colorful book, her brow pressed into a frown. "What's wrong?"

Charlie gathered her into her arms and hugged her close.

Ghost slammed through the front entrance, his eyes wide and his face tense until he spotted Charlie and Lolly. "Are you two okay?"

Charlie nodded and then tipped her head toward the kitchen door. "But Rebecca isn't. Could you take Lolly while I help her?"

"You stay with Lolly. I've had training in first aid." He stepped past her and entered the kitchen.

A few minutes later, a young sheriff's deputy entered the library, his gun drawn.

"I don't think you'll need that," Charlie said. They didn't need some rookie deputy shooting a man who was only attempting to render aid. "Jon Caspar is in the kitchen with Ms. Florence. He's one of the good guys."

The deputy didn't lower his weapon, instead, he entered the kitchen. Voices sounded through the wood paneling of the door.

Moments later the fire department paramedics entered. Charlie directed them to the kitchen and then pulled Lolly into the front parlor of the old house that Rebecca had designated as the children's room.

While she waited for Ghost to emerge from the kitchen, she read a story to Lolly.

"Mommy, you're not doing a very good job," Lolly said.

"Then *you* read it to *me*," she said, too tired to argue with her daughter.

Lolly read the story, slowing over some words, but far advanced for her age.

Charlie only half listened, her chest tight, her stomach knotted. When she saw the paramedic wheel Rebecca through the house on a stretcher, she stood.

Ghost followed, stopping in the doorway.

Charlie ran into his arms and hugged him around the middle. "Is she going to be all right?"

Ghost smoothed the hair on the back of her head. "I believe so. She took a pretty hard hit to the forehead. They'll keep her in the hospital to observe for concussion. Before she passed out, did she say who did it?"

"She didn't know. Apparently he wore a mask." Charlie wrung her hands. "I think she was attacked because of me." She stared up into Ghost's eyes, her own filling with tears. "I couldn't live with myself if something happened to her because of me."

"Why because of you?"

Her stomach roiled. "She said he attacked her because she told."

"Why would he attack *her*, if he was looking for *you*?"

"He might have thought she was me. I was tapped into the library Wi-Fi when I was looking at the social media site. I have auburn hair, Rebecca has strawberry blond. The picture he sent was not absolutely clear, he could have mistaken her for me."

"That's it. I'm staying with you and Lolly."

"Okay."

He went off as if she'd never spoken. "Until we know what's going on, you and I need to stick together. No argument."

Her lips twitched as she touched a hand to his chest. "I said okay."

Ghost stopped talking and stared down into her eyes. "About time we agreed on something." He bent to capture her lips in a soul-defining, earth-shattering kiss that left her boneless. She leaned against him, completely dependent on his strength to hold her up.

He glanced down at Lolly staring up at them. "Yes, Lolly, I kissed your mother."

GHOST KEPT IT together all the way back to Charlie's house. He couldn't tell her that hearing her crying out Lolly's name with a touch of panic in her voice had made his heart practically explode out of his chest. Then seeing what had happened to Rebecca and knowing it could have been Charlie made him nearly crumple to his knees.

He'd been back only a day and already he was as deeply in love with Charlie as he'd been seven years ago. The connection they'd shared had never quite gone away, instead it was there and stronger than before. The things he knew, the places he'd been and the experiences he'd survived made him even more aware of how fleeting life could be. One day a man could be on the earth, alive and healthy. The next, he could be six feet under or in the case of the two

BLM men, they could have fallen into a toxic pit, leaving nothing left to identify.

He'd had friends die in his arms. He carried the pain with him every day of his life, never quite able to erase the images of them. They seemed to line up at night and dare him to sleep.

Knowing that could have been Charlie on the floor of the library left him feeling more panicked and uncertain than ever. He hadn't come back to find her, but fate placed her directly in his path and revealed to him the fact he had a child. How could he not stay and protect the two women who meant the most to him?

"You two stay here." Before he could allow them to go much farther than the front entryway, Ghost thoroughly searched the entire house. As soon as the guy who had attacked Rebecca discovered she wasn't the one he was after, he'd come back.

Ghost had to be ready.

When he returned, he found Charlie holding Lolly in her arms. The little girl was sobbing on her mother's shoulder.

Ghost's heart broke at the sound of the child's sobs. "Hey, what's all this?" he said softly.

"Ms. Florence is hurt." She sniffed and leaned back to look at Ghost. Her eyes were red-rimmed and puffy and tears stained her cheeks.

"Come here." He held out his arms. When Lolly went to him, his chest swelled two times bigger. She trusted him enough to come to him when she was distressed. That meant a lot.

Charlie stood with her hand on her daughter's back, her own eyes suspiciously glassy.

Holding Lolly in one arm, he opened the other.

Charlie stepped in and wrapped her arms around him and Lolly. For a long moment, the three of them remained in the tight hug.

Ghost had no desire to break it off anytime soon. The scent of Lolly's hair filled his nostrils. Baby shampoo and fresh air. He inhaled deeply and kissed the top of her head. Then he dropped a kiss on Charlie's temple, wishing he hadn't been such an idiot when he'd been there last. If he hadn't told her he wasn't interested in a long-term relationship, she might have let him in on the secret of his child. He wouldn't have missed all of her firsts. The first tooth, the first time she giggled. Her first step.

As he stood with his arms full of the two women he loved, he came to the conclusion he had to give up something. His career as a Navy SEAL or the family he'd just discovered.

He didn't want to give up either, but he had no right to ask Charlie and Lolly to wait around for him when he went out on missions. So many SEALs were divorced or never married. The waiting killed relationships. Most women wanted their man at home at night. Every night. And the worry of whether or not he'd come home alive, not in a body bag, was real and destructive to a spouse's peace of mind.

When his leg started aching and he couldn't stand still another minute longer, he asked, "Who wants hot cocoa?"

Lolly lifted her head from his shoulder. "Me."

"Me," Charlie agreed. "I'll fix it."

"No. Let me. Just point me in the right direction." He handed Lolly to her mother. "I can make a great cup of cocoa."

"We can all help." Charlie set Lolly on her feet and took her hand.

Lolly slipped her free hand in Ghost's and they entered the kitchen together. In a few short minutes, Ghost had the hot cocoa ready and Charlie made hot dogs for lunch.

"I know I bought ketchup," she said, sorting through the bottles of condiments in the refrigerator. When she didn't find it there, she went to the pantry. After a moment, she came back to the table with mustard. "I'm sorry. I must have forgotten it at the store."

"I put it in the refrigerator," Lolly said. She jumped up and went to the appliance and yanked open the door. "I put it right here." She pointed to an empty spot in the door.

"Well, it's not there," Charlie said. "You'll have to have mustard or eat your hot dog plain."

Lolly's bottom lip stuck out and she frowned. "I guess I'll eat mine plain." She sat at the table, and nibbled at the naked hot dog and drank the hot cocoa, gaining a white melted-marshmallow mustache on her upper lip.

Charlie slathered mustard on her hot dog and ate.

Ghost filled his bun with mustard and sweet relish and savored every bite. "That was delicious."

"Sweetheart," Charlie said softly to Lolly. "If

you're done with your lunch, you can take your plate to the sink and go play in your room."

"Okay." She slid out of her chair and carried the plate to the sink.

As the child left the room, Charlie grimaced. "She usually won't eat a hot dog without the requisite ketchup."

Ghost smiled. "A girl who knows what she likes. We'll have to ease her into mustard and relish. It's an acquired taste. But so good."

Charlie stared at him for a moment, her brows pinched lightly.

Ghost tried to think of what he'd said that would make her stare at him with that look of concern.

"Now that you know about Lolly, what are you going to do?"

He glanced in the direction Lolly had gone, not wanting to discuss the future of their daughter in front of her. "If you're finished with your meal, let's take this discussion out on the back porch."

He gathered her plate and his and carried them to the sink.

"Leave them. I'll take care of them later." She led the way to the back door and waited for him to follow before she opened it wide, stopped dead in her tracks and gasped.

Ghost nearly bumped into her, she stopped so fast.

There on the porch was the bottle of ketchup and written in bright red tomato sauce were the words *I KNOW WHERE YOU LIVE.*

Chapter Six

Charlie staggered backward into Ghost's arms. He pulled her away from the door and closed it between them and the damning writing on the porch.

"How did he get in?" Charlie turned and buried her face in Ghost's chest. "I'm positive I locked the doors."

"I double-checked the windows, as well as the doors." He smoothed his hand over the back of her head, his voice low and steady. "He must have picked the lock."

"He knows who I am, and he knows now where I live. He must have figured out Rebecca wasn't the one who tapped into his messages. We're not safe. I should pack up, take Lolly and leave."

"Then he wins."

"Good God, Ghost!" She slapped her palms on his chest. "This isn't a game."

"To him, it might be." He held her arms and stared down into her face. "He might follow you wherever you go."

"Or not. He might be trying to scare me away from Grizzly Pass until he and his following do whatever dastardly deed they have planned." She shook her head and stared at the closest button on his shirt. "I can't risk Lolly's life on a game some psycho is playing with me."

"You forget something."

"What?" She stared up at him, her eyes a little wild, scared.

"You forget that you have me."

"I could have been in the library when he attacked Rebecca," she said, a shiver slithering down the back of her neck. "You weren't there."

"I will be from now on. And you can't go anywhere without me until we catch the bastard."

"Then he wins by making me a prisoner in my own home." Charlie spun out of Ghost's grip and walked across the kitchen and back. "Look, you can stay until we figure this out. But you have to sleep on the couch. We're not picking up where we left off seven years ago. I'm a different person than the naive girl I was back then."

He nodded. "Agreed." He grinned. "About the couch and about being different. You're a much more beautiful woman, you're more independent and an incredible mother."

"And…" Her chin lifted and she captured his gaze with a cool steady one of her own. "I don't need anyone else in my life to make me happy," she insisted, if not to convince him, to convince herself.

"And you don't need anyone else in your life to make you happy," he repeated. "I get that. But when you're ready to talk, I want to discuss who Lolly needs in *her* life."

Charlie pinched the bridge of her nose and shook her head. "Can we postpone that one for another day? I have ketchup bleeding in my mind. And I'm not ready to start a custody battle."

He stepped toward her, his hand outstretched. "It doesn't have to be a battle."

She backed up. "No? I can't see anything but a battle in our future." When he opened his mouth, she held up both hands. "Please. For now, let's not go there. I can't deal with everything and a terrorist out to kill me." She looked at the floor, seeing Rebecca's limp body lying in her own blood. "I can't believe he attacked Rebecca. She wouldn't hurt a fly." She glanced up. "And it's my fault. If I hadn't been snooping on the internet for a few measly dollars extra, none of this would have happened."

"Darlin', you can't blame yourself. You didn't hurt Rebecca. *He* did. We'll deal with this together."

Though her heart warmed when he referred to her as darlin', she couldn't ignore the most important part of the equation. "What about Lolly? I don't want her to be collateral damage. She's just a child." God, what had she done? This was supposed to be an easy gig. She was supposed to be anonymous. No one would know she was the one surfing, searching for terrorist activities.

"Tell you what," Ghost said. "I'll have Garner bring new locks and keys. I can install them today."

She shook her head. "What good will that do? He'll just pick those, too."

Ghost shrugged. "It'll make *me* feel better."

She flipped her hand. "Fine. And I can get online and see if I can find the IP address of the social media group. Maybe we can chase down the leader through it."

"Garner will have Hack working on that, as well."

She nodded. "I did give him the URL. I would think Hack could find it before I can, but two heads are better than one."

Ghost clapped his hands together. "Good. You have a plan. I have a plan. Let's get to it."

Charlie went back to work in her office, searching through the internet, looking for the IP address that the Free America group occupied.

She could hear Ghost placing a call to Kevin, explaining what had happened with the ketchup. Half an hour later, a man she didn't know arrived at her door.

Apparently, Ghost did, calling him by an unusual nickname. "Hey, Caveman. Thanks for bringing these."

"I'm staying to help install them," Caveman said.

"That'll get it done faster," Ghost agreed. "Thanks."

They didn't ask her opinion or assistance, which was perfectly okay with her. Charlie didn't leave her office, except to check on Lolly. She spent the afternoon trying everything she knew, and searching the internet for techniques she didn't know that could help her find the man who'd threatened her online.

About the time Caveman left, Charlie could hear

the two men talking softly near the front door, their voices carrying down the hallway, but not clearly enough to make out their words.

Charlie didn't care. She trusted Ghost to keep her and Lolly safe. She had to get to the bottom of who was threatening her, or she'd have no peace.

Ghost appeared in the doorway a few minutes later, carrying a cup of hot tea. "Any luck?"

"I wish I could say yes, but I'm no computer forensics expert. That's not what I studied in my Information Systems degree."

"So you've been in school again?"

She nodded.

"You had just completed a degree when we met seven years ago."

"In business. It was pretty general. When I realized I was pregnant, I knew I had to get something with more of a skill I could work with at home. So I went into Information Systems and learned about databases, data management, design and programming."

"I'm impressed."

She shrugged. "My goal was to work from home so that I could live wherever I wanted." And she'd wanted to come home to Grizzly Pass to raise Lolly. It was a more laid-back and safe environment. Until now.

"I'm impressed. You've been busy."

"What about you?" She'd been dying to ask, but hadn't wanted to know more about him that would make her fall more deeply in love with the man. Still she couldn't resist knowing what he'd gone through in the past seven years. "Are you still based out of California?"

"I'm out of Virginia, now. I completed some training in riverine ops with SEAL Boat Team 22 out of Stennis Space Center in Mississippi. I've had over forty deployments since last we saw each other. But I've also managed to complete my online degree in financial management. Since I'm rarely in town, I don't have time to spend the money I make. I invest it."

She smiled up at him. "You've been busy, too."

He nodded. "Anything I can do to help?"

Her lips twisted and she shook her head. "Not unless you're an experienced hacker, along with being a trained SEAL."

He disappeared, leaving her to her work.

Charlie's senses were tuned into his movements. She could tell when he'd gone into Lolly's bedroom. Their voices drifted to her, making her want to give up on her search and join them. Normally, she would break from her work for the Bozeman software company to spend time with her daughter. But what she was doing was more important. She couldn't let the man threatening her get away with it. And since he'd attacked Rebecca, apparently he would follow through on his threat.

Charlie shivered and dug deeper, following leads on the computer, searching through videos on how to find an IP address. Everything she tried ran her into a brick wall.

The smell of cooking onions drifted into her office and brought her out of her focused concentration.

Ghost was in the kitchen and, by the sound of it, Lolly was helping. Charlie smiled. At least her daughter had a chance to get to know the man who was her father.

Ghost was a good man. Charlie shouldn't have kept the news of his daughter from him. He'd missed so much of her life already and it wouldn't be fair of her to keep him from seeing her in the future. They'd have to come up with a plan to trade off on weekends and holidays.

The thought saddened her. Charlie had grown up with parents who had been married for more than thirty years. They were still as in love with each other as the day they'd met. Their marriage was the standard by which Charlie measured all other relationships.

Perhaps theirs was the exception, not the rule. Wasn't having a part-time father who loved her better than no father at all? She had a lot of thinking to do, and perhaps this wasn't the time to do it. Her problems were more immediate than setting up a visitation schedule.

Lolly appeared in the doorway with a hand-folded paper hat on her head and a towel over her shoulder. She stood straight, her lips twitching. "Your dinner is served," she said in her most formal tone. She spoiled the effect by giggling. "Come on, Mommy. Mr. Caspar and I set the table. We made a lasagna for dinner."

"Lasagna?" Charlie's stomach rumbled. "It smells wonderful."

"It is wonderful." The child grabbed her hand and pulled Charlie to her feet. "Hurry. I'm hungry."

Charlie chuckled and let her daughter practically drag her down the hallway to the kitchen.

Ghost stood at the sink, an apron looped around his neck and tied around his narrow waist. He glanced over his shoulders. "Have a seat. Dinner is just about done."

"Can I do anything?" Charlie asked.

"You can sit down and look beautiful with Lolly." He winked at the little girl. "She even brushed her own hair and changed into that dress."

Lolly nodded. "All by myself."

Charlie stood back, studying her daughter's clothes and hair. "Good job." She gave her a high five and pulled out a chair for her daughter to slide into.

Dinner was perfect. The lasagna tasted so good, Charlie accepted a second helping and ate until she was so full, she couldn't form a coherent thought. "What did you put into that pasta? I suspect it was some kind of sleeping potion." A yawn slipped out and she covered her mouth. "I think I'll get a shower and go to bed." She glanced at Lolly. "Are you about done?"

"Don't worry about Lolly. She and I have a date with her favorite book tonight. I'll help her through bath time and pajamas. Go. Get your shower and sleep."

Charlie didn't argue. The stress of the day and

not being able to sleep the night before had left her exhausted. She trudged her way to the bathroom, stripped down and stepped beneath the spray. If she wasn't so tired, she'd be tempted to invite Ghost to join her.

Her eyes widened. What was she thinking? Invite Ghost in the shower with her? She wasn't a twenty-two-year-old anymore. Ghost wasn't going to be around forever, and she refused to put herself and Lolly through the heartbreak of a man entering and leaving her life with no commitment to return.

He might be okay with that lifestyle, but she couldn't take that yo-yo effect. Lord forbid if he should bring back a wife on one of his visits to Lolly.

Her hands clenched and heat burned through her body. She twisted the knob on the faucet to cold and stood beneath the showerhead, letting the water chill her until she shivered.

Then she remembered she hadn't grabbed a towel from the hall linen closet. She stepped out of the shower onto the bath mat, dripping wet and chilled to the bone. Grabbing her shirt, she held it up to her chest and opened the door a crack. No one was in the hallway. She could hear voices in the kitchen. With the coast clear, she darted across the hall to the closet, flung open the door and snatched a towel. She had just turned to dash back into the bathroom when the wood floor squeaked at the other end of the hallway and she heard Ghost say, "I'm going to check to see if your mother is finished in the shower. I'll be right back."

She didn't make it across the hall. Her feet froze to the floor. Holding the towel in front of her, she couldn't think, couldn't move and only stared at Ghost.

His gaze slipped over her, traveling slowly downward from her face to her breasts, where she'd pressed the towel to the swells. Lower still, his gaze moved to the flare of her hips, clearly visible with the towel draped down only the middle of her torso.

His eyes flared and his body stiffened.

Heat rose from Charlie's core and spread throughout her body. The moisture from that short, cold shower steamed off her body as passion flared and burned a path outward, making her ache for him in every part of her existence.

"Charlie." The word came out in a low, sexy tone. He stepped toward her, his hand reaching out.

Charlie was caught in the spell, the temptation to run into his arms so strong, her arm relaxed, the towel inching downward.

"Mr. Caspar?" Lolly called out from the kitchen.

And snap. Just like that, the spell was broken.

Charlie flung herself into the bathroom, closed the door and leaned her back against it, breathing hard as if she'd run a marathon instead of three feet across the hallway.

From sleepy to wide-awake in two seconds flat. She scrubbed her body with the towel, hoping the added abrasion would push Ghost out of her mind. It had the opposite effect. Her skin tingled from the heated gaze he'd spread over her body. Her nipples were tight, puckered for his touch.

She moaned, threw the towel onto the floor and stomped it. "No. No. No. I will not make love to that man."

"Everything all right in there?" Ghost's voice sounded through the door. Was that a chuckle she heard?

Charlie channeled her desire into something just as heated. Anger. Shoving her head into her nightgown, she pulled it down over her body and slipped her arms into the matching robe. Then she frowned, fearing the garment was a little too revealing. Since she didn't have anything else with her in the bathroom, she sighed. It would have to do. She reached for her panties, but the counter was bare.

Damn. Had she forgotten them? She opened the door and peered out.

Ghost stood in the hallway, dangling a pair of soft blue bikini panties from his index finger. "Missing something?"

Her eyes widened and she reached for the panties.

He pulled them back at the last minute.

Charlie's forward momentum carried her toward him and she slammed into his chest.

Ghost clamped an arm around her waist and held her tight against him. "You felt it, too, didn't you?"

"I don't know what you're talking about." She reached for the panties again, her breasts rubbing against his chest through the thin fabric of her nightgown. "Let me have those."

He raised his eyebrows. "Say *please*."

She gritted her teeth, her core tightening, the ache building the longer she stood with her nearly naked body pressed to his. Instead of arguing over underwear, she wanted to wrap her legs around his waist. Hell, she wanted him inside her, filling that space that had been empty for so long. God, she'd missed him. And she'd miss him when he was gone.

Charlie slumped in his arms. "Fine. You can keep them. But let me go. There really can't be anything between us."

His arm tightened around her. "Why?"

"You have your responsibilities. I have mine. I gave you my heart once. I'm not willing to do it again."

For a long moment, he held her in his arms, his gaze locked on hers.

She refused to look away first. Losing him the first time had been so hard. Carrying his baby, knowing he wouldn't be a part of their lives had nearly killed her. She couldn't let him back into her life, only to have him leave again and break not only her heart, but Lolly's, too.

FINALLY, GHOST LOOSENED his hold. He could see the hurt in Charlie's eyes and he wanted to take it all away. He'd caused that. He'd been the one to break her heart. If he wanted her back, he'd have to earn her trust.

He released her, but he didn't hand back her panties. Instead, he wadded them up and shoved them into his pocket. Yeah, it might be juvenile, but he wanted something that belonged to her, should she end up kicking him out of her life. "Lolly's ready for her bath and bedtime story."

"I can take care of her."

"Get her through her bath. I'll take it from there."

"You don't need to. I'm awake now."

"I don't care if you're awake. I want to read to my daughter—to get to know her." His mouth formed a thin line, his brows dipping low. "At least give me that."

She nodded. "Fair enough." Charlie stepped away from him, spun on her heels and walked into her bedroom.

Knowing she wasn't wearing panties nearly made Ghost come undone. The sway of her hips and the way she flung her damp hair over her shoulder was so enticing, he almost went after her. The way her nipples puckered, making little tents in her silky nightgown, was proof she wasn't immune to him.

Yeah, he had a long way to go to convince her he was worth a second chance.

You broke my heart once…

Was he selfish to want her back? He adjusted his jeans to accommodate his natural reaction to her bare-bottom state. Hell, yeah, it was selfish. What he needed to consider was if he was the man for her. Charlie was special. She deserved someone who could be there for her always.

As a Navy SEAL, he couldn't be in Wyoming except when he took leave. If she and Lolly wanted to be with him, they'd have to leave Wyoming and join him at Little Creek, Virginia. Even then, they'd only see him when he wasn't deployed. The advantage to living on or near a Navy base was the support network of the military and other military spouses.

God, she deserved so much more.

After his last deployment and being injured, Ghost had worried he wouldn't get the medical clearance to return to his unit. Now he wondered if it wasn't time for him to step down. Take a medical retirement, find a less dangerous job that allowed him to be home more often.

He walked back into the kitchen to find Lolly drying the last plate.

"I couldn't reach the cabinet." She pointed upward.

Ghost opened the cabinet and set the cleaned and dried plates inside. Then he dropped his hand to the top of Lolly's soft, red hair. He wanted the chance to be with his daughter. To get to know her, and for her to get to know him. Dragging them around the nation was selfish. But, damn it. He wanted to be a part of Lolly's life, even if Charlie didn't want anything else to do with him.

"Come on, it's time for your bath and a bedtime story." He held out his hand.

Lolly laid hers in his, so trusting. Would she be better off with a stepdad who could be there for her? Would he be kind to her and treat her like she was his own daughter?

Ghost couldn't imagine Lolly with any other father, any more than he could imagine Charlie with another man.

"You get your pjs while I run the water."

"Roger," she said and grinned up at him. "I said that right, didn't I?"

He'd been teaching her how SEALs talked to each other. The child picked up quickly. Smart as a whip. Just like her mother.

"Roger." He gave her a nudge toward her bedroom. "Go. Get those pjs." Ghost entered the bathroom. It still smelled like Charlie's shampoo, making him want to skip Lolly's bath and go straight into her mother's bedroom, climb into her bed and make crazy, passionate love to her.

Instead, he sat on the side of the bathtub, turned the handles on the faucet and adjusted the temperature to just right for a six-year-old.

Lolly entered carrying her colorful pjs, tossed them on the counter and stuck her hand in the water. "Just right."

"Need any help here? If not, I'll go find the perfect book for us to read together."

"I can take my own bath. Mommy thinks I need help, but I don't." She puffed out her chest and lifted her chin, just like Charlie did when she was standing up for herself or someone else. Lolly was so much like her mother, it made Ghost's chest hurt just looking at her.

"Okay, then." He dropped a kiss on top of her head and left her to do her thing, propping the bathroom door open so he could listen for her.

He walked back to the living room, found the phone and dialed the number for Garner.

"Charlie, how's it going?"

"It's Ghost," he said. "So far we're okay. What's the status on the librarian?"

"She's holding her own. Minor swelling on the brain. They're watching her closely and keeping her sedated. By all indications, she'll live."

"I also wanted to know if Hack found anything in those messages that would lead us to whoever has targeted Charlie."

"Nothing so far. He's close to finding the IP address. As soon as he does, I'll send one of the guys out to recon."

"I'd like to be the one to corner that man."

"You and me both. He's a slick bastard. But I find it hard to believe a rancher or pipeliner is crafty enough to pull off a takeover without some help from outside."

Ghost's fists clenched. "You think the ranchers and pipeliners are too dumb to pull this off?"

"No, no. Don't get me wrong. I think they're plenty smart. I just don't know that they could pull it off without some tactical training and influence from outside the ranching and pipeline community."

"So far, all I've seen in the way of an uprising was the ranchers protesting the confiscation of a herd of cattle. Was anyone arrested?"

"No. As long as there was no harm to anyone and no property damage, they were free to protest."

"Did you or one of the others get some names of the primary instigators?"

"Hawkeye spoke with one rancher who had twenty-eight hundred head of cattle confiscated, LeRoy Vanders," Garner said. "He was hopping mad and ready to rip into the BLM."

"And?"

"The sheriff managed to calm him. The crowd has since dissipated, but there are a lot of angry ranchers. Hack's checking online records for some of the names Hawkeye came up with from the protesters. T-Rex will be positioning himself at the County Line Bar tonight to make some new friends among the survivalist groups."

"What about Hawkeye?"

"He'll be downstairs in the Tavern striking up conversations with the ranchers and unemployed pipeline workers who come in each night to get a drink and commiserate."

"Mr. Caspar?" Lolly called out from down the hall.

Ghost lowered his voice. "I have to go. Let us know anything you might find out about the man stalking Ms. McClain. As *soon* as you find out. Even if it's in the middle of the night."

"Roger," Garner said. "I'll have Caveman swing by a couple of times during the night."

"Thanks," Ghost said. "Out here." He ended the call and hurried down the hall to the bathroom.

Lolly was out of the tub, wearing her panties,

her nightgown pulled over her head, but stuck half-way down.

Ghost untangled the gown and dragged the hem downward to her knees.

She smiled up at him. "Thank you." Then she skipped past him to her bedroom and selected a book from her shelf. "Read this," she demanded.

Ghost took the book from her. "Did you brush your teeth?"

She clapped a hand to her mouth and darted for the door. "I'll be right back."

He grinned and waited for her, thumbing through the book she'd chosen about a little girl pretending to be a beauty shop lady. He chuckled at some of the descriptions. Then he turned down the comforter on Lolly's bed and sat on the edge.

Lolly was back in two minutes, smiling wide. "Clean. See?"

He frowned down at her. "You sure you brushed long enough?"

She nodded. "I sang 'Happy Birthday' all the way through twice."

"Okay. Let's find out what's going on in this book." Ghost opened the book and started reading, getting as caught up in the character's plight as Lolly by the end of the story.

"Now, this one," Lolly insisted, opening another book and handing it to him.

After reading two more books, Ghost told Lolly it was time to close her eyes and go to sleep.

Lolly pouted for a brief moment and then flopped

down on her back and burrowed into the sheets and comforter, until all Ghost could make out was Lolly's cute little head poking out of the big bed. "Aren't you going to stay?" She patted the bed beside her.

Ghost sat on the edge of the bed and bent to kiss her good-night. She captured his head between her palms and kissed him soundly on the cheek.

He laughed and kissed the top of her head. "Good night, princess."

"Good night, Mr. Caspar." She yawned, stretched and closed her eyes. "I love you."

Ghost's heart squeezed hard in his chest. Those three little words practically brought him to his knees. The child hardly knew him, but she trusted him to take care of her and to be there when she woke up.

He wanted to gather her in his arms and hold her tight. Forever. His little girl.

In less than five minutes she was asleep, her breathing slow and steady. But Ghost remained perched on the side of her bed, watching her angelic face as she slept, and his heart grew fuller by the minute.

If anyone tried to hurt her... His fists clenched. He'd rip the attacker apart, one limb at a time. No one messed with his family.

"No one," he whispered.

Chapter Seven

Charlie woke with a start and stared into the darkness. She'd had a dream about someone chasing her through the rooms of the library next door. He'd almost captured her, when she'd forced herself to wake.

Her heart thundered against her ribs and perspiration beaded on her forehead. A glance at the clock indicated she'd been asleep for four hours. She hadn't even heard when Lolly went to bed. That was a first in the six years she'd been a mother. Going to sleep before her daughter wasn't something she ever did. It was a testament to the trust she had in Ghost.

Which reminded her. Though she trusted him to keep her and her daughter safe through the night, she shouldn't trust him with her heart. She wasn't sure she would survive a second time around of a broken heart.

Shoving aside the covers she got out of bed and padded barefoot down the hallway to Lolly's bedroom.

Her daughter lay curled on her side, an arm wrapped around her favorite teddy bear and sleeping peacefully with a smile curling her lips. A few books lay on the nightstand beside her bed.

Charlie smiled, imagining Ghost reading them to her daughter. She'd have him reading more than that if he let her talk him into it.

Tucking the blanket around Lolly's chin, she bent to kiss her daughter's cheek.

Lolly rolled over and whispered, "I love you, Mr. Caspar."

Charlie's breath caught at the constriction in her throat. Her daughter was already falling in love with the man who'd broken Charlie's heart seven years ago. Would Lolly's little heart be broken as well when Ghost left to return to his SEAL team?

On silent feet, she tiptoed down the hallway where she peered into the living room.

Ghost lay in the lounge chair, shirtless, wearing boxer shorts and nothing else. He leaned back, his arms crossed over his chest, his eyes closed and his breathing deep and regular. Asleep.

Charlie took the opportunity to drink her fill of him, studying his face, chest, arms and thick, muscular thighs. How she wished she could go to him, straddle his waist and press her hot center to him. She had yet to find another pair of panties. She wondered what he'd done with the ones he'd taken.

That he wanted to keep them must mean something. But what? That he wanted to make love to her? She had no doubt about that. When he'd held her close, the ridge beneath his jeans had been firm and insistent, pressing against her belly.

Warmth spread through her body, igniting the flames at her center. She burned uncontrollably, wanting the man more than she'd wanted anyone or anything in her life. If she gave in to her carnal lust, he wouldn't resist. Hell, he'd welcome her with the same level of passion. Their sex life had never been the problem between them.

Yeah, Charlie had told Ghost she didn't care if a relationship with him was only temporary. But that had been before she'd discovered she was in love with him. When he'd left, she'd held it together until that night when she'd been alone in her bed. Then she'd cried. And cried some more. Two weeks later, she was crying even harder when she discovered she'd missed her period and the early pregnancy test proved positive.

Seven years ago, she'd given her heart to this man. And based on the way she felt at that moment, she still loved him. If not as much, then even more.

Her eyes stinging, Charlie backed away from the living room and escaped into the kitchen. She peered through the curtain over the window on the back door. Moonlight shone onto the porch, bathing everything in a dark blue glow.

The ketchup had been cleaned off the wooden planks. She'd have to thank Ghost in the morning. It was one fewer thing she had to face on her own. Though the message was gone, it remained seared into her mind.

Unable to face going back to her lonely bed, Charlie tiptoed into her office, half closing the door. She booted her computer and went to work, trying to find the man responsible for the attack on Rebecca and the ketchup message on her back porch. The threats had to stop. Both to herself and to whatever government facility he had in mind by his call to arms.

She returned to the site with the entries from people who had legitimate gripes with the way they'd been treated by local and national authorities. One by one, she followed each posting, tracking them back to their own social media pages. Each had pictures of their families posted. These were real people with loved ones. All they wanted was to be treated fairly. They were all upset about the confiscation of LeRoy Vanders's herd, wanting the authorities to return the man's animals as they were his livelihood. If he couldn't get them back, he wouldn't have the means to provide for his family. He'd posted, You might as well shoot me now. I'm worth more to my family dead than alive.

She followed LeRoy to his page. There he had posted messages from Bible scripture, praying for a peaceful resolution to the current crisis. It didn't sound like a man crazy enough to threaten someone for spying on his messages.

But then Charlie didn't know what set a man like that off. If desperate enough, he might go off the deep end and come out fighting.

She tried scanning the internet for other terrorist threats that could be tied to the state of Wyoming. At one point she found a message from a man claiming to be a member of ISIS. His threat was to all American infidels. He was coming. Be prepared to convert or die.

A shiver rippled across her as she stared into the

eyes of a man who looked like he could kill without it impacting him in the least. His brown eyes had that intense crazy look that burned into her, even from a computer screen.

Charlie pushed her chair away from the monitor and keyboard. She stood, stretched and walked to the window overlooking the street in front of her house. Moonlight streamed through the window, bathing her in its pale, blue glow.

Why did something so beautiful three nights ago seem so sinister now? She'd always loved nighttime in Wyoming. She'd loved staring up at the stars with her father, identifying constellations and planets.

The night she'd spent in the back of Ghost's pickup, they'd had fun naming different stars as if they were the scientists who'd discovered them. They laughed and rolled into each other's arms. A kiss led to a caress. The caress moved from outside their clothes to bare skin. Soon, they were naked, bathed in starlight, making love.

Charlie wrapped her arms around her middle and sighed. Why couldn't things have remained the same? That had been their last night together. The next day, he'd driven to his new assignment in California and she'd stayed in Wyoming, nursing a broken heart.

She raised her hand to push her hair back from her forehead.

Seven years later, he was in her living room, wearing nothing but boxer shorts, sexier than ever, and she was staring out at the night sky wishing for something that would only bring her more heartache.

"Hey." Ghost's voice echoed in her head, like a memory she couldn't forget. Why had she never been able to forget him? Why couldn't she ignore him now?

"Charlie, darlin'." That voice again, made the ache in her belly grow.

Big hands descended on her arms, turning her to face the man she'd never stopped loving.

GHOST HAD REMAINED in the doorway to Charlie's office for a long time before he'd made a sound.

She'd stood by the window, her body swathed in a pale glow turning her into an ethereal blue image of lush, unaffected beauty.

She was sexy, but appeared sad, staring out into the darkness. He wanted to tell her to step away from the window in case someone decided to take a shot at her. As still as she was, she'd make an easy target.

When she raised her arm to push her hair back the moonlight shone through the thin fabric of her nightgown, exposing the silhouette of her naked body beneath.

His breath lodged in his lungs, or he would have moaned aloud. Every cell in his body burned for her. His pulse sped through his veins carrying red-hot blood angling south to his groin. He had to have her, to hold her in his arms. To feel her skin against his.

"Hey," he managed to say.

When she didn't turn to face him, he eased into the room. Perhaps she'd been sleepwalking and wasn't hearing him through her dream.

"Charlie, darlin'," he whispered. Gripping her arms, he turned her toward him.

She glanced up at him, recognition in her gaze and something else. Longing. Pure, unrestricted passion.

Charlie pressed her hands to his chest and slid them up to lock around the back of his neck. Then she stood on her toes, pulling his head down to hers. "Call me all kinds of a fool, for making the same mistake twice, but I want you."

"If wanting you is a mistake, I don't care what you call me. Just let me have you for a moment," he said, drawing her into his arms. He wrapped his hands around her waist and pressed her hips against his. His erection swelled, pressing into her belly, when he'd rather be pressing it into her.

He claimed her mouth in a long, hard kiss. When he traced the seam of her lips, she opened to him, meeting his tongue with hers in a twisting tangle of urgency.

She drew her arms down his chest and around to his backside, sliding her fingers beneath the elastic of his boxers. Slim, warm hands cupped his buttocks and squeezed gently.

He broke the kiss, dragging in a deep breath, barely able to hold back, when wave after wave of lust washed over him, urging him to take her now. In the office, on the desk, against the wall. Anywhere he could get inside her. Now.

He bunched her nightgown in his hands, pulling it up over her bottom and groaned.

She hadn't found another pair of panties. Her sex was bared to him, there for the taking.

Ghost slid his hands down the backs of her thighs and lifted her, wrapping her legs around his waist.

She locked her ankles behind him and captured his face between her palms. "This is for now. Nothing has changed between us. Don't expect anything from me tomorrow."

His heart tightened in his chest. He understood why she said these things. She didn't trust him. Didn't expect him to stay and she had to guard her heart and Lolly's from the hurt she expected him to inflict when he left.

He knew all of this as the truth, but he couldn't stop. He had to have her. He'd work on the trust later. When he wasn't consumed by his need to feel her against him. The need to lose himself inside her.

He carried her down the hallway to her bedroom, careful not to make enough noise that would wake the little one. Once inside, he pushed the door half-closed with his foot and carried Charlie to the bed. "Protection?"

"I'm on birth control and I'm clean."

"I'm clean, too."

She kissed his lips and whispered against his mouth, "Then what are you waiting for?"

He sat her on the edge of the bed, grabbed the hem of her nightgown and pulled it slowly over her head.

She raised her arms to accommodate the removal of her only garment. Charlie leaned back on her elbow in the glow of a night-light and spread her knees wide. She ran one hand down her belly to the triangle of curls covering her sex and threaded her fingers through them. She tipped her head toward his boxers. "Are you going to wear those all night?"

"Oh, hell no." Ghost shucked the shorts and stood before her, his shaft jutting out, his body on fire for her. His first inclination was to take her, hard and fast, to thrust deep inside her glistening entrance. But he didn't want to scare her away. He wanted her to know the depth of need and passion he was experiencing. Hell, he wanted to bring her to the very edge and make her beg for him to take her.

Ghost dropped to his knees in front of her and draped her legs over his shoulders.

Her eyes widened and her breathing became more labored. She threaded her fingers through the fluff of hair over her sex to the folds beneath.

Ghost stroked her hand and her fingers and brushed them aside to take over. He parted her folds, exposing the narrow strip of flesh between. Leaning in, he flicked her with the tip of his tongue.

She moved her hands, weaving them into his hair, while digging her heels into his back, urging him to continue.

He tongued her again, this time swirling around, laving until she pulled on his hair, a moan rising from her throat.

Ghost remembered how she had given herself to him so completely when they were younger, yelling out his name in the throes of their shared passion. He wanted to capture that same sense of abandon.

While his tongue took control of her nubbin, he thrust one of his fingers into her slick channel, reveling in how wet she already was, knowing it would ease him inside her soon. He added a second finger in with the first and stretched her, feeling her muscles contract, gripping his fingers.

Teasing and tasting, he licked, swirled and flicked that amazing bundle of nerves that made her crazy with desire.

And she responded by raising her hips, pumping them upward, pulling on his hair to keep him focused on her pleasure.

He didn't need the encouragement. Making her come apart was his goal. If he read her right, she was nearing her climax.

Charlie's body tensed, her heels dug into his back and she thrust her hips upward.

Ghost didn't relent, continuing his frenzied assault until he stormed past her resistance.

Charlie's fingers curled into his scalp and she cried out softly, "Ghost!" as she gave in with abandon, her body shaking with her release.

Ghost continued to stroke her with his fingers and tongue, slowing the movement as she relaxed and sank back to the mattress.

"Oh, my," she said, her head tossing from side to side. "I didn't know it could be even better than before."

Ghost chuckled and scooted her up farther on the bed. He lay beside her, his hand cupping her sex, his shaft throbbing with his need. He wanted her to be sure.

She finally looked into his eyes, her own narrowing. "Why did you stop?"

"I want you to be sure."

"Sweet heaven. I've never been more sure." She dragged him over her, parted her legs and let him slide between them. "Please. Don't make me wait another minute."

Releasing a long breath, he eased up to her entrance, dipping in slowly. "Tell me to stop and I will."

"Don't you dare." She raised her legs, clamped them around his waist and dug her heels into his buttocks, urging him to take her. "I want you. All of you. Inside me. Now."

Unable to hold back another second, he drove into her, thrusting all the way until he was completely encased in her slick, tight wetness.

He bent to kiss her, taking her tongue with his as he moved out and back into her. Slowly at first, then faster and faster until he pumped in and out of her like a piston in an engine.

The faster he went, the harder he got, the tension building, pushing him to the edge. One. Last. Thrust. And he shot into the stratosphere, spiraling to the stars, his body exploding with electric shocks that spread through him from his shaft to the very tips of his fingers. He dropped down on her, still buried deep inside and held steady until his shaft stopped throbbing and he could breathe normally again.

At long last, he rolled to his side and pulled her with him, curling her up against his body.

Charlie laid her cheek against his chest and chuckled. "Your heart is racing."

"You do that to me."

She sighed and circled her fingers around his hard, brown nipple. "I'd say I could get used to this, but I can't."

"Can't, or won't?"

"Does it matter?" she whispered. "You're here today. But you'll be gone soon."

"What if I come back?"

"In another seven years?" She snorted and shook her head.

"How about in a couple of months?"

"Would it be fair to Lolly?"

He thought about it. "I want to know my daughter. I want to watch her grow."

"You can't do that if you aren't here."

He knew what she said was true. But lots of SEALs had families willing to be there when they got home.

"Charlie, I want you—"

She pressed a finger to his lips. "Shh. I just want to hold you for tonight. We don't have to talk. In fact, I'd rather not ruin what we shared with words we might regret."

Ghost clamped his teeth down on his tongue, wanting to say more, wanting to force her into some kind of commitment, but he didn't want her to kick him out of her bed. For that night, he would shut up and hold her. Tomorrow, they'd have to make time to talk. They had too much at stake to remain silent for long.

Chapter Eight

Charlie lay in the warmth of Ghost's arms, listening to the beat of his heart. This was where she'd always wanted to be. She didn't want the night to end. For a long time, she lay awake, until her eyes closed and she drifted into sleep.

A sharp ringing sound jerked her out of a lovely dream, jarring her awake. She sat up, thinking it was the smoke alarm. When it stopped and then rang again, she realized it was the phone on the other side of the bed.

Ghost grabbed the phone from the cradle and handed it to her.

She took it, almost afraid to answer. "Hello," Charlie said, her voice hoarse with sleep.

"Ms. McClain, Hack here. You wanted me to call when we got a hit on the IP address."

Charlie sat up straighter, pushing the fog of sleep out of her head. "Whose is it?"

"We traced it back to a man who died several months ago, but I have one of our guys headed out to the physical address. Apparently it's local. I thought you'd want to know."

"I do. Is that all?"

"So far. I'm still tracking some of the people in that chat room. When I have more, I'll let you know."

"Thank you." She handed the phone to Ghost and he set it back on the charger.

"They're sending someone out to the physical address associated with the IP address," she said, draping her arm over her eyes.

Ghost rose up on his elbow and stared down at her. "Whose was it?"

She moved her arm and stared up into his eyes, her own narrowing. "That's the strange part. Hack said it was registered to a dead man."

"A what?" He brushed a strand of her hair from her face, tucking it behind her ear.

She leaned into his hand and kissed his palm. "Someone who'd died several months ago."

Ghost bent to kiss her forehead. "I would like to know if he died of natural causes, or if he was murdered." Then he kissed her nose.

Charlie closed her eyes, loving the feel of his lips on her skin, while blocking the thought of someone who might have been murdered for his connection to an IP address. She opened her eyes. "What time is it?"

Ghost leaned back to glance at the clock on the nightstand. "Nearly seven o'clock."

Her heart leaped. "Lolly will be up any minute."

She shoved against his chest. "You have to get out of here."

"Why?"

"She's super curious and asks a lot of questions. Frankly, I'm not prepared to answer any about you."

"Like, 'Mommy, why are you in bed with Mr. Caspar? And why are you naked?'" He lowered the sheet and tweaked the tip of her nipple.

Her core responded with an answering ache. But she couldn't allow herself to go for round two with the chance of Lolly running in and jumping into the bed, like she did so often. As much as she would have liked to see his tweak and raise it to a much more satisfying conclusion, she didn't feel like facing a lot of questions from her daughter.

"Out." She rolled away and shot out of the bed.

Ghost got up and stretched, his body naked in the light peeking around the edges of the curtains. God, he was gorgeous.

A sound from the room down the hallway made her race to her closet, grab the first pair of jeans she could find and jam her legs into them. "For the love of Mike, cover yourself," she hissed. "Lolly's awake."

Ghost grabbed his boxers from the floor and slipped them up his thighs.

Charlie pulled a sweatshirt over her head and ran for the door. "I'll distract her while you find more clothes."

His laughter followed her out the door and down the hallway to Lolly's room.

Her chest swelled with an unbidden joy at the

sound. The joy faded when she thought about the end of the week and his ultimate departure. She wasn't certain her heart could take the pain again. Refusing to think that far ahead, she entered Lolly's room and found her standing by the bed, pushing her bright auburn hair out of her face. "I'm hungry," she said.

"Let's get you dressed and then you can help me fix breakfast." Charlie spun her daughter away from the door and walked her over to her dresser.

As Charlie helped Lolly choose an outfit, out of the corner of her eye, she saw Ghost pass by in the hallway, with a big grin and a little wave.

When Lolly was dressed in a hot pink shirt, jeans and her pink cowboy boots, she was hard to hold back.

Charlie stepped out of her way, hoping Ghost was completely dressed and presentable. Apparently he was, because she heard Lolly in the kitchen talking to him.

With a few minutes to herself, Charlie washed her face, brushed her hair and her teeth and dressed in something more attractive than jeans and a bulky sweatshirt. Feeling a little more put together in dark jeans, a white blouse and her cowboy boots, her curly hair secured behind her head in a barrette, she entered the kitchen to find Ghost and Lolly waiting for her, the stove cold, the kitchen table empty.

"We're going to have breakfast at the tavern," Lolly said, grinning.

"We are?" Charlie's gaze met Ghost's, her brows rising.

"We are. My treat," he said. "Shall we go?" He took Lolly's hand in his and cupped Charlie's elbow.

"Actually, it sounds good." She hadn't treated herself or Lolly to a breakfast out in a very long time. Eating at a fast-food restaurant in Bozeman on her way to drop Lolly at the daycare didn't count.

Ghost insisted on taking his truck, moving Lolly's booster seat into the back center seat of the crew cab. Lolly liked being high above the ground, claiming she could see everything.

Charlie climbed into the passenger seat and waited for Ghost to slip into the driver's side and start the engine. "Anything else from Kevin?"

He shook his head. "No."

"We could stop by there on the way home, if you like."

With a nod, he reversed, turned around and headed down the road to the tavern.

Since it was early on a regular workday, the tavern parking lot was full, with vehicles lining the street, as well.

Charlie suspected they might not get a table as full as it was. But once inside, they waited for only ten minutes before they were seated in a booth near the door.

"Hi, Charlie." Lisa Lambert, a young, bleach-blonde waitress, set a cup in front of Ghost, one in front of Charlie and poured coffee into both. She winked at Lolly. "Juice or chocolate milk?" she asked.

Lolly rocked in her seat. "Chocolate milk!"

After Lisa left, Charlie tried to focus on the menu, when she'd rather stare at the man she'd made love to the night before. When the waitress returned with Lolly's chocolate milk, Charlie still didn't know what she wanted to eat.

"We don't see you in here for breakfast often, Charlie. Who's your fella?"

Charlie's face heated. "He's not—"

Ghost stuck out his hand and smiled at Lisa. "Jon Caspar. Nice to meet you." He leaned close to read her nametag. "Lisa, is it?"

She shook his hand, blushing. "That's right. You must be new in town. I know I'd remember you, if I'd seen you around."

"I'm not actually. But I'm so much older than you, you wouldn't remember me. I'm back in town for a visit." He reached across the table and laid his hand over Charlie's. "Charlie was good enough to put me up for the week."

"Are you thinking of moving back?" Lisa asked, taking a pad and pen out of her apron pocket.

Charlie's breath caught in her throat and she leaned forward, wanting to hear his answer, even though she knew he was putting on a show for Lisa.

He gave Lisa a friendly smile. "I don't know yet. It depends on the job."

"We're ready to order," Charlie interrupted.

"Oh, right." Lisa pressed her pen to the tablet. "What would you like?"

They placed their orders and Lisa left, her cheeks

flushed with color from the smile Ghost gave her before she turned away.

Charlie wanted to smack the grin right off his face. She'd slept with him the night before. How could he flirt with the waitress in front of her?

"Nice one, that Lisa," he said, with a smile playing around his lips. "Why don't I know her?"

Charlie's lips thinned. "Because she was practically in diapers when you were in high school."

He cocked his brows. "Jealous?"

"Not in the least. She's barely out of high school. What use would you have with her? She's not much older than Lolly."

Lolly glanced up from her chocolate milk, her gaze curious.

Ghost's smile faded. "Okay, I'll behave myself, if you'll stop being so serious. Deal?" He held out his hand.

Charlie took his, knowing as soon as they touched, she'd feel that electric shock running through her body. And there it was, searing a path straight to her heart. "Deal."

GHOST DIDN'T KNOW why he'd flirted with the young waitress. He supposed he wanted to get a reaction out of Charlie when she was holding him at arm's length that morning.

He didn't let go of her hand immediately, staring across the table at her. "Just to set the record straight, you're the only woman who interests me."

"For now," Charlie added, trying to pull her hand from his.

He held tight, refusing to release her yet. "For always."

"Please." She finally freed her hand and placed it in her lap, out of his reach. "I find that hard to believe when you haven't been back for seven years."

She was right. He'd tried to forget her in those seven years, but he'd been unsuccessful. The intensity of his training and deployments had made the time seem to fly. But always in the back of his mind, she was what kept him sane and focused.

The tavern door opened behind Charlie.

Ghost glanced up, his gaze taking in the newcomers entering.

Charlie turned in her seat.

A man in a law enforcement uniform and a woman who appeared to be his wife stepped through the door. They waved at the man behind the counter and were shown to a seat at a table beside Charlie and Ghost's.

Charlie smiled at the man. "Good morning, Sheriff and Mrs. Scott."

The woman smiled. "Good morning, Charlie, Lolly. It's always a pleasure to see you two." She turned to include Ghost in her smile and greeting. "And you are?"

The sheriff nodded, his gaze narrowing on Ghost. "Aren't you Tom Caspar's son?"

Ghost nodded and reached across to shake the sheriff's hand. "Tom is my father."

"Used to be the foreman out at the Dry Gulch Ranch, wasn't he?" the sheriff asked.

"That was him," Ghost said.

"How's he doing down in Florida?"

Ghost grinned. "They love that they haven't had to shovel one scoop of snow since they moved."

The sheriff smiled, nodding. "That's good. Thinking about taking Fran down there for a vacation to see if it's something we'd like for our retirement."

"You should visit my folks," Ghost said. "I'm sure they'd love to see you."

"Might do that." The sheriff turned his attention to the menu.

Lisa returned with three plates of food, setting them in front of Charlie, Ghost and Lolly. "Enjoy," she said and walked away.

The door behind Charlie swung open again with a bang that shook the booth they were sitting in.

Ghost frowned, his gaze following the man who'd entered. He thought he recognized him. His father had met with him on more than one occasion to discuss trading bulls. He'd called him Vanders.

"Sheriff Scott, what are you going to do about the cattle thieves who stole my herd?" the man shouted.

Charlie spun in her seat. "LeRoy?"

He ignored her, his attention on the sheriff. LeRoy Vanders stomped toward the section where the sheriff and his wife sat. He planted his fist on the table and glared at the man.

"LeRoy, we've been over this. You signed on to graze your herd on government property. You read the contract. So, they raised the rates. The contract you signed gives them the right. And it's still cheaper than leasing private property." Sheriff Scott tilted his chin up and narrowed his eyes. "Pay your fees and I'll bet they'll give back your herd."

"My family has been grazing our cattle on that land for over a century. As far as I'm concerned, the government stole that land and is extorting money from me." He pounded his fist on the table.

"What do you expect me to do, LeRoy? You have to take it up with the Bureau of Land Management."

"I expect you to arrest the rustlers who stole my cattle." LeRoy's voice rose. "I was due to take them to the sale. That's the money I use to feed my family and heat my house through the winter. How am I supposed to make do until spring without that money?"

"I can't help you. You have to pay your fees." The sheriff started to rise.

LeRoy pushed him back into his seat and pulled a gun from beneath his jacket.

Mrs. Scott screamed.

Charlie gasped and used her body to block any stray bullets from hitting Lolly.

LeRoy pointed the gun in the air. "I'm tired of being pushed around on my own land. I'm tired of the government taking what belongs to me. I'm tired of the law protecting the criminals and not me and my family."

Ghost eased out of his seat, keeping low, staying out of LeRoy's peripheral vision. He didn't want to startle the man into pulling the trigger. At the angle he was currently holding the gun, LeRoy would put a sizable hole in Ghost if he fired the weapon.

"LeRoy, put down the gun and discuss this like a reasonable man."

"I'll show you reasonable," LeRoy said. Before LeRoy could pull the trigger, Ghost grabbed the man's hand, jerked it into the air and yanked the gun from his grip. Then he twisted the rancher's arm up behind his back.

"Let go of me, damn you!" LeRoy shouted. "Mind your own business. This discussion is between me and the sheriff."

Ghost leaned close to LeRoy's ear. "This discussion stopped being just your business when you pulled the gun." Ghost nodded toward the sheriff. "You want to take him away, or should I?"

A young sheriff's deputy burst through the door. "Got a call from dispatch. Where's the perpetrator?"

The sheriff shook his head. "Over here, Matthews."

Matthews hurried to where Ghost held Mr. Vanders immobile. He snapped the cuffs on the man's wrists and led him toward the exit.

Vanders twisted out of Matthews's grip. "This isn't over by a long shot, Sheriff. I'm not the only one angry about what's going on. You just wait. This isn't the last you'll be hearing from us." He glared at Ghost and Charlie. "And we don't take kindly to interference."

Matthews hooked LeRoy's arm and dragged him out of the door.

Ghost waited until the man was out of the building before he relaxed.

Sheriff Scott held out his hand. "I'll take that. It's evidence."

Ghost gladly handed over the gun.

"Thank you for taking charge," the sheriff said. "I never would have thought Vanders would pull a gun on me. He used to be a reasonable man." He touched his hand to his wife's shoulder. "Are you okay?"

She nodded.

The sheriff sighed. "I'm thinking Florida is looking pretty good about now. How about you, dear?"

Fran pressed a hand to her chest, her face pale, her eyes worried. "People are getting crazy around here. I've never seen them so mad about so much."

A man rose from the table behind the sheriff and shook Sheriff Scott's hand. "You handled that well, Sheriff."

The sheriff frowned. "Should I know you?"

The man smiled. "Randall Gaither. I work with the Apex Pipeline Authority. It's good to see local law enforcement enforcing the laws."

The sheriff's brows twisted. "Just doing my job. Now, if you'll excuse me, I'd like to have breakfast with my wife."

The man nodded. "Of course. Of course." He resumed his seat at the table on the other side of the sheriff and lifted his coffee cup.

Ghost took his seat and stared down at his plate for a moment before he raised his chin and met Charlie's gaze.

Charlie stared at him across the table. "You're as cool as a cucumber." She lifted her glass and her hand shook so much orange juice spilled onto the table. "And I'm shaking like a leaf. You were amazing."

He shrugged. "I was hungry. I figured I wouldn't get to eat my eggs while they were hot, if someone didn't shut him up." He winked at Lolly. "How are your Belgian waffles?"

And just like that, they continued their breakfast as if a man hadn't just pulled a gun in a public place. The less he made of the incident, the better they all were. For Lolly's sake, he didn't let on that he'd been almost as shaken as Charlie. A man had entered the tavern with a gun. He could have started shooting and hurt Charlie or Lolly.

Ghost couldn't let that happen. Wouldn't let it. Hopefully, their problem was solved by the arrest of LeRoy Vanders. Maybe now, they could relax and enjoy the rest of the week.

He shook his head. Nothing ever was that easy. Hadn't Vanders said he wasn't the only one unhappy about the current state of government in Wyoming? If he was right, he might have been only the tip of the iceberg.

The week ahead didn't look like it was going to be a picnic.

Chapter Nine

"Is today Mother's Day Out?" Lolly asked as they left the tavern.

Charlie had barely been able to choke down her food. After all of the excitement, the patrons of the tavern had either gotten up to leave or stayed to gossip about LeRoy's tirade and Ghost's handling of the situation.

Lisa had been all over Ghost. Forney, the tavern owner, had offered to give them their meal for free.

Ghost had insisted they could pay and did so. He didn't look comfortable with the notoriety. As soon as Lolly finished her meal, he hurried them out the door.

Charlie nodded. "As a matter of fact, today is Mother's Day Out. Would you like to go play at the center?"

"Yes, please. Can I go?" Lolly danced around Charlie, her eyes wide, her hands pressed together. "Please?"

Charlie glanced over her head at Ghost. "Think it would be okay?"

"Are they inside much of the day?"

"They have arts and crafts and play games in the center."

"It should be okay. We can give the teacher a heads-up to be watchful."

Charlie stared down at her daughter and sighed. The threats had been against her, not her daughter. With LeRoy detained, perhaps the problem had been solved. "Okay," she said to Lolly. "You can go for a couple of hours." It would give her time to meet with Kevin and his computer guy to see if they had anything more to tell them. She was anxious to hear what they found at the address Caveman was supposed to check out that morning.

"Do you remember where the community center is?"

Ghost nodded. "I think so."

"That's where they have the Mother's Day Out. Lolly goes three times a week to play with her friends during the summer." She started to help Lolly up into the truck, but Ghost nudged her aside.

He lifted Lolly, settled her into the booster seat and buckled the seat belt around her.

When he rounded the truck to hold the door for Charlie, he whispered in her ear. "Are you sure it's a good idea to leave her at the daycare?"

"The threats were against me," Charlie said. "Not Lolly. And she so looks forward to going. I hate to disappoint her." Though she'd had the same misgivings. "How about we let her stay long enough for us to do some digging here in town? We won't be far, if anything happens."

He nodded. "Okay." Ghost helped her up into the truck and climbed into the driver's seat.

The community center was on the edge of town, with a wide, open field used for baseball, soccer and football practice. The center was a converted US Army Armory. The inside was a gymnasium with basketball hoops on either end of the open room. Back when the US Army National Guard occupied the building, they had used the gym for formations on bad weather days and for hip-pocket training in buddy care and field stripping their weapons.

Now the gym was used by locals for the occasional game of basketball and for the Mother's Day Out program, offering the community children a place to play with others their age.

As they drove up to the center, Ghost commented, "Looks better than when I used to come here."

Charlie smiled. "We recently had a Fix It Day. Everyone turned out to paint and do much-needed roof repairs."

"What's with the signs?" He pointed to a grouping of signs outside the center, indicating other businesses besides the community center.

"The city overhauled the old armory offices. The mayor and the county treasurer occupy two of them and the others were rented out to a real estate agent and an insurance salesman. They have access to the outside without going through the gymnasium where the kids play."

Charlie remembered spending a lot of time in the community center as she was growing up. From the annual Halloween parties and Christmas craft shows, to the Fall Festival dances. The community center had been a hub of social gatherings in the Grizzly Pass area.

Ghost parked and helped Lolly out of her seat.

The little girl ran toward the entrance, her face alight with excitement. She had to wait for Charlie to enter the pass code to open the outer door. But once inside, she ran through the front lobby straight into the gym.

Ghost and Charlie followed at a more sedate pace.

Inside, a dozen children were playing four square on the wooden floor of the gymnasium, their shouts echoing off the walls.

Charlie found the woman who ran the Mother's Day Out, her friend from high school, Brenda Larson.

Brenda pushed a stray strand of hair out of her face and smiled as she weaved through a couple of smaller children to where Charlie and Ghost stood. "Charlie, I'm so glad Lolly was able to come today. Ashley and Chelsea missed her yesterday."

After hugging Charlie, Brenda stood back, her gaze raking over Ghost. She tipped her head, her eyes narrowing. "You look familiar…" Then her face lit. "Jon? Jon Caspar?" She flung her arms around him and hugged his as tightly as she'd hugged Charlie. "You look so much larger than life. You were all buff when you came through several years ago, but look at you." She stood back and ran her gaze over him again. "I barely recognized you. When did you get back in town?"

"Yesterday," he said. "It's good to see you, Brenda."

"What a wonderful surprise." She glanced from Charlie to Ghost and back. "Any special reason you're here?" She paused.

Heat rose up Charlie's neck into her cheeks. "No. Not really. He's here on leave."

Brenda's brows rose again. "Your parents moved south several years ago. I would think you would vacation in Florida with them."

Ghost shrugged. "I haven't been back here in a while. It's nice to be here and explore all of my old stomping grounds."

"I'm sure." Brenda's lips curled up on the corners. "Where are you staying?"

Charlie wasn't up for answering her friend's questions with Ghost standing beside her. "I'm only leaving Lolly for a couple of hours while I run some errands."

Brenda crossed her arms over her chest and nodded. "I see how it is. Ignore the questions and maybe she'll stop asking." She winked at Ghost. "Have it your way." She turned toward the kids. "We're making sock puppets today. I think Lolly will enjoy that. Don't forget we're going on a field trip tomorrow to the Yellowstone Nature Center. You won't want Lolly to miss that. We were able to get an educational grant from the state to fund the bus and the snacks for the trip. If you want to come and help supervise, I'd gladly take all the help I can get."

Charlie frowned. "I'd forgotten that was tomorrow. Lolly's been looking forward to the trip all summer."

"Have her here a few minutes early." Brenda touched her arm. "And don't worry if you can't come along. I know you work from home and it's hard to get away sometimes."

Charlie took Brenda's hand. "About Lolly. Could you keep an extra special close eye on her?"

Brenda glanced toward the happy child, bouncing a ball with three other little girls. "Is she not feeling well?"

Charlie explained the situation with the threats. "I don't know if she'll become a target because of my meddling."

"Wow." Brenda squeezed her hand. "I'm sorry to hear this is happening to you. I'll be sure to keep her close. We don't plan on leaving the building until after lunch."

"I'll be sure to get her before then."

Brenda's lips twisted as she stared at the little girls. "She'll be disappointed that she won't get to go out on the play set with her pals." Charlie's friend turned back to the adults. "But I understand completely. I'd be leery, as well."

"Thank you, Brenda." Charlie touched her friend's arm.

"We should get together for a girl's night out in Bozeman sometime soon."

"I could use a break," Charlie agreed. "When this mess clears, you're on."

Brenda smiled. "You sure tall, dark and hunky won't mind?"

Charlie glanced up at Ghost. He wouldn't be around when that time came around.

"Whatever makes Charlie happy," Ghost said. His gaze met hers and held it for a long time.

A flash of hope filled Charlie's chest. If Ghost really believed that sentiment, he'd stay in Grizzly Pass with her and Lolly and give up his life with the Navy SEALs. But as much as he loved the path he'd chosen, the likelihood of him leaving it behind was slim to nada.

"Come on, we have some things to check on. And I really do have a job I need to work on. My boss is patient, but he likes it when I meet my project deadlines."

After one last glance in Lolly's direction, Charlie turned toward the door.

Ghost hooked her elbow and walked with her.

The familiarity of his grip on her arm gave her comfort at the same time as it fanned the smoldering embers burning inside. If they didn't have bigger problems to solve, she'd have him take her back to her house to make love to her until it was time to pick up Lolly.

And if wishes were horses...

He handed her up into his truck and closed the door. Then he rounded to the driver's side and climbed in behind the steering wheel. "Where to?"

The first word on the tip of her tongue was *Home*.

But she tamped down the urge and answered, "Kevin's. I want to know what they've come up with."

GHOST DROVE BACK to the Blue Moose Tavern and parked in back of the building. Because it was broad daylight, he sent Charlie up first and followed, shortly after.

Garner answered on the first knock. "Come in. I'm glad you stopped by. And, by the way, thank you for disarming LeRoy before he shot through the ceiling and hit one of us or the computers."

Caveman rose from a chair beside Hack's and held out his hand.

Ghost shook it and nodded toward the computer screens. "Find anything at the physical address for the IP address?"

The D-Force man stretched and shook his head. "Nobody there, only a server and a satellite internet setup. What I gather from the neighbor a half a mile away is that Old Man Huddleston died in his sleep and no one found him until he'd stopped picking up his mail for two weeks."

Garner continued the story. "The mailman notified the sheriff who checked on him and found him in his lounge chair, dead. No one turned off the electricity or gas to the place and someone has been mailing in the payments with cashier's checks."

"The satellite internet is a hack job. Someone with a little know-how is tapped into several satellites. No subscription or paid service."

"Seems like a lot of trouble to keep a social media site up and running."

"And anonymous," Hack said.

"After the demonstration yesterday, I ran into Vanders's wife at the grocery store. She was stocking up on pantry staples, as if she was getting ready for a big snowstorm. I asked her if she'd seen the internet reports about the demonstration. She laughed and said she rarely looked at their computer and didn't know how to use it, anyway."

"That rules out Vanders's wife, but not Vanders himself as the one who'd been leaving threats with Charlie."

"You would think he would have singled me out more at the tavern, if he was angry with me," Charlie pointed out.

"We're still researching Don Sweeney. There's not much on him."

Caveman nodded. "He was the other name I came out of the demonstration with. He's younger and likes to hear himself get loud. He might be in his late twenties. I imagine he knows a little about the internet. Most kids under thirty have been exposed to computers and the internet. Hell, most of them can run circles around me."

Hack turned to face the others. "I found his name on a list of recent layoffs from the Apex Pipeline Authority. I traced him through state birth records. He's the son of a local cattle rancher, Raymond Sweeney, who fell on hard times and had to sell several hundred acres to pay for his wife's cancer treatments.

Apparently Don wanted to work on the ranch but had to take a job with the pipeline as soon as he left high school. His mother died last year. Don was laid off this year when the oil prices plummeted."

Ghost narrowed his eyes. "Has he had any run-ins with the law?"

"He had a DUI when he was nineteen, right after his brother died in a farming accident," Hack said, "But other than that, nothing else showed up on his record."

"No tie-in between him and the server setup at the Huddleston place?" Charlie asked.

Caveman rubbed his fist into his opposite palm. "Want me to have a talk with the man?"

"Supposedly, he's up in Montana looking for work in Bozeman."

"Can you verify that?" Charlie asked.

"Already did. His credit card purchases are around the Bozeman area as late as this morning."

Charlie shook her head and drew in a deep breath. "I feel a need for more groceries."

"What?" Ghost shot a glance at her, wondering why the sudden urge to buy more food when she'd been to the store the day before.

A smile tilted Charlie's lips. "Mrs. Penders, one of the owners, is a notorious gossip. If anyone knows anything, she does."

"What are we waiting for?" Ghost turned toward the door.

"*I'm* going. Alone." She gave him a stern look.

"She might clam up with both of us hitting her with questions."

Ghost frowned. "I don't like it when you're out by yourself."

"I've been managing on my own for years," she said.

Taking that punch to the gut, Ghost nodded. "Maybe so, but not with someone threatening your life."

"It's walking distance." She pressed her lips together for a moment before adding, "If you want to walk with me, you can." She held up her finger. "But you're *not* going in."

Caveman, Hack and Garner watched their interchange, their lips twisting.

Heat flooded Ghost's cheeks. He didn't like being told what to do. Still, Charlie didn't belong to him. He had no right to order her around. Even if he and Charlie were a thing, he wouldn't be able to control her. She had a mind of her own.

"She'll be okay," Garner reassured. "And you'll be right outside the store."

"Fine." He turned toward the door. "Let's go."

As they descended the stairs to the ground, Ghost worried. "I don't like leaving you unprotected."

"I'll be fine. I have my gun in my purse."

"You carry?"

"I have since before Lolly was born."

He stared at her. He'd taught her how to shoot a 9 millimeter pistol when he'd been back in town seven years ago. She'd been pretty good, even after only one lesson. "Do you practice?"

"Every chance I get. At the very least, I make it a point to go quarterly. I figure it's no use having a weapon if you don't know how to use it."

Ghost chuckled. "Okay. I feel a little better knowing you can defend yourself."

"And Lolly," she reminded him.

"And Lolly," he agreed. "But it doesn't hurt to have someone covering your six."

"Your six?"

"Navy speak for your six o'clock position," he said with a grin.

"Oh, you mean my back." She smiled. "I like it when you go all military on me. As long as you explain it to me. I don't know much about what you do."

His smile faded. "It's probably just as well. Most of it isn't pretty or something you write home about."

She touched his arm. "I hope someday you'll tell me about why you limp."

"That's easy." He shrugged. "Took shrapnel in my thigh."

She shivered. "You say that like it's no big deal."

"It happens in wartime situations."

"It must be hard to go into battle knowing you or some of your friends might not come out alive."

"Not as hard as thinking about the ones we leave behind. Most SEALs aren't worried about themselves."

"They're worried about their families," she said, finishing his thought. "Is that why you pushed me away when you were setting off for your first assignment as a SEAL?"

They walked along the sidewalk in front of the hardware store, their pace slowing as they neared Penders Grocery.

"I knew what I was getting into would be difficult. I couldn't ask you to wait for me. I'd already heard too many stories about SEALs' wives and girlfriends leaving them when they were on deployment. Some came back to an empty house. Others came back to find other men had taken up residence in their beds."

She stopped short, her hands going to her hips. "And you thought I would do that?"

"No. But other women cracked under the pressure of waiting, not knowing if their men were coming back alive or in a body bag."

"So you decided to spare me the pain?"

He nodded.

"Without giving me the choice." She stared at him a moment longer.

Ghost had left her, convinced he was doing the right thing by letting her live her life without the worry of losing him. Looking at the color in her cheeks, the anger blazing from her eyes, he decided he might have been wrong.

They'd arrived in front of the grocery store.

"Are you sure you don't want me to go in with you? I can keep my distance while you're talking to Mrs. Penders."

She dropped her hands from her hips, inhaled and exhaled before she responded. "I'm quite capable of taking care of myself, and making my own decisions. And have you ever considered that you might need someone back home to cover your six? To be there when you get back and to take care of you when you were wounded?"

He stiffened. "What if I'd lost my leg or an arm? Or hell—what if I came back a paraplegic?"

"You'd still be you where it counts." She touched his chest. "And Lolly would have had a father."

"Lolly has a father. And I want to be a part of her life."

Charlie nodded. "I was wrong to keep her from you, but now isn't the right time to break that to her. We have to figure out who the hell is stirring up trouble. When the dust settles, we'll figure out how to make sure you get to see her." She lifted her chin and stuck her hand out. "Deal?"

He took her hand in his and yanked hard enough to pull her off balance.

Charlie fell into his chest, her hand trapped between them.

"Deal." He pressed a kiss to her lips, taking her mouth with a searing-hot passion he hadn't felt since the last time they'd been together. Whatever happened with the stalker, Ghost refused to walk away from this woman ever again. It had taken him seven years to figure out what was wrong with him, why he felt like he was walking through life with a hole in his chest. He'd been missing a part of himself. The part that was Charlie.

He broke off the kiss, wanting to say so much to

her, but the timing wasn't right. Somehow, it never felt right. "Go. Before I say to hell with it and take you back to your house and make crazy love to you."

She stared up at him, her tongue sweeping across her bottom lip. "And that's a bad idea?"

"When someone's after you and we don't know who it is?" He nodded. "Probably not a good idea. See if Mrs. Penders has anything to go on. Find out who has been having trouble besides Vanders."

She cupped his face with her palm. "After all of this, we need to talk."

"Damn right we do," he said. Then he turned her and gave her a gentle nudge toward the store entrance.

Chapter Ten

"Charlie!" Mrs. Penders exclaimed.

Still reeling from Ghost's kiss, Charlie had barely entered the store when the older woman swept her into her arms and hugged her.

"I heard about what happened in the tavern with LeRoy." She stood back and stared at Charlie, running her gaze over her as if searching for injuries or blood. "You're not hurt, are you?"

"No, I'm fine. No bullets were fired. No blood was shed."

"I heard LeRoy went crazy with the sheriff and threatened to shoot him."

Charlie nodded, encouraging the woman to go on about the earlier tussle with the angry Mr. Vanders. "I can't get over how LeRoy behaved toward the sheriff."

"He's just the first rancher in the county to stand up to the law. The man has to be feeling pretty desperate. With his cattle confiscated, he has no way to support his family."

"He said there were others who felt the same.

What did he mean by that?" Charlie asked. "Are there more people in the county struggling to make ends meet?"

"Oh, sweetie, there are so many."

"How could I not know this?"

"Most of them keep their troubles to themselves." Mrs. Penders leaned close. "But I hear things as they check out here at the grocery store."

Charlie almost felt guilty for prying into her neighbors' affairs. But it if helped to find Rebecca's attacker and her own stalker, then so be it. "What do you hear?"

"The Parkers are selling their prized, registered quarter horses to pay the mortgage on their place. Because of the increased fees per head of cattle, they aren't making enough off the sale of their steers to keep feeding all of their horses and pay the bills."

"Circle C quarter horses?" Charlie's stomach fell. "They've raised quarter horses for a century."

Mrs. Penders nodded. "I imagine Ryan's grandfather is turning over in his grave. And then there's Bryson Rausch."

"The richest man in the county? I remember his daughter driving a Cadillac convertible to high school. He's having trouble?"

Mrs. Penders nodded, glanced around at the store to make sure no one else was listening. "He bet on the wrong stock in the market and lost everything."

Mr. Rausch had always been very nice to Charlie when she'd run into him in town or at the county fair. Though she'd been envious of his daughter Sierra, she'd always liked Mr. and Mrs. Rausch and hated to know they were in financial trouble.

"Then there's Timothy Cramer," Mrs. Penders went on.

Charlie frowned. "Timothy?"

"Goes by Tim. You might have known his wife, Linnea."

"Oh, yes. Linnea." Her frown deepened. "Her second child died of SIDS not long ago."

Mrs. Penders nodded. "So tragic. It broke Linnea's heart and busted up their marriage."

"That's awful."

"Tim went on a drinking binge and disgraced himself with some floozy in Bozeman. Linnea tried to forgive him, but she couldn't. Not when he didn't even show up for the baby's funeral. She filed for divorce and took half of everything he owned. He's having to sell his grandmother's farm north of town because he can't afford to buy her out. And to add to his misery, he worked as an inspector for the pipeline and lost his job when he was caught falsifying reports.

"The Vanderses and the Parkers aren't the only ones hurting from the increase in range grazing fees. The Mathis family, the Herringtons, Saul Rutherford and the Greenways are all angry with the changes made by the Bureau of Land Management. They can't afford to pay the fees and they can't afford to lease private land. They'll end up selling their cattle at a loss and not having a way to support their families and pay their mortgages next year."

"I'm so sorry to hear that. It makes me sick to know so many are hurting."

"And some are more vocal than others. I wasn't surprised when I heard LeRoy was hauled off to jail. He was a powder keg set to go off. Thankfully someone stopped him from taking others down with him."

"Are there any others as angry and vocal as Mr. Vanders?" Charlie asked.

A customer walked into the store and waved at Mrs. Penders. She waved back and lowered her voice. "Oh, sure. Ernie Martin is angry because the government cut subsidies to his production of angora wool. He's been raising those goats for the past couple of years, making a killing and spending it as fast as he made it. But the money comes from the subsidies, not from the goats or the wool. Now that he's been cut off, he needs it more than ever to make payments on the second mortgage he took out to purchase all of those goats. Ernie's been madder than a hornet about losing the subsidies. He was forced to take a job with the pipeline company, but was laid off when the gas prices dropped. The poor man has had nothing but bad luck."

"Anyone else?" Charlie pushed, knowing she was running out of time with Mrs. Penders. As soon as her customer came to the counter, she'd be interrupted and remember she had a store to run and clean.

"Just about any of those folks who were tagged with bigger grazing right fees. None of them are happy. And they don't know where they'll get the money to pay the fees. Some of them have said they'll stand and defend their herds of cattle from being confiscated by the BLM. Some are willing to die." Mrs. Penders clucked her tongue. "I've never seen people so hot or determined."

"Mrs. Penders. Charlie, what are you ladies doing?" Linnea Cramer stepped up to the counter, carrying a quart of orange juice and carton of eggs. "You two look entirely too intense. What's going on?" Then her eyes widened. "Oh, wait. You have to be talking about the near-shooting at the tavern this morning. Is that it?" Linnea leaned closer. "I heard that you were there when Vanders tried to shoot the sheriff. Someone said Jon Caspar was there and subdued the man. You weren't hurt, were you?"

Charlie smiled and shook her head. "I'm fine. I feel sorry for Mr. Vanders. He was not happy about his cattle being taken."

"We're all struggling a little from the economy tanking and the oil prices falling. People in this area don't have a lot of choices for jobs. That's why we lose so many young people to the bigger cities."

Mrs. Penders squeezed Charlie's hand. "I was so glad to see you come home to Grizzly Pass."

Charlie's eyes misted as she hugged the older woman. "Mrs. Penders, you're so sweet to say that." She moved away to allow Linnea to reach the counter with her purchases.

"I wish I could say I was happy to be in Grizzly Pass, but I'm not. As soon as my ex-husband sells his property, I'm free to go wherever I choose."

"And where will that be?" Mrs. Penders asked, adding Linnea's grocery items as they spoke.

"I think I'll move to Seattle. At least there I can go to the theater, visit a museum and see the ocean whenever I want."

"I thought you liked it here in Grizzly Pass," Mrs. Penders said.

Linnea's lips thinned. "I did. But things change." She shoved the items across the counter toward Mrs. Penders.

"Is this all?" the store owner asked.

"All I can afford for now," Linnea said.

Mrs. Penders placed the items into bags and counted out Linnea's change. "I hope things work out for you."

Charlie touched Linnea's arm. "I hope you find the happiness you're searching for."

"Me, too. And the same to you, Charlie. At least, in our daughters, we have someone to love, who loves us unconditionally. Count your blessings. I know I would." She gathered her bags and left the store in a hurry, her eyes suspiciously shiny.

"Poor woman. To lose her second baby and her husband all in less than six months. Thankfully, her first child keeps her grounded." Mrs. Penders transferred her gaze to Charlie. "Here I've been talking all this time. What did you come into the store to get?"

Charlie glanced at the clock on the wall. She'd been there the better part of half an hour. Already it was getting close to lunch and time to collect Lolly. She thought about everything happening in her community, the families falling apart, losing their homes and loved ones. All she wanted to do was gather hers closer. She couldn't wait until her parents were back from their river cruise in Europe. For now, she wanted to spend time with Lolly and Ghost. "I was wondering if you had something I could take out on a picnic. I'm feeling the need to spend time with my family."

Mrs. Penders smile spread across her face. "All of the gloom and doom talk getting to you? You're a smart woman to put your family first." She grabbed Charlie's hand and walked her to the bakery section of the store where she and her husband stocked the glass cases with fresh bread and pastries. "Let me make up some sandwiches and a tub of potato salad and baked beans for you to take with you."

While she waited, Charlie thought about all of the people she knew who had reason to be mad at the world, who might want to take it out on the government. Their list of suspects had grown from one or two to what felt like an entire town. Her heart ached for all of them. But it made it abundantly clear that she, as a mother, needed to focus on what was most important. Her family.

GHOST HAD FOUND a bench in front of the hardware store and settled back to keep an eye on Penders Grocery. In the meantime, he watched as people passed in cars, trucks or on foot. Some stopped to say hello and renew acquaintances with Ghost, taking him for a short stroll down memory lane before they moved on to conduct their business or duck into the tavern for an early lunch.

He'd been there for five minutes when a man around his own age, stopped by and sat next to him. "Heard you were back in town." He held out his hand. "Tim Cramer. You might not remember me. I was a couple years ahead of you in school."

"I remember. You were our star quarterback. You helped the Grizzlies win state that year for the first time in nobody could remember how long."

Tim's lips turned upward on the corners. "That was a long time ago. Back when nothing could stop us." He stared out at Main Street. "What about you? What brings you back to this hellhole?"

"Felt like visiting the place I grew up," Ghost said.

Tim's lip lifted in a half smile bordering on a sneer. "Not someone in particular?"

Ghost shrugged. "Not really." Not at first, anyway. Now that he was there, he wanted to spend all of his time with Charlie and Lolly.

"Didn't you join the Navy?" Tim asked.

Ghost nodded.

Tim glanced his way. "What happened with that?"

"Injury sidelined me."

"Sorry to hear that." He leaned back again. "I hope you're not looking for a job. You'll have to get in line. Half the men in the county are unemployed or barely making it by."

"That's what I'm hearing," Ghost said. "They don't have to worry about me taking their jobs. I won't be here more than a week."

"Yeah, well, enjoy your vacation and tell Charlie hello. See ya around." Tim rose from the bench and walked away, his hands in his pockets.

Ghost remembered Tim as being a lot bigger. Or was it that Ghost had been a lot smaller, being three years behind him in high school? The man had been cordial and friendly, but something about him struck Ghost wrong. He tried to pinpoint it, but he couldn't. Soon Charlie emerged from the store with a sack full of food.

"What did you find out?" he asked.

"Let's go to Garner's loft before we talk." She crossed the street and stopped at Ghost's truck. He unlocked it and helped her load the bags into the back seat.

She led the way up the stairs to where they found Hack and Garner bent over a computer screen.

"Anything?" Charlie asked.

"We did some digging into LeRoy Vanders's family. Seems his sons have been in trouble with the law on more than one occasion. Some of their arrests include driving under the influence." Hack read through a report he had up on one of the monitors. "Both Vernon and Dalton have a couple of DUIs each. Vernon has been arrested on multiple occasions for hunting out of season and poaching on federal land. Dalton has been in several fistfights and has a restraining order against him. LeRoy's oldest son did some time in federal penitentiary, for shooting at a law enforcement officer."

Garner nodded toward Charlie. "What did you learn from Mrs. Penders?"

She listed a number of names and circumstances that made the men potential suspects. One jumped out at Ghost.

"Tim Cramer?"

Charlie nodded. "Divorce. He's losing his daughter and half of everything he owns, including the land and house his grandmother left him."

"I spoke with him while waiting for you to come out of the store."

Charlie's eyes narrowed. "What did he say?"

Ghost shrugged. "Nothing incriminating. He asked if I was looking for work and told me I'd have to get in line since half the men in the county were unemployed. He also told me to say hello to you." He captured Charlie's gaze. "I couldn't read anything into what he said."

"I ran into his ex-wife in the store. Was he watching for her to come out, do you think?"

"Was that the woman who came out before you did?"

"Yes."

"No, he was gone before she emerged."

"We'll look into his background and see if we can come up with anything." Garner half sat on the edge of a table, his leg dangling over. "I feel like we're searching for the needle in the haystack."

"I checked the Vanderses' utility bills," Hack said. "They have a phone line and internet. They are all on the same plan. They might be involved in whatever takeover they're planning, but we don't know if it's one of them, or all of them. And we don't know if they are computer savvy enough to tap into Charlie's webcam. That takes more sophistication and technical knowledge."

"Check Cramer, Rausch and Parker," Charlie said. "Any one of them would have to be computer savvy to do their business. Raising prized horses would require a website and email in these times. A man who makes and loses his wealth in the stock market is heavily involved with technology. And a man working for the pipeline as an inspector has to have the ability to communicate using modern technology."

"On it," Hack said.

"In the meantime, we're heading out to lunch," Charlie said.

Ghost shot a glance her way. "We are?"

She nodded. "After we pick up Lolly."

As they descended the stairs, he asked, "Where are we going for lunch?"

She responded, "Out."

Ghost wasn't sure he liked the vague answer, but he went with it. "Just promise me we're not going into the lion's den."

She shot a sideways glance at him. "Huh?"

"You know. We're not taking Lolly into a potentially dangerous location where crazy men wield guns."

Her lips twitched and a smile spread across her face.

Ghost swallowed hard on the constriction in his

throat. This was the Charlie he remembered from seven years ago. Happy, carefree and in love with life.

"Uh, Ghost, we've already done that today. You remember. The tavern?"

He would have laughed at her teasing, but the thought of LeRoy Vanders shooting that gun inside the restaurant where Lolly and Charlie were close enough to be killed with a single bullet made his chest hurt. "Yeah."

She was right, but it wasn't funny.

Lolly was in the middle of playing hopscotch with her girlfriends when they arrived. She dragged her feet, her bottom lip sticking out just a little. "Can I stay longer?"

"No, sweetheart," Charlie said, taking her daughter's hand. "But I have a special surprise I think you'll like."

Lolly's face perked and she hopped up and down. "What is it?"

"My question, exactly," Ghost muttered.

"Now, it wouldn't be a surprise if I told you, would it?" Charlie winked at Lolly and lifted her chin when she glanced toward Ghost.

He liked this teasing, fun Charlie. She didn't seem as weighted by responsibility. She appeared to be making an effort to include them in the fun.

Ghost went along with her. "Come on, sugar bear." He swung Lolly up in his arms and carried her toward the truck. "The sooner we get going, the sooner we discover what this big surprise is."

Minutes later they were on the road heading toward Charlie's house.

As Ghost neared the turn, Charlie put her hand on his arm. "Keep going."

"Where to?" he asked.

"I think you'll know when you get there." She sat back in her seat. "Follow the highway heading south out of town."

He increased his speed as he left the town limits and hit the open road. Before long, his instincts knew where they were going without Charlie telling him. "We're going to the Dry Gulch Ranch, aren't we?"

She smiled.

His chest tightened, his mind filling with memories of growing up on the Dry Gulch Ranch. Five generations of Whitakers had owned the ranch. Ghost's father had worked for the fourth of the five. Ghost had grown up with Trace Whitaker, riding horses, swimming in the creek, hunting and fishing on the Dry Gulch. They'd been best friends even though his father had worked for Trace's father.

"Has Trace returned from his stint in the Army?" Ghost asked.

"Not yet. But the foreman is aware we're coming out and Trace left word with him that you're welcome to have run of the ranch anytime you're home on leave."

"I haven't been back since my parents moved away."

"It hasn't changed a whole lot. I came out once to help the foreman's wife set up her new computer."

Ghost focused his attention on maneuvering through the huge gate with the cattle guard over the road. Then he drank in the view leading up to the first place he'd ever called home. The winding drive through pastures with the mountains as a backdrop was forever seared into his memory.

He rolled down the window to smell the scent of the pinion pines as he neared the ranch housing compound. The drive wove through a stand of trees. At the last curve, the trees seemed to part and the big rock-and-cedar house with the wide porches and huge expanses of windows appeared.

To Ghost, it felt like coming home. He turned before he reached the house and drove around to the back where the foreman's quarters sat near the huge old barn.

Charlie had been right. Nothing much had changed, except one major item. His parents wouldn't be there to welcome him and he wasn't home. This was another foreman's lodgings now.

Still, the surprise was one he could enjoy anyway.

Jonesy, the wiry cowboy with salt-and-pepper hair who'd taken over from Ghost's father, met them in front of the barn with a friendly smile.

Charlie helped Lolly out of the truck while Ghost went to greet the older man.

"Jon Caspar, you're a sight for sore eyes." Jonesy had been one of the ranch hands Ghost's father had trained to take over his position as foreman. He'd been there as Ghost was growing up on the ranch.

Ghost engulfed the man in a hug. "How are you and Mrs. Jones?"

"The missus is doing fine. She would have been here, but she's in Bozeman picking up some ranch supplies and some fabric for her quilting bee or some such nonsense." He stepped back and looked at Ghost. "You look great. The Navy must be treating you right." His smile slipped. "Heard you were injured." He tilted his head from side to side, his gaze skimming over Ghost. "Nothing permanent, I hope."

Ghost laid a hand on his leg. "Took a bit of shrapnel to the thigh. I'll be okay." He didn't go into the detail of how long the doctors spent in the operating room removing all of the shards of metal and reattaching major veins. Or the physical therapy it took to get him back to where he was, standing on his own two feet, with only a limp.

He knew he still had a long way to go before they would allow him to return to his unit. Hell, he still had to face the Medical Review Board. They might decide to medically retire him. He refused to think of that now. Not when the sun was shining and he could smell the hay in the barn and the earthy scent of horse manure.

"I saddled a couple of horses and a pony for your ride. I think you'll like the ones I picked." Jonesy's brows drew down. "I didn't think about it, but can you ride with your injury?"

Ghost wasn't sure. "I'll let you know after I've given it a try."

"I gave you a gentle gelding, and Charlie has one of our sweetest-tempered mares."

"What about me?" Lolly asked, her eyes wide, excited.

Jonesy bent to Lolly's level. "You get to ride Annabelle, a rescue pony Mr. Whitaker insisted on giving a home. She's just the right size for a little girl like you." He straightened and gave Charlie a direct look. "Annabelle is very well trained and will behave herself with the little one."

Charlie smiled. "I know you wouldn't give Lolly anything she couldn't handle. She's been taking riding lessons at the Red Wagon Stables on the other side of town, so she knows a little bit about sitting in the saddle and handling the reins."

"That's great. You can't start them too young. If you ever want to come ride, you can come out here. Mr. Whitaker would like knowing his horses are getting some exercise besides what me and the missus are giving them."

Charlie shifted the bag she carried into one arm and hugged the man with the other. "Thank you, Jonesy. It's good to see you. I don't get out here nearly enough." She glanced down at what she was carrying. "I brought the food for a picnic. I don't suppose you have an old blanket and some saddlebags?"

"A picnic?" Lolly clapped her hands. "We're going on a picnic."

"When you called to tell me what you wanted to do, I got things ready for you. The saddlebags are on Jon's horse and the blanket is tied to the back of yours."

"Thank you." Charlie kissed the older man's cheek.

A moment later, Jonesy brought out the horses and the pony and tied them to a hitching post.

Ghost helped Charlie put the food in the saddlebags and then he stood at the ready while Lolly mounted the chocolate brown pony with the cream-colored mane and tail. Annabelle stood patiently while Lolly settled into the saddle.

Jonesy adjusted the stirrups to fit her legs and handed her the reins. "If you tap her gently with your heels, she'll walk. Pull back on the reins when you want her to stop."

"I learned this at my lesson," Lolly said. She tapped her heels and the pony moved forward.

Lolly's grin filled Ghost's heart with joy. He'd never thought about children of his own, but deep down, he'd wanted them, and he'd wanted his children to ride horses and have a love of the outdoors.

Ghost held the mare's head while Charlie mounted. Then he approached the gelding, praying he could hoist himself into the saddle. Thankfully, it was his right leg that had been damaged the most. He set his boot in the stirrup and swung his leg over. So far, so good. He had trouble setting his right foot in the stirrup, but eventually managed. "Where to?"

Charlie shook her head. "You know the ranch better than I do. Lead the way."

Jonesy opened the pasture gate for them and

waited as Charlie and Lolly passed through. When Ghost rode abreast of him, he leaned toward him. "Take them to the pool in the creek where you and Trace used to swim. That's about the prettiest place on all of the ranch."

Ghost nodded. "You're right. I will."

Jonesy glanced up at the clear blue sky. "The weatherman calls for rain this afternoon."

"We'll be back before then," Ghost said.

"If you get caught up on the mountain—"

"I know of a place we can hole up until we can get down."

Jonesy smiled and nodded. "You should. You spent most of your youth in those hills." His smile faded. "Keep an eye out for bears. I've seen bear scat and claw marks on trees out that direction. They're around."

"Will do," Ghost promised.

Jonesy closed the gate behind them and headed back to the barn.

Ghost nudged the gelding into an easy trot to catch up with the others. When they came abreast, he was glad when the horse settled into a steady walk. The constant jolt of a trot was too hard on his recovering leg.

The three of them ambled across the pasture, their pace set by the pony.

Ghost pointed to wildflowers and trees, naming them for Lolly. She asked questions, curious about the birds and the ground squirrels they saw along the way. They spied antelope in the distance and admired a bald eagle flying overhead.

By the time they arrived at the creek pool it was well past lunchtime. As soon as they tied the horses to the bushes, they worked to spread the blanket over the grass and set out the food Mrs. Penders had prepared for their picnic.

Ghost ate in silence, enjoying the sounds of the birds and the rustle of leaves as a gentle breeze rippled through the branches. When they finished, they packed the leftover food in the saddlebag and set it aside.

Charlie stretched out on the blanket, her arms crossed behind her head, a smile lifting the corners of her lips.

Lolly played nearby, skipping stones in the pool.

Ghost leaned up on one elbow, his gaze on Charlie, Lolly in his peripheral vision. "I understand why my parents moved to Florida, but I can't help thinking that this is as close to heaven as you can get."

She closed her eyes, her smile widening. "I thought you might like to get away from town for a little while."

"What made you think of coming here?"

Her smile slipped as she looked up at him. "After listening to Mrs. Penders talking about all the troubles people were having, I needed a pick-me-up, and I figured you could use one, too. Life's too short to go around looking for what's wrong with it. If you just open your eyes, you can see the beauty all around you."

Ghost nodded, soaking in the beauty that was Charlie. "I agree."

"Seriously, look around us. Have you seen anything more beautiful?"

"Never."

She turned toward him. "You're not looking at the trees and the sky."

"No. I'm not." He touched her cheek with the back of his knuckles. Her skin was as soft and smooth as it had been seven years ago. And her lips… He bent to taste them.

She didn't resist. Instead, she opened to him and met his tongue with her own in a long, languid caress that stirred his blood and made his heart beat faster.

Eventually, he lifted his head to stare down at her.

"Remember the last time we were here?" she asked, cupping his cheek with her palm.

He nodded. "We skinny-dipped in the pool."

She smiled. "Uh-huh. I think this is where Lolly was conceived."

He shook his head, his heart full to bursting. He glanced across at Lolly, the beautiful little girl with hair as fiery as her mother's.

A movement behind the child made Ghost refocus his attention on the dark brown woolly mass on the other side of the pool, rearing up on its hind legs.

Grizzly!

Chapter Eleven

Ghost lurched to his feet. "Lolly," he said, his voice low and urgent. "Lolly," he said a little louder.

She was bending over picking flowers.

Charlie rolled to her feet and stared in the direction Ghost was looking. Her gasp indicated she'd seen what he was looking at. She started forward, but Ghost put out a hand to stop her. "Get to the horses and be ready to mount with Lolly. I'm going to distract the bear while you two get away."

"You can't run on that leg. I should distract her while you and Lolly get away."

"Just do it," he said, his voice low, his tone unbending.

Charlie left the blanket and the saddlebag and eased toward the horses, quickly untying them from the bushes.

Lolly had yet to see the grizzly. She glanced up and looked in Ghost's direction. "Aren't these pretty?" she called out.

Ghost froze, his gaze on the grizzly across the

pool from Lolly. Then he saw movement in the brush behind the big bear. Two cubs emerged.

Holy hell. It was a mama grizzly and her two cubs. Lolly was in mortal danger.

"Lolly, look at me," Ghost said. He bent to gather the saddlebag and blanket. "Sweetheart, go to the horses." In a commanding tone, he said, "Now."

She frowned, looked down at the flowers and back up at him, "But—"

"Now," he repeated swinging wide, away from Lolly toward the narrower end of the pool. If the grizzly charged, it would be slowed by the deeper water. In which case, Lolly would have time to run to the horses. Hopefully, Charlie would get her in the saddle and the hell out of there before the grizzly cleared the pool.

If the bear was smart enough to go around to the shallow end, she'd focus her ire on Ghost and he'd use the saddlebag and the blanket as distractors to give himself time to get away.

That was the plan and the backup plan. It was up to the bear to make the first move.

Lolly frowned and started toward the horses.

The grizzly mama roared and ran into the water.

Lolly spun toward the sound, saw the grizzly and screamed.

"Run!" Ghost yelled.

"Run, Lolly!" Charlie said. She had the horses' reins in her hands. They'd spotted the grizzly and were dancing backward, pulling her away from Lolly.

The girl seemed to be frozen for a moment. Then

she dropped the flowers, turned and ran as fast as her little feet could carry her, straight for her mother.

The grizzly started into the water. When it got too deep, she changed direction toward the shallow, narrow end where Ghost was waiting. He waved the blanket, catching her attention.

The bear roared again and ran toward him.

Ghost took off, pain shooting through his bum leg. Too late, he remembered he wasn't as agile as he used to be. He sure as hell couldn't outrun a grizzly. His only hope was to fool her into attacking the blanket while he climbed a tree. He wasn't fool enough to believe she wouldn't climb up after him, so he'd have to make the blanket convincing enough to keep her occupied while he made good his escape.

The mama bear roared again and charged out of the deeper water toward him.

Ghost ran for the brush. As he passed a big bush, he lifted the blanket letting it catch the wind enough to spread it out, then he laid it down over a tall bush and ran behind it.

Moving from bush to bush, he ran as fast as he could, careful not to let the grizzly see him. When he reached a tree he thought he could climb, he popped his head above the bushes enough to locate the grizzly.

She was mad, slapping at the blanket and the bushes with her murderous claws. Once she'd ripped the blanket to shreds, she reared up on her hind legs again and gave another terrifying roar.

Ghost eased himself up into the tree, reaching only for the branches on the far side of the thick trunk. Several times he leaned around the side to spy the grizzly sniffing through the bushes, trying to find him.

He kept climbing, higher and higher. The narrower the branches, the less likely the grizzly could reach him. Despite common misconception, he knew grizzlies could climb trees. It was harder for them than for the black bears, because of their giant claws, but they could climb. His best bet was not to draw attention to himself.

When he'd gone as high as he could, he stopped and remained absolutely still.

The bear kept coming, her nose to the ground, sniffing for him. When she reached the base of the big tree, she circled it several times, sniffing and looking up into the branches.

Ghost held his breath, praying she didn't see him and hoping Charlie and Lolly had gotten far enough away that the grizzly couldn't easily catch up to them.

Several minutes crept by. The bear reared on her back legs and hugged the base of the tree. For a heart-stopping moment, Ghost thought she would climb.

Then the sound of a cub calling out in the woods came to him and the grizzly at the same time.

For a moment, she continued to stare up into the branches of the tree. With one last roar, she dropped to all fours and hurried toward the sounds of her cubs.

Ghost watched her until he couldn't see her anymore. Then he gave it another two or three minutes before he eased his way down through the branches.

As he got close to the ground, he paused, took a moment to scan the area. When he was absolutely positive the bear had gone, he slipped to the ground and crept through the woods, making his way toward the pool. The grizzly and her cubs had moved on.

Ghost walked back along the trail they had arrived on earlier, hoping to catch up to Charlie and Lolly. His leg ached and the clouds had settled in over the hills.

Soon fat drops splattered on the ground and in his face. Part of him hoped Charlie and Lolly had gone back to the barn. Another part hoped they were just ahead of him on the trail.

The drops turned to a deluge of cold rain soaking through his clothes, chilling him to the bone.

He was wiping his eyes for the tenth time when he glanced up to see dark masses blocking the trail ahead. For a moment his heart skipped several beats. His first thoughts were of the bear and her cubs. Then he could make out the shapes of two horses and a pony, a woman leading them and a little girl huddled close to her mother's legs.

Limping faster, Ghost hurried toward them. "Charlie! Lolly!"

They turned as one and ran toward him, flinging their arms around him.

"We were so scared," Lolly said, her words coming out on a sob.

"Are you all right?" Charlie asked, rain streaming down her face. She leaned back and studied him, her gaze going over him from head to foot.

"I'm fine. I don't think I've climbed a tree that fast since I was a kid." He grinned and lifted Lolly into his arms. "Come on, I know of a hunting cabin close by. We can take shelter until the storm passes."

He settled Lolly on the pony, helped Charlie into her saddle and pulled himself up onto his horse.

Within a few minutes, he'd found the cabin they'd used during the fall hunting season, years ago. The door opened easily and the inside was dry, even if it wasn't warm. Fortunately, someone had stacked dry cordwood next to the potbellied stove. Matches and tinder were right where they had always been. Soon Ghost had a fire going and the interior of the cabin grew cozy warm.

The one-room structure had two twin beds, the thin mattresses folded over to keep the dust from settling on the surface.

Charlie stood at the window, staring out at the rain coming down. "It doesn't look like it will let up soon and it'll be getting dark soon."

Ghost removed his soaked shirt and hung it on a nail on the wall, close to the stove. "We might as well get comfortable. Looks like we'll be spending the night."

Lolly sat on one of the two chairs, her eyes wide. "Will the bear find us here?"

"No, sweetheart," Charlie reassured her.

"If she does, will she break down the door?" Lolly shivered.

"You'll be okay here in the cabin," Charlie said.

"She only chased us because she was protecting her babies."

"I'm scared," Lolly whispered, a violent shiver shaking her body.

Charlie smoothed a hand over her daughter's damp head. "You know what I do when I'm scared?"

Lolly shook her head.

"I get busy." She drew Lolly to her feet. "Let's get these beds ready to sleep in."

Ghost pitched in to help them shake the dust from the mattresses. They found sleeping bags rolled up in an airtight plastic container in one of the corners. On one of the shelves they found cans of beans and corned beef and hash. Another shelf contained a pot and an old, manual can opener. Soon, they had dinner of beans and corned beef and hash.

Charlie stripped Lolly out of her damp clothing and tucked her into a sleeping bag. She hung the items near the stove to dry.

With the warmth of the fire, a full belly and the people he loved surrounding him, Ghost couldn't think of a place he'd rather be.

Could he have a different life than that of a SEAL? Was he ready to leave it to the younger, more agile men coming out of BUD/S training?

He looked around at the small cabin, tucked away from the world and realized this was his world. These were the people he cared most about. He wasn't sure of what he'd do career-wise, but he would take into account the need to be with his daughter. If Charlie gave him a second chance, he'd spend the rest of his life making up to her for the past seven years.

CHARLIE ARRANGED THE sleeping bags over the thin mattresses and settled Lolly into one of the small beds.

Lolly reached out for her mother's hand. "Will you sleep with me?"

"You bet." Charlie had already decided the beds were too small for her to sleep with Ghost. With Lolly in the same room, she didn't think it right for her to be in bed with a man who was more or less a stranger to her daughter.

She lay down beside Lolly, pulled her close and sang the soft ballad she'd sung to her daughter since she was a tiny baby.

Ghost settled in the bed beside them and turned on his side, his gaze on her and his daughter.

Soon, Lolly's breathing grew deeper and her body went limp. With her hand tucked beneath her cheek, she slept.

Charlie stared past her to the man who'd risked his life to save them from being mauled by a grizzly. With an injured leg, he'd run through the woods, providing a sufficient distraction for them to get away.

Her heart squeezed hard in her chest like it had when she'd ridden away with Lolly, not knowing if he would escape the bear. For all Charlie knew, Ghost might have been killed or wounded so badly, he could have been lying on the ground bleeding to death.

She and Lolly had ridden hard, putting half a mile

distance between them and the pool where the grizzly had appeared.

About that time, the clouds lowered on them. It began to drizzle and Charlie couldn't go any farther without knowing. She'd turned back the way they'd come, determined to find Ghost. Lolly had been just as worried about him, insisting they go back.

The sky had opened up, dumping rain on them. They couldn't see ahead and the horses slipped on the trail. She'd gotten down from the saddle and set Lolly down beside her. If Ghost was to be found, she had to be close enough to the ground to see him.

When he'd emerged from the deluge, walking toward them, Charlie's heart had nearly exploded with the joy she'd felt.

She and Lolly had run to him, hugging him close. At that moment, Charlie knew she was still hopelessly and irreversibly in love with the man.

And she'd been terribly wrong to keep news of his daughter from him.

"I'm sorry," she whispered, capturing his gaze in the soft glow coming from the potbellied stove.

His brows dipped. "For what?"

She smoothed a hand over her daughter's drying hair. "For keeping Lolly from you."

"I didn't make it easy for you to come out and tell me," he said. "I'm sorry I was so selfish when I left, that I didn't consider what I was leaving behind."

"You were just starting your career. You didn't need to be saddled with the worry of a family."

"And you shouldn't have had to go it alone with a child to care for."

"We made mistakes," Charlie said.

"The question is, do we continue to make the same mistakes, or do we make things right?"

His words were softly spoken, but they were heavy, weighing on Charlie's mind. "You still have a career with the military. I can make sure you see Lolly on holidays."

"I want to be with her more than that."

Charlie's gut clenched and her breath caught in her throat. Was he going to sue for custody? God knew he had a right to.

"Being back…being with you…makes me want more." He swung his legs over the side of the little cot and winced. "Being a SEAL used to be everything to me. The training I went through made me want to prove something to my team and to myself. But after the first year or two, I realized there will always be another battle and another enemy to fight. I didn't think it would be right to bring someone else into my personal life, when my life wasn't guaranteed."

"Nobody's life is guaranteed," Charlie argued. "I could be hit by a bus tomorrow. Or worse, we could be targeted by homegrown terrorists. You can't live thinking about what *could* happen. You have to muddle through with what you know and what you have."

"I know that, but a SEAL's life expectancy is a hell of a lot lower than most people's. It wouldn't be fair to subject a loved one to the constant worry."

Charlie stiffened, the heat of anger rising in her chest. "So you make that determination unilaterally? Have you ever thought it isn't fair to exclude a loved one from the decision?"

His lips twisted. "I thought it was the right decision."

"Well, you might be the only one who thought it. If you bothered to include all involved in the decision-making process, you might have come to an alternate conclusion."

Charlie flipped over onto her other side. Her eyes stung and she swallowed hard. She wouldn't cry another tear for Ghost. The man could be so thickheaded. The way he was thinking would doom them to the same mistake they'd made seven years ago. When would he ever learn?

With a child to care for and protect, she couldn't spend her days mooning over a man who couldn't commit.

"Charlie, I've never stopped loving you," he said.

"Yeah, yeah," she muttered, without turning over. "You have a funny way of showing it." The last of her words came out garbled as she choked back a sob.

"Please don't turn away from me," he said.

"I have a job, Lolly has plans for tomorrow and I need sleep. I have two lives to think of. Figure out your own life."

"But—"

"Please," she whispered. "Just leave me alone. I'm too tired to think or argue."

"We're not through with this conversation," he said, his tone firm.

She lay silent, tears slipping down her cheeks. She refused to sniffle. He couldn't know that he was breaking her heart all over again.

Charlie lay awake, pretending to be asleep long after Ghost settled back in his bed.

She hurt so much it was a physical pain she couldn't ignore. Before the sun rose, she was up, looking out the window at the gray light of predawn.

"How long have you been awake?" Ghost whispered.

"Not very." She didn't face him. She couldn't. Her heart weighed heavily in her chest and one little word from the man she loved and she might burst into tears.

"I'm hungry," Lolly said. She stretched in the bed and rubbed her knuckles against her eyelids. "Are we going home?"

"As soon as you get your clothes and boots on, we can start back," Charlie said.

Lolly rolled out of bed and dressed in her dry clothing and then pulled on her pink cowboy boots. "My boots are still wet."

"We'll get you into some dry clothes and shoes when we get back home."

"And breakfast?" Lolly asked.

"And breakfast." Charlie forced a smile to her lips and turned in Lolly's direction. "Ready?"

Ghost had his boots on and had tucked his shirt into his waistband. Without saying a word, he left the little cabin, gathered the horses and waited for

Charlie and Lolly to mount before he swung up onto his horse.

They rode down the mountain as the sun edged over the horizon.

Charlie's gaze scanned the hillside and the brush for grizzlies, not wanting a repeat of their encounter from the day before. The ride remained blissfully uneventful.

Jonesy greeted them at the barn, leading a saddled horse, his brows furrowed. "I was just about to ride out to find you three."

"We had a grizzly sighting and got caught in the rain," Ghost informed the man.

Jonesy shook his head. "I'd noticed bear scat in that area, but I'd hoped you wouldn't run into one."

"It was a mama and her two cubs," Lolly said. "She didn't like it that we were around."

"Glad you got away without injury. Some aren't as fortunate." Jonesy grinned. "Did you stay in the hunting cabin?"

Ghost nodded. "I'll bring some canned goods and firewood to replenish what we used."

"No, don't do that. I was going to run some up this week anyway. Glad you found dry wood and something to eat."

"We are, too," Charlie said. "Otherwise it would have been a much more uncomfortable night." She slid out of her saddle and started to lead the horse into the barn.

"I'll take care of the horses. You three look like

you could stand some breakfast. The missus has extra scrambled eggs if you're hungry."

"I'm hungry," Lolly exclaimed.

"Are you sure it's not a bother?" Charlie asked.

"She'd be happy to have someone to fuss over," Jonesy reassured her.

"We can't stay long," Charlie glanced down at Lolly. "Today is the day for the field trip to Yellowstone National Park. We have to be there early."

"I'll hurry," Lolly promised.

They made their way to the foreman's little cottage where Mrs. Jones had breakfast waiting on the table.

"How did you know we were coming?" Lolly asked.

Mrs. Jones blushed. "I was watching through the window."

"We don't want to burden you," Ghost said.

She waved her hands. "It was no trouble at all. We get so few visitors, it's a pleasure to cook for someone else."

Ghost, Charlie and Lolly took seats at the table and dug into the scrambled eggs and thick slices of ham Mrs. Jones served.

Charlie hadn't felt much like eating, but the ham and eggs hit the spot and helped lift her flagging spirits. By the time she left the Dry Gulch Ranch, she was resigned to whatever happened.

Lolly's chatter filled the silence on the drive home.

While Lolly took a quick shower, Charlie changed into dry clothes and shoes, washed her face and brushed her hair back into a ponytail. She'd considered wearing makeup, but decided it was too late to impress a man who wasn't going to stick around. Resigned to going without makeup, she ducked into her office and powered up her computer. Once the monitor flashed to life, she clicked on the URL of the Free America group and scrolled through the messages. She'd just about reached the bottom when Lolly called out.

"I'm ready." Her daughter entered her office wearing jeans and her community center T-shirt and sneakers.

"You were fast," Charlie remarked. She glanced at the computer one last time and frowned.

A message popped up on the group that caught her attention.

Let it begin with a meeting of the mines

A chill slithered down Charlie's spine as she turned toward Lolly. The message wasn't directed at her, this time. It was directed toward the Free America group. So much for assuming LeRoy Vanders was the leader. He was safely in jail with no access to the internet.

Though Charlie wasn't sure what the message meant, one thing was certain, something was about to start. What, she didn't know.

"Come on, Mommy. We're going to be late and miss the trip." Lolly spun on her heels and ran down the hallway.

Charlie rose and met Ghost by the front door where he held Lolly's hand.

What did it mean? Had they meant to spell mines

or had it been a misspelling intended to be minds? The hills were dotted with abandoned mines from the gold rush era. "Ready?" Charlie asked, her mind on the message, her stomach churning.

"Yes!" Lolly jumped up and down. "We're going to Yellowstone today. We get to ride on a bus."

Her excitement brought a small smile to Charlie's lips. As she gathered her keys and purse from the hallway table, the phone next to them rang.

Charlie froze, almost afraid to answer. Would it be another harbinger of potential doom? She lifted the phone from the charger. "Hello."

"Charlie, Kevin here."

"Hey, Kevin," she said. "What's up?"

"We have some satellite images that might interest you and Ghost."

Her gaze met Ghost's and a tremor of awareness rippled through her. "We're on our way to town. I have to drop off my daughter at the community center, then we'll be there."

"See you in a few, then." Garner ended the call.

Ghost met her gaze with a question in his eyes.

"He has some satellite images he wants us to look at." She looped her purse over her shoulder and followed Ghost and Lolly outside.

"We can take my Jeep. I feel like driving." She might as well get used to being that single parent again. It wouldn't be long before Ghost left.

Ghost didn't argue, but moved the booster seat from his truck into the backseat of her Jeep and buckled Lolly in.

Once again, Lolly jabbered away. If the adults weren't responding, the little girl was too excited about riding in the bus to notice.

As they neared town, Charlie pulled up in front of the tavern first. "Why don't you get started reviewing the images? I'll be back in less than five minutes."

"I can wait," he said, not budging from the passenger seat.

"Please," she said, staring straight out the front window without looking into his eyes. "I need just a few minutes alone."

He hesitated.

In her peripheral vision she could see his jaw harden and his lips press into a thin line. Then he leaned into the backseat and chucked Lolly beneath her chin. "Have a great time at Yellowstone. Don't pet any bison while you're there."

"Don't be silly. Bison are wild animals," she said.

He climbed out of the Jeep and stood on the sidewalk watching as they drove away.

Charlie felt as if she was leaving him for good, knowing perfectly well she'd be back to study satellite images. But she couldn't help looking at him in the rearview mirror. He looked so sad, and that made her heart hurt even more.

What were they going to do? How could they fix a relationship that wasn't meant to be?

More immediately, she worried about the message.

Let it begin with a meeting of the mines.

Chapter Twelve

Ghost wanted to kick himself. Hard. Last night he could have made things right with Charlie. He could have told her he loved her and wanted to be with her more than he wanted to breathe. Instead, he'd fumbled the pitch and struck out.

She'd dropped him off like she wanted nothing to do with him. If he didn't know better, he'd bet she didn't come back to view the images Garner's team had come up with.

And then there were the threats against Charlie that had him worried. She ran around town without him as if no one would attempt to harm her. And maybe no one would, but that didn't make Ghost any more confident. He had half a mind to jog down to the community center and make sure she was all right. It was only a few blocks. But wait. He wasn't quite up to jogging. Not without a whole lot of pain.

He didn't believe LeRoy Vanders was the one posting the threats. Frankly, the man didn't seem technologically advanced enough to track her back to her webcam. But if not Vanders, then who?

Yeah, he was being foolish. Instead of following her, he climbed the stairs to Garner's office and knocked.

Caveman opened the door. "Good, you're here. You'll want to see this." He stepped aside.

Garner, Caveman and Hawkeye stood at the large monitor mounted on the wall, staring at a satellite image.

Garner glanced over his shoulder. "Ghost, glad you made it. Where's Charlie?"

"She went on to the community center. She'll be here in five minutes."

"Do you want us to wait until she gets here to go over what we found?"

"No, she said to get started without her." Ghost stepped up beside Garner. "What's this a picture of?"

"The mountain between Grizzly Pass and the highway turnoff that leads to Yellowstone National Park. The image is from a week ago." Most of the mountain was dark and dense with lodgepole pine trees. Garner pointed to a place that appeared to be a gash in the landscape. "See this?"

"Looks like an old mining camp," Ghost noted.

"It is. We looked it up. It's the abandoned Lucky Lou's Gold Mine. It played out about forty years ago and has been closed since." Garner glanced back at Hack. "Show two nights ago."

Hack clicked his mouse and the screen in front of the others flickered. For a moment, it appeared unchanged. Until Ghost leaned closer and noticed a change in the mine area.

"Are those vehicles?"

Garner nodded. "We counted half a dozen. And if you look here at that bright dot, we think that's a campfire, and next to it are people. Show the infrared shot," he called out.

Hack clicked and another image appeared with green spots of color. Where the campfire had been was brighter, almost white.

Garner pointed to several smaller dots of green lined up from the back of one vehicle to the side of a hill. "Why would they be lined up at the back of one of the vehicles and all the way to the mine entrance?"

"Are they unloading something?" Ghost asked.

Garner nodded. "That's the only thing we could think of. Caveman, Hawkeye and I are headed out this morning to check on it."

"I want to go," Ghost said.

"Do you think Charlie will be okay without you to keep an eye on her?"

Ghost wrestled with his desire to go with her and his desire to find out what someone was storing in an old mine in the middle of the night. "I'd better stay."

The phone rang in Kevin's office.

Hack lifted it. "Yeah." A moment later, he held it up. "It's for you, Kevin."

The DHS team leader grabbed the phone. "Kevin, here." He listened for a moment and nodded. "Are you sure you'll be all right?" He paused. "Okay. I'll tell him." The man handed the phone back to Hack and turned to Ghost. "That was Charlie. The woman who was scheduled to go with the field trip got sick and couldn't make it. Charlie offered to go with them."

Ghost stiffened. "When are they leaving?"

Garner looked at him. "Now. Do you want to try to catch up to them?"

Ghost hesitated. He didn't have transportation to follow the bus and if he risked running to the community center, he might miss them. Apparently Charlie wanted a little more time to herself without him. "No."

"She should be all right. No one was expecting her to be on that field trip."

"I guess it will have to be all right."

"You could take my SUV if you want to follow and make sure they're safe," Garner offered.

"No." Ghost shook his head. Charlie hadn't wanted him along. "Let's go see what's in that mine."

Garner grabbed his keys. "We can go in my vehicle." He stopped at a large safe near the door and twisted the combination back and forth until it clicked and he opened it. Inside was an arsenal of weapons. He reached in and pulled out an AR-15 military-grade rifle and handed it to Ghost. "We don't know what we're in for at the mine. If they have stashed something illegal or deadly, they might have guards positioned there." He reached in again and handed Caveman another AR-15. To Hawkeye, he handed a specially equipped sniper rifle with a high-powered scope.

Then he moved to a footlocker beside the safe and unlocked the padlock with a key and threw it open. Inside were rifle magazines and boxes of ammunition.

"Most of the magazines are already loaded. Grab what you think you might need. You can load everything into these duffel bags. We don't want to alarm the natives as we carry them out to the SUV."

Ghost wasn't sure what they'd run into at the mine. Being armed to the teeth was better than being outgunned.

Once they had everything they could possibly need for a prolonged standoff with a small army, they headed out the door and down the steps.

Caveman carried the duffel bag with the rifles, Ghost and Garner carried gym bags filled with ammo. Hawkeye carried the case with the sniper rifle. One by one, they loaded them into the back of Garner's SUV.

With the smell of weapons oil in his nostrils and the hard shell of armored plating strapped around his chest beneath his shirt, Ghost closed the hatch.

He'd started around the side of the SUV when an explosion rocked the street.

Ghost automatically dropped to the ground and rolled beneath the SUV. His pulse pounded and flashbacks threatened to overwhelm him with memories he preferred to forget.

For a moment, he was back in that Afghan village, being fired on by a Soviet-made rocket-propelled grenade launcher manned by a Taliban fighter positioned on top of one of the stick-and-mud buildings. He lay pressed to the ground, trying to breathe past the panic paralyzing his lungs.

Chapter Thirteen

Charlie sat beside Brenda Larson in the front seat of the bus headed north toward Yellowstone National Park, wondering what Kevin had found that they'd needed to see. Though she knew Ghost had their best interests at heart, she would have liked to have been there to gauge for herself the importance of the new information.

They were ten miles out of town and the children had settled back in their seats when Brenda hit her with, "So what's up between you and Jon Caspar?"

"What do you mean?" Charlie stalled, not really wanting to talk about Ghost or what was or wasn't happening between them.

"He's back. You're in love." Brenda sat back, her brows raised, her gaze direct, unflinching. "When can we expect an announcement?"

"There won't be an announcement." Charlie stared out the window, her chest tight, her eyes stinging. A tear slipped free and trailed down her cheek. Damn. And she'd promised herself she wouldn't cry that day. The field trip was all about the kids, not her

pathetic excuse for a love life. She swiped at the tear
and grit her teeth to keep others from falling, hoping
Brenda wouldn't see them. Then she glanced at her
reflection in the window and Brenda's beside it. Too
late, Brenda could see everything in her reflection.

Her friend laid a hand on her arm. "What's wrong,
Charlie?"

What was the use holding back now? And she
really needed a shoulder to lean on. "He's going to
leave again and I love him."

Brenda's face brightened. "Maybe he'll take you
with him? Not that I want you to leave Grizzly Pass.
Friends our age are hard to come by around here."

"He doesn't think his life is conducive to having a
family." Charlie sniffed and wished her voice hadn't
sounded so wobbly.

Brenda tilted her head to the side and touched
her finger to her chin. "He might have a point. They
move around a lot."

Charlie frowned. "You're not helping. Besides, I
already knew that."

"He's a Navy SEAL. They are in a high-risk
job. He might get killed on a deployment." Brenda
smiled. "Perhaps he doesn't want you to be just another military widow."

"He won't give me that choice."

"Would you be okay with him staying in the military?"

"Of course."

"Would you move to be with him when he's not
deployed?"

Charlie nodded.

Brenda raised her hands, palms up. "Then what's the problem?"

"He hasn't asked." Another tear slipped down her cheek.

"Have you given him a chance?" Brenda chuckled. "I've seen you when you get all stubborn and hardheaded. It's pretty intimidating."

Charlie thought about how she'd shut Ghost down the night before and how she hadn't encouraged a frank conversation since. "Maybe not."

"Then wipe your tears, have fun with the kids today and when you get home, hit him up with how you feel. If he feels the same, he'll ask you to go with him. If he doesn't, at least you will know and you can stop crying over him."

"You're right." Charlie wiped her tears and straightened, forcing a smile to her face.

She squeezed her friend's hand. "Thank you. I needed someone to talk to."

"Glad to help. Anytime."

The bus lurched, flinging her forward.

Kids screamed and the brakes smoked.

"What the—" Charlie glanced up in time to see a big, army-style dump truck straddling the highway in the middle of a curve.

The bus driver had jammed his foot on the brake and now stood on it in an attempt to stop the bus before it slammed into the truck.

"Hold on!" Charlie yelled and braced for impact.

Brakes smoked and the bus skidded across the

pavement toward the truck. With a bluff on one side and a drop-off on the other, they didn't have a choice.

As if in slow motion, the bus went from fast to slow, the truck rising up before them, filling the windshield. Charlie braced herself, but couldn't close her eyes as the bus slowed, slowed, slowed but not fast enough for her. Just when she thought they would crash into the truck, the bus stopped, its front bumper scraping the side of the truck.

When the smoke from the brakes cleared, Charlie sat up and glanced back at the children, her gaze darting to the seat Lolly had occupied with Ashley Cramer and Chelsea Smith. At first she didn't see them. Then, one by one, their heads popped up over the top of the back of the seat in front of them and they looked around.

The rest of the children crawled up off the floor and into their seats, some crying, others looking frightened and disoriented.

Brenda stood and walked toward the back. "Hey, guys. Everyone okay?"

Most children nodded. One little boy shook his head, his nose bleeding, tears streaming down his cheeks.

"Come here, Elijah." Brenda gathered him up into her arms. "For now, stay in your seats until we figure out what's going on. Everything will be all right."

Charlie leaned over the back of the seat and touched the bus driver, Mr. Green's, shoulder. "Are you all right?"

He nodded. "Didn't see that coming." The old man

wiped the sweat from his brow and peered through the windshield. "That could have been really bad."

Charlie looked to either side of the truck for a driver to find out why the truck was parked in the middle of a dangerous curve. Movement around the rear of the truck captured her attention and she watched as a man emerged, wearing camouflage pants, camouflage jacket and a black ski mask. He carried a military-grade rifle with a black grip and stock and he was headed straight for the door of the bus.

Charlie's heart fluttered and a cold chill shivered down her spine. "This doesn't look good. I think the truck is the least of our worries."

Another man dressed from head to toe in camouflage followed the first, also wearing a ski mask and carrying a rifle with a curved magazine loaded in it.

They stopped at the bus door.

"Open the door," the guy in front ordered.

The bus driver shook his head, shoved the shift in Reverse and pressed the accelerator.

"Go. Go. Go!" Charlie said.

He popped the clutch in his hurry and the bus engine stalled.

The men holding the rifles pointed them at the door and opened fire.

Charlie staggered backward, the seat hit her in the backs of her knees and she sat hard.

Mr. Green grunted and slumped forward over the steering wheel.

One of the men kicked what was left of the door

open and entered the bus. "Stay down and don't move!" he yelled and waved his rifle at the occupants of the bus.

Charlie wanted to go to Mr. Green, but was afraid if she moved, the attackers would open fire in her direction and hit one of the children. So she stayed down, praying Lolly would remain seated.

The second man entered the bus, pulled the driver out of his seat and dragged him to the side. Then he slipped into the driver's seat and started the engine.

The dump truck engine roared to life. The big vehicle turned away from them and lumbered north along the highway until they reached a dirt road on the left. The truck turned onto the road and disappeared between the trees.

Charlie held her breath, as the bus turned as well and followed the dirt road the truck had taken. She wanted to go to Lolly and hold her in her arms, but she didn't want to draw any attention to herself or the children.

The kids sat in silence or softly sobbing, holding on to the seatbacks in front of them as they bounced along the rutted road.

Where were they going? What was going to happen to the children?

Charlie wished Ghost was with them. He'd know what to do. With only two men wielding guns, surely he would have been able to subdue them before they shot Mr. Green. She glanced down at the old bus driver, her stomach knotting.

The man's face was even paler than before and

his chest didn't appear to be moving. Dear God, he was dead.

Charlie closed her eyes briefly and prayed for a miracle. Then she opened them and focused on the road ahead. She had to keep her wits about her to ensure the safety of the children.

The bus slowed around a curve in the dirt road and came to an open clearing, facing a giant hill that had been carved away at the base. It appeared to be an old mine.

The hills and mountains of Wyoming were dotted with the remnants of old gold mines from the gold rush era of the 1860s. This was just one of many that had been abandoned when the gold played out.

The man driving the bus slowed, as he headed toward the entrance to the mine.

Charlie leaned forward, her heart leaping into her throat. "What are you doing?"

"Shut up!" the man wielding the rifle backhanded her, knocking her across the seat.

She picked herself up and watched in horror as he drove right up to the mine, parking the bus so that the door opened into the mine entrance.

The driver parked the bus and clicked on a flashlight.

"Everyone out!" he yelled. He grabbed Mr. Green and dragged him down the steps and into the mine.

Charlie pressed a hand to her bruised cheek. "What are you going to do with us?"

"You have two choices—shut up and get out, or die." He pointed his rifle at her chest.

She raised her hands. "I'm getting out." Charlie eased to the edge of her seat. The rifleman backed up, giving her enough room to pass.

For a moment, she thought of all the self-defense classes she'd taken. None of them had prepared her for the possibility of children being used as target practice or shields. Her instinct was to jam her elbow into the man's gut and shove the heel of her palm into his nose. But she couldn't. If he jerked his finger on the trigger, he could shoot a kid.

Charlie could never live with herself if her actions were the cause of one of these babies being killed. She glanced back at Lolly as she stepped down off the bus.

The man with the flashlight waved Charlie to the side. "Do something stupid and one of these kids will get hurt."

She raised her hands. "Please don't hurt the children. Just tell me what you want me to do. I'll do it."

"Stand over there and keep quiet." He shone the flashlight toward a stack of crates.

Charlie followed the beam and stopped when the light swung back toward the bus.

Three children dropped down from the bus, huddling together, sniffling in the dark. The flashlight swung her way.

Charlie opened her arms and the kids ran into them.

She counted them as they emerged, one by one. When Lolly reached the ground, she looked for her mother.

Charlie nearly cried. Again the flashlight swung her way and Lolly ran to her. Charlie held her in her arms, smoothing her hand over her hair. "It's going to be all right," she whispered. "I promise." Somehow they'd get out of this in one piece. She refused to break her promise to her daughter.

Brenda brought up the rear with Lolly's friends Chelsea and Ashley.

Another man joined the two in camouflage. This one was dressed all in black with a matching black ski mask. He stood beside the other two as Brenda walked by with the two little girls.

He grabbed Ashley and swung her up into his arms. "I'll take this one."

Brenda leaped forward. "Don't you hurt her!"

The man with the flashlight swung it, clipping Brenda in the side of the head.

Brenda crumpled to the ground and lay still.

Chelsea dropped down beside her, crying hysterically.

"Take the brat before I hit her, too," Flashlight Guy shouted.

Charlie rushed forward and dragged Chelsea back to where the rest of the children huddled. She told them to stay where they were and then she eased forward to where Brenda lay with her face down, her eyes closed.

"Get back!" the man with the gun yelled.

Charlie inched back to stand with the cluster of kids and waited for the men to leave or at least back up enough to let her get to Brenda and the bus driver.

The bus moved away from the opening of the mine and a triangle of sunlight shone in.

Charlie studied everything around her, looking for an escape route, counting the number of men involved, evaluating her options and coming up with no plan that would save twenty children.

Yet another man wearing camouflage stepped into the cave entrance where the original captors stood. He was bigger than first two, and he carried a 9 millimeter pistol. "Where's Cramer?"

"Hell if I know. He drove the truck," Flashlight man said.

"He was here a minute ago," the rifleman said. "Took one of the kids and walked out."

The man muttered a curse. "Dalton, find him. Vern, help me move the plate in place."

"What about them?" Vern said.

"If one of them moves, we'll shoot them," the big man said.

Based on the names they were calling each other, Charlie knew who they were. The Vanders brothers. And it appeared Tim Cramer had come along for the ride in order to steal his daughter away. Charlie would bet Cramer had already escaped the compound with his girl. Dalton wouldn't find them.

For the next few minutes, the two men worked to move a huge metal plate into position over the entrance of the mine.

Charlie took the opportunity to study the boxes lining the walls. She reached into an open one. Inside were sticks of dynamite and dozens of empty cartridge boxes. She searched for a weapon among the boxes, only to find more empty boxes. Another crate contained empty cases of what appeared to have at one time contained new AR-15s. More than the number carried by the men holding them hostage. A lot more. In one crate alone, she counted over twenty empty AR-15 boxes. And there were a lot of crates lining the walls of the mine. What were they planning? A total takeover of the state?

Once the metal door was in place, most of the light was blocked. A little at the top and sides gave just enough for Charlie to make it over to Brenda and Mr. Green. She felt for a pulse on the bus driver. His skin was cold, he lay very still and no matter how long Charlie pressed her fingers to the base of his throat, she couldn't find a pulse. The man was dead.

Her heart hurt for his wife. They were a childless couple who loved each other and their menagerie of dogs.

Moving to Brenda she touched the caregiver's shoulder. "Brenda."

Brenda moaned.

"Sweetie, please. Wake up and tell me you're all right."

She moaned again and rolled onto her back. "Why is it so dark?" she croaked.

"We're in a mine."

"Oh, God." She tried to lift her head but dropped it back to the ground. "The kids?"

"All here and okay, except Ashley Cramer."

"Where's she?" She rolled to her side and tried to push to a sitting position. "Linnea will be frantic."

"I think Tim took her."

"That bastard." Brenda pressed her hand to her lips. "Sorry."

Charlie wanted to say a whole string of curses, but it wouldn't get them out of the mess they were in. "Tim was in on this."

"What is *this*, anyway?" Brenda asked, blinking her eyes before staring around at the walls of the mine.

"The Vanders brothers have taken us hostage. We're in some mine shaft."

"Those idiots?" She tried to get up, but couldn't quite make it on her own. "What do they hope to accomplish?"

"I don't know." Charlie helped Brenda to her feet and she staggered over to the children where she collapsed to a sitting position.

The children gathered around her, all wanting to be held and comforted, every one of them frightened out of their minds.

Charlie knelt beside Lolly. "Are you doing okay?"

She nodded. "Are those bad men going to let us out of this cave?"

"I don't know if they will, but someone will find us and let us out." She hoped it was true. As far as she knew, nobody would know where to look for them.

"Mr. Caspar will find us. He's a real hero."

Charlie hugged her close. "Yes, Lolly, he is."

That's what he did. He fought for his country. For her and Lolly and everyone else. He was the real hero.

"Miss Brenda told me." Lolly snuggled against Charlie. "I'm cold."

Charlie rubbed her arms and pulled her closer.

"I hope my daddy comes soon."

Charlie swallowed the lump in her throat to say, "Your daddy?" Had she overheard them talking about her? Had she put the pieces together and guessed?

"Mr. Caspar. He's nice and he's a hero. I want him to be my daddy."

"Oh, baby." Charlie held her tight and fought the tears. She wanted Ghost to be Lolly's daddy, too. And Charlie wanted him to be her husband. If she had another chance, she'd get right to the point and ask him if he would marry them. If he said no, she'd figure out how to live without him. But on the slim chance he said yes, she'd be the happiest woman alive and follow him to the ends of the earth, if that's what it took.

"WHAT THE HELL was that?" Caveman called out from behind a parked pickup.

The sound of the Delta Force soldier's voice penetrated the fog of memories and yanked Ghost back to the present and Grizzly Pass, Wyoming.

Caveman and Hawkeye had sought cover behind vehicles while Garner knelt near the corner of a brick building. Ghost waited a moment, trying to determine where the sound had come from. When no other explosions shook the ground, he rolled from beneath the SUV and stood.

"Sounded like it came from the south end of town," Garner said.

A siren wailed from the north, heading toward the tavern.

Ghost hurried toward the front of the building in time to see a sheriff's vehicle racing south along Main Street.

"Come on," Garner said. "Let's go check it out."

All four men climbed into the SUV and took off after the sheriff.

At the other end of town people were coming out of their homes and businesses, standing in clumps, talking to each other, holding their small children close. The sheriff's car was positioned at the end of Main Street, blocking traffic from entering or leaving town.

Garner parked a block away. The men piled out and hurried toward one of the abandoned buildings on the edge of town. The front wall had been blown out, the bricks scattered across the street.

Behind them, another siren sounded and the volunteer fire department engine truck rolled down the street, passing them to stop next to the sheriff's vehicle. Firefighters jumped to the ground and started unrolling a long hose.

The sheriff emerged from the building, covered in dust, shaking his head. "You won't need that. Looks like someone set off a stick of dynamite. No fire, no smoke, just a big mess."

Ghost inhaled and let out a long, slow breath and asked, "Why?" He turned to Garner and the others. "Why would someone want to blow up an old building in a little town?"

"Kids bored in the middle of summer?" Caveman offered.

No. Ghost wasn't buying it. Someone had deliberately set that dynamite to blow in that particular building at that particular time.

"It didn't do much damage." Hawkeye studied the scene. "It was an old building not worth anything. Whoever did it, did the town a favor, getting the demolition started."

"Why would they pick this building on the south end of town?" Ghost asked, his mind wrapping around the possibilities and coming up with one. "Unless they were creating a diversion to draw all of the attention away from something."

The radio clipped to Sheriff Scott's shoulder chirped with static. "Sheriff, we have a problem," came the tinny voice.

Sheriff Scott touched the mic. "Give it to me."

Ghost's attention zeroed in on that radio and what was being said, his gut clenching.

"Someone's demanding LeRoy Vanders's release."

"Demanding?" The sheriff snorted. "On what grounds?"

"They want to negotiate his release in exchange for a busload of our kids."

The words hit Ghost like a punch in the gut.

The sheriff's face paled and everyone standing in hearing range of the sheriff's radio froze.

"What is he asking for?" Sheriff Scott asked.

"He wants you to bring LeRoy Vanders to Lucky Lou's Gold Mine in one hour, in a helicopter. If you aren't there in exactly one hour, they will blow up the entrance to the old mine with dynamite. With the children inside."

Ghost grabbed Garner's arm. "That's my woman and my kid on that bus."

"We have to work with the sheriff to get those kids to safety," Garner said. He stepped toward Sheriff Scott. "Sir."

"Don't bother me now. I have a crisis to avert." The sheriff hit his mic. "Who the hell can we call with a helicopter?"

Garner got in front of the sheriff. "I can get one in under an hour."

The sheriff looked at Garner and nodded. Then he keyed the mic. "Get Vanders ready. I'll let you know when the helicopter lands." He stared at Garner. "If you're wrong, you might cost us the lives of those kids."

"I can get one from Bozeman in thirty minutes." He gave the sheriff instructions on how to contact his resource at the Bozeman airport. A helicopter would be dispatched in less than ten minutes.

Ghost paced the pavement, desperate to do something. "We can't wait for them to make the trade. What if they decide to bury those kids in the mine anyway? They could have that whole place rigged with explosives."

"We'll make the exchange," the sheriff said. "We can't risk the lives of the children."

"Sheriff." Ghost planted himself in front of the sheriff. "You have four of the most highly skilled military men at your disposal. Let us get in there, recon the situation and report what we see."

"I don't know." The sheriff shook his head. "If they see you, they might detonate the explosives."

"We know how to get in without being seen. We can get a count on the number of combatants. You'd be better off knowing numbers in case they start shooting at the men delivering Vanders."

"He has a point," Garner added. "Let us be your eyes and ears while you're putting the exchange in place."

The sheriff stared at Garner. "How do I know you won't do something stupid?"

Ghost grabbed the man's arm. "The woman I love and my little girl were on that bus. I wouldn't do anything that would cause them harm. Please. Let us do this."

The sheriff stared into Ghost's face. "I've known you for a long time. I knew your father. He was proud that you made it through SEAL training. From what they say, only the best of the best can be a SEAL." He stared at the others. "I trust Jon Caspar. If he trusts you, I guess I have to, as well. Go."

Ghost turned to run.

The sheriff snagged his arm. "We have to bring those kids back alive. One of them is my grandson."

Ghost nodded and took off for the DHS agent's SUV. Hawkeye, Garner and Cavemen beat him to it, climbing in. Ghost settled in the seat and leaned forward, staring through the front windshield as they blew through town and north toward Lucky Lou's Gold Mine. He prayed they could get in without being seen and that none of the passengers on the bus had been hurt in the hostage takeover.

Chapter Fourteen

Lolly fell asleep, leaning against Charlie.

Unable to sit still without coming up with a plan, she eased Lolly to the floor and stood, stretching the kinks out of her muscles. She wondered how long it had been since they'd been captured. Thirty minutes? An hour? More?

Some children were still sniffling, huddled up to Brenda, seeking comfort from each other.

Charlie crossed to the metal plate covering the opening of the mine and strained to hear what was happening outside.

"They'll be here on time if they want to see those kids again," a voice said.

Charlie recognized it as the man who'd been carrying the flashlight, Dalton Vanders.

"What if they bring in the feds?" The slower, deeper voice of Vernon Vanders said. "We aren't equipped for a standoff."

"We have the detonators." The third voice could only be the man in charge. The oldest of the Vanders brothers, GW. "The mine entrance is rigged to blow.

If they don't give us what we want, we blow the entrance."

Charlie gasped. If they blew the entrance, everyone inside could be buried alive. Should, by some miracle, they live through the blast, they might suffocate before anyone could dig them out.

"They better hope they bring Dad in that helicopter," Dalton said.

"Ten minutes. If they don't show by then, we blow and go," GW said, his voice moving away from the mine entrance.

Ten minutes. Charlie looked around in the limited lighting. They had ten minutes to figure out how to get out of the mine.

Going deeper without lights was suicide. They could fall down open vertical shafts in the floor, or die due to poisonous gases. She went back to the boxes and searched for something, anything she could use to move the door enough they could slip out.

The only thing she could find was a broken slat from one of the crates. If she could use it as leverage, she might be able to move the heavy metal plate that had taken two men to slide in place.

Charlie jammed the slat into the sunlit gap at the base of the metal barrier. Holding on to the end, she leaned back as hard as she could, putting all of her weight into it. The plate budged, but only half an inch. She pulled the slat out and lay down on the floor.

She could see a little bit of daylight and movement. A couple of yards from the entrance, stood someone wearing camouflage pants and black work boots.

She didn't know where the others were, but she couldn't wait for them to appear. She had to get a wide enough gap to slip the children out and away from the men before they got really stupid and detonated the charges that would seal twenty children and the adults in the mine.

Fitting the slat back in the gap, she pulled again, the gap widening until a four-inch opening stretched from the top to the bottom of the entrance.

On her third attempt, the slat cracked and broke. Charlie fell on her butt with a bone-jarring thud and groaned. The additional space she'd gained was less than another inch. Five inches wide might get a small child out, but not Brenda and Charlie. And the children would need to be guided into the nearby trees and underbrush to hide. Without the leverage of the slat, she'd have to work with her bare hands. As heavy as the metal plate was, she doubted she'd get far, but she had to try.

The sky darkened, as if clouds had blocked the sun.

Charlie crawled to the widened gap and peered out. She spotted all three Vanders brothers. They stood near the dump truck. Two of them held the AR-15s. The one she figured was GW had the 9 millimeter in a holster on his hip and his hand wrapped around a small gadget Charlie assumed was the detonator.

Her teeth ground together. Any man who could contemplate blowing up the entrance to a mine with children trapped inside was no man at all. He was an animal.

She looked to her right and her left. If she remembered correctly from their drive in, the mine entrance had several bushes growing next to it and a young tree sprouting near the base of the hill. If they could get the kids to the bushes they might make it to the forest before their escape was discovered. The men outside must have felt pretty confident in the ability of the rusty metal plate holding their hostages inside. Either that or they were too busy watching for whatever they'd demanded to arrive to keep a close eye on a bunch of kids and two women.

Charlie leaped to her feet. Time was running out. She had to get the children to safety before the crazy brothers sealed their fates inside a mine shaft tomb.

Brenda disentangled herself from the children and rose to assist. "Let me help," she said.

With her heart pumping adrenaline through her veins, Charlie grabbed the metal plate.

Brenda curled her fingers around the rusty steel.

Together they leaned back, straining to move the heavy sheet of metal. By God, they'd move that barrier if it was the last thing they did.

Charlie prayed it wasn't.

ARMED WITH A headset radio and an AR-15 rifle, Ghost lived up to his nickname and eased up to the edge of the mine compound, clinging to the brush.

"Three targets, two carrying rifles and one with the prize."

"I got one vehicle leaving by road." Caveman was working his way toward the mine by paralleling the road in and out. "Notifying 911. They have the state highway patrol on standby. They should pick him up on the highway."

"I'm in position in the bird's nest," Hawkeye said from his position on a ridge high above the mine clearing.

"Ready when you are," Garner added.

The big guy in the middle had his fist closed around a small box of some sort. If it was a detonator, they'd have to get him to let go of it before they took out the other two men. It would do no good to kill any of them, if the guy holding the key to the show pressed that button.

He studied the layout. An older model dump truck was parked a couple of yards away from the mine entrance. One of the men stood near the rear of the truck, watching the road in. Another used the other end of the truck as cover, also monitoring the only road in.

The man with his hand on the detonator pulled what appeared to be a satellite phone off the web harness he wore and hit several buttons.

"Where's Vanders and our bird?" he demanded. "My thumb is a hair's breadth away from the ignition button." He listened for a moment. "I don't care if it takes time to get a helicopter here. Five minutes. That's all that's left between you and those kids. Five." He jabbed the phone, ending the call. "Get ready. Either they'll show up with him and the bird, or we set off some fireworks and get the hell out of here."

"I think I hear something coming," one of the men shouted.

"'Bout time," the guy at the other end of the truck said. "I need a beer."

The sound of rotor blades beating the air came over the top of the hill.

"Got my sights on the prize holder," Hawkeye reported.

"Do not engage," Garner reiterated the sheriff's instructions. He was positioned to the right of Ghost and twenty yards to his rear. He was to transfer data to the sheriff as the others took their positions.

"Holding steady," Hawkeye reassured.

Ghost scanned the area for other bad guys but was surprised there were only three. It didn't take an army to take a school bus full of children and un-armed adults. And with the lives of those children held in the balance, these men could demand the world and get it.

The helicopter crested the hill and hovered over the mine.

"What are they waiting for?" one of the men shouted.

"I don't know," the man holding the detonator yelled back over the roar of the helicopter.

"There's someone with a gun in there!" One of the men with a rifle pointed his weapon at the helicopter.

"Don't shoot!" detonator man yelled.

"They've got a gun!" He raised his weapon to his shoulder and fired.

Ghost shook his head. Just what they needed, a trigger-happy bad guy firing at the helicopter carrying their bargaining chip. "The situation has escalated, request permission to move in and take out the targets," Ghost said.

"Sheriff said do not engage," Garner reminded him.

"The sheriff didn't get the word to the bad guys. Things are about to get really bad." Ghost bunched his muscles, ready to charge into the gray.

"I've got the shooter in my sights," Hawkeye reminded them.

"I'm in position and have the other dude with the gun in mine," Caveman said.

Ghost couldn't wait for the men to freak out and blow up the mine entrance. "I'm going in for the man with the prize. Boss, either you're with me or you're not."

"I got your six, coming up on your left," Garner said. "Sheriff gave the go-ahead. They're lifting off."

As the helicopter climbed higher into the sky, the team moved in.

Hawkeye took out the man firing at the bird. Caveman fired at the other, nicked his leg and sent him to the ground. Unfortunately, he still had his gun in hand and was firing back in the direction of Caveman.

Ghost was almost across the open ground when

the man with the detonator turned toward the mine entrance and raised his hand.

Making a flying tackle, Ghost hit the man in his midsection, sending him staggering backward. He stumbled and hit the ground flat on his back. The detonator flew from his grasp and skittered across the dry ground, landing in front of the man firing at Caveman.

He flung his rifle to the ground and low-crawled toward the detonator.

Ghost punched the man he'd tackled in the nose and scrambled to his feet, flinging himself at the man as he reached for the detonator.

Before he could get to him, the man's hand slammed down on the red button.

The world erupted behind Ghost, sending him flying forward and slamming him to the ground. He laid for a moment, stunned, his ears ringing. The man who'd hit the button lifted his head and stared at him, then reached for his rifle.

Ghost lurched to his feet and kicked the rifle out of the other man's grip.

A shot rang out behind him and the big guy he'd tackled stood facing him, his eyes wide, blood spreading across his camouflage shirt. He took one step and fell forward like a tree toppled by lumberjacks.

Garner lay on the ground nearby, his rifle up to his shoulder. "Told you I had your six."

Ghost scanned the area. Caveman came out of the woods, the helicopter dropped lower and landed on the other side of the dump truck and people rushed toward the mine entrance.

"Charlie. Lolly." Ghost's head still rang and his leg ached, but none of that mattered. The woman he loved and his only child were trapped behind the rocks and rubble blocking the entrance to the old mine.

He ran toward the jumble of boulders and rocks. Dust swirled in a cloud making it hard to see clearly. Or were those tears clouding his vision?

"Charlie! Lolly!" Oh, dear God, how was he going to get them out of there? He lifted a boulder and tossed it to the side. He lifted another and threw it to the side, too.

"Ghost!" Hawkeye said his name several times before he heard the sound through his headset.

"They're in there," Ghost said, his heart ripped to shreds, his mind numb. "They're in there, and I can't get to them."

"Ghost, listen to me," Hawkeye said. "I have them in my sights."

"What?" Ghost straightened from the pile of rocks. "How?"

"They're in the woods to the south of the mine. I count more than a dozen kids and two adults."

From desperation to hope, Ghost left the rocks and ran toward the south side of the mine. He crashed through brush, tripped over logs and fell several times before he spotted something pink through the dense foliage.

When he broke through the underbrush, he stumbled and fell to his knees in front of all the children and two women. "Charlie! Lolly!" He coughed, choking with the dust he'd inhaled and the emotion he couldn't hold back.

"Ghost?" Charlie ran forward and knelt beside him. "Is that you?" She rubbed her hands across his face, her fingers getting coated with a fine layer of dust. "Oh, thank God." She flung her arms around him and kissed him, dirt and all.

He held her close for a long time. His leg hurt like hell and his ears still rang, but Charlie, Lolly and the rest of the kids were okay.

"Mr. Caspar?" Lolly inched forward, her brows knit, her cheeks streaked with dried tears.

"Lolly, baby, come here." He held out an arm, making room for her in his embrace.

She ran to him and wrapped her arms around his neck. "I was so scared."

He laughed. "So was I." He kissed her cheek with a loud smack. "But we're okay now."

She leaned back and stared at his face. "You're dirty."

He laughed out loud, his heart filled with so much joy, he was afraid it might explode. "Yes, I am. And I'm so happy you and your mama are all right."

Her eyes filled with tears. "Mr. Green didn't come out with us."

Charlie smoothed a hand over her hair. "No, sweetie, he didn't. But the sheriff will make sure they get him out of there. You'll see."

Ghost's gaze connected with Charlie's.

"The bus driver," she whispered and shook her head, her eyes filling.

He nodded. With Charlie's help, Ghost lurched to his feet and straightened his leg, the pain shooting up into his hip. He ignored it, looking at the children huddled around another young woman. He shook his head, thankful they were all alive. "How did you get them out of the mine?"

Charlie held up her hands, stained with rust and marked with cuts and scrapes. "Brenda and I moved the metal plate they'd used to block the entrance. They thought it could keep a couple of women with a bunch of children contained." She snorted. "They didn't count on the adrenaline rush we'd get at the mention of blowing the entrance." Charlie lifted her chin and smiled at the other woman. "The important thing is, we got it open enough to get all of the children out while the Vanders brothers were shooting at the helicopter. It was close, but we were able to get all of the children out of the mine before the explosion."

Ghost shook his head, a grin spreading across his face. "You are amazing."

"And you should have seen Lolly, herding the kids into single file like the little soldier she is." Charlie smiled down at their daughter. "She's so much like you it hurts sometimes."

Lolly stared up at Ghost. "Mr. Caspar, will you be my daddy?"

Her words hit Ghost in the gut and he sucked in a breath before responding. "I don't know." He turned to Charlie. "What does your mother think about the idea?"

Charlie's eyes filled again, tears spilled over the edges and her bottom lip trembled. "I was going to wait until I was wearing a pretty dress and my hair was fixed." She stared down at her wrecked hands. "And after a manicure." She laughed, the sound coming out as more of a sob. "But I don't want to wait another minute to know." She dropped to one knee and took Ghost's hand.

"What are you doing?" he asked. He tried to lift her back to her feet, but she resisted.

"Jon Caspar, you big, sexy SEAL, with a heart as big as the Wyoming sky, will you make an honest woman of me and marry me?" She stared up at him, tears running down her dirty face, her hair a riot of uncontrollable curls, her clothes torn and smeared with rust. She was the most beautiful woman in the world.

Ghost's heart swelled in his chest to the point he thought it could no longer be contained.

Lolly clapped her hands together, her eyes alight with excitement. "Please say yes!"

Ghost laughed and drew Charlie up into his arms. "I would have liked a shower before I proposed to you. But since we're here, the sun is shining and I'm holding the most beautiful woman in the world, I can't think of a better answer than yes." He drew in a deep breath and bent to kiss the tip of her nose. "Yes, I'll marry you. Yes, I'd love to have Lolly as my very own daughter. And yes, we'll work things out, somehow, because that's what people do who love each other as much as we do. I love you, Charlie, from the tips of my toes to my very last breath."

"Jon, I've always loved you," Charlie said. "From our first date, I knew you were the one for me. I just had to wait until *you* knew I was the one for you."

He brushed a strand of her hair out of her face and tucked it behind her ear. "I've always loved you, but I didn't want to hurt you by dragging you through the life of a SEAL's wife."

Charlie laughed. "So you hurt me by leaving me behind?" She shook her head. "That's man thinking." She cupped his face and leaned up on her toes to kiss him. "I'd follow you to the ends of the earth, and I'd always be there for you when you came back from deployment."

"Me, too." Lolly hugged him around his knees. "I love you, too. I'm going to have a daddy of my own." She looked up at him with his blue eyes and her mother's red hair and grinned. "We're going to be a family."

"You bet, we are." Ghost lifted her up on his arm and wrapped the other around Charlie. Together, they led the others out of the woods and back to the clearing in front of the mine.

CHARLIE FELT AS if she'd gone from one movie set to the other and wondered if she had been dreaming through all that had happened. She had a hard time wrapping her mind around all of it from having the bus hijacked to being trapped in a mine, to the fairy-tale proposal in the woods and back to the cacophony of every kind of motor vehicle and dozens of uniformed personnel filling her vision.

A fire truck had arrived, along with rescue vehicles from across the county. Every sheriff's deputy on duty was there along with the Wyoming Highway Patrol. The sheriff was in the middle of all of it speaking with the DHS representative, Kevin Garner.

When Charlie emerged from the woods with Ghost, Brenda and all of the children, a round of applause erupted from the rescue personnel.

Paramedics rushed forward to check out the children, Brenda and Charlie.

She suffered through the delay of having her hands cleaned and bandaged, while Ghost carried Lolly over to where the sheriff directed the remaining efforts.

Charlie hurried over as soon as she could break away.

Tim Cramer was tucked into the backseat of one of the Wyoming Highway Patrol cars, his face angry, his hands cuffed behind him.

A deputy escorted a pale and shaky Linnea Cramer into the fray where she was reunited with her daughter, Ashley, in a tearful reunion.

"Thank God, they got Ashley back," Charlie said as she joined the group gathered around the sheriff.

"We had a roadblock set up on the highway headed toward Montana. We figured he'd make a run for Canada with the child," the sheriff said. "Wyoming Highway Patrol picked him up. If he thought he had problems before, he's in a heap more trouble now. Rebecca Florence came to this morning and said it was Tim Cramer who'd attacked her in the library. He'd worn the ski mask he was found with today, but she knew it was him when he told her it was her fault he was losing his wife."

Charlie frowned. "What do you mean it was her fault? I didn't think she and Linnea were even friends."

The sheriff's mouth twisted. "Apparently, Ms. Florence was in Bozeman for a library conference staying at the same hotel where Cramer was entertaining a young lady who wasn't his wife in a room on the same floor as Rebecca's."

"And she told Linnea." Charlie nodded. "So he beat her up for squealing on him."

The sheriff nodded.

"What about the Vanders brothers?" Charlie asked, looking around as paramedics loaded a sheet-draped body into the back of one of the waiting ambulances.

"Dalton is dead, Vernon and GW will live to face time in the state prison," the sheriff said.

Charlie couldn't feel sorry for any of them. How long would it be before the children got over the terror they'd faced on the bus and in the dark mine? "I hope they get what they deserve."

Ghost slipped an arm around her.

She leaned into his strength, glad he was there.

"If not for Garner's team, it could have been a whole lot worse," Sheriff Scott said. "The chopper took hits from Dalton's gun. The pilot is being treated for a gunshot wound to his leg and Dalton shot his own father." The sheriff shook his head. "LeRoy Vanders took a bullet to the chest. They're working on him now and loading him into the helicopter his son tried to shoot down. I doubt he'll make it all the way to the hospital in Bozeman."

"What about Mr. Green?" Charlie asked. Her heart ached for the old man who'd done nothing to deserve being killed for driving a busload of kids. "He's still inside the mine." She shook her head. "He didn't make it. Vernon took him out on the bus."

The sheriff's lips thinned and released a long sigh. "His wife will be devastated." He pinched the bridge of his nose before continuing. "I ordered excavation equipment in case we had to dig you and the kids out. It's on its way. We'll get him out."

Charlie nodded.

Sheriff Scott shot a glance at the crumbled mine entrance. "What I don't understand is where they got all the explosives and detonators."

Ghost's jaw tightened. "From what I saw of the detonator, it was military grade. I knew the Vanderses had an arsenal of guns from all the hunting they do. But the explosives are an entirely different game."

Charlie touched the sheriff's arm. "I found at least a dozen wooden crates in the mine. They were filled with empty boxes from what appeared to be a large number of rifles, boxes of ammo and the curved magazines I've seen used with the semiautomatic weapons the military use. What would the Vanders brothers need with that many weapons?"

"Unless they aren't the only ones stockpiling weapons," Kevin Garner said. "We have infrared satellite photos of a group of people unloading items from a truck into the mine. It was from only a few days ago."

"Those crates were empty except for the boxes the weapons came in."

"Where did all of those guns and ammo go?" the sheriff asked. "And who shipped all of them? There has to be a paper or money trail."

Garner nodded. "I have my tech guy working on that. In the meantime, getting into that mine and going through those crates might help us trace the weapons back to the buyer."

The sheriff's face grew grim. "Sounds like someone is trying to build an army."

"Then we better find out who before they succeed," Garner said.

Charlie shivered in the warm country air. Her peaceful hometown of Grizzly Pass, Wyoming, had darker secrets than she'd ever expected. She began to wonder if bringing her daughter there to raise had been a good idea after all.

Ghost tightened his hold around her waist, reminding her that if she hadn't come back, she wouldn't have found Ghost again.

Everything happened for a reason. And she couldn't be happier that she now had her family back together. Whatever the future held, wherever they went, it would be as a family. Anything else, they could deal with, as long as they were together.

An hour later, Kevin Garner loaded his team of specialists into his SUV along with Charlie and Lolly and took them back to town.

He dropped Charlie, Lolly and Ghost at the community center where Charlie had left her Jeep.

Charlie handed over her keys. "If you don't mind, my hands are shaking too much to drive."

He took the keys in exchange for a kiss and helped her and Lolly into the vehicle.

Once they were all inside, he glanced over at Charlie and took her hand. "Just so you know, I plan on staying until the situation is resolved here in Grizzly Pass. After that, I hope you'll be patient and flexible with where we go next."

Charlie squeezed his fingers. "I'm one hundred percent okay with that plan. As long as you're here with us. I don't think we've found the people at the crux of what's been going on around here."

"Me either," he said. "But I know one thing."

"What's that?"

"I'm not leaving until we do. And when I do leave, you and Lolly are coming with me." He lifted her hand and pressed a kiss to the backs of her knuckles.

"Good," Charlie said. "Because I'm not letting go this time."

"How do you feel about being a Navy wife?"

"I couldn't be prouder, as long as my Navy husband is you."

"Good, because once we've completed this assignment, I want to rejoin my unit in Virginia."

"I've always wanted to go to Virginia," she said, a happy smile spreading across her face.

"And if the medical board invites me to leave the military?"

She turned her head toward him. "We could come back to Wyoming."

"I'm glad you feel that way. Being back reminded me how much I love this state. More than that, it reminded me of how much I love you."

* * * * *

0217/46

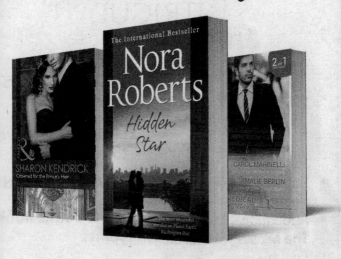